Mark Billingham has twice won the Theakston Old Peculier Award for Crime Novel of the Year, and has also won a Sherlock Award for the Best Detective created by a British writer. Each of the novels featuring Detective Inspector Tom Thorne has been a *Sunday Times* bestseller. *Sleepyhead* and *Scaredy Cat* were made into a hit TV series on Sky 1 starring David Morrissey as Thorne, and a series based on the novels *In the Dark* and *Time of Death* was broadcast on BBC1. Mark lives in north London with his wife and two children.

Also by Mark Billingham

The DI Tom Thorne series
Sleepyhead
Scaredy Cat
Lazybones
The Burning Girl
Lifeless
Buried
Death Message
Bloodline
From the Dead
Good as Dead
The Dying Hours
The Bones Beneath
Time of Death
Love Like Blood
The Killing Habit
Their Little Secret
Cry Baby
The Murder Book

Other fiction
In the Dark
Rush of Blood
Cut Off
Die of Shame
Rabbit Hole

MARK BILLINGHAM

THE
LAST
DANCE

SPHERE

SPHERE

First published in Great Britain in 2023 by Sphere

1 3 5 7 9 10 8 6 4 2

Copyright © Mark Billingham Ltd 2023

The moral right of the author has been asserted.

All characters and events in this publication, other than those
clearly in the public domain, are fictitious and any resemblance
to real persons, living or dead, is purely coincidental.

All rights reserved.
No part of this publication may be reproduced, stored in a
retrieval system, or transmitted, in any form or by any means, without
the prior permission in writing of the publisher, nor be otherwise circulated
in any form of binding or cover other than that in which it is published
and without a similar condition including this condition being
imposed on the subsequent purchaser.

A CIP catalogue record for this book is available from the British Library.

Hardback ISBN 978-1-4087-1712-7
Trade Paperback ISBN 978-1-4087-2633-4

Typeset in Plantin by M Rules
Printed and bound in Great Britain by Clays Ltd, Elcograf S.p.A.

Papers used by Sphere are from well-managed forests
and other responsible sources.

MIX
Paper from
responsible sources
FSC® C104740

Sphere
An imprint of
Little, Brown Book Group
Carmelite House
50 Victoria Embankment
London EC4Y 0DZ

An Hachette UK Company
www.hachette.co.uk

www.littlebrown.co.uk

For Claire, remembering our first dance ...

'You dance love, and you dance joy, and you dance dreams.'

GENE KELLY

'Almost nobody dances sober, unless they happen to be insane.'

H. P. LOVECRAFT

The coloured lights from more than a million lamps seem to dance above the town's main street and their reflections shimmer on the surface of the black sea just beyond. On the street itself, a thousand neon signs dazzle and buzz and the slow-moving traffic has become a pulsating necklace of red and white beads. To the casual observer, gazing down from the top of the Tower perhaps, or from a penthouse apartment in one of the expensive blocks that have sprung up in recent years, this might be Las Vegas.

If that casual observer *really* squinted.

And had never been to Las Vegas.

A minicab pulls up on the Promenade and, once the passenger door has been opened for her, a glamorous-looking woman who could easily be a celebrity of some sort, but isn't, steps slowly out. She hands over a ten pound note, tells the driver to keep the change and walks up the steps to the entrance of the Sands Hotel.

The concierge opens the door for her and touches his dusty cap. The woman nods and hands over another ten pound note. The concierge palms it, touches his cap a second time and says how lovely it is to see her again.

'Likewise, I'm sure,' she says.

'Yeah, whatever,' the concierge mutters when she's gone.

She sashays across the lobby, heels click-clacking, and steps into an empty lift. She presses the button for the top floor and straightens her dress. She's checking her handbag to make sure she has everything she needs as the doors close.

All her bits and bobs.

A few minutes later, she's tapping lightly on the door of a room on the fifth floor. She takes out a compact mirror and quickly freshens her lipstick, then leans close to the spyhole. Sensing movement beyond the threshold and hearing a noisy, desperate breath, she turns on a smile to put any of those megawatt lightbulbs outside to shame. She blows a kiss and waits, knowing full well that the man she's here to see is watching her from the other side of the door.

An hour or so later, the only occupant of the hotel room still breathing steps out into the corridor and closes the door softly behind them.

A mobile phone is immediately produced and a number dialled. Almost done and feeling satisfied with a job perfectly executed, the owner of the phone, and of the gun, begins to walk quickly – but not too quickly – towards the lift.

Stops. Freezes, then slowly turns.

A phone has begun to ring behind them, close behind them.

The call is terminated fast, the number dialled a second time and, for reasons the caller is struggling desperately to fathom, that nearby phone begins to trill again.

A few steps back, an ear pressed to a door.

It makes no sense, but that hardly matters now and the situation will be sorted because it has to be. It is what it is and the fact is that a phone which should be ringing *anywhere* but there is now ringing behind the door of another room.

STEP ONE

CHALLENGE POSITION

ONE

Miller stared at the rat and the rat stared right back.

'So, what's it to be, this morning?'

The rat raised itself up, bead-black eyes bright and whiskers quivering.

'A nice bit of kedgeree, maybe?' Miller waited, smacking his lips. 'Eggs Benedict or a cheeky full English?' He sighed and let his head drop so the furry little buggers would know just how disappointed he was, then shuffled forward on his knees and shook the plastic container. 'OK, if you want to be boring.' He opened the cage and took out the two food bowls, filled each one with the same old mix of cereal and oat flakes, then, before setting down their breakfast, he reached into the cage to take Ginger out. He held her on his lap and ran a finger gently across her head. 'You know you've always been my favourite, right?' He lifted her up and nodded towards her partner in the cage, whispering as she scrabbled for a few seconds then snuggled against his neck. 'For God's sake don't tell Fred, though. Nobody likes a sulky rodent.' He leaned back to look Ginger in the eye. 'Don't rat me out.'

He sat on the sofa after that and watched them eat. He'd brought a mug of coffee across, but fifteen minutes later, by the time he'd stopped worrying about the day ahead – the walking into the office and the strange looks he was very likely to get – and thinking about what he should say to people and what he definitely shouldn't and picking at the loose threads on his tatty old dressing gown and remembered that there was coffee, it was lukewarm, so Miller carried it back to the kitchen and poured it away.

He couldn't be arsed to make himself another.

He'd have one when he got to work.

He was pretty sure he'd need one.

Dressing slowly, like it was something he'd all but forgotten how to do, he listened to some irritating rent-a-gob sounding off about the state of the NHS on Capital Lancashire, so he argued with him, same as he always did. Muttering, or occasionally shouting, at the radio. It was a daft habit that had become a kind of ritual, whatever the host or caller or so-called expert happened to be pontificating about, and Miller always enjoyed it.

He put on pants and socks, then picked out a shirt.

'... and you can't get an appointment to begin with, not unless you've got one leg hanging off, or you're an immigrant or something ...'

'You're an idiot, mate. On second thoughts, I take that back, because it's insulting to idiots.'

He stepped into itchy grey trousers and the shoes he'd polished the night before.

'I mean, wasn't that why we voted for Brexit in the first place? That, and the fish ...'

'This is drivel, mate. You're talking drivel.'

He put on his least offensive tie – which wasn't saying a lot because he had quite the collection of horrific neckwear – then immediately undid the top button of his shirt, because it felt like he couldn't breathe. 'I swear to God, I could eat a tin of Alphabetti Spaghetti and *shit* more sense than you're talking . . .'

As conversations went, Miller was fully aware that these chinwags were somewhat one-sided, but that wasn't the point. Along with the ratty chit-chat, it got his brain moving in the morning, or at least moving in the right direction, and it reminded him what his voice sounded like. He needed the kick of that and the distraction.

He needed the noise.

Truth be told, he also argued with the radio in the afternoons, and in the evening. Middle of the night, quite often.

But that wasn't the point.

A few minutes later, wearing a jacket that more or less matched the trousers, he stood in front of the large mirror next to the front door. He tried out a few expressions until what passed for a smile didn't seem too scary. He had a bash at a couple of casual nods and shrugs that he was hoping would do the trick. After the habitual brief skirmish with his hair, he settled for a draw and turned back towards the multi-level cage-cum-playpen that had cost him a small fortune and now took up most of the living room floor.

He gave the rats a twirl.

'So, what d'you reckon? I think it's going to have to do.'

Predictably, Fred and Ginger were otherwise occupied chasing each other from one end of the cage to the other. Miller tried not to take their lack of interest as a bad sign and turned to pick up Alex's mobile phone which was lying there where it always was; plugged in on a table by the door. That sparkly red case which looked nice enough, but – like he'd told her a hundred times – would have been totally useless if she ever dropped her phone. Not that she ever did drop the bloody thing, certainly not as often as Miller dropped his, because she was always careful.

But that wasn't the point.

He reached across and touched the screen, a picture of Alex and him. Some competition from a few years back. The pair of them looking pretty tasty, even if he did say so himself.

He grabbed his rucksack from the chair by the door and threw it over his shoulder. He bent down for the crash helmet that was underneath it, then stood and raised his eyes to the ceiling. Shouted up.

'Alex . . . I've fed Fred and Ginger, OK . . . ?'

He stood and listened. He stepped back across to the mirror and *watched* himself listen. The silence seemed to thicken and settle for those few long seconds before it was broken by the painful squeak of the rats' wheel; before Miller sucked in a fast breath and finally reached to open the door, like a brave soldier. Or a very stupid one.

Sofia Hadzic tied on her apron then stepped out, yawning, into the basement corridor, pushing the trolley she had spent the previous twenty minutes loading with fresh supplies. Bobbly towels with a faded letter *S* and sheets that might once have been white. The postage-stamp sized slivers of soap wrapped in plastic, the tiny bottles of shampoo that looked fancy enough but were filled up every few days from a huge plastic flagon of cheap stuff. The toilet roll that your fingers went through.

8

The Sands was not a hotel she would choose to stay in herself.

She exchanged a nod with one of the other girls as she shunted the trolley into the lift. She didn't know the girl's name and seriously doubted that the girl knew hers, but it didn't much matter. She was only there to work and she wasn't looking to make new friends.

She put on her headphones then stabbed at the button for the top floor.

Sofia yawned again, nodding her head in time to an old Little Mix song she loved as the lift doors clattered shut.

The motorbike – a red and black Yamaha Tracer 9 with six-speed transmission and an 890cc liquid-cooled beast of an engine – roared along the seafront. It cut through the morning traffic like the cars and lorries were going backwards, the North Pier and the glowering Tower there and gone. It raced past the sea-life centre, the mini-golf course where Miller had once copped off with a girl called Sandra Bullimore, and innumerable arcades that were just blinking into life. It burned up the tarmac and swerved skilfully round the potholes, while away to its right the Irish Sea frothed and spat against the damp sand; the same colour as the coffee Miller had poured away and a damn sight colder.

Half a minute after the bike had turned towards town and stopped at traffic lights by the Morrisons, Miller pulled up next to it. The leather-clad biker glanced across and, even though his expression was hidden behind a dark visor, it was a fair bet that he was less than impressed by Miller's pale blue moped and high-vis tabard; those seventy pitiful ccs that he probably thought had sounded like a hairdryer behind him. Or maybe a wasp, trapped in his helmet.

Miller stared back, watching as the biker revved his engine, keen to get moving. 'Race you,' he said.

The lights turned to amber and the biker just shook his head like Miller was an idiot. Miller winced when the light turned green and the Yamaha shot away; within seconds it was just a dot in the distance, though Miller could still hear the noise of that engine as he shouted after it. 'Yeah, off you go. Pussy . . .'

A few seconds later, some twonk behind him started leaning on his horn, indicating less than politely that it was time for Miller to move. Miller was in no hurry, though. He wasn't kidding himself that the day ahead was going to be easy, but right then he was in a pretty good mood.

He gave the twonk the finger anyway, because why not?

The carpet in the long straight corridor was ugly, with brown and yellow swirls. Sofia thought it looked like someone had been sick on it. Given the state of this place, of some of the guests she'd encountered, she guessed that plenty of people *had* been sick on it.

She pushed her trolley towards the far end, though it wasn't easy as one of the wheels was bent and she kept veering towards the wall. It was annoying, but what could she do? The whole of the top floor was hers, so starting with the room at the end and working back seemed like the best plan.

The first bedroom was nice and straightforward. Sheets changed, sink and shower scrubbed, tea and coffee making facilities replenished. In and out in ten minutes. The second room was closer to what she was expecting and took twice as long. Wet towels and dirty clothes all over the place, bins full of empty beer cans *and* it smelled like someone had been smoking in there.

Some people were pigs.

She knew she should probably say something to the manager, but it wasn't her job to spy on anyone, so she just snapped on her rubber gloves turned up her Little Mix and got on with it.

She paused for a few seconds outside the door of her third bedroom, took out her phone and skipped a couple of tracks she wasn't fond of. Once she'd found the song she wanted, she leaned forward to slide her key card into the slot below the door handle. When the light flashed green she spun round and nudged the door open with her backside.

She heaved the trolley in from the corridor and turned as the door slammed shut behind her.

Initially, it struck her that the room wasn't in too terrible a state, certainly nothing like as bad as the last one. There wasn't a great deal of . . . mess, to speak of. Aside from the blood on the bed and the body it had come from, obviously.

Sofia's scream was loud enough to wake a dead man.

Not this one, though.

TWO

Miller wasn't sure how long he'd been standing there like a lemon waiting to go in, peering through the window of the incident room. Too long, probably. Long enough to clock several of the usual faces, anyway; the looks on a few of them when they noticed him. Like someone had slapped them in the gob with a wet fish or they'd spotted George Clooney in Tesco's. Like they'd coughed and followed through.

Eventually he just got fed up with himself and walked in.

Breezed in, like it was any other day and what was the big deal? It was a bit forced, maybe, but there was even a smattering of bantz as he sauntered across the office.

Sauntered, which was bloody ridiculous and only went to prove that he was brimming with misplaced confidence. Miller might have ambled now and again and may even have meandered on occasion, but he had never been one for sauntering anywhere.

He was more of a lolloper.

'Oh . . . hey, Dec.'

'Hey yourself. That is a seriously brave haircut, by the way.'

'How's it going, Dec?'

'Mustn't grumble. Yourself . . . ?'

All fine and dandy until he reached his desk. What had been his desk, at any rate. Tony Clough – who was looking nice and comfy sitting behind it – was a decent enough bloke and a fair-to-middling DC, but he was a bit of a lump sometimes. Also, he'd turned up at the pub one night wearing a rugby shirt with the collar turned up, on top of which Miller had once heard him say *nucular*. So . . .

Clough finally realised Miller was standing there and looked suitably shamefaced.

'Well, this is me,' Miller said. 'At least it used to be me.'

Clough moved as fast as Miller had ever seen him. On his feet and gathering up his things like it was going-home time or someone had announced they were giving pies away.

'Sorry, Dec, here you go . . . I mean, nobody said, so we weren't . . . you know.'

Miller shrugged, like it wasn't a big deal. 'Jump in my grave as quick, would you, Tone?'

The blood drained from Clough's face and they just stared at each other for a few seconds, nodding like idiots. Miller felt a bit guilty, because he certainly could have said something that would have made the man feel less uncomfortable. Actually, he couldn't think of much that would have made him any *more* uncomfortable, but that's what had popped into Miller's head, so that's what came out of his mouth.

That's how it tended to be.

As Clough stalked away in search of a different desk, Miller made himself back at home. He shifted the computer screen round an inch or two and whistled for a bit. He adjusted the height of the chair, opened and closed a few drawers then noticed some godawful gonk thing that Clough had left behind and lobbed it into the bin.

He looked up to see DS Andrea Fuller hovering.

Miller reckoned that, himself aside, Fuller was probably the smartest copper on the team and, if she wasn't, she certainly had the shortest fuse. He knew her parents were knocking on a bit and that she had to take care of them on top of the Job, so it was understandable that she got somewhat ... frazzled sometimes. They once had an argument about whether wearing only socks counted as being naked and things had got a bit heated.

She'd been wrong, obviously.

'Boss wants a word,' she said.

Miller sat back and held out his arms, but he could see that a simple gesture of disbelief wasn't going to be enough. 'Andrea, you know when people use the word "literally" and you want to punch them, because they don't really mean literally?'

She just grunted and Miller could tell by the way she rolled her eyes how thrilled she was that he was back.

'Like, there were *literally* a million people in the pub. No, there almost certainly weren't. He was *literally* pissing himself laughing. No, I think you'll find he wasn't. Well, I have literally been here two minutes. *Literally.* So how the hell can I be in trouble already?'

Andrea grunted again and threw in a shrug for good measure. 'I think you've just got a gift.'

He knocked and bowled straight through DCI Susan Akers's door before she had a chance to say 'come in'. Using the same long-perfected tactic, he sat down before he was invited. He knew it would be fine, because even though Akers was his boss, they'd known each other a long time and were close. Well, as close as you could be to someone you were inordinately fond of, but who was also well capable of scaring you half to death whenever she fancied it.

Whenever you ... whenever *he* messed up.

'Balloons would probably have been a bit much,' he said. 'I get that, but a cake would have been nice. Not a massive cake, I mean not the kind of cake someone could jump out of. Well, maybe a child or a very small person. That sort of size. I mean, now I think about it, any sort of cake was unlikely, bearing in mind nobody knew I was coming in. But there's still time, if anyone fancies making the gesture. That's all I'm saying. I promise I'll act surprised.'

He grinned at her, but Akers stayed stony-faced.

'Have you finished, Detective Sergeant?'

He pretended that he was thinking about it, then leaned forward to pluck a dead leaf from the potted plant on her desk. It looked nasty. 'Grey mould.' He shook his head to let her know just how nasty it was. 'You need to keep an eye on that.'

'What the hell are you doing here?'

'Oh my God I must have missed it!'

'Missed what?'

He grabbed the newspaper that was sitting on her desk and began leafing quickly through it. 'You know, crime being ... over. Is it in here somewhere? I didn't hear anything on the radio. I mean that's fantastic news, obviously. So what are you going to do, now none of us are needed any more? You and your missus will have plenty of time for the amateur dramatics now, and the golf, so it's a win-win when you think about it ...'

15

He stopped because, even though he was not always great at taking a hint, on this occasion Miller could see very clearly that she wasn't remotely charmed or amused. Best to cut his losses, he reckoned.

Best to tell the truth.

'I was bored, Susan. Fair enough?'

'It's only been six weeks.'

'I know exactly how long it's been.'

'That's not enough time. You were given twice that long.'

'Rattling around in that house—'

'That's not a good enough reason—'

'I need to work.' He looked at her, made sure she knew he meant it. 'I need to do something.'

He let his head drop back for a few seconds, and when he lifted it again the DCI was straightening papers on her desk. It was probably an effort to distract herself from wanting to throw something at him. He saw her look past him and he didn't need to turn round to know that people in the incident room were watching through the big window of her office.

'Look, don't get me wrong, Dec,' she said. 'Nobody's more delighted than I am to see you're doing better.'

'Me,' he said. 'I'm more delighted.'

'But it's still my job to see that this team runs efficiently and that means all officers doing their jobs properly. I know you think you're up to it, but ...' She looked at him and he saw her eyes close for a second or two which was usually a sign that he was wearing her down. He tried not to do anything too obvious like cheer or punch the air. 'OK, but I'll need to re-jig things a bit.'

Unable to resist it, he turned to give the incident room audience a thumbs-up.

'Clough and Fuller are a team now,' she said. 'So I'll have to find someone else to pair you up with. I could put you with the officer who came across to replace you, but that would be cruel and unusual punishment.' She left a beat, which he thought was impressive. 'For them, obviously.'

'Obviously,' he said.

'I'll have a word with DI Sullivan, see what he thinks.'

That pissed on Miller's chips, somewhat. 'Sullivan's a *DI*?'

'Came through last month.'

'Honestly, you turn your back for five minutes and everything turns to shit.' Tim Sullivan's promotion was genuinely bad news, but seeing Susan working to suppress a smile made him feel a little better.

'Leave it with me, Dec,' she said.

Miller stood up to leave but stopped at the door. 'I'm serious, by the way.' He pointed to her sorry-looking plant. 'Grey mould. *Botrytis*. Nasty if you don't sort it. Just remove the infected bits, do something about your ventilation and you'll be right as ninepence. See, Susan?'

Akers pulled a face, like she knew she'd regret asking. 'What?'

'Back on the job less than an hour and I've already saved a life. To be honest, I don't know how you've managed without me.'

THREE

It was true that Miller wanted to be busy, but he hadn't been counting on picking up such a big case on his first day back. That was the way things went, though. You were desperate for a day or two to catch your breath or even just looking to recharge your batteries after a major inquiry and someone decided to poison their husband or stab a passer-by because they didn't like their trainers.

People were so bloody inconsiderate, sometimes.

Before that though, before he'd caught the aforementioned case, he'd needed the rest of the team to know where he was at. He'd needed to lay down a marker and let everyone know that they could relax.

He was forced into it, really.

After his meeting with DCI Akers, he'd spent an hour or so at his computer, looking through the squad's open cases, trying to see if there was an inquiry he could easily slot into. It was hard to concentrate though, because every time he so much as glanced up or went to make himself tea, he was aware that he was still being ... studied. He'd catch Tony Clough or one of the others staring and whenever he did, there was always that irritating, sickly smile or even worse the annoying slow nod.

It was tense and awkward and it was starting to get on Miller's nerves.

After one too many sympathetic cocks of the head, he'd had enough and found himself standing up and clambering a little awkwardly on to his desk, then clinking a spoon against an empty mug until he had everyone's attention.

Found himself, because that was the way it went a lot of the time. Impetus or say something and five minutes later – if someone was to ask him why he'd done such and such or made that stupid/inappropriate/offensive comment –_he wouldn't be able to come up with much beyond feeling strongly that it had been the right thing to do at the time. That was usually all he had. The right thing, despite all available evidence and expert opinion pointing to the fact that it was very much the wrong thing. Miller did not make any apologies for who he was. Well ... sometimes he *had* to.

So, desk, mug, clink-clink with the spoon ...

All heads turned and it went very quiet.

'OK, well ,. thank you all for coming.' He manufactured that smile he'd been practising in the mirror before leaving the house. 'I'll try to keep this brief because we've all got crimes to solve ... alcohol habits to support, gambling debts to pay off, whatever. So, just to say, my wife Alex, who some of you knew, is dead. She's ... dead. It's a pisser, but there you are.

'Obviously, if you knew her, you're well aware of the fact

that she's dead and you might well have been at the funeral, so I could probably have skipped that bit ... but I suppose what I really want to say is ... I'm dealing with it and if *I* am, then you lot should.'

He stared down at the shocked faces and momentarily lost his thread a little.

'Also. Be dealing with it.'

Miller looked across and saw that Susan Akers had moved to the window of her office and was watching along with everyone else. He was trying to keep it light, which had become even more of a default position lately, and he'd thought he was doing a decent job of it.

Still, she looked upset.

'So, there's really no need to creep around or lower your voices or have that expression like I've got cancer, and *please* don't put your hand on my shoulder and give it a little squeeze of condolence. God, I hate that. If you do, I might well have to break a couple of your fingers and at the very least you'll get a nasty Chinese burn, so please don't say I didn't warn you ...'

He paused and looked around to make sure everyone had got the message. There were a good many blank stares, but it wasn't like he'd been expecting a round of applause, so he decided they would have to do.

'I'm just saying, shit happens and we've all got jobs to do, so just ... get over it. OK? Right then, thank you so much for your attention. As you were.'

There were a few long seconds of very stunned silence when he'd finished, before people began muttering and started to drift back to work and Miller tried to climb down off the desk.

It was a lot harder than climbing up.

When a hand reached up to help, he happily grabbed it,

then, once he had both feet back on the floor, he stood staring at the woman to whom the hand belonged as it began shaking his.

'Thanks very much,' he said. 'Who the hell are you?'

She was somewhere in her early thirties, had short dark hair and was, he guessed, of Chinese descent. Guessed, because making a presumption about such things was always dodgy, not least because you could end up looking like someone who was not culturally sensitive.

Or just a pillock.

He glanced down at the ID on her lanyard, wondering if he should apologise for the Chinese burn thing, and he was about to have a bash at her surname when she saved him the trouble.

'I'm DS Sara Xiu.'

'Right, like ... *jus.*'

She blinked then said her name again. They were still shaking hands.

'Like the stuff you get in fancy restaurants, you know? *Jus.* I mean, it's basically just posh gravy, if you ask me.' Miller smiled, pleased with it. 'Maybe I should call you "Posh Gravy".'

'Why would you do that?'

'I don't know.'

'Hmm.' She let go of his hand.

'It's just a daft nickname—'

'I'm your replacement,' she said. 'Well, I *was.*'

'Oh,' he said. 'Sorry about that.'

'It looks like we're going to be teaming up.'

'Even sorrier.'

She smiled. 'That's a joke, right?'

'Not really.'

She carried on smiling and then she started nodding, which was when Tim Sullivan – now, sadly, *DI* Tim Sullivan – marched out of Akers's office and shouted across.

'Miller, Xiu, you're up . . .'

Miller looked at Xiu. 'What are you, cursed?'

They walked across to where Sullivan was still talking to someone on his phone. He paused his call to give them their instructions, the voice even more nasal and grating than Miller remembered.

'Suspicious death at the Sands Hotel, so get yourselves over there and see what's what. I'll be fifteen minutes behind you.'

'Sir,' Xiu said.

Miller's new partner was clearly raring to go and he watched her hurry across to a desk and gather up her things. He waited for her at the door, staring expectantly at a couple of his fellow officers as they wandered past. He held out his arms.

'So, definitely no cake, then?'

Nobody, least of all Miller himself, would have claimed he was the world's most natural driver.

He could do it when he needed to, obviously, and workwise he'd done the compulsory highspeed chase training and all the surveillance courses. With the day-to-day stuff, though, the getting from A to B, he was not always as confident as you needed to be behind the wheel. He could lack a little focus, sometimes, he was well aware of that, and was just as likely to be thinking about why a particular blood-spatter pattern looked like an elephant or how on earth Scotch eggs are made as he was about the lights changing up ahead or the driver in front of him slowing down. He was easily distracted. All in all, it was safer for him, and a whole lot safer for everyone else, for Miller to do as little driving as possible.

Which is why, when they got to the assigned pool car – a Honda something-or-other – and Xiu climbed into the driver's seat, he wasn't about to argue.

She started the car then turned to him.

'I'm sorry about your wife,' she said.

There was no sympathetic tilt of the head or soppy smile. She just said it quietly, like it was a statement of fact.

'Not as sorry as I am,' Miller said.

Xiu just stared at him, but Miller wasn't bothered because it happened a lot. He gave it a few more seconds, just to see if she had anything further to add, then nodded towards the car park exit. 'Come on, Posh, let's get a shift on. This murder isn't going to solve itself.'

FOUR

Pippa Shepherd had not slept well.

She'd been wide awake since the early hours – rigid and unblinking under clammy sheets or curled around a pillow fighting back the tears – before eventually giving up and dragging herself downstairs just after five-thirty. She hadn't bothered getting dressed, because she couldn't see the point. Instead, she'd sat in her neat and tidy living room and watched the sun come up like it couldn't care less, then let the bright and breezy noises of morning TV slop over her while she'd drunk a lot more tea than anyone needed and made the same phone call every few minutes.

Now, she reached for the phone again and hit the redial button.

'I'm sorry, but I'm not around to take your call . . .'

Telling herself she was being stupid and over-dramatic really didn't help, not for very long anyway, but she kept doing it all the same. What else could she do? She was an idiot and she was panicking for no good reason and why did she always have to dwell on the worst case scenario? A doom-monger, wasn't that what Barry always called her?

24

After all, there were any number of reasons why . . .

One reason, there was *one* . . . and much as she told herself not to think about that, it was impossible to think of anything else. Like trying to kid herself she wasn't hungry when she was actually ravenous. The feeling that she knew would be so much worse than anything she was going through right then; the pain, for which this was only a rehearsal.

Empty, hopeless and done with. Dead inside.

She dialled again, held her breath while she listened, then threw the phone across the room as soon as his recorded voice had repeated that same pointless apology.

'I'm sorry . . .'

She got up and scampered to retrieve her phone, quickly hanging up the call so the line was free in case he called and setting it back down on the arm of the chair.

She let her breath settle.

A minute later, or maybe fifteen, she found herself drifting slowly back to the kitchen for more tea, staring around the room like she didn't recognise it, then stopping when she caught sight of the bottle she'd all but emptied the night before. Drinking and dialling as the evening had crawled by. The anxiety turning to dread.

'. . . I'm not around . . .'

She could still taste the red wine, thick on her tongue, and though it wasn't quite eight-thirty in the morning and she was still wearing pyjamas, finishing that bottle off felt like the most sensible decision Pippa would make all day.

Michelle Cutler gritted her teeth and pushed on into the last half-mile of a tough uphill climb in the Italian Alps. The scenery was pretty, but God, it hurt. Her instructor – a nicely-ripped young thing called Eduardo – told her that she was nearly there, that she needed to feel the burn, so she pushed even harder, staring at the screen and thinking of all the ways in which she'd have enjoyed feeling the burn with Eduardo that didn't involve riding a pricey and over-complicated exercise bike.

Five minutes later she was still thinking about it as she stepped into the shower. Her mobile chirped just as she was reaching for the tap, but she ignored it, letting the call ring out as she moved beneath the hot water. She knew it would be Jacqui calling and that Jacqui would only be calling to ask, *again*, about the whereabouts of her beloved son.

Bloody Jacqui.

Michelle worked herself into a lather in every sense, thinking about it. It always used to be fat male comedians making jokes about their mother-in-law, but she reckoned that actually far more women than men had those . . . issues. Well, they certainly did if their mothers-in-law were anything like Jacqui.

Once she was dry and had made herself up, she dressed in comfy sweats then wandered down to the kitchen. She sat at the enormous marble-topped island and, after wondering what to do with herself for a few minutes, she reached for a shiny green apple from the fruit bowl. They were almost never eaten, being purely for decoration and replaced when they went soft, but she fancied one, so sod it.

The scissors were still sitting there at the other end of the island.

Seeing them made her smile as she remembered what she'd done with them the night before. She'd been using her phone to track his, so she'd known where he was and what was happening and putting those nice sharp scissors to good use had seemed like a very clever thing to do.

26

And Michelle knew she was clever.

Far cleverer than the likes of Jacqui gave her credit for, anyway.

She bit hard into the apple, enjoying the crunch, relishing every moment of the tearing with her teeth and the sweetness afterwards. She swallowed, then barked at the smart speaker on the worktop, asked it to play a Bon Jovi track. Her karaoke song of choice. That to rock out to, or the sad one from *Titanic* if she'd had a few too many and was feeling a bit teary.

As she danced around the island, she imagined Eduardo dancing opposite her, so she gave him all her best moves. She shimmied and dipped and thrust her hips, showing off a body perfected at the gym and at Pilates classes and on those punishing bike rides through Italian mountain passes or along Californian hillsides. She raised her arms and sang along with the chorus, belting it out until her throat hurt and hearing her voice bounce back at her off the marble and the stainless steel, the polished tiles they'd had shipped over from Venice. She heard the echo rising up to the vaulted ceiling then dying away.

She stopped and quietly told the speaker to shut up.

She was singing and dancing in her stupidly expensive kitchen and there was nobody there to see it. Nobody to tell her how great she sounded and how fantastic she looked.

Michelle sat down and tore into the apple again.

That was all right though, she decided, it was no big deal. Being alone was not a problem, being alone would be good for her.

More to the point, it was something she'd have to get used to.

FIVE

Miller could never get very excited about hotels. Most of the ones he ever needed to stay in for work were predictably bog-standard and, if he was shelling out for it himself, then as long as the bed was decent enough he was happy. You only ever *slept* there after all, so Miller could never understand the need for all the fancy stuff. He and Alex had treated themselves to a high-end establishment a couple of times – on her birthday one year and for a competition in Scarborough – but even then he wasn't exactly bowled over by the chocolates on the pillow (nasty, like dog-chocolate) or the towels folded so they looked like swans (they didn't) and who the hell needed their toilet paper arranged into a nice pointy V-shape?

There was only one way to fold a towel, bog-roll origami was idiotic and he could always pop a Malteser on his pillow at home if he felt like it.

So, no, a hotel was not a place that set him all a-quiver with anticipation.

Unless there'd been a murder in it, obviously.

The Sands was a big old monstrosity on the seafront and maybe it had been smart and stylish a hundred years ago. Maybe it had been the place to be. Miller guessed that it was still impressive enough to anyone checking in, but once you stepped out of the lift into one of the tatty, snot-green corridors, it was obvious that the lobby was where all the money had been spent and that the establishment was barely worth its three stars. If a guest staying at the Sands was to discover something that looked like chocolate on their pillow, Miller would have strongly advised against eating it.

By the time Miller and Xiu got there, room 503 was already a hive of activity. Crime scene tape had been stretched across the doorway and tied to the handles of the adjacent rooms. While they changed into their forensic romper-suits in the corridor, CSIs crept around with their brushes and scrapers or carried boxes of equipment in and out. Glancing into the room as he pulled up his plastic hood, Miller could see that there were already several similarly clad force photographers snapping away inside and that Prisha Acharya, the on-call pathologist was already at work.

'Right, shall we have a look at him?' Xiu asked.

'Well, I don't think he's going anywhere.'

Xiu led the way.

Miller exchanged a few grunts of greeting with some of the officers and CSIs already in there. Nobody seemed awfully surprised to see him. Most of them, who he only ever really met at crime scenes, probably didn't even know he'd been away, and if they did they may not have known why, which was fine by him. Acharya glanced up from the body on the bed and nodded.

The man they were all there to see was face down in a puddle of blood. There was a tattoo of some kind on his shoulder, which Miller guessed was meant to be an eagle but thought looked more like a demented budgie, and he was wearing white boxer shorts with what looked like penguins on them. Underwearwise it was clearly an unforgivable choice, but Miller supposed that the man sporting them was long past caring. He walked across to the window and took in the breathtaking vista of dirty cement and blackened rooftops, a sliver of what might have been the sea.

'Well, if he paid for a room with a view, he should ask for a refund.' Miller turned back into the room. 'Oh, wait . . .'

'OK,' Acharya said. 'Ready to turn him.'

She counted to three and Xiu and Miller stepped closer to the bed as a couple of CSIs heaved the body over.

'Small calibre, looks like.' Xiu was pointing to the nice, neat bullet hole in the middle of the man's forehead. 'Nine millimetre, maybe.'

Under normal circumstances, Miller would probably have said something unnecessary to Acharya at that point and, because they'd worked together a while, she'd have been expecting him to.

I don't want to leap to conclusions or tell you your job, but might that be the cause of death?

Instead he just stared at the dead man's face, feeling like he'd been punched.

'You OK?' Xiu asked.

He nodded and began to breathe a little more easily as an officer wandered across with something dangling from his gloved fingers. 'Found this, sir.' The officer proffered an expensive-looking brown wallet. 'No money inside, but I think there's enough in there to identify him.'

'Don't bother.' Miller was already on his way out of the room. 'I know who that is.'

Back in the corridor, they lowered their hoods.

'His name's Adrian Cutler,' Miller said. 'His father's Wayne Cutler. They're not . . . a nice family.'

Xiu was nodding and Miller could see that she recognised the name. It was probably the first one mentioned to her when she'd joined the team. He knew very well what the second name would have been.

'Drugs and sex work,' she said.

'Well, I'm a bit busy right now.' Miller waited, but there was nothing. 'But yes, those are indeed the areas of criminality with which Mr Cutler senior is primarily associated.'

'We should talk to Ralph Massey,' Xiu said.

And there was that other name. That other punch.

'Laundering money through a network of ballrooms and casinos and Cutler's main rival, right?' Xiu nodded back towards the bedroom. 'I mean this certainly looks professional, so Massey should probably be our first port of—'

Miller raised a hand to stop her and thankfully it worked. 'First off, well done for being, hands down, the winner of the Lancashire Police Job-Pissed Swot of the Year Award.' Xiu blinked slowly. Miller was starting to notice that she did that a lot. 'And second of all, there are more than two gangs. It's not *West Side Story*. There's plenty of others bumping up our overtime, plus these days we've got the county lines drug gangs to think about.'

'Of course. I'm aware.'

'But yeah, obviously we'll be having a word with Ralph Massey.' It was hard not to gag, just saying his name. He watched as a uniformed officer came bowling down the corridor towards them, alongside a pudgy individual with a blue suit and a red face.

'This is the hotel manager,' the officer said. 'He wants a quick word.'

As the officer walked away, the manager marched across and shook Miller's hand with both of his, which was usually a sign that someone cared about something a great deal or else was just a bit of an arse. He talked directly to Miller, as though Xiu wasn't even there.

'Paul Mullinger,' Paul Mullinger said. 'Well, this is horrible ... goes without saying, and I know you have a job to do, but I just wanted to make sure that I wouldn't have to close the hotel completely. I mean, surely that won't be necessary, will it?'

Miller extricated his hand and pointed at Xiu. 'This is Detective Sergeant Xiu. Maybe you didn't see her.' Mullinger may have reddened a little but it was hard to tell. He leaned across and gave Xiu's outstretched hand the same creepy-clutchy treatment as he had Miller's. 'Good, now we're all friends,' Miller said, 'and no, I don't see any reason why the hotel needs to close.' *Well, aside from what I can only presume are reasons of health, safety and food hygiene standards.* 'This floor will need to be shut off for a day or two, though. Have all the rooms up here been cleared?'

'Well, checkout time was over an hour ago.'

'You might want to make sure.'

'Right. Yes, of course.'

Mullinger scuttled away towards the room at the far end of the corridor, removing a pass key that was attached to a chain on his belt.

'I can stick up for myself, you know,' Xiu said.

'Never said you couldn't.'

'Thanks, though.' She glared at Mullinger as he opened a bedroom door and peered inside. 'Knob!' Mullinger closed the door again and gave them a wave.

'So, why's Adrian Cutler staying in a crappy hotel?' Miller smiled at Mullinger who was moving towards the next door. 'No offence.'

'Is he married?'

'Yep, with three young kids. Big house on North Park Drive.' Miller knew the area well, one of the pricier parts of town; a million miles away (though actually only six) from the area in which he himself had grown up. Not that Miller was from a particularly deprived area, though there were plenty of those, too. He'd grown up in an ordinary part of town midway between 'rough-as-a-badger's-arse' and 'all-fur-coat-and no knickers', even if his childhood (thanks to a mother who was only sporadically healthy and a father who was only sporadically present) had been anything but ordinary.

Miller watched Mullinger open another door and check that the room was empty. A thumbs-up.

'Trouble at home, maybe?' Xiu suggested.

'Maybe.'

'Business meeting that went wrong?'

'In his penguin boxers?'

Things were now getting a little tricky for the manager. He'd reached the room next door to the one that contained the body and the handle had crime scene tape wrapped around it. He pointed and shrugged, not sure what he was allowed to do. Miller waved and told him to take the tape off.

'Are you sure?'

'It's fine,' Miller said. 'We'll put it back afterwards.'

'If Cutler wanted to treat himself,' Xiu said, 'there's plenty of nicer places he could have chosen.'

Miller knew she wasn't wrong. 'There's an alleyway round the corner with a few old mattresses in it. That's a step up.'

'Secret assignation, you think? Didn't want to be anywhere he might be recog—'

Xiu stopped when Mullinger cried out and they turned to see him stagger back from the open door of the adjacent bedroom and press himself against the wall.

'Oh, Jesus . . .'

Miller and Xiu stepped quickly across, peered into the bedroom and saw what the manager had seen. The body of a man lay at the foot of the bed. Unlike the one in the room next door, this victim was fully clothed, but there was just as much blood and the bullet wound was virtually identical.

'I reckon we should *probably* call this in,' Miller said.

Xiu reached into her bodysuit for her mobile.

'I'll tell you one thing.' Miller nodded towards the hotel manager. Mullinger was gasping like a beached fish and his previously ruddy complexion was now the colour of old porridge. 'This is not going to look good on Tripadvisor.'

SIX

An hour or so later, Sullivan had arrived and gathered the team for an ad hoc meeting in the small lobby area on the fifth floor outside the lifts. There was a plastic potted plant, a low table and two armchairs, though Miller had no idea why. Did people really need to make themselves comfortable while they were waiting for the lift in a five-storey building? Thumb through a magazine? How long did the bloody thing take?

Staff had brought up a Thermos of coffee and there was a basket of biscuits; two of each sort in plastic wrappers, same as the guests might find in their rooms. Miller rootled through the selection on offer while Sullivan did his bit.

'So, aside from the fact that we're all looking at a very long day, based on observations and the intel gathered so far, what do people think?'

Nobody – not Clough or Fuller or Xiu – seemed hugely keen to speak up.

Miller stepped forward, brandishing a pack of biscuits

in each hand. 'I think that a ginger snap is far superior to a shortbread finger, so I'm frankly gobsmacked that the finger outnumbers its gingery counterpart by about three to one. I'm not sure there's much point in complaining about the discrepancy, but still.' Sullivan didn't look impressed, but that was never Miller's intention. 'Oh, you meant, what do we think about the *case*? Sorry, but you weren't very specific. Well . . . I think we're looking at a hitman who went to the wrong room.'

'Sullivan studied him. 'You're kidding, right?'

'Why not? Everyone makes mistakes. So . . . in he goes, bang bang . . . checks his instructions, calls the client, whatever . . . *oh, shit, number 501 not number 503! What am I like?* Knock knock, bang bang. Two for the price of one. Job done.'

'You're not quite back up to speed, Dec,' Sullivan said. 'So I'll give you the benefit of the doubt. Anyone else?'

'We've got two wallets,' Xiu said. 'No cash in either, but two solid IDs. Barry Shepherd – they're checking him out back at base – and Adrian Cutler, who I'm obviously aware of and who the rest of you are clearly very familiar with.'

Xiu looked across at Miller and so did Sullivan. Something *knowing* in his expression, which made Miller wish that lift shaft was empty so that he could toss the new DI down it. The rest of them just looked sheepish.

'The empty wallets are weird,' Fuller said. 'If this is a professional hit, why bother nicking cash?'

Sullivan nodded. 'It's a good point. We need to look into that. And where's Shepherd's phone . . . ?' He stopped as he saw Acharya and Penny Dawson, the CSI team leader, walking towards them from the crime scene.

'So, what's the verdict?'

'Well, they've both been dead approximately twelve hours,'

Acharya said. 'They were almost certainly killed at around the same time. Possibly within a few minutes of each other.'

'Right, thank you. PMs in the morning.'

'I'll do my very best, Detective Inspector.' Acharya walked away towards the lift and waited. She didn't bother taking a seat. As she passed, she gave Miller a sly wink, which was very much appreciated.

Sullivan turned to Dawson.

'Been busy, Penny?'

Dawson looked at him like he was an idiot, which again was very nice to see. 'What do you think? A hotel room is pretty much a CSI's worst nightmare.'

'No shortage of trace, then?'

'Put it this way, if you wanted me to process all the DNA in those two rooms, I could probably turn it round for you in . . . oh, eighteen months?' She turned and smiled at Miller. 'Good to see you back, Declan.'

'Good to be back, Penny,' he said.

Sullivan sniffed and adjusted his collar. 'You've got *something*, though.' He nodded towards the plastic evidence bag in Dawson's hand.

She held it up, dangling it like treasure. 'Physical evidence, which, as of now, is our best bet. Quickest, certainly. Hairs found in Mr Cutler's bed and they don't appear to be his.'

Sullivan stepped across to take a closer look.

'There's bulbs attached, which means I can get a solid DNA profile. We can assume the sheets were changed before the victim checked in, right?'

Miller thought that, as assumptions went, it was on the bold side, but he was willing to go with it for the time being. 'So, Adrian had a visitor.' He gave the word just enough stress to

37

make it clear he wasn't talking about the visitor who'd put a bullet in Cutler's head, though he was well aware they might have been one and the same person.

Tony Clough made his first contribution. 'Prossie, you reckon?'

'You mean "sex worker", Tony?' Xiu said.

Clough was speechless and, if Miller had had anything in his mouth, he might well have spat it out like he was in an old sitcom.

'Thank you, Sara.' Sullivan nodded enthusiastically. 'That's exactly what DC Clough means.'

'Yeah, course,' Clough said.

'Right then. I'll get back and brief the DCI, get the death knocks organised. The rest of you, stay here. We already know there's no CCTV on any of the floors, but there are cameras in the lobby, so we can have a good look at all the comings and goings last night. Tony, can you get on to that?'

'Boss,' Clough said.

'Everybody else, we need to talk to the staff. Find out if any of them had dealings with either of our victims.'

Miller thought it was about time to chip in again. 'On the subject of staff, it might be worth finding out if any of them didn't show up for work this morning.'

Clough actually snorted. 'What, you think one of the staff might have killed them?' He looked towards Sullivan and shook his head.

'All these doors have spyholes, right?' Miller pointed and waited while everyone looked and saw that he was correct. 'Whoever it was, Cutler and Shepherd were happy to let them in. Just saying.'

Sullivan was clearly getting impatient. 'OK, whatever. Let's

38

just get this all done on the hurry-up and we'll meet for a debrief back at base at five o'clock.'

While Sullivan stayed where he was and Penny Dawson walked back towards the crime scene, Miller moved to the lift along with Clough and Fuller. He pressed the button for the ground floor, looking forward to getting stuck in.

He was not oblivious to the fact that Xiu had hung back.

Sara Xiu watched the lift doors close. She glanced at Sullivan who smiled, then wandered across and dropped, sighing, into one of the two armchairs near the lift. Xiu followed the DI and perched a little gingerly on the edge of the chair next to his.

'So, how's it going?' Sullivan asked.

'Fine.' Xiu nodded.

'Good to hear.'

'It's an interesting case—'

'With DS Miller.'

'Oh . . . it's a bit early to tell, if I'm honest.'

Sullivan grunted, hitched up his trousers and crossed his legs. 'Well, you know where my office is, if there's anything you need to tell me.'

'Sir.'

'My door's always open, Sara.'

'He's certainly . . . different,' Xiu said. 'DS Miller.'

'One way of putting it.'

Xiu saw the muscles working in Sullivan's jaw. She was eager to join the rest of the team downstairs, but something was nagging at her. 'I just wanted to ask, sir. DS Miller seemed a bit . . . weird about Adrian Cutler. I mean, is there anything I should be aware of?'

Sullivan appeared to relax a little as he leaned forward and

39

nodded, knowingly. Like there was something that would be painful to impart, but which, as a helpful colleague, he would force himself to share with her all the same. 'DS Miller's wife was a DI on Serious and Organised. The Cutlers were one of the organisations she was investigating when she was murdered. The Cutlers and the Masseys.'

Xiu was stunned. Why hadn't anyone seen fit to tell her?

'Oh, I didn't know she'd been . . .'

Sullivan nodded again, solemn. 'Afraid so. Shot in the head. Just like Adrian Cutler.'

SEVEN

While Xiu and Fuller interviewed various members of staff and Clough scrolled through CCTV footage from the lobby, Miller walked to the manager's office, where the chambermaid who had discovered Adrian Cutler's body was waiting for him.

Together with a uniformed officer, Mullinger had been inside comforting her and he stepped out for a word when Miller knocked on his door.

'She's being very brave,' he said. He nodded, as if to remind Miller that having only recently stumbled upon a corpse himself, he knew exactly what the poor girl had been through. When he leaned in to say 'but she's *very* upset', his breath made it clear that he'd had a stiff drink or three to deal with his trauma.

She was sitting in a chair in front of the manager's desk, her hands folded in her lap, rubbing one against the other as she stared at the wall. Once the uniformed officer had left, Miller walked around the desk and sat in Mullinger's chair. He waited until she finally raised her eyes to him.

'I'm Detective Sergeant Miller, Sofia. Is it all right if I call you Sofia?'

She nodded.

Sofia Hadzic was twenty-six years old and looked even younger. She was slight, her dirty-blonde hair tied back with a scrunchy, and she had clearly been crying a good deal.

Miller took out his phone. He pressed the record button and set it down on the desk. 'Do you mind if I use this? I'm getting on and my memory's going a bit.' There was a smile then, or something close to one, but he couldn't be sure because it wasn't there long enough. She sat up and he could see that she was trying to pull herself together. 'Can you just talk me through what happened this morning? Take your time . . .'

She took a deep breath, then leaned towards Miller's phone on the desk. Her voice was soft, barely above a whisper. There was a pronounced accent, Eastern European, Miller guessed. Croatia perhaps, or Serbia, but he certainly wasn't going to presume. Cultural sensitivities, again.

He knew she wasn't from Glasgow.

'It was normal, you know?'

'OK . . .'

'I collect my trolley and I go up to the fifth floor. I go to the room at the far end because that is the best place to start. This was the third room I clean. I knock on the door to make sure the room is empty. Then I open it—'

She flinched at the sudden knock on Mullinger's door and both she and Miller turned to see Xiu poke her head round.

'I just need a quick word.'

Miller apologised to Sofia, turned off the recorder on his phone and stepped out into the corridor.

'I checked the log at reception,' Xiu said. 'Both victims were booked in for one night. They actually checked in within five minutes of each other.'

'Interesting,' Miller said.

'You think?'

'God knows.' Miller shrugged. 'It's just something you say, isn't it?'

'The receptionist who was on duty last night has gone home, but I've left a message and asked them to call me back.'

'Good work.'

Xiu looked momentarily pleased, then hesitated. 'Just something you say, right?'

'Yep.'

Miller turned away, stepped back into Mullinger's office and sat down again. He restarted the recording app on his phone and leaned slowly towards Sofia. She still looked shell-shocked.

'Sorry about that,' he said. 'You'd just opened the door . . .'

'Yes, and then I go in, and . . .' She stopped, her mouth hanging open, remembering. She shook her head and lowered it.

'I'm sorry,' Miller said. 'I know this is difficult.'

She looked up again and now he could see that she was clutching a balled-up tissue in her fist. She pressed it to her eyes.

'I see him straight away. On the bed. He just has underwear on . . . with those birds on them. What are they called?'

'Penguins.' Miller still hadn't recovered himself.

'Yes, penguins. He's just lying there and I can see all the blood, you know? All the blood where he's been shot in the head. Such a lot of blood . . .'

She paused, frozen and staring. She quickly composed herself and carried on, but the tears were falling now and her voice had become tired and almost robotic.

'I think I will be sick.' She pressed her hands to her stomach and closed her eyes. 'I scream. I just keep screaming until somebody comes.'

Miller gave her a few seconds, waited until her eyes were open again. 'Had you seen the man on the bed before?'

She shook her head.

'Is there anything else you can remember, Sofia? Anything at all?'

'It's stupid, I know, but while I was standing there screaming, I remember thinking that it would be very hard, you know? Very hard to wash all that blood out of the sheets.'

Miller thanked the young woman for her help and told her that they would do everything they could to help her, that there were people she could talk to if she wasn't coping. He gave her a card with his number on. He called the uniformed officer back in, then stepped out to find Mullinger lurking.

'Everything OK?'

'Three quick questions,' Miller said. 'First off, as far as the ratio of gingerbread to shortbread goes, why so skewed in favour of shortbread?' He waved away the manager's confusion. 'OK, I'll leave that one with you. Second, are there any members of staff who should have been at work this morning and weren't?'

Mullinger thought about it. 'Well, this time of year there's always a quick turnover, but ... no, I don't think so. I'll double check.'

'If you could. Finally, and perhaps most importantly, on a scale of one to ten, how disgusting is your bar food?' Mullinger opened his mouth to answer, but Miller quickly cut him off. 'Be honest, now. I'm a highly experienced police officer and I'll know if you're lying.'

*

He sat with Xiu at a table in the corner, tucking into a BLT that wasn't altogether inedible and watching Xiu pick at a salad and sip water that was a lot more sparkling than the conversation.

'You OK?' he asked, eventually. Miller had already sussed that his new partner wasn't the gobbiest of souls, but she seemed unusually subdued.

'All good,' she said.

'Only I can barely get a word in edgeways.' He smiled and she didn't. 'Is it edge*ways* or edge*wise*? I'm never sure.'

She'd clearly never thought about it. 'I was just thinking about the case,' she said.

'Oh, right. Very good. Cracked it yet?'

She shook her head, then forked a tomato rather more viciously than was strictly necessary and they descended into silence again. Miller finished his sandwich. He looked round and could only marvel at the interior décor of the Sands bar, the faux leather banquettes and the hideous artwork that took up every available inch of wall space. While it wasn't quite in the same league as dogs playing snooker, it was in the same ballpark of atrocity. He made a mental note to have serious words with Paul Mullinger and suggest he get rid of it all in favour of something less offensive. A chimp sitting on a toilet, perhaps, or an inspirational print saying LIVE, LAUGH, LOVE (Miller was all in favour of adding PUKE).

'I didn't think your suggestion was stupid, by the way,' Xiu said suddenly.

Miller waited, because there were several to choose from.

'The whole "wrong room" scenario.'

'Well, that's good to hear,' he said.

'It isn't what you would call thinking in a straight line, but that's not a bad thing.'

'I won't hand in my resignation just yet.'

She looked at him, fierce suddenly, which was properly disconcerting if not a little scary. 'Of course not. No, you should definitely *not* do that.'

'I just said I wouldn't, didn't I?'

'Why would you even think about doing that?'

'Are you sure you're OK?'

She sighed and shook her head. She pushed her unfinished salad away from her and necked what was left of her water. She looked at her watch.

'Yeah, we should probably crack on,' Miller said.

EIGHT

Back at the station, while the extended team was gathering in the meeting room, laying out information packs and ensuring that pencils were sharpened, Miller took the opportunity to put in a quick call to his dead wife's phone. He only did it a few times a day because he wasn't barking mad, but it always made him feel better to hear her voice when the call – inevitably – went to her answerphone. Alex, telling him she wasn't there right now, like he needed reminding. Asking him to leave a message, which he obviously didn't do, but . . .

It was just nice to hear her voice.

He didn't want to forget it.

He dialled and, listening to it ring out, he imagined Fred and Ginger's ears pricking up, same as he always did, as the tinny theme to *Strictly Come Dancing* chimed around his living room.

For years he'd taken the mickey out of that bloody ringtone, but Alex had loved it. She'd said it made her happy and reminded her of good times even when she knew that her phone ringing usually meant bad news, for her or for someone else. She'd played it just to annoy him sometimes, waving her phone at him and singing along, and he'd pretended that it did, even though secretly he'd loved it too.

Now, that music just killed him.

'This is Alex and I can't talk right now, because I'm out somewhere fighting crime, or doing serious damage to a bottle of red. Either way, beep, message, you know . . .'

There were more people around the table in the conference room than Miller remembered seeing in a long time. Then again, he couldn't remember anyone discovering two bodies in adjacent hotel rooms, so it was probably fair enough. Xiu, Clough, Fuller and half a dozen other members of the team were all seated, leafing through their packs. Several ancillary staff were standing, including Carys Morgan from the Digital Forensics Unit and someone who might have been called Brian from the Press Liaison Office.

Sullivan stood up at the head of the table and talked the team through a hastily assembled PowerPoint presentation on the screen behind him. As always, Miller found himself idly fantasising that the wrong file had been loaded and that they would be treated to a selection of Sullivan's holiday snaps or, better yet, his and Mrs Sullivan's private collection of saucy bedroom videos.

'Oh, Tim, you're the best.'

'Yeah . . . who's your Daddy?'

It would not be pleasant, but it would certainly ease the tension.

'So . . .' Sullivan pointed to the screen, as the first pictures of the victims appeared. 'Adrian Cutler, thirty-one. I don't think I need to tell anyone about him. Youngest son of Wayne Cutler. It's safe to assume Adrian was the prime target, so it goes without saying that his old man is going to be looking very closely at the activities of the Massey family and that could all get very nasty. Obviously we've given Serious and Organised a heads-up.' He glanced at Miller. *The unit your dead wife used to work for.*

'I don't quite understand the *safe* bit,' Miller said.

'Sorry?'

'Why is it a safe assumption that Cutler was the target?'

Sullivan stared as though it was a very daft question. 'Er . . . because he's the son of a gangland boss?'

'True, but not necessarily relevant.'

'Because it looks very much like he was executed?'

'Yes, that's certainly what it looks like,' Miller said. 'Then again a fried egg can look very much like a tinned peach, which, trust me, isn't a mistake you want to make more than once. More to the point, even if Adrian Cutler was executed, so was the other bloke. Never mind safe, I'm not even sure it should be an assumption.'

Sullivan nodded slowly. 'In his own . . . unique fashion, DS Miller has provided us with a timely reminder that we shouldn't take anything for granted. But, until such time as he produces any evidence that the target in this case was actually the forty-four-year-old IT consultant in the next room, we'll move forward on the . . . hypothesis that Adrian Cutler was the killer's intended victim.'

'I don't think an assumption and a hypothesis are the same things,' Miller said.

Sullivan ignored him. 'We must not forget however that we are investigating two murders here and whatever our killer's primary motivation proves to have been, we can't ignore the second victim. Barry Shepherd. A very different kettle of fish. An IT consultant, as I said, married with no kids. So, how the hell does he end up going the same way as Adrian Cutler and, crucially, what were both of them doing at the Sands Hotel in the first place? Tony ... ?'

Clough began sorting through his notes. 'Right, so we've found our ... *sex worker.*' He nodded at Xiu, who did not react, then began handing out photographs captured on the CCTV cameras at the hotel. 'That's definitely what she was.'

'The concierge recognised her,' Fuller said. 'Told me she's been there several times. No ID as yet, though.'

'Well, we need to put that right,' Sullivan said. 'Let's find out who she is and bring her in as quickly as possible. Anything else from the CCTV?'

'I've gone over all the comings and goings in the key time-frame, and in terms of anyone using the lift to access the upper floors, we've got one individual who currently remains unaccounted for and who nobody can identify as a guest.' Clough handed out copies of a second photograph, which were quickly passed around the table and studied.

A man who, as of that moment, was their prime suspect.

Miller stared down at the picture. The features of the man walking across the lobby were not exactly pin-sharp, but Miller thought he looked a bit like celebrity gardener, TV presenter and national treasure, Alan Titchmarsh. It was unlikely, obviously, but still, he couldn't help but imagine the headlines.

Green-fingered Alan Caught Red-handed.

Something about evidence being planted ...

Sullivan nodded. 'I don't need to tell you that finding this individual is our number one priority.' He nodded to the man who might have been called Brian. 'We'll get copies of this photo circulated to the media ASAP.'

The man who might have been called Brian nodded back.

'What if our killer never left the hotel?' Miller asked, having temporarily stopped thinking about Alan Titchmarsh. 'What if he's hiding in plain sight?'

'Hiding where?' Sullivan stared at him and so did everyone else.

'Well, if I knew that, we'd all be home in time for *Countdown*, wouldn't we?'

'This thinking outside the box, is it?'

'Just mooting the possibility,' Miller said.

'Oh, right. *Mooting.*' Sullivan shook his head. 'So, where are we on Cutler's phone?'

Carys Morgan took a step forward. A ferociously bright and proud Welshwoman, she had also proved herself adept at decision making. Once, when a beat officer had made a sheep noise in her hearing, she had been forced to decide quickly between reporting the officer to IIR or dealing with the matter herself in a fashion that would not require any paperwork. She had plumped for the latter, distinctly more forthright option and the officer in question had pounded his beat somewhat gingerly for a fortnight afterwards.

Miller was a big fan.

'We're going through it right now,' she said. 'Also trying to trace his movements prior to checking in. There was no sign of Mr Shepherd's phone at the scene, presuming he had one, but hopefully there's a computer at home.'

'Get someone to pick it up,' Sullivan said.

'Talking of checking in.' All heads turned to Xiu. 'The book at reception shows that Shepherd checked in to the hotel only five minutes after Cutler. Unfortunately the receptionist who spoke to them both has gone off duty. I've left a message and asked him to call me back.'

'Right. Thanks, Sara—'

'And while I don't think DS Miller's suggestion was *completely* off beam . . .' she smiled at Miller '. . . the whole "wrong room" scenario, I can also see what *you* were saying, sir. You know, weighing it up. I mean we're definitely talking about someone professional, right? Nobody heard anything, so the killer must have used a silencer.'

'That's certainly the obvious explanation,' Miller said. 'But it might be worth checking there wasn't a convention of deaf people staying there last night. Cross the *t*s and dot the *i*s, right?'

Xiu stared. Sullivan sighed and moved towards the door.

'Right. The wives should be on their way to identify the bodies. Miller and Xiu, can you get down there?'

'To the morgue?'

'Well, it's not going to happen at the newsagent's, is it?' Sullivan's face didn't change, but it was clear he was pretty pleased with himself.

It felt to Miller like he was deliberately being handed the shitty end of the stick and that Xiu, who hadn't said anything Sullivan could take exception to, had been given no choice but to get her hands dirty too.

It was not a part of the job that any copper relished.

Certainly not one who had himself stood all too recently where the victims' wives would soon be standing.

Miller did not respond, did not even move for just long enough to make Sullivan think he might flat out refuse. Or become emotional and storm out. Or perhaps march purposefully across the room and do to Sullivan's nether regions what Carys Morgan had done to that bleating flatfoot's.

'Always a pleasure,' Miller said, eventually. 'Never a chore.'

NINE

Miller and Xiu gently led Barry Shepherd's widow into the room where her husband's body was lying. As soon as she had nodded to let them know she was ready, Miller signalled to one of Acharya's assistants, who drew back the sheet that was covering the body. A smaller, linen cloth had been placed carefully across the top of the dead man's head to mask the bullet wound.

Pippa Shepherd's hand moved quickly to cover her mouth, to stifle a gasp or a scream or the sudden rush of vomit.

Miller had seen all of them at one time or another.

Six weeks before, staring down at his wife's body on the same slab, that same discreet square of linen, he had done none of those things. He had felt every bit as dead as she was. Every bit as absent. Now, all too aware that Xiu was looking at his reaction as much as she was at Pippa Shepherd's, he tried desperately to keep those memories from his face. He tried, but he knew he'd been unable to manage it. He might even have groaned quietly or closed his eyes for a few seconds. It could not be helped and it was a small mercy that, despite having called her 'Job-pissed' once already, he didn't have Sara Xiu down as one of those who'd go rushing into Susan Akers's office first chance she got.

You were right, ma'am, DS Miller's definitely *not ready . . .*

Miller could not always control his instincts, but he trusted them.

Once the formal ID had been made, they escorted Pippa Shepherd back out into the corridor, where Michelle Cutler was waiting her turn. Miller stepped across to greet her, to say how sorry he was for her loss, but their paths had crossed before in very different circumstances, so he got only a perfunctory nod in return.

Xiu, meanwhile, was showing Pippa Shepherd out and could not help but notice the look she had given Michelle Cutler as they'd moved past her. Adrian Cutler's widow had paid her counterpart no attention whatsoever, but the lack of interest had certainly not seemed mutual.

It was only fleeting, and of course Xiu might have imagined it, but Pippa Shepherd had looked seriously thrown.

Startled, even.

Ten minutes later, Xiu was driving them back into town. Miller hadn't done much more than issue the occasional grunt since leaving the mortuary and was now staring blankly out at the landscape as it rushed by, his head against the car window.

The Tower loomed ahead of them and it was starting to rain.

'Did you catch that look back in there?' Xiu asked. 'I'm pretty sure there was a look. The look Pippa Shepherd gave Adrian Cutler's wife?'

Miller said nothing, miles away.

'So, what was all that about, then?'

Finally, Miller turned to her. 'Probably no more than a justifiable reaction to velour.'

'What?'

'I mean, who wears a velour tracksuit to identify a body? I know there's not really any formal dress code as such, but even so.'

'It looked to me like Pippa knew her—'

'Pull over!'

Miller was pointing, so Xiu did as she was told, hitting the brakes hard, veering across the road and bumping the Honda up on to the pavement.

'What's the—?'

Miller was out of the car before Xiu had even turned the engine off. She followed him as he strode across to a shop doorway where he bent to talk to what looked like a homeless girl, crouched inside and sheltering from the rain.

'Hey, Finn.'

'Hey, Miller,' the girl said. 'How's tricks? Apart from the . . . ?' She waved her hands around vaguely to fill in the gap and it was clear that she knew Miller well enough to appreciate what he'd been through.

'Apart from the . . .' Miller mimicked the girl's gesture '. . . it's all good. You?'

'Oh, you know. I've only collected thirty-seven pence all morning and a dog pissed on my sleeping bag last night, but aside from that . . .'

The girl looked up at Xiu, wary suddenly. She was in her mid-twenties, Xiu reckoned. Pale and with hair that looked like she'd hacked at it with nail scissors. She seemed ill and it was fairly obvious what kind of medicine she needed.

'Oh, don't worry, this is Sara,' Miller said. 'She's down with the kids.' He clenched his fist in the air. 'A friend to the homeless massive. Sara, this is Finn.'

Xiu exchanged nods with the girl, then watched Miller squat down next to her.

'Just wondering if you might have heard any whispers about the county lines lads. Any moves that might have been made.'

'Moves?'

'We've had a bit of an incident.'

The girl nodded. 'The shootings at the hotel, yeah?'

'Wow,' Xiu said. 'You've certainly got your ear to the ground.'

'Quite literally, most nights.' The girl looked back to Miller. 'I've not heard anything, but I'll see what I can find out.'

Miller nodded and took the photograph of the as yet unknown sex worker from his pocket. He unfolded it and handed it across. 'Recognise her? We can't ID her, so she's probably new.'

The girl took no more than a cursory glance. 'Yeah, I think I can remember her name.'

'You *think?*'

'I'm not a *hundred* per cent sure.'

Miller nodded again and took out his wallet. He opened it, then turned to Xiu. 'You couldn't bung me a tenner, could you? I appear to be financially embarrassed.'

'Seriously?'

'I'm good for it.' Miller nudged the girl. 'Tell her I'm good for it.'

'Oh yeah, he's properly minted.'

The girl was a picture of innocence as Xiu rummaged in her purse and dug out a ten pound note. 'I won't forget,' she said.

Miller grinned. 'Oh, I know you won't.'

Xiu handed it across just as her phone rang and, seeing the caller ID, she stepped away to answer, missing what Miller and the girl said to each other for a few vital seconds after that. The information she was paying for. She inched back towards them, only one ear on her call.

'Oh, and I could really do with finding out where Chesshead is,' Miller said.

'I heard he went to London.'

'What, to see the King?'

'Just telling you what I heard.'

'Well, try and find out if he's still there, if you can. I need to speak to him.'

The girl looked hard at the banknote in Miller's hand. 'That's quite a lot of work for a tenner.'

'Well, maybe my parsimonious partner can be persuaded to part with a little bit more if you come up with anything.' He nodded towards Xiu. 'Did you see the moths fly out when she opened that purse? *Moths*, I swear.'

The girl laughed and Miller handed over the cash.

'Now, make sure every single penny of that goes on drink or drugs, OK?'

'Obviously.'

'Don't go wasting it on, I don't know . . . food.'

The girl tucked the money away. 'What do you take me for?'

'And call me if you hear anything.'

The girl gave Miller a small salute as he heaved himself upright and walked back towards the car. Xiu quickly ended her call and followed him.

'So what's her story, then?' Xiu started the car.

Miller already had his phone out and was online searching for a number.

Xiu nodded back towards the doorway. 'The girl?'

'Aha.' Miller began dialling.

'And who the hell is Chesshead?'

'I'll tell you later,' Miller said. 'Not that you'll believe me.'

'Why don't you—?' Xiu stopped when Miller shushed her, his call having connected, and from that point on she could do little but listen.

'Hello there,' Miller said. 'Is that Bootylicious Babes?' He gave Xiu a thumbs-up. 'Splendid. Yes, I'd like to book one of your "top-class escorts" if I may ... specifically, a Miss Ribbons. Yes, Scarlett Ribbons ... like the song?' He waited then shook his head. 'It doesn't matter.' He waited again, staring at Xiu. '*How* much? Look, I should stress that it probably won't be the full hour, it will be strictly vanilla and that is rather more than I was expecting to pay.' He listened again, nodding. 'OK, well, let me give you the address ... it's Gerry Richardson Way, off Clifton Road. You can't miss it, it's the big white building. The one with all the police cars outside.' He grinned at Xiu, then nodded again, evidently happy with the response. 'Yes, first thing tomorrow morning will be perfect. Many thanks ...'

Miller ended the call and put his phone away. He leaned to beat out a frantic rhythm on the dashboard, delighted with all he'd accomplished in the previous ten minutes.

He said, 'It's nice when people are helpful, don't you think?'

TEN

Miller lurked next to his moped, eating crisps and watching a steady stream of officers and civilian staff leave the building at the end of their working day, while others arrived to start late shifts. It was not surprising that one group moved a little faster and seemed a mite more cheery than the other. Miller, on the other hand, had almost always come to work with a spring in his step. With the notable exception of today – which was never going to be easy – he enjoyed rocking up to play his small but significant part in making the ceremonial county of Lancashire, and this bit of it in particular, a slightly less horrible place to be.

Even if he often felt like a square peg in a round hole.

Or a peg with no discernible shape at all.

With one or two obvious exceptions, he largely enjoyed the company of other coppers. When it was actually funny, he relished the black humour and edgy repartee that was born of shared experience, that forged a bond between men and women who often struggled with the demands of a difficult job. Miller was more than happy to do his bit, readily contributing to everyday exchanges such as those he now instigated with a group of male officers on their way into the building.

'Hey, Faruk, did that nasty fungus on your doo-dads ever clear up?'

'What is *wrong* with you, mate?'

'Nice to see the diet's working out, Trevor.'

'Bugger off, Miller.'

Some people struggled more than others.

With time to kill, Miller decided to deal with some of the dozens of unanswered texts and voice messages that had been left on his phone in the previous few weeks. Messages that, however well-meaning or heartfelt, he had felt unable or unwilling to address. As far as most of those he looked at now went, 'deal with' meant 'ignore' and in a few cases 'delete', but there were still plenty of people who deserved a response.

A few days after Alex had been killed, he had recorded a voicemail greeting that simply said *'Dead wife. Busy. Leave message'*, but had decided it was perhaps a touch brusque and tasteless, even for him, and reverted to the automated one.

It was probably time to record something new . . .

Keeping an eye on the station doors, he texted Alex's sister to let her know that he was back at work and busy as all hell, and promised that he would try and find a good time for her to come round. He sent variations on the same message (with 'come round' replaced by 'get a coffee' or 'meet up in the pub') to several of Alex's friends and one or two of his own, before calling his mate Imran.

He wasn't too disappointed to get his friend's own voicemail message.

'Hey, it's Dec. Sorry I've been so rubbish . . . more rubbish than normal, I mean. I'm back at work now, which is probably a massive mistake, and things are pretty full-on . . . but if I can sneak off a bit early one of the days, shall we meet up for our customary competition? What do you reckon . . . usual place, usual stakes? I hope you've been practising, mate.' Miller glanced up and saw the officer he'd been waiting for emerge. 'I'll try you again later . . .' He hung up, emptied the last of the cheese and onion into his mouth and followed.

His target moved quickly, clearly in a hurry to get some-where, or just to get anywhere else, so Miller jogged across the car park and finally caught the man up as he was approaching his very shiny Volvo.

'Dominic . . .'

The man turned and, after a second or two, raised a hand. 'Oh, hey Dec.'

'Nice car.'

'I heard you were back.'

'Is it new?'

The man stared down at the car keys in his hand. 'Yeah . . . newish. Listen, are you OK? I mean, are you sure you're doing the right thing? Coming back this quickly.'

Miller smiled and took a step closer. 'You're looking very serious, Dominic.'

'I'm concerned, that's all. A lot of people are.'

'Mind you, I suppose you have to be, right? Serious. Serious and organised.'

Dominic Baxter said nothing, but finally returned Miller's smile, though his was thinner than a politician's excuse. He was rangy and athletic-looking, with a goatee beard and hair which Miller was convinced should have started to grey

62

by now. More important, he was someone who had worked closely with Miller's wife for several years.

Baxter took half a step towards his car.

'Oh, right . . . well, I'll try not to keep you,' Miller said. 'It's just a quickie really . . . only I was wondering what you'd told Forgeham about the night Alex was murdered. You know, about where she was, or where she was supposed to be.'

DCI Lindsey Forgeham was part of a separate homicide unit, heading up the investigation into Alex Miller's murder. An investigation which, for obvious reasons, Miller himself could not be part of. Miller was yet to be reassured that much investigating had actually been done, certainly any that had yielded a single thing worth writing home about.

'Come on, Dec,' Baxter said.

'Come on *what*, Dom?'

'If they haven't told you stuff, it's because they're not allowed to. I get that must be hard, but it's procedure.'

'I've got every right to know.' Miller was spinning his wedding ring. He had no desire to take it off, though truth be told he had fingers like sausages and he wasn't convinced that, short of amputation, he'd ever be able to. 'We were married. Alex and me, I mean, not me and you. Remember what that's like, matey? Watching shit TV together and putting the bins out and having daft arguments about nothing. Knowing that person better than anyone else in the world, while they know you every bit as well, and thinking about them a thousand times a day and only ever being happy if they are.' Miller stopped and smiled again. 'Ringing any bells, Dom?'

Baxter glanced around and, when he finally spoke, he lowered his voice which Miller thought was ludicrous, because there wasn't anyone else within fifty yards of them.

'I told them I didn't know where Alex had gone that night, because I didn't.'

Miller whispered, just to play along and so Baxter wouldn't feel quite such a tit. 'Is that normal?'

'It's not *ab*normal,' Baxter said. 'It's . . . unusual, maybe.'

'Shouldn't all that stuff be logged?'

'Yeah, it should be, but it doesn't always happen. Sometimes you have to do things on the hoof, you know? This kind of work.'

Miller knew that Baxter was right, having heard much the same thing from Alex often enough. It didn't make him feel any better, though. 'Why didn't she take her phone?'

'I've no idea.'

'What about her work phone? I know she had a separate one, but strangely nobody seems to know what happened to it.'

'She had it with her,' Baxter said. 'I'm pretty sure she did, anyway. I heard the tracking was turned off, though.'

'Heard from who?'

'Someone on Forgeham's unit.'

'So they tell *you* stuff, but they won't tell me.'

'They can't. Look, we've already . . .' He stopped when Miller began shaking his head.

It wasn't as if they'd never told him *anything*, of course. Almost every week – for the first month or so anyway – Miller had received a dutiful call or an email and, on one memorable occasion, there'd even been a visit at home. There'd been a card signed by everyone on Forgeham's team which Miller had swiftly binned and a bottle of wine which he'd necked in twenty minutes. Each time, in so many words he'd been told – sorrowfully, but firmly – that the investigation was ongoing.

Miller always tried to stay calm, to not laugh out loud or throw anything, but he knew what that meant.

Ongoing nowhere, ongoing backwards.

'What was she working on?'

'Sorry?'

'She must have talked to you about that.'

'Well . . . nothing that you don't already know,' Baxter said. 'The usual stuff. Cutler, Massey, one or two others.'

Cutler and Massey. The two arseholes of the apocalypse who, thanks to the very recent murder of Cutler junior, were individuals Miller would have to deal with in the days to come. He knew he should probably tread carefully and that he had about as much chance of doing that as a three-legged giraffe on ice skates.

'Listen, I need to get going,' Baxter said.

'Course you do.'

Baxter keyed his remote and the central locking on his newish motor honked like an emphysemic goose.

'You know where I am, right?' Miller winked. 'If there's anything you're itching to tell me.'

'It's good to see you back, though.'

'Is it, though?'

'If you're sure you're OK.'

'Oh, I'm ticking along nicely, Dominic,' Miller said. 'I'm raring to go.' He turned and began walking back across the car park, hearing the Volvo start up and accelerate away behind him.

Back at the moped, Miller tightened his high-vis jacket and fastened the chin strap beneath his crash helmet. He yelped and shouted 'Ballbags' when the plastic clip snagged a piece of skin on his neck. He'd just fired the hairdryer up when he heard the familiar roar of a Yamaha Tracer 9 and turned to see the big bike pulling up next to him.

The leather-clad biker revved the engine, then reached to lift up the black visor.

'Race you,' Xiu said.

For the second time that day, Miller watched the black and red bike speed away into the distance and he was grinning as he stamped the moped into gear and puttered after it. Stalled, started the bloody thing again and *then* puttered after it. No, coming back to work had not been a walk in the park and he knew the day was going to get harder before it was finished, but teaming up with Posh Gravy had definitely been a highlight.

ELEVEN

From the end of a small street high above the town, Miller stared out to sea, hoping that the shushing of the waves against the shore far below, the stillness and the dark, might clear his mind a little and help him make the decision. It didn't. The only decision he'd ever reached where the sea was concerned was to avoid it whenever possible and certainly to steer well clear of ever getting *in* it. It was cold and wet and there were things in there he didn't want to think about for very long.

Alex, of course, had felt very differently. She'd swum on mornings when the sand had glittered with frost for God's sake and had greedily sucked in the smell of the water and the weed at every opportunity; closing her eyes and humming with contentment, the same way he might if it was deep-fried doughnuts or bacon sizzling in a pan. She couldn't get enough of it and had laughed at Miller's aversion to the water, even when he'd discovered there was an actual word for it.

'It's called thalassophobia,' he'd told her. 'I'm a thalassophobe.'

She'd told him he was a wuss.

It was what she'd call him now, Miller knew that. He turned back to look at the shabby, single-storey building he was far more nervous about entering than the one he'd just left.

It made sense, that's what he told himself, because there was so much more in there to be afraid of. There just *was*. So much he didn't want to face up to or remember. He had every right to be a little apprehensive, more than a little, and surely nobody who'd been through what he had could be blamed for saying 'sod this for a game of soldiers', climbing back on to their moped and going straight home.

It's what anyone in his position would do.

If they were a wuss . . .

When Miller eventually stepped through the cracked and creaky door carrying his crash helmet, they all turned to look at him and a couple of them even gasped. It wasn't unlike the moment he'd stepped back into the incident room that morning, except that most of the people in here were a good deal older – a lot older in some cases – and, more important, they all looked pleased to see him.

At a variety of different speeds, the group hurried across to greet him.

Howard and Mary were certainly in their mid-seventies while Gloria and Ransford could not have been that far behind them. Ruth was in her early forties, same general ballpark as Miller, and Nathan (the baby of the group) wasn't yet thirty. Nathan and Ruth weren't a couple, but Miller had long suspected that Nathan harboured ambitions in that direction.

Miller liked the lad immensely, though it was fair to say

68

that they hadn't bonded over a shared taste in music. Nathan had – for example – casually declared that Jay-Z was the new Shakespeare. As Miller didn't know an awful lot about the *old* Shakespeare, he'd felt unqualified to comment, but he wasn't about to let Nathan's next pronouncement go unchallenged.

'The Beatles? They're not even the best band to come out of Liverpool, never mind the best band in the world. One word – overrated!'

Miller had responded with a word of his own and, even if it was one they'd all heard before, it was said with such vehemence that Mary had needed to take a break for fifteen minutes and sit down with a large gin.

'We knew you'd be back,' Mary said now.

'Oh, yeah?'

'Didn't we, Howard?'

'Yeah, we knew,' Howard said.

Miller shrugged and looked around, taking it all back in. It was just a big old shed, basically. The Sea Scouts used it at least one night a week to practise not drowning, and assorted community groups held jumble sales there, or sparsely attended coffee mornings, but three nights a week it became something else.

'Well, I'm glad *you* did,' Miller said. 'Because I wasn't sure. I'm still not.'

'You can't just give up,' Ransford said. His voice was surprisingly high and light for such a big man, the Jamaican accent now tinged with a Lancashire burr.

'I wouldn't have been ... giving up.'

'No, right. I didn't mean *giving up.*'

'Things are just different, obviously.'

Ruth stepped across and punched him on the arm. 'You'll be grand, love.'

'Yeah, course you will.' Nathan leaned in for a slightly unco-ordinated high-five. 'It's good to see you, mate.'

Mary nudged her husband and beamed at Miller. 'It's wonderful, and what's more, Alexandra would have thought you being back here was wonderful, too.'

Miller nodded. He was still wondering if it wasn't too late to turn tail and get back on the moped, but Mary made sure that wasn't going to happen when she reached across and took his hand. He felt some of the weight lift when she squeezed. These were friends, after all, and this shitty old scout hut was an escape. It had been their escape, his and Alex's, but there was no reason why it shouldn't still be his. Somewhere he could come for a few hours to leave murder behind and all the nonsense that rattled round his stupid head when he was at home on his own.

All the same, it remained to be seen if—

Mary, who was as bossy as she was arthritic, clapped her hands. 'Right then, let's start with something nice and easy, shall we? Declan . . . you can partner me.'

Miller quickly raised his hands. 'Whoa, not yet, Mary.' He began walking across to the knackered old piano in the corner, shouting back to the others who stood and watched him. 'Just some accompaniment tonight, I think. Ease myself back in gently.'

He dumped his jacket and crash helmet on the floor, sat down and began to play. Miller was happier on guitar than piano, but he could bash out a tune if he needed to. After no more than half a minute's bashing, he became aware that Mary was standing directly behind him. He stopped playing like they were in a saloon and a badass gunslinger had just walked in.

'You need to get back on the horse, love.'

Miller stared down at the keys.

'Seriously?' Her voice was stern, suddenly, like she had every mind to slap his legs. 'You're going to stand me up? I'm a bloody pensioner!'

'I don't think I can do this,' Miller said. 'Not without . . .'

'Well, there's only one way to find out, isn't there?' Mary clapped her hands again. 'Nathan, you come and play . . .'

Reluctantly, even though he knew that arguing with Mary was pointless, Miller stood up and Nathan moved across to take over. Miller sighed and hoped the tremor in his legs wasn't too evident as Mary led him to the centre of the room. He tried to smile when she put his arms where they needed to go and leaned in close.

'Just a simple paso doble, a double-step . . . get you back into the swing of things.'

'No.' Miller stepped away. 'Not that one.'

'Oh, right.' Mary shook her head like she was an idiot. 'Of course not that one. How about a waltz, then? Nathan . . . ?' She pulled Miller back and repositioned his arms. 'I promise I'll be gentle with you.'

Nathan started to play, more or less in time and, a few moments later, Miller, Mary and the rest of them began to dance.

It had always been, to put it politely, a mixed ability group, but none of them fell over very often. Gloria needed to sit down fairly regularly, Howard was known affectionately as the 'toe-crusher' and on one occasion Ransford had turned his ankle quite badly during an over-ambitious tango, but generally speaking, everyone was . . . competent.

Miller watched them over Mary's shoulder, remembering.

'That's it,' she said. 'Just relax and ... one two three, one two three ... there we go, love. See? It's all coming back ...'

Miller relaxed, because it genuinely felt like it was.

He closed his eyes, and when he opened them again, everything had changed.

It was Alex looking up at him and a smile spread across her face as the lights from a huge glitterball floated across it. The orchestra kicked in and everyone else moved back to the edge of the floor to watch as Miller and his wife began to move in perfect sync. Miller's tuxedo was immaculate and he could feel the sequins on Alex's dress beneath his fingers as the two of them rose and fell together, stepped and slid and stepped again, living and breathing their dance.

It was faultless, it was effortless.

Their shoulders moved smoothly and stayed perfectly parallel to the polished floor. Intuitively they lengthened their steps and Alex's eyes were fixed on his while Miller led her into space.

Every move, silk on silk, like they'd done it a million times.

Box step, natural turn, reverse turn, backward passing change until finally, as the music swelled and grew louder, the routine moved like clockwork towards its climax. Miller's arm snaked around Alex's slender neck. It slid down to support her as she slowly arched her back and let her head drop, staring up at him with love and with the widest smile, as the audience got to its feet and began to cheer ...

... and Miller opened his eyes.

Nathan's final, somewhat iffy piano chord echoed off the grubby white walls as Miller awkwardly hoisted Mary back up. He was struggling to get his breath back and to stay on his feet. All smiles and equally breathless, Howard, Gloria and the others were already gathering around and they nodded enthusiastically when Mary announced that it was a mightily good effort for someone who was understandably rusty and you know, *considering*.

'Let's all have a cup of tea,' she said. 'Then we'll try something else.'

She rubbed Miller's arm and said that he should feel very pleased with himself. She told him that he'd be back to his sparkling best in no time at all and that, most importantly, the tears were nothing to be ashamed of.

TWELVE

It would have been hard to slip a cigarette paper between Michelle Cutler and her mother-in-law, pressed tightly against her on the sofa in Michelle's living room. Michelle stared at the wall or down at her hands, looking anywhere but at her brother-in-law Justin, and especially not at Wayne, who was watching her from an armchair on the other side of the room. When her father-in-law wasn't giving her evils, he was up and down every five minutes, slipping into the hall to make phone calls he clearly did not wish to be overheard.

Michelle sat there and wished that she'd cried more, or even at all.

Somehow she just hadn't been able to manage it, so instead she'd done her bit keeping the teas and whiskies coming, while everyone else did the weeping for her. That said, she was relieved that the kids weren't around to see their grandparents so upset. They'd already seen enough blubbering and heard enough raised voices to last them a lifetime. Michelle had packed them off to stay with her mum first chance she'd got, which was a treat for all of them. Although her mother only lived fifteen minutes away, she barely got to see her grandchildren because Jacqui always had first dibs; smothering them the same way she smothered everyone else, with what looked like affection but Michelle knew was something else entirely. It was about staking a claim and marking out what was hers, same as she'd always done with her precious son.

Jacqui sighed and leaned into her again; the reek of perfume and that soggy cheek – *she'd* done *plenty* of crying – pressed against Michelle's noticeably dry one.

'How did this happen?'

Michelle had been asking herself the same question for a long time. She'd been to a good school, which her mum had sacrificed everything to pay for. She'd worked hard and got good grades, had ambitions which everyone told her she could easily fulfil.

Journalism, maybe, or something in fashion. Plenty of people had said she could have been a model. Still said it.

The world had been Michelle Conroy's oyster.

So how did she end up being crushed against a woman like Jacqui Cutler while Wayne Cutler eyeballed her like he knew something she'd rather he didn't? How did she end up being a bloody Cutler in the first place?

Because Adrian was not like his father. That's what he'd told her. Because he could charm the birds out of the trees whereas his old man would simply have taken a shotgun to them. Well, Adrian had charmed Michelle out of her knickers on their second date and that had been that. The world wasn't her oyster any more, however many they ate and however many pearls Adrian bought for her. Welcome to the family . . .

Now, six years and three kids later, what was she left with? Well, the kids, obviously and she'd die for her babies, but even keeping hold of them might be a struggle. Jacqui wouldn't let them go anywhere without a fight, least of all now, when Wayne didn't even have to pretend that he liked her any more.

He was looking over at her again and Michelle was damn sure, same as always, that he knew exactly what she was thinking. What she'd been thinking for a while.

What the hell was going to happen now?

The Family Liaison Officer had been with her from that first knock on the door, and she was nice enough, but Pippa Shepherd wasn't daft. She knew that the woman wasn't just there to make sympathetic noises and keep the kettle boiling. The spouse was always a suspect, wasn't that how it worked in detective novels and on TV shows?

The jealous wife, the greedy wife, the wife who'd lost control.

Pippa wasn't any of those things, so she felt like looking the woman straight in the eye and telling her that she was wasting her time. That not only was she never going to get a confession, but that she wasn't actually needed. Yes, for those first few hours it had been a comfort, Pippa supposed, but ever since they'd got back from the mortuary all Pippa had wanted to do was scream, maybe smash a few things, and there was no way she was going to do that with a police officer hanging about. She'd always been a bit . . . buttoned up, she knew that. Not as much as Barry, of course, not even close, and part of her desire to hold things in was knowing how much Barry would have disapproved were she to . . . lose it. She could picture the look on his face if she started wailing and throwing stuff around.

Come on now, Pip . . .

No, not *disapproved*, that was unfair of her, that was actually a horrible thing to think. Her husband hadn't been a man who'd worn his heart on his sleeve, that was all. He'd bottled things up. Everyone was different, weren't they?

Everyone kept secrets, too . . .

Barry hadn't been where he'd told her he was going to be last night, and even though she knew that she shouldn't be worried about that now – that she should be far more concerned about the fact that he was gone and how that made her feel dead and empty, like she would be falling through blackness for ever – she couldn't stop thinking about it.

Why hadn't he answered her calls?

He always answered, always called her when he said he would.

She tried to recall their last conversation, but couldn't. Something terribly ordinary, probably, same as they usually were. She'd been doing other things while he'd been packing his bag, gathering up all his work stuff, then she'd watched him leave from an upstairs window. She remembered that he'd honked his horn as he'd eased out of the drive. That was him saying all the important things in his own strange way, wasn't it?

See you tomorrow, love. I'll miss you.

She hoped so, because Pippa knew that, watching him drive away, she hadn't been thinking those things and that was what would torture her every day from now on as she tumbled through the dark.

She bent double suddenly and there were sounds coming out of her mouth she'd never made before. *Keening*, was that what they called it?

What had he been doing at that hotel?

The Family Liaison Officer – Fiona was it? Or Phoebe? – stood up and asked her again if she wanted tea or something to eat. Pippa shook her head and raised it to stare at the ornaments arranged on the bookshelves above the television. Things they'd picked up over the years.

That hideous china seahorse Barry had bought her in Malta one time.

'It's actually a piggy bank, Pip. See, there's a rubber plug in the bottom? I knew you'd like it.'

Now, Fiona or Phoebe was stepping across with the box of tissues and the smile that spread across Pippa's face was wet and crooked as she thought, *If and when I do lose it and start hurling stuff at the wall, that bloody seahorse will be the first thing to go.*

THIRTEEN

Years before, when he and Alex had first started dancing, the trip to the Bull's Head afterwards – knackered and footsore – had been pretty much the main reason for doing it at all. No, the only reason. In those few months after Alex had first dragged him along, stumbling his way through some bloody foxtrot and feeling like a pillock had been the price Miller would have to pay to earn himself a couple of pints and a bag of pork scratchings. They'd both got a lot better, of course. They'd begun to enjoy themselves and the evenings spent dancing had become the highlight of their week, but the hour or so in the pub once they'd finished was still very much part and parcel of their nights out.

As was feeling like a pillock doing the foxtrot. However good he'd become, Miller had never quite got over that.

While Gloria, Ransford and the others were seated together near the bar (Nathan and Ruth sitting *very* close together), Miller sat with Howard and Mary at their usual table in the corner. Where the four of them had used to sit. They touched glasses.

'You've still got it, lad,' Howard said. 'Great to see.'

Miller managed a smile, then sank a third of his beer in short order.

'Alex would be very proud,' Mary said.

'You reckon?' Miller tore open a bag of scratchings and got stuck in. As always, knowing how bad these crunchy slices of fried pigskin were for him and being well aware of the possibility that he might break a tooth at any moment only made the experience more enjoyable; gave it a salty frisson. It was basically Russian roulette with snacks. As far as the consumption of dangerous foods went, it wasn't quite as exciting or potentially deadly as eating pufferfish sushi or even dodgy chicken, but it was about as far as Miller was prepared to go.

'I *know* she would, love. It took a lot to come back and dance again.'

Miller lifted his glass and drank some more. He had not forgotten that the moped was parked outside and told himself to take it easy, but decided that the drink was necessary as it would lessen the possibility of choking on a particularly large or hairy scratching.

On top of which, he seriously needed it.

Howard put his pint down and leaned across the table. 'So, no news, then?'

Mary smacked her husband on the arm. 'Howard!'

'It's fine, Mary.' Miller leaned over and gave Howard a smack of his own for good measure. 'And no. There isn't.'

Howard shook his head. 'It's all gone to pot if you ask me.'

'Nobody's asking you,' Mary said.

'Since me and Mary were in the Job.'

'That was a long time ago.'

'Hang on, Mary, I think your old man's got a point.' Miller licked the salt off his fingers. 'You certainly knew where you were back then.'

'Too bloody right you did,' Howard said.

'When you only had to blow your whistle to see a villain carted off to the gibbet for stealing a loaf of bread. When you could happily set about ruffians and cutpurses with your wooden truncheon. Happy days.'

Howard said, 'Sod off,' but he was smiling, well used to Miller's ribbing.

'I know you're only being comical, Declan,' Mary said. 'But things *are* different now. Nastier.'

Miller nodded. 'Right, and Jack the Ripper was just a bit of a scamp.'

'Basic policework is still basic bloody policework,' Howard said. 'I mean, they should have done more with Alex's phone for starters.'

Miller said nothing, thinking about what Dominic Baxter had told him.

'Whoever called her that night—'

'The number on her phone was withheld.' Miller had begun methodically tearing up a beermat. 'Carefully hidden, so there's no way to trace it.'

'There's got to be something they can do.'

'Leave it now, love.' Mary had reached over to pat her husband on the arm. 'Let's just have a nice drink, shall we?'

Howard sat back and shook his head. 'That night, though. So bloody tragic.' Mary nodded and Howard stared sadly down into his beer for a few seconds before looking over at Miller. 'I mean . . . you two would have made the final, no danger!'

'Howard!' He got another smack.

'That tango was bloody epic—'

And another one.

Miller smiled, because he'd missed this. When it came to saying something at the wrong time and without quite thinking it through, Howard was very nearly in his league. Watching the retired copper put his foot in it was almost as enjoyable as seeing the one he was married to berate him for it. Much as Miller couldn't resist taking the mickey, Howard and Mary were people he was always happy to go to for advice.

'I'm just saying. Pair of them were on bloody fire that night.'

Mary held up her glass. 'Why don't you do something useful and get another round in?'

Howard drained his glass and heaved himself out of his chair. Miller said he'd have the same again, thanks very much, scratchings included.

'Those things'll kill you.'

Miller emptied what was left of the packet into his mouth. 'There's worse ways to go,' he said.

Sara Xiu didn't even know the name of the band. They were almost certainly called The Screaming Bastards or Skullshag, but it didn't much matter. As long as they were loud.

Which they definitely were.

The function room above the King's Arms was not the most spacious in town and, as soon as the band had begun to assault their instruments, the few dozen local devotees of thrash metal willing to pay seven pounds fifty to risk permanent hearing loss had quickly coalesced into a frenzied, sweating mass of hair and leather. Men and women – mostly men – enthusi-astically slammed themselves into one another. Some pulled disconcerting faces as they soloed on invisible guitars or just kept on furiously nodding, like they were very much in agreement with themselves. Had it been possible, one or two looked as though they'd have been perfectly willing to swing a cat, but with that out of the question, the metal-heads made do with the feverish crush and, throwing herself around with the rest of them, ears ringing and denim jacket drenched in lager, Xiu was exactly where she wanted to be.

Lost in the noise and the crowd and, for an hour or so at least, trying not to think about the strange murder case she was working.

The even stranger man she was working it with.

'Better lock the doors, gotta stay inside . . .'

Next to her, two portly and impressively bearded devotees of the band were joining in with their latest banger, punching the air as they shouted along with the lead singer.

'You don't wanna be dinner, time to run and hide,
They'll eat your flesh like it was fish 'n' chips,
It's the zombie . . . apocalypse!'

No, to be fair, she hadn't quite . . . got Miller yet, but then none of the others on the team seemed to get him either, and they'd been working with him for a lot longer than she had. It wasn't like Sullivan and Akers hadn't warned her. It wasn't like Miller hadn't warned her himself.

Grief could do funny things to people, she knew that.

'You'll be people pudding and human stew . . .'

Mind you, she guessed that Miller was funny enough before.

'Or you'll be served up as undead barbecue,
They'll gnaw on your knackers and they'll nibble your nips,
It's the zombie . . . apocalypse!'

Squeezed between the two screaming beards, Xiu used

what little arm movement she was capable of to raise her plastic glass and take a drink. With her back to the makeshift stage she looked through the crowd and noticed a man staring at her from the corner of the room. He looked a bit like Keanu Reeves, she thought, albeit a lot shorter and with a few more piercings. His T-shirt was plastered rather nicely to his chest by sweat or beer and there was a fancy tattoo just creeping up from the neck of it.

There were other ways to take your mind off work.

'With your bodily fluids as a selection of dips, it's the . . .'

As the crowd chanted the song's title, Xiu smiled and watched short-arse Keanu stop nodding to smile back.

He'll do, Xiu decided.

FOURTEEN

There had been a time when, if Miller had found himself unable to sleep, the soothing voices of night owls on phone-in radio had done the trick, their low level, soporific conversation proving far more effective than sleeping pills, or 'Now That's What I Call the Relaxing Sounds of Waves', or even three and a half pints of IPA.

Not tonight, though.

He'd *had* three and a half pints of IPA and even that plus the radio wasn't helping. In truth, the radio didn't really help at all anymore, not since he'd started arguing with it.

'. . . and they're all the same. These film stars and pop singers . . . all paedophiles.'

'What, even the Cheeky Girls?'

'It's all there on the internet . . .'

'Oh, put a sock in it, you cockwomble.'

'. . . and to keep themselves young, a lot of them drink the blood of our children. It's a mystery to me why something isn't done about it.'

'No, mate. The mystery is how you manage to get yourself dressed in the morning.'

Wide awake, Miller climbed out of bed and sloped, muttering into the living room. He made himself a bowl of corn flakes and stared across at Fred and Ginger, dead to the world beneath their tiny shredded-cardboard duvet.

'Jammy buggers,' Miller said.

He watered his plants. He picked up his guitar and noodled for a while, then put it back and turned on the TV. He spent fifteen minutes struggling to choose between the cerebral delights of the curiously named *Celebrity Catchphrase* (they aren't catchphrases and they weren't celebrities), *Four in a Bed* (not as much fun as it sounded) and QVC. The latter was oddly compelling, but Miller knew it was best not to get too involved. A heavy-drinking desk sergeant he knew had once confessed to spending a night on the sauce, then splashing out on a diamonique collar for a cat he didn't have and an inflatable dinosaur costume.

'I've taken a few serious drugs in my time, Dec,' the sergeant had told him. 'I've even slept with a hooker or two, but I've never hated myself quite that much in the morning.'

Miller made himself tea, drank it while flicking through an old copy of *Dancing Times* and, by half-past stupid in the middle of the night, found himself doing what he usually did. What he'd known he'd end up doing from the moment he'd got out of bed. He sat on the sofa scrolling through Alex's phone, and when he wasn't doing that, he was staring down at a tatty square of cardboard with the number 37 written on it.

'Busy first day back?'

Alex was standing in the kitchen doorway, wearing her

favourite stripy pyjamas under the dressing gown she'd
pinched from that hotel they'd stayed in on her birthday.

'Ridiculously busy,' Miller said.

'Better than mooching about in here like a tit in a trance.'

'Oh, and to make matters worse, Sullivan's a bloody DI.'

'Couldn't happen to a nicer bloke.' Alex wandered across
and perched on the arm of the sofa. 'Funny old case to come
back to though, don't you think?' She stared down at the rats'
cage. 'Adrian Cutler.'

'Yeah, funny.'

'So, what do you reckon?'

'Bit of gangland business by the looks of it.'

'Hitman with a silencer.' Alex nodded. 'Nice clean shot.'

'Yeah, fairly straightforward, so all the usual suspects.'

'Massey?' Alex looked away again.

'I'll be . . . talking to him.'

'You think the prostitute's involved?'

'You mean "sex worker"?'

Alex smiled. 'Oops. Cancelled.'

'Maybe she is,' Miller said. 'They might have used her to
catch Adrian off guard, relax him a bit. Anyone's going to get
a bit sloppy wearing penguin boxer shorts.'

'Mmm . . . sexy.'

'OK, maybe I'll get some.'

'So, what about the other bloke . . . ?'

'Barry Shepherd.'

'Yeah, him.'

'Well, it might just be like I told Sullivan, or like I tried
to tell him. Our hitman messed up and went to the wrong
room. Come on, we've all tried to get into the wrong car in
a car park, haven't we? Kids calling their teacher "Mum" or

a parent walking out of the supermarket with the wrong kid. Everyone makes mistakes.'

'You included.'

'Rarely,' Miller said. 'Very rarely.'

Alex stood up and walked to the window. There was a view of the sea which predictably she'd always enjoyed far more than Miller. 'I think you got lucky with your new partner, by the way.'

'We'll see.'

'Come on, she seems nice.'

'Lots of people seem nice,' Miller said. 'Charlie Chaplin seemed nice and he married three teenagers. Three! Ted Bundy seemed nice. Michael Palin seems nice, but I heard someone on the radio who said she saw him shouting at a dog.'

'Well, I like her,' Alex said.

'She doesn't laugh at my jokes enough.'

'Which is definitely a point in her favour.'

Miller reached for the phone again. He unlocked it and began scrolling. The contacts list, the text messages, the calls received.

'What are you looking for?' Alex asked.

'I've got no idea.'

'Well, I can't help you. I wish I could ...'

Miller started flicking through the photos: a selfie holding Fred and Ginger; Alex beaming and raising a glass after a successful court case; her mum and dad on the beach. He stopped and stared at a photo of the two of them, what was probably the last photo. Mary had taken it, just before that semi-final. Miller in his rented tuxedo and Alex in the dress her sister had made, their number written on cardboard and fastened to their backs.

37 ...

Miller held up the handset in its sparkly red case and waved it at her. 'Why didn't you take your phone?' There was an edge of desperation to his voice – how could there not be? – but he hoped he didn't sound angry. 'You always took your bloody phone.'

Alex said nothing.

'You can't tell me, can you?'

'Course not,' Alex said. 'I can't tell you anything you don't already know.'

'Because I'm only imagining you.'

'Well, I'm not a bloody *ghost*, am I?' She was shaking her head and smiling as she walked back towards the kitchen. 'Come on, Miller, have you lost it ... ?'

'No, obviously not.' He laid the phone back down on the table and pushed the piece of cardboard away. He fell back and closed his eyes, hoping that he might at least manage a couple of hours' sleep before the sun struggled up and he was forced to do the same. 'I think I might have temporarily ... mislaid it. That's all.'

FIFTEEN

The early morning briefing had lived up to its name, lasting no more than fifteen minutes (including coffee and pencil sharpening). Within the first five, it had become obvious to Miller that their esteemed leader was starting to panic a little at the lack of immediate progress. That's the kind of copper Tim Sullivan was, though; the kind that would start flapping if there wasn't a super-quick result. Making all the right noises, obviously, demanding more effort and commitment from everyone on his team, then nipping back to his office to play with paper clips or finish a sudoku. Of course, he was also the kind that would happily step up and accept the plaudits if and when there was a result.

A *glory hunter*, that's what some people would have called him.

In the three or four years he had been unlucky enough to work with the man who was now his boss, Miller had amassed an impressive collection of altogether different words and phrases.

Today, he favoured *pointless spunktrumpet.*

Now, settling down in the interview room, Miller wondered what kind of copper his colleagues would say that *he* was. Maybe he should stop wondering and just ask them. He could put up a form on the noticeboard or, better yet, distribute questionnaires. *Is your fellow officer DS Declan Miller, (A) Quirky but exceptional. (B) Unorthodox but brilliant. (C) Other.*

He decided against it.

While Sara Xiu gathered her papers together next to him, Miller studied the young woman on the other side of the table. He smiled at her and she rolled her eyes. She'd already been offered tea and a biscuit, been thanked in advance for her cooperation, and still her pinched expression and surly body language made it perfectly clear that being there at all was only marginally more tolerable than root canal work or listening to Piers Morgan.

She didn't *look* like a 'Scarlett Ribbons', Miller thought, certainly not the glamourpuss in that CCTV image. Then again, he reminded himself, she wasn't dressed for work. Not unless her clients had a thing for grubby hoodies and beanie hats.

'Thanks for coming in so early,' Xiu said.

'Like I had any choice.'

'All the same.'

'Do you mind if I call you Scarlett?' Miller leaned forward. 'Miss Ribbons seems a bit . . . formal.'

'I don't care.'

'Plus, it makes you sound like a character in a surprisingly racy "Little Miss" book.' He turned to Xiu. '*Little Miss Ribbons took the punter's money and stepped slowly out of her fishnet tights* . . . see what I mean?'

Xiu clearly didn't.

'Look, as long as we get this over with as quickly as possible you can call me whatever you want.'

Miller gave her a thumbs-up.

'Or we could just call you Pauline,' Xiu said. 'Because that's, you know ... your name? Pauline Baker.'

Pauline/Scarlett finally smiled but managed to make it look like she was giving them two fingers.

Xiu got down to business. 'Two nights ago, you were booked to provide ... personal services to a guest at the Sands Hotel.'

'Was I?'

'Oh yes, you definitely were,' Miller said. 'Say what you like about Bootylicious Babes, you can't fault their record-keeping.'

'Oh, and there's this.' Xiu slid the CCTV photograph of Scarlett in the hotel lobby across the table.

Scarlett didn't even bother looking at it. 'OK, so I was at the Sands.'

It was Miller's moment to act on the hunch he'd discussed with Xiu before Scarlett had arrived.

'Look,' he'd said. 'All we've got so far is the photo of her in the lobby, right? We don't know yet if the hair found in Adrian Cutler's bed is hers. So, what if he wasn't the one she was there to see?'

'Worth a bash,' Xiu had said.

'I mean, of the two of them, Shepherd's the one you'd think might have to pay for ... personal services.'

'That's a bit harsh.'

'I'm not wrong though, am I?'

Now, Miller slid a photograph of Barry Shepherd across the table. 'Was this the man you visited at the hotel two nights ago?'

Scarlett shook her head. 'He looks as though he could do with it, though.'

'That's what *I* said.' Even if his hunch about the identity of Scarlett's client had been wide of the mark, Miller was pleased he'd been right about something.

'So ... you went to see Adrian Cutler,' Xiu said.

'Yeah, course.' Scarlett was starting to sound bored. 'Why didn't you just ask me? His family's got some kind of stake in the agency and Adrian liked to sample his own goods. Check out what was on offer.'

'Talking of *checking out* ...' Miller said.

Xiu picked up the cue. 'I'm sorry to tell you that Mr Cutler won't be requiring your services again.'

Scarlett didn't look shocked. She looked like someone had just told her it was Wednesday or she needed to empty her vacuum cleaner.

'Yeah, everyone's talking about what happened to Adrian. It's a real bloody shame.'

'Of course it is,' Xiu said. 'Not to mention the fact that you've lost what I'm guessing was quite a lucrative little arrangement.'

Scarlett looked at her.

'I think that's what she meant,' Miller said.

Xiu nodded, like she was well aware of that. 'When you were with Mr Cutler, did he ever say anything to you about someone wanting to hurt him?'

'Only me,' Scarlett said.

'Sorry?'

'Nothing too ... rough or anything.' The young woman leaned forward and eyeballed Miller, starting to enjoy herself suddenly. 'Some blokes like that.'

Miller sat back and folded his arms. 'See ... I've never really got it with S&M. Far too easy to confuse it with M&S if you ask me. Mind you, if you were dripping candle wax on to somebody's nipples while wearing a sensible and reasonably priced cardigan, you'd actually be combining the two.' He shrugged. 'So . . .'

'How was Mr Cutler when you left him?' Xiu asked.

Scarlett smiled. 'Happy.'

'*Well* and happy?'

'Are you for real?'

'Could you please answer the question?'

If Xiu thought her tone was in any way intimidating, she was clearly mistaken. Scarlett appeared to be perfectly confident, amused even. 'Listen, Adrian liked a little bit of pain, all right? Because it got him off. So yeah, I whacked him across the arse with a belt now and again, but I think shooting him in the face would have been a bit over the top. Don't you?'

Xiu began gathering up her papers. She was about done.

Miller wasn't, though.

'Takes all sorts, I suppose,' he said. 'Personally, I'd need a safe word if we were playing conkers.'

Watching Scarlett Ribbons walk away, Xiu said, 'So you think we should eliminate her?'

'That's probably a bit over the top,' Miller said.

Xiu sighed and waited.

'Oh, from the inquiry, you mean?'

'Even if Adrian Cutler was alive and well when she'd finished, you know . . .'

'Spanking him with a wooden spoon?'

'. . . doing *whatever*, that isn't proof she wasn't involved. I know they'd had an arrangement for a while, but that doesn't mean it wasn't set up by someone else.'

'No, it doesn't,' Miller said.

'Someone who wanted Adrian dead and had been planning it for quite a while. Or maybe Scarlett was still in the room with Adrian when the shooter arrived. Because of the spy-holes, we've been presuming the victim knew who was at the door, but what if it was Scarlett who opened the door and let the killer in?'

Miller doubted it, but all the same he remembered his 'conversation' with Alex the night before. She'd suggested something similar. If Xiu was someone who thought along the same lines and had the same instincts as Alex, then Miller knew he'd got very lucky with his new partner.

Well, I like her.

Of course, Xiu was only thinking along the same lines as he had, and those same instincts had been his.

But that wasn't the point.

Xiu began walking back towards the incident room.

'So, what's next?' she asked.

Miller followed her. *Well, promotion would be nice,* he thought. *So I wouldn't have to answer to a pointless spunktrumpet, and the subsequent pay increase would mean I could buy a new moped or a plastic buffet ball for Fred and Ginger.* 'The widows,' he said.

SIXTEEN

Xiu ended the call she had taken as they were walking up to the front door. 'That was the receptionist who was on duty the night Cutler and Shepherd checked in,' she said. 'Apparently, Shepherd specifically requested a room near his "friend".'

'Interesting,' Miller said.

'So, maybe they weren't quite the strangers we thought they were.'

'Just "friends we haven't met yet".'

'Sorry?'

'Strangers are just friends we haven't met yet. I heard some-one say it on the radio this morning.'

'Oh, I like that.'

'Why?' Miller stared at her. 'It's ridiculous. Strangers are strangers. Precisely *because* we haven't … met. Them. Yet. People get on my nerves sometimes.'

The door was opened. 'Lovely to see you, Dec.'

'Lovely to see you too, Fiona,' Miller said. 'Shame it's not under more pleasant circumstances.'

It was a well-established greeting that he and Fiona Mackie had never tired of. A daft joke that still made her smile, because Mackie was a Family Liaison Officer and she and Miller only *ever* met under unpleasant circumstances. She had tried to change the routine up once, suggesting that perhaps they could see each other for a *pleasant* evening at the theatre or one afternoon at a picnic. Miller had winced and quickly pointed out that a picnic was one of the least pleasant things he could think of, what with bad weather and food you could just as easily have at home and wasps or whatever, so Mackie had stuck to the previously agreed exchange from then on.

Miller introduced Xiu, then Mackie stepped back to let them into the house. She nodded towards the living room. 'Mrs Shepherd's in there. You want something to drink? Tea? Coffee?'

Xiu was hanging up her coat. 'A coffee would be lovely, thank you.'

'I'll have a Cosmopolitan,' Miller said. 'But don't bother if it's too much of a faff.'

Xiu and Mackie exchanged a look. *What are you going to do?*

Pippa Shepherd was hunched up on the sofa. The TV was on – some programme about doing up old houses – but the sound had been turned down. Miller wandered straight across to the window.

'Mrs Shepherd?' Xiu waited, but the woman did not look up. 'I'm Detective Sergeant Xiu and this is Detective Sergeant Miller. We met yesterday when you came to identify your husband's body.' She sat down in the armchair opposite. 'We're very sorry for your loss.'

Pippa finally glanced up and managed a small nod. It was obvious that she hadn't slept.

'We just have a couple of questions, if that's OK?'

Pippa nodded again.

'What colour would you say these are?' Miller pointed to the curtains, which were still closed. 'Is that pea-green or would you call it avocado?'

Pippa turned and stared. 'I don't . . . I've got no idea.' She turned back and looked at Xiu like she needed help.

Miller walked across and perched on the arm of Xiu's chair. 'It's fine, don't worry . . . but I'm leaning towards avocado.'

'We won't be long, I promise.' Xiu gave Miller a long, hard look. 'We were hoping you might be able to tell us why Barry was at the Sands Hotel the night before last.'

Pippa shook her head.

'Is that where you thought he was?'

It took a few moments and, when she finally spoke again, the woman's voice was barely above a whisper. Miller and Xiu both had to lean across to hear her.

'He told me he was at an IT conference in Liverpool.' A half smile. 'He said it would be really dull, but that he couldn't get out of it.'

'Did you speak to him that night?' Miller asked.

'I tried to call, but he wasn't answering.'

'But you had no reason to worry?'

'No. Just . . . it was odd that I couldn't get hold of him, that's all.'

'Was there anything about his behaviour recently that was different?' Xiu leaned a little closer. 'Out of the ordinary?'

'There was never anything different about him. He was always just . . . Barry. He was reliable, you know? Nice and reliable, so how can something like this happen?' She was starting to get upset, tears brimming as she clutched at the sofa cushions. 'Was it some kind of mistaken identity thing?'

'We're still making enquiries, so—'

'I mean, it must have been, right?'

Xiu looked at Miller. 'Maybe we should come back tomorrow—'

'And why have they taken his computer? They came first thing and took away all sorts of his bits and pieces and it doesn't make sense, because that's what they do when they suspect someone of something, isn't it? I've seen it on the TV shows.'

'It's just routine, Mrs Shepherd,' Xiu said. 'I promise you.'

'Absolutely.' Miller lowered his voice, as though he had a secret to reveal. 'Plus, you don't want to believe anything they do on those daft TV shows.' He smiled when she looked at him. 'Trust me, I've never met a single copper who likes opera or drives a quirky yet distinctive car.'

'How could you suspect Barry of anything, though? I mean, he's the one that's . . . dead.'

'Well, he's one of them,' Miller said.

The woman stared at them, stunned. 'I don't understand.'

'Yeah, it's definitely an odd one, but the fact is that another man was killed at the same time as Barry. In the room right next door as a matter of fact. A man named Adrian Cutler. Does that name mean anything to you?'

The woman was still staring. She shook her head. 'No. Sorry.'

'So, obviously, we're working on the theory that the two murders are connected.'

Pippa began to cry again. 'No . . . that doesn't make sense.'

'Well, it would be one hell of a coincidence if they weren't, Mrs Shepherd.' Miller reached for the box of tissues on a side table and handed them across. 'Don't you think?'

Fifteen minutes later, Fiona Mackie was seeing Miller and Xiu out.

'To be honest, that's the most she's said since I've been here. I spend most of my time just trying to get her to eat some-thing—' She stopped, seeing that Xiu and Miller were staring at something behind her. She turned and saw Pippa Shepherd drifting towards them along the hallway, so stood aside so that the woman could come to her doorstep.

'It doesn't feel real,' she said. 'It's like I'm in some stupid film. Like you are, too.' She looked at Miller. 'I don't know what I'm supposed to do.'

Miller walked slowly towards her and Xiu and Mackie could do little but move out of the way and watch.

'You carry on,' Miller said. 'That's what you do. You make ... the arrangements. You say goodbye and then you come home and you do the things that seem inconceivable right now. Horrible things. You bag up clothes for Oxfam and you carry boxes into the loft. You move things around. You eat and you sleep and you wake up again, even though it seems pointless, because it's not just your husband that's gone, but your entire future. That's what's been taken away. The trips you won't ever take together, the holidays and the long week-ends. The children and the grandchildren the pair of you can't ever fuss over. That's how it feels right now, I *know* that ... but I promise you that's not how it's always going to feel.'

He took another step towards her and opened his arms.

'Come on ...'

Pippa Shepherd stepped out on to the path, closed her eyes and gratefully let Miller pull her into an embrace.

Xiu and Mackie looked at each other again. *What* are *you going to do?*

'Something like this happens, the very worst thing, and we don't think there's any way there can ever be light again. But there is. There *will* be. Until then, we put one foot in front of the other and we carry on. We just ... carry on. Because we have to.'

SEVENTEEN

Forty minutes later they sat, parked up in an altogether swankier postcode a few miles out of town. Xiu had insisted on turning off the radio at which Miller had been ranting all the way there. Now, she stared out at houses that looked like they might have gift shops attached, or mazes in the back garden, while Miller watched a video on her phone.

It only gave him another reason to rant.

'Social media platforms are supposed to have standards of some sort. They should block content that's this offensive.'

'There's dozens of these on YouTube,' Xiu said.

Miller shook his head. 'This is bloody torture.'

The face of Barry Shepherd filled the small screen. Sandy hair, wire-rimmed glasses, shaving rash. The words that had materialised when the video started – *INFORMATION TECHNOLOGY: TUTORIAL 6* – had been enough on their own to fill Miller with an apocalyptic dread, but the content, delivered in an unfortunate monotone that sounded like a Dalek on Mogadon, was an altogether different level of horrific.

'As an IT infrastructure technician, you'll be supporting clients, assisting with troubleshooting and providing solutions so as to problem-solve business-wide infrastructure concerns.'

'I think I'm actually slipping into a coma,' Miller said.

'You'll be responsible for workflow management, as well as applying structured IT techniques to both common and non-routine computing issues . . .'

'I mean, look at the poor bloke,' Xiu said. 'He's just . . . I don't want to say *boring*—'

'So don't say "boring",' Miller said. 'Try "unutterably tedious". Or "Oh my God, this makes watching paint dry seem like white water rafting".'

'Yeah, OK . . . but why would anyone want to kill him?'

'So there wouldn't be any more of *these*.' Miller thrust the phone back at her, then reached for his own when it *pinged*. 'If he wasn't already dead, I'd be tempted to do it myself.'

Xiu's look of disapproval was no more than fleeting, having already realised that censure of any sort was all but designed to encourage him. She watched him reading the email he'd just received. 'Anything interesting?'

'Spam,' Miller said.

'You shouldn't open them.'

'Well, you don't know they *are* spam until you open them. Besides which, there's a Nigerian prince making me some seriously interesting business propositions. Not to mention what I've been promised in terms of . . . physical enhancements.'

'I'd prefer it if you *didn't* mention it,' Xiu said. 'Ever again.' She turned to stare up at the house they were here to visit.

'Shall we go and see how the other widow's getting on?'

'You fancy going on your own?'

'Not especially.'

Miller climbed slowly out of the car and followed Xiu as she marched up the long drive to the house. He hung a little way behind, in no hurry to catch her up, and by the time he did Xiu had already rung the bell. Inside this house were the bereaved relatives of a murder victim, Miller knew that. He needed to be here. All the same, calling on this particular address without an arrest warrant made him distinctly uncomfortable and suddenly a viewing of Barry Shepherd's seventh IT tutorial seemed like an attractive alternative.

The door was opened by a man who looked like a slightly older version of Adrian Cutler, probably because he was.

'Good afternoon,' Xiu said. 'I'm—'

Justin Cutler – Adrian's older brother – raised a hand and squinted at the ID Xiu was brandishing. 'This isn't a good time, all right? There's been a family bereavement.'

Miller stepped towards him and raised his own ID. He held it close to Justin's face, in case Justin thought it was a Tesco loyalty card. 'Well, duh!'

Justin showed Miller and Xiu through to a vast living room. Miller guessed it had been furnished at Kingdom Of Leather, with décor courtesy of Republic Of Crystal and accessories supplied by Dictatorship Of Leopardskin.

He did not need any introduction to most of the occupants.

Michelle Cutler was sitting on a sofa, squeezed between her mother-in-law Jacqui and one of Adrian's sisters. Wayne Cutler sat clutching a tumbler of what looked like whisky in an armchair beneath the window. There were several other men dotted around the room, perched on chairs clutching

bottles of beer or leaning against the wall. They were probably cousins, Miller thought, or just blokes brought in by
Wayne Cutler – generous supporter of the gig economy that
he was – and employed on zero-hours contracts whenever
there were legs to be broken or testicles that needed wiring
up to car batteries.

Justin Cutler walked across to stand next to his father's chair.

'Please excuse the interruption,' Xiu said. She introduced
herself and looked at Michelle Cutler. 'I'm very sorry for your
loss.' She turned to the dead man's parents and siblings. 'And
for yours.'

'Bless you, love,' Jacqui Cutler said.

'What about you, Detective Sergeant?' Wayne Cutler was
trying, without much success, to hide the fact that he was
balding and the money he'd spent on having his teeth done had
left him looking like there were too many of them to fit in his
mouth. He was a big man, but there was rather more fat than
muscle and he was not nearly as intimidating as he thought he
was; not physically, anyway. He stood slowly up from his armchair and Miller was pleased to hear the clumsy power-move
somewhat undercut by the soft farting noise from the leather.

'What about me, *what*?'

'You not sorry?'

'Yes,' Miller said. 'I am.'

'Well, that's nice to hear.'

'Yeah, nice,' Justin said. 'Presuming you mean it.'

Cutler senior took a sip of whisky, his eyes never leaving
Miller's. 'Though, to be honest, I am a little surprised to see
you back on the job quite so soon.'

Miller returned the man's stare, watched him take
another sip.

You can stand there all day long, thinking you're sending me some kind of message, but there is no way I will rise to this. You do not get that satisfaction. And no, I'm not sorry, not remotely, and don't think for even one second that we have anything in common or that your grief is the same as mine, because it isn't.

It isn't . . .

'So, the whole . . . leopard print thing.' Miller nodded towards the assorted throws and cushions. 'Was there some kind of sale on, or—?'

'We'd like a word with Mrs Cutler,' Xiu said quickly. 'If that's OK. With Michelle, I mean.'

Miller watched Michelle glance at her father-in-law, as though she was looking for permission.

Cutler was still staring at Miller. 'So, go on then. Have a word.'

'It's more of a private conversation,' Xiu said.

'It's fine, Wayne.' Michelle Cutler leaned across to kiss her mother-in-law, then got to her feet.

'See, Wayne?' Miller said. 'It's fine.'

EIGHTEEN

Michelle Cutler and Xiu sat on either side of a gleaming marble island while Miller, having set his phone to *record* and placed it on a worktop, wandered around, as usual. The kitchen could have contained his own five times over and was kitted out to a level he reckoned would have kept Gordon Ramsay happy. If Gordon Ramsay was ever happy. Miller was actually more of a Jamie Oliver man himself, because the chirpy Essex everyman didn't swear quite as much as the spiky-haired Scot, or pronounce *restaurant* wrong, or punch underlings for over-crisping a rissole. He didn't say *pukka* any more either, which was definitely a major point in his favour. Miller was no great shakes in the kitchen himself (spag bol, chilli, a fish pie if he was feeling fancy), but looking around at the spotless surfaces, he doubted that much cooking, cordon bleu or otherwise was done in Michelle Cutler's culinary pleasure dome.

'Yeah, I knew exactly why Adrian was at that hotel,'

Michelle said. 'He always had a thing for tarts. For sleaze and tarts.'

'Right,' Xiu said.

Miller glanced across at Xiu, both of them clearly wondering if Michelle knew precisely what manner of 'sleaze' her husband had been paying said 'tarts' for.

'Made him feel like one of the lads or something.' She caught her breath and sniffed. Much as she was doing her best to brazen it out, the spasm of grief was unmissable. She reached for a shiny green apple from the fruit bowl and bit into it. 'Silly bastard.'

'Blokes, eh?' Miller said. 'What are you going to do?'

'Divorce him, that's what *I* was going to do. Doesn't matter now though, I suppose.' She looked up and saw Miller staring. 'What's the matter? Not had your lunch yet?'

Miller shrugged. 'I'm quite partial to a Granny Smith, that's all.'

Michelle picked up another apple and tossed it across.

'Owzat!' Miller held up the successfully caught apple, then proceeded to polish it against his thigh, before biting into it.

'Did your husband ever say anything about threats?' Xiu asked.

'Only the ones from me.'

Xiu waited.

'If he didn't stop treating me like I was daft.'

'Apart from that, though?'

'Nothing that I knew of.'

'Did he seem . . . concerned about anything?'

'The only thing Adrian was ever concerned about was Adrian. Oh, and his precious model trains, obviously. Don't think any of the "lads" ever knew about *that*.'

108

'I had a train set when I was a kid,' Miller said, chewing.

'Yeah, when you were a *kid*. Adrian never grew up, that was always his problem. Spent a fortune on those stupid trains. Well, unless his mummy was buying them for him, of course.' She barked out a bitter laugh and nodded towards the basement. 'I'm telling you, it's like bloody Manchester Piccadilly down there.'

'Did he wear a hat?' Miller asked.

Michelle looked at him. 'Hat?'

'A signalman's hat or whatever.' Miller was looking for somewhere to dispose of his apple core. 'The real enthusiasts wear hats and blow whistles while they're playing with their trains. No, it's not my idea of a hobby either, but you've got to admire that level of commitment.'

'So, there was nobody in particular that Adrian was worried about?' Xiu had one eye on Miller, who had opened the pedal bin and was now staring down at its contents. 'He didn't mention any names?'

'Well, I wouldn't dream of telling you your job ...'

'At this stage, anything at all would be helpful.'

'I presume you'll be talking to Ralph Massey.'

Miller walked across to the island, hands thrust into his pockets. 'Any reason in particular that we should?'

'I'm not in the mood to play games, Miller.' Michelle looked upwards as the sound of noisy conversation drifted down from the sitting room. Wayne Cutler's voice, raised. 'I'm not ... in the mood, OK?'

Xiu slid down from her bar chair. 'Please let us know if you think of anything else, Mrs Cutler.'

Xiu and Miller walked towards the door, but Michelle didn't move and it was obvious that she wasn't really listening. She was still staring at the ceiling and looking nervous.

'Anything at all,' Miller said. 'I'd be especially keen for clarification on the hat.'

To the impartial observer, it might have looked as though Wayne Cutler was politely showing them out, but to Miller it felt rather more as if he and Xiu were being escorted from the premises.

'You'll do everything you can to find out who killed my son, right?' He half closed his front door. 'I don't need to worry about that, do I?'

Miller could not help but admire his partner's reaction to what was clearly a threat wearing a see-through veil. Xiu was all business.

'We'll do our jobs, sir.'

Cutler nodded. 'Course you will, and DS Miller here's the perfect man for the job, when you think about it. Because he knows what it's like to lose someone. He knows how it feels.' Now, he looked at Miller. 'Don't you?'

Miller opened his mouth, not altogether sure what was going to come out of it and how much trouble it might get him into, but Cutler closed the door without waiting for a response.

'I do,' Miller said, quietly.

They turned and trudged back down the long drive.

'So, how come Michelle Cutler didn't get a hug?' Xiu asked.

'I don't think she needed one as much.'

A few steps further on, Miller stopped, said, 'Oh, yes,' and fished out a handful of dark blue material from his pockets: the cut-up strips and stained scraps he had surreptitiously fished out of the pedal bin in Michelle's kitchen. He held a few against his chest and struck a pose as though he was modelling the very latest in high-end menswear. 'What do you reckon?

I think I could rock some bespoke tailoring. *Declan Miller is wearing a "deconstructed" two-piece by Armani ...*'

Xiu stared. 'What am I supposed to be looking at?'

'One of Adrian Cutler's fancy Italian suits. Well, it *was*, until Michelle Scissorhands got hold of it.'

'So ... what? You think—?'

Miller shrugged. He shoved what was left of the suit back into his pocket and started walking towards the car. 'Come on, I'm bloody starving.'

NINETEEN

They ate fish and chips out of paper on the promenade, waving away the ubiquitous attentions of seagulls, each of which looked just as capable of snatching up a small dog as a gobbet of haddock.

'What is that?' Miller said.

Xiu popped a chip into her mouth. 'What?'

'That song you keep singing to yourself.'

'Wait . . . do I?'

'Sounds awful . . . something about zombies?' Miller watched Xiu redden and look down, fascinated suddenly by what she'd been eating for the last few minutes. He very much wanted to know what she was so embarrassed about but decided not to push it. Not right then, anyway.

'So . . .' Xiu looked up, herself again. 'You seriously think she had her old man killed because he couldn't keep it in his pants?'

'His boxer shorts, if you want to be accurate about it. With fetching penguin motif.'

'I remember and my question still stands.'

'Well, it's certainly a motive.'

'A lot of men sleep around,' Xiu said.

'A lot of men who aren't married to Michelle Cutler. She's almost certainly got "hitman" in her phone book somewhere. Right between "hairdresser" and "homeopath".'

'I'm not convinced.'

'You're probably right,' Miller said. 'I doubt she has a homeopath.'

They ate. On the beach below a woman shouted at her children, her voice more strident than the mechanised beats from the rides and arcades behind them, screechier than the wheeling gulls.

'So, what the hell made you want to do this?' Miller asked, suddenly.

'It was your idea to have chips.'

'This *job*.'

Xiu looked a little thrown at the conversation taking a personal turn. She pointed to her mouth, just in case Miller couldn't see that it was full of chips.

'I can wait,' Miller said.

Xiu finally swallowed. 'So . . . I used to be an estate agent.'

'Oh, Christ, I'm so sorry.'

'And I thought it was about time I did something a bit more useful.'

'Which is just about anything—'

'I'd thought about joining the police when I was at school and never did anything about it. Anyway . . . when I finally got fed up showing people round hideous flats, I just went online and googled *how to become a detective*.'

'Well, that's sound detective work in itself. You're obviously a natural.'

'I already had a degree, which meant I was eligible for the fast-track scheme, and that was it really. I did eighteen months with the Met before this, which was ... pretty horrible.'

Miller waited for her to elaborate.

'Well ... the obvious issues. Some people were harder than others to work with, because I had a funny-sounding name and, you know ... a vagina.'

'Really?'

Xiu looked at him.

'Oh, I don't mean "*really*, have you got a vagina?" I just presumed you had. No, not *presumed*, because you shouldn't really presume anything in this day and age, should you? Just ... my money would have been on a vagina. As it were.' He nodded. 'I'm sorry you had to go through all that business with the Met.'

'What about you?' Xiu asked. 'How did you get into it?'

'How long have you got?'

'Give me the short version.'

Miller dug out a fat chip and leaned back against the wall. 'Well, my old man was a copper, same as his old man. A few uncles, too. So it was kind of the family business. I tried to resist the ... pull of it at first, you know? Go my own way. Then, when he was dying, my dad ... Sidney James Miller ... said how much he wanted me to continue the tradition. Told me how proud it would make him if I was to ... carry on coppering. So, what was I supposed to do?'

'That's nice,' Xiu said.

Miller felt a twinge of guilt. *She doesn't laugh at my jokes enough.*

'The truth is, I just quite liked the pointy helmets. Do you know, there's still a law on the statute books saying that any pregnant woman in urgent need of emptying her bladder can legally urinate in a policeman's helmet? Happened to me at the pleasure beach once and I smelled like a toilet for a month.'

'I never know when you're winding me up,' Xiu said.

'I get that.'

'Are you?'

'Sadly not.' Miller scrunched up his fish and chip paper and dropped it into a bin. He looked across the road at the building opposite, a name in lights which he still had nightmares about. 'Let's get this over with . . .'

Xiu disposed of her own leavings, then the two of them waited for a gap in the traffic before walking across the road towards the Majestic Ballroom.

As they walked along the corridor and up the steps to the main ballroom, Miller noticed that the purple carpet looked a little less plush in daylight, the stains and cigarette burns rather more obvious. The place smelled musty. There were lingering top notes of Lynx Africa and Carling Black Label, and they passed a pair of elderly cleaning ladies in branded pinafores fighting a losing battle with a 'Henry' vacuum and a can of Febreze.

While Miller was happy to keep his head down, all too familiar with the place, Xiu seemed oddly fascinated by the framed posters that lined the walls. She *oohed* and *aahed*, seemingly starstruck by the various dance spectaculars and variety performers that had graced the Majestic in years gone by.

Glenda Brunt is 'Queen of the Cha-Cha-Cha'.

The Stars of TV's 'On the Buses' in 'Stop It, Nurse'.

Keith Hedges and 'Jasper' the naughty duck. (Adults Only.)

Miller decided that Xiu definitely needed to get out more.

Standing at the back of the ballroom, they watched a solitary figure throwing extravagant shapes on the otherwise empty dance floor. There was no music and all the lights were on, but the scattered pattern of a glitterball was just visible as it moved across him. He was immaculately dressed in shiny black trousers and a loose-fitting cream shirt, his long silver hair swishing around his head as he stepped and twirled.

'Someone told me you dance a bit,' Xiu said.

'Did they?'

Miller was not going to commit himself. He knew there were rumours, of course. The circumstances of Alex's death had rather let the cat out of the bag, but still, he hated the idea that what he did in his free time had become common knowledge. It wasn't even the inevitable mickey-taking that bothered him. If you dished it out you had to be prepared to take it, but dancing was a part of his life that was his alone, had been *theirs* alone, and he wasn't ready to share that just yet.

He was spared any further questioning when a member of staff appeared suddenly behind them, like a scary Mr Benn. The man looked as though he'd been smacked repeatedly in the face with a shovel. He probably fancied himself as *front of house* and wore a nice suit of an evening, but his duties would also have included chucking out drunks. Or selling them drugs *then* chucking them out.

'Can I help you?'

Xiu produced her warrant card. 'We're here to see Mr Massey.'

Shovel-Face nodded and walked away towards the lone dancer.

'Oh,' Xiu said. 'Well ... you have to admit he's got some moves.'

Miller grunted. He knew that Ralph Massey had all sorts of moves, none of which you'd see on a dance floor.

The bouncer whispered in Massey's ear. Massey turned and looked across to where Miller and Xiu were standing. He smiled and waved. The man they were here to see might have been dancing like nobody was watching, but Miller guessed he'd known all along that someone was.

Xiu took half a step. 'Should we go over . . . ?'

Massey pointed upwards to where Miller knew his office was and moved towards the stairs at the rear of the building. He threw in a dramatic twirl for good measure before he stepped off the dance floor, stabbing at his mobile as he went.

TWENTY

Ralph Massey's office was in stark contrast to the rest of the building, which he owned and managed and from where he oversaw what might euphemistically be called a successful laundry business. It was all very clean and what Miller guessed was 'on trend'.

The desk was made of thick Perspex and the chairs arranged – apparently at random – around the room were glossy plastic, in a range of primary colours. Artfully dis-tressed industrial lamps hung from the high ceiling, a collection of vintage radios had been arranged beneath the window and a stuffed animal of some sort was perched on a stripped filing cabinet in the corner. A polecat, maybe, or a weasel. Miller hoped it was a weasel, which might just as well have been Ralph Massey's spirit animal.

The room was putting on a hell of a show, much like its owner.

Massey had been on the phone, sitting at his desk, when

Miller and Xiu had appeared in the doorway. He'd beckoned them in and carried on his conversation.

'It's just a few stars on the ceiling, love. It's not the Sistine Chapel . . .'

Having taken in the room, Miller turned his attention to its two other occupants. Massey was accompanied by a pair of pretty young skinheads, seated a few feet away; one on either side of him, like bookends. They wore matching outfits – jeans, boots, buttoned-up polo shirts – and both stared forward, expressionless. Until he saw one of them blink, Miller had idly wondered if they were stuffed too, like the weasel.

'Yes, another quote would be wonderful. That's very kind . . .'

Massey himself had now donned a raffish scarf, but even with that on top of the shimmering trousers and blousy shirt, he seemed what was, for him, a little underdressed. Performing as the Fabulous Miss Coco Popz ('she'll have you for breakfast!'), the businessman had once made a decent living as a drag queen and was still known to pull on one of his many flamboyant stage outfits from time to time. On special occasions, or if there was something to celebrate. Miller wondered if Massey had put the slap back on any time recently; if perhaps he'd dug out a frock and feather boa when he'd heard about Adrian Cutler's murder.

'Well, thank you again and next time please don't take me for an imbecile or I might not be quite this polite.' Massey ended his call and gestured for Miller and Xiu to sit. Xiu pulled a bright orange chair a little closer to the desk, but Miller was happier to stay standing.

'Doing the place up a bit?' he asked.

'Well, it's looking a bit tired.' Massey sat back and gave Miller the once-over. 'As are you. Not sleeping well?'

Miller said nothing.

Xiu was staring at the two skinheads, who Miller was already thinking of as the *twinheads*. Massey saw her looking and grinned.

'My nephews.'

The skinheads continued to stare. Miller side-eyed Xiu and whispered theatrically, 'They're *not*.'

'So, this'll be about Adrian Cutler, then. The business at the Sands.'

'Actually, there were two victims.'

'I only knew one of them.'

'You're very well informed, as always, Ralph.'

'This is Blackpool, Miller, not Los Angeles. A double shooting *is* still rather shocking.'

'Oh, definitely. But I just want to be clear. The son of your closest business rival is murdered and you're … shocked, are you?'

Massey smiled. 'Well, mixed feelings if I'm being strictly honest. You see, I'm not a father myself—'

'A loving uncle, though?'

'Yes, very much so … and I can't really imagine what Mr Cutler senior must be going through. But on the other hand, as per your clumsy implication, it does present a business opportunity. On top of which, Cutler the younger was the most dreadful little shitehawk.'

'Charming,' Miller said.

'Well, you did ask.'

'Mr Massey.' Xiu waited until she had the man's attention. 'Would you mind telling me where you were between ten p.m. and midnight the evening before last?'

Massey looked at Miller and nodded towards Xiu. 'Who's this one?'

'*This one* is Detective Sergeant Xiu,' Xiu said. 'And I'd be grateful if you could answer my question.'

Massey sighed and shrugged. 'I was here, same as I am every night, being fabulous. There are several hundred people who can confirm that because it was a very busy night, but do feel free to check.'

'Oh, I will, and I'll need the same information as it pertains to all your employees.'

'Seriously?'

'She doesn't do jokes,' Miller said.

'Well, it's an entirely pointless exercise, but if you insist.'

'I do,' Xiu said. 'And finally, can you tell me if the name Barry Shepherd means anything to you?'

Massey puffed out his cheeks, like he was thinking about it. 'There was a vent act called *Gary* Shepherd about fifteen years ago. Or maybe that was *Larry* Shepherd ... you don't mean him, do you?'

'I do not.'

'In which case, I'm afraid that name means precisely bugger all.' Massey looked bored suddenly, irritated. He picked up his phone, stared at it for a few seconds and put it down again. Then he spun around in his chair suddenly to face Miller, as though he'd just remembered something.

Miller knew very well that he'd simply been biding his time.

'Oh, I meant to say ... I was so sorry to hear about your wife, Detective Sergeant.'

'I'm sure you were.'

'She'll be greatly missed around here.' He held out his arms. 'Won't she, boys?'

The twinheads nodded sadly, in unison.

'Seeing her dance, I mean. She was quite the little mover. I didn't really know her that well . . . professionally.'

Aware that Xiu was watching him every bit as closely as Massey, but not really giving a monkey's, Miller walked slowly across to the desk and leaned down on it. 'She knew you, though.'

Massey nodded slowly and leaned towards him. With one slender finger, he began to drum out a simple rhythm on the desk and to whistle softly, a melody that gradually got louder. The *Strictly* theme tune.

Alex's ringtone.

It was an odd feeling, Miller thought. Agony and frustration fighting it out. Feeling like something was trying to kick its way out of your stomach, while you so wanted to do some good, hard kicking of your own.

Wanted to, but couldn't.

He turned away and walked towards the door. Behind him, Xiu stood up to follow as the pair of dead-eyed skinheads picked up the cue from their master and began to whistle right along.

'What was all that about?' Xiu was a few steps behind him as they walked back downstairs.

Miller kept on walking.

'Something you want to tell me?'

He didn't.

'Listen, what you said in there, about me not . . . doing jokes? I mean, is that all right?'

'Yeah, whatever.'

'I just don't really *get* jokes. Never have.' They were back in the ballroom. Miller stopped at the edge of the empty dance floor and stared up at the glitterball. 'Someone says "knock-knock", I just want to open the door.'

Miller wasn't listening any more. The kicking in his guts had eased a little and now a different sort of pain moved through him, hardening like boiling water turning suddenly to ice. Hearing music that wasn't there, he froze over in one beat of a quickstep, remembering the worst night of his life.

TWENTY-ONE

It was six months or so after he and Alex had started dancing – when the waltzes, the jives and the rumbas had become every bit as important as the beers afterwards – when Mary suggested that the pair of them might want to take things up a notch. That maybe they should think about dancing more seriously. She and Howard had done it years earlier, she told them, without a great deal of success, admittedly, but apparently it had all been 'good experience'.

'You two should definitely give it a go,' she said.

'What do you mean, "give it a go"?' Alex asked.

'You should start entering some competitions.'

'*What?*' Miller almost spat out a pork scratching. They were all in the Bull's Head, obviously, and he could only assume that Mary had put away a few more gin and tonics than he'd thought.

'Trust me, you're good enough.'

'Well, yes, we're probably the best in the group,' Miller

said. 'Just about. But with all due respect, that's not saying much, is it?' He looked around at their fellow dancers. 'I mean, no offence.'

'None taken,' Ransford said.

'I'm doing my best, mate,' Nathan said, looking a little hurt.

Howard was quick to agree with his wife, though Miller reckoned it was only because he was scared not to. 'If Mary says you're ready for the big leagues, then you're ready.'

'Big leagues?'

'Oh, yes.' Howard nodded and began to reel them off. 'The Thistleton Open, the Mereside Invitational, the Elswick All-Comers League Championship—'

'Third division's probably best,' Mary added, quickly.

'Well, obviously,' Howard said. 'Nobody's suggesting they should run before they can walk.'

'Better make some room on your mantelpiece,' Ruth said.

Nathan nodded. 'For all the trophies.'

'Whoo-hoo!' Gloria clapped her hands and she and Mary began talking about which new outfits they would wear to cheer Miller and Alex on in their first final.

Miller stood up to get another drink. 'You've all lost your minds.'

An hour or so later, after a couple more rounds and a good deal of well-meaning badgering, Alex had put her hand on his arm and leaned in to whisper, 'Come on, why not?'

Miller told her he could think of a hundred good reasons. At least.

Alex started making chicken noises and the others joined in.

He gamely fought his corner for a while, because it felt like he was being ganged up on, but by chucking out time it was obvious he was fighting a losing battle. Plus, he'd drunk rather more than he'd intended to. On top of which, he'd started to think that Alex might be right.

Because she usually was.

'Fine,' he said, eventually. 'But if I make an idiot of myself, we don't ever mention it again.'

'It might be fun,' Alex said as they were leaving.

'As long as I never have to do a bloody foxtrot . . .'

To begin with, Miller had felt like the two of them were Accrington Stanley going up against Liverpool in an early round of the FA Cup, and there was certainly no giant-killing. After a few early embarrassments, Miller vowed to get better, because he knew that he was the one letting the side down and even Alex was impressed by his efforts to improve. He stayed longer at their practice sessions, he worked harder. Using what little space was not taken up by the ever-expanding rat-world, he would go through steps at home. On the job, filling in unnecessary paperwork would take even longer than it might have done otherwise, as Miller sat at his desk working through routines in his head.

Accrington Stanley were about to have their day.

The Liverpool in Miller's footballing analogy had turned out to be a couple from Bolton named Ted and Sue Dixon. The Dixons always seemed to show up whenever Miller and Alex thought they might be in with a chance and won virtually everything. Alex was not keen on being party to any petty rivalry though, because they were *better than that*, and Miller couldn't deny that the Dixons were seriously good. Then, Ted Dixon had collared him at the bar one night after doing Miller and Alex out of a placing yet again. He'd winked, and said, 'Your rumba is *really* coming on, pal,' and things took a bit of a turn.

'That Ted Dixon is a proper little arsehole,' Mary had said. The gloves were off.

The night Miller and Alex finally beat the Dixons into second place was one to remember, even if, after several hours celebrating in the Bull, neither could actually remember very much of it the following day. They had won their first competition (the Swinton Seniors' Ballroom Shield) and although they didn't actually have a mantelpiece, and the trophy looked like something you bought from somewhere that also cut keys and mended shoes, they were inordinately proud.

Nathan said, 'The first of many.'

Howard said, 'We knew them when they were nothing.'

'Bollocks to the Dixons,' Mary said.

They moved up a level after that and began travelling further afield to compete (Morecambe, Blackburn, Keighley), juggling entry to competitions at weekends to fit in around busy work schedules. There were more wins than near misses and a few more trophies to show Fred and Ginger. There was the occasional write-up in a local paper and, on one occasion, a small photograph in *Dancing Times* that Miller had framed and which, of course, necessitated another big night in the Bull.

'Surprised you're even talking to us any more,' Ruth said.

'Didn't I tell you?' Mary said.

Howard rubbed his hands together. 'The big one, next.'

Alex even changed her ringtone ...

The big one, in amateur ballroom circles, was the North-West Lancashire Over Forties and they had finally decided, after three years of local stuff, that they were ready to enter. They were doing well. They'd come through several heats and three knockout rounds (where they'd knocked out the Dixons and tried not to gloat) and, even though Miller had made a couple of stupid mistakes in a routine he'd thought he could perform backwards, they'd squeaked a win in the quarter-final.

Mary and Gloria went shopping for those new outfits.

Miller and Alex had put more than a few killers away in their time, and both came face to face with dangerous individuals on a regular basis, but they were happy to confess (to the rats and to each other) that this was about as scared and excited as they had ever been.

The semi-final.

A warm Saturday night, on home turf at the Majestic Ballroom.

'Are you all right ... ?'

Only dimly aware that Xiu was even talking to him, Miller stared up at the glitterball. It was spinning faster now, scattering multi-coloured lights across the freshly polished floor and the four-piece band the organisers had hired for the occasion ...

Each couple was required to dance twice that night.

Miller thought that he and Alex had aced their first routine. They'd danced a traditional tango, which was Miller's favourite. He loved it because at one time it had been considered immoral, because it was the 'forbidden' dance and had once been banned by the Pope, but mainly because, whenever they finished, he could lean down to whisper 'you've just been tangoed' and Alex would always pretend to find it funny.

The judges loved it when Alex smiled.

Alex was quick to point out that, even though the tango had gone well, they were only halfway there and Miller shouldn't get too cocky. He promised to dial the cocky down. They waved to Howard, Mary and the rest of the gang who had been cheering them on all night, got multiple thumbs-up, then hurried backstage to change into their outfits for their second dance.

At the door to the female dressing room, Alex stopped and said, 'Listen, if we *do* win this—'

'*When* we win this.'

'Cocky!'

'Sorry ...'

'You should go out and buy a flipping tuxedo. For the final. I'm fed up with telling you, but renting one every single time we enter a competition is a bit of a false economy. Don't be so tight, Miller!'

Miller laughed and told her he would treat himself. Alex had no such worries, of course, always looking fabulous in one of the amazing dresses her sister knocked up for her. Tonight's was one of the loveliest ever and Miller knew she had something even better lined up for their second routine.

Had he told her how spectacular she looked?

He thought he probably had ...

'Break a leg,' Miller said. 'I mean, obviously *don't* because then we'll have no bloody chance.'

Alex kissed him and walked into the dressing room. 'See you in a bit ...'

Fifteen minutes later, the Master of Ceremonies stepped up to the microphone. 'Please welcome back to the floor couple number thirty-seven, Declan and Alexandra Miller ...'

The lights went down as the decent-sized audience applauded politely, except for the slightly more raucous section where Mary and the others were gathered. They whooped and cheered and Nathan produced a super-loud whistle with his fingers in his mouth.

Miller walked on in semi-darkness and took up his opening position.

The band struck up the first notes to 'Another One Bites the Dust', the song Alex had chosen for their climactic paso doble. Eight bars in, the spotlight picked Miller out and he thrust his arms towards the opposite side of the floor, where the second spotlight hit Alex.

Where it was *supposed* to hit her . . .

Because Alex wasn't there.

The band stuttered, then stopped and, after some feverish discussions at the technical desk both spotlights went out. Half a minute later, the whole routine began again, but the result was the same. There was silence, then murmured questions and the stirrings of muffled laughter from some of those watching.

Where the hell was she?

Miller stared helplessly at the empty space where Alex should have been, then out at the crowd. He could just make out Mary and Howard, the shock and confusion on their faces. Shielding his eyes against the glare of the spotlight, he looked up and saw the unmistakable figure of Ralph Massey gazing down from the balcony as the embarrassing fiasco unfolded below him. Miller couldn't swear to it, but even from that distance, Massey did not appear to be awfully bothered.

He might even have been smiling.

As the muttering from the audience grew louder, and one or two began a slow handclap, Miller ran across the floor and away into the wings. Behind him he could hear the MC saying something about disqualification, but that was the last thing Miller was concerned about.

Maybe Alex had somehow managed to lock herself in the dressing room, or had fallen asleep or, God forbid, she'd hurt herself . . .

He rushed along the corridor, past smirking members of staff and several of the other competitors, who pressed themselves against the wall as he bolted towards the dressing room.

He burst through the door without bothering to knock.

The room was empty and Miller's eye was drawn immediately to the sequined dress Alex had been planning to wear. It had been tossed across the back of a chair. Abandoned on the counter, beneath a smeared mirror with lights around it, he saw the cardboard square with their number – 37 – drawn on it and next to that was Alex's phone.

Miller snatched the handset up and entered Alex's PIN. He looked at the call log and saw that she had received a call just ten minutes earlier from a withheld number. He checked her emails, but there was nothing. He scoured the room for a note, but there was . . . nothing.

Clutching the phone, Miller wandered out of the room in a daze. The band was playing and the competition was back in full swing. He found Mary, Howard and the others waiting for him in the foyer and he could do little but stand there shaking his head, his mind racing, as they fired questions at him.

'Maybe she just wasn't feeling well and didn't have time to let you know,' Mary said, finally.

'She gets those migraines, right?'

'Yeah, that'll be it.'

'She's probably waiting for you at home,' Howard said.

*

Miller was not surprised when he arrived home to an empty house.

He watched the rats for a while and stared at Alex's phone and he was still sitting in his tuxedo two hours later, when the uniformed officers arrived at the door.

He'd known, as soon as heard the knock.

TWENTY-TWO

Miller and Xiu had been summoned back to the station before they'd even left the Majestic Ballroom. Xiu had taken the call from DI Sullivan. He'd told her that he was in the process of collating the case intelligence and was *very* keen to hear what information had been gained from the conversations with Scarlett Ribbons, Michelle Curler and Ralph Massey as soon as possible.

'Well, we mustn't keep the incompetent wankspangle waiting,' Miller said.

'You're not a big fan of his, are you?'

'Blimey, there's no flies on you.'

Xiu was working her way slowly through rush-hour traffic, trying to get them out of town.

'He doesn't seem too bad.'

'People said that about Hitler,' Miller announced. 'And Prince Andrew.'

'I don't think that's true.'

'Well, someone probably did. "Oh, look at his nice big teeth and his lovely . . . ears, and he does such a lot for charity." I'm talking about Prince Andrew now, by the way.'

'It doesn't sound like you're being very fair—'

'He made a pass at Alex once.'

Xiu turned, open-mouthed. '*What?*'

'Sullivan, I mean, not Prince Andrew.' Miller was about to say something pithy about Alex not being young enough, but Xiu didn't give him the chance. She wanted details.

'This was while you two were married?'

'No, it was well before we met, actually . . . but that's not the point.'

'Oh, I kind of think it is.'

Miller nodded and smiled conspiratorially. 'Sullivan doesn't know I know about it, and I've got no intention whatsoever of telling him. I don't want him to know why I don't like him. Let him lie awake, moaning and drenched in sweat, trying to work it out.'

'I'm not sure he's that bothered,' Xiu said.

They caught a red light which Miller would have been happy to jump, but Xiu had no intention of doing any such thing. She hit the brakes instead and swore under her breath.

'Potty-mouth,' Miller said. 'So, to be clear . . . I didn't like our beloved leader a lot even before he was promoted. It's not just because he's now my boss, OK? I mean, you can accuse me of a lot of things . . .'

Xiu looked sideways at him as though she'd already compiled a healthy list.

'. . . but you can't say I'm inconsistent.'

Once they'd pulled away from the lights, Xiu was able to speed up a little, the traffic thinning out as they turned inland.

'So, what information have we gained?' she asked. 'From the interviews.'

134

'Well, we can't rule Miss Ribbons out just yet,' Miller said. 'Though I'm fairly sure the fact that Adrian Cutler enjoyed a light spanking isn't relevant. Quite funny, but not relevant. His widow, though . . . she seems a bit too nervous, if you ask me. I mean, that might just be because Michelle's worried she's now become a suspect, and she's scared that we're on to her. She's certainly scared about something.'

'What about Massey?'

'Yeah, well Massey . . .'

Xiu waited, but Miller turned and stared out of the window, rather less talkative suddenly.

'Some of that stuff between you and him, in his office. It wasn't about this case, was it?'

'Not really.' Miller knew that he'd have to tell Xiu about it all eventually. It would certainly be a lot better coming from him than the likes of Clough or Sullivan. He knew that various heavily embroidered versions of the story had been flying around ever since Alex had died, but he'd already decided that Xiu deserved to know the truth.

Just not quite yet.

'Massey has to be in the picture,' he said. 'Somewhere. Even if the slimy bugger's got alibis up to his carefully sculpted eyebrows.'

'I'll start looking at his associates first thing tomorrow,' Xiu said. 'See if their alibis are quite as solid.'

'Nice.'

'So, you still think it's a gangland thing?'

'Well, it was obviously professional,' Miller said. 'So that has to be favourite. I reckon we'll know a lot more when I manage to catch up with Chesshead.'

Xiu turned to him. 'Right, *him* again.' She sounded a little

135

irritated. 'Are you ever going to tell me who this mystery man is? There's obviously some story and all you've said so far is that I won't believe it.'

'You won't.'

'So—'

'*Hello* . . . look who it is.'

Miller pointed to a familiar figure walking briskly along the pavement up ahead and asked Xiu to slow down. They stopped once they were level and Miller wound down the window.

'Do you need a lift, Mrs Shepherd?'

Pippa Shepherd looked a little alarmed initially, and Miller quickly apologised for startling her.

'I'm a bit surprised to see you out and about, if I'm honest.'

'I *had* to get out.' She stepped closer to the car and bent down. 'I was going mad just sitting there, so I sent that police-woman away for a few hours. I mean, is that OK?'

Miller knew that a good Family Liaison Officer like Fiona Mackie was well used to the mood-swings of those recently bereaved and guessed she would probably be waiting on the doorstep when Pippa Shepherd got home. 'It's entirely up to you,' he said. 'So, can we run you somewhere?'

Pippa shook her head. 'Thanks, but I'm just on my way to work and it's only five minutes from here. I'm quite enjoying the walk.'

'Work?' Miller didn't know that Pippa Shepherd had a job. It hadn't been in any of the notes.

'You know Gemelli's?'

Miller told her that he did. It was actually a place he and Alex had been to several times. Decent seafood, though he thought the pizzas were a bit on the pricey side.

'I work on the desk in there, answering the phone or whatever.

136

A bit of waitressing too, if they're short-staffed. It's just a couple of nights a week, but it gets me out of the house and, like I said . . .' She turned away briefly and took a few deep breaths.

Xiu leaned across from the driver's seat. 'We can't tell you what you should and shouldn't do, Mrs Shepherd, but it has only been a couple of days. Are you quite sure you're ready for this? To go back?'

The woman shrugged and tried to smile. 'No, I'm not sure at all. I might be being very stupid, but what else am I going to do?' She stepped away from the car. 'Sorry, but I really don't want to be late—'

'Just quickly, then,' Miller said. 'We've got a bit more information on the man who was killed at the same time as your husband.'

'Oh . . .'

'Yeah, the man in the next room. Adrian Cutler. That name still not ringing any bells?'

Pippa shook her head. 'I'm afraid not.'

'Anyway, I just thought you'd be interested to know.'

'So, who was he?'

'Well, weirdly, it turns out he's from a family with well-established links to organised crime.'

'Seriously?'

'So, I just wondered if that made any sense to you.'

Pippa stared at him, confused.

'As far as any connection to your husband goes, I mean.'

'No . . . it makes no sense at all.'

'Because organised criminals need the likes of your husband from time to time. Accountants, computer experts and so on. To actually do the organising, help them hide their ill-gotten gains or whatever.'

Xiu leaned over again. 'Please don't think that we're suggesting your husband might have been *knowingly* involved.'

'Right,' Miller said. 'Sometimes people don't know who they're actually working for, that's all. I mean, your nice Italian restaurant might be a front for the Mafia for all we know. All ... spaghetti carbonara and friendly smiles one minute, then the next thing you know, the manager from the Domino's over the road is waking up next to a horse's head.'

Pippa smiled and thrust her hands into the pockets of her overcoat. 'I get what you're saying, detective, but no ... not my husband. Knowingly or otherwise. The idea that Barry might have been involved in anything like that, or even known those sorts of people is just ... ridiculous.' For a moment it looked like she might even laugh. 'It's totally ridiculous.'

'Yeah, I thought you'd probably say that,' Miller said. 'It never hurts to ask though, right?'

Pippa took half a step away. 'OK, then ...'

Miller started to wind the window up, then stopped and wound it down again. 'By the way, is there actually a Mr or Mrs Gemelli?'

'No, I don't think so.'

'Well, would you mind having a quick word with whoever's in charge for me? You know, if you get a chance. The pizzas are nice, don't get me wrong, but considering what they charge for them, they're a bit mingy with the toppings.'

138

TWENTY-THREE

Back in the days when performing had been his primary source of income, Ralph Massey had never considered himself vicious. Naturally, if some other drag queen had decided to get particularly catty, he'd been able to hold his own and spit a few choice insults right back. He had bitched with the best of them and doled out plenty of withering tongue lashings in his time, but there had never been anything ... physical. That had all changed one night, after a try-out show in Preston, when the flinty-eyed manager of the Boilermaker's Arms had tried to stiff him – or rather to stiff Miss Coco Popz ('she'll have you for breakfast') – out of her fee.

'I'll give you half and that's me being generous,' he'd said. 'I don't think *that* kind of thing is what my regulars are going to go for.'

The manager had quickly seen sense when Coco held a pair of nail scissors close to his eye and had not only agreed to cough up, but to hand over twice the original fee.

Massey/Miss Popz had been pleasantly surprised.

He/she hadn't known he/she had it in him/her.

That was definitely the turning point.

Reputation counted for a good deal, he'd always known that. Up to then, he'd made a good enough living thanks largely to his reputation for lavish outfits and, above all, for selling a number. For being able to out-Liza Liza and to be even more Cher than Cher (he had fantasised about working with his idol one day and the pair of them being billed as 'Cher and Cher-Alike'). When he found out that he'd earned himself a reputation as someone not to be messed with, Massey began to think that there might be easier ways to earn a few quid. Or better yet, a few thousand.

As it happened, he'd been considering a career move anyway. His voice was not what it had once been and though he'd never stopped being a crowd pleaser, he was definitely starting to feel his age a little. There *were* one or two older acts on the circuit, but he'd always found that a little bit sad. He didn't want to wear corsets because he had to, or still be flouncing about when arthritis kicked in. Much as he loved to drag *up*, he didn't want to still be doing it when dodgy knees and liver spots were dragging him *down*.

It was tacky and undignified.

So, eventually, the performing had become a hobby. Coco had slipped somewhat reluctantly into semi-retirement, and Massey was delighted to discover a remarkable aptitude for business of an altogether different sort. One that was a little easier on his hips. He'd rarely needed to 'get the nail scissors out' since that transformative night in Preston, but it had never really mattered because, if that brand of viciousness became absolutely necessary, he employed plenty of people who would.

It was a rule he tried to live by, one of the many things experience had taught him.

Never get your hands dirty.

Shaving your legs is a pain in the arse.

If a piece of business needs doing, it's always better to do it fast.

The visit from DS Miller and his absurdly serious partner – though it had not been entirely unenjoyable – meant that now, a piece of business did need attending to. It was annoying, because he had the ever-more-expensive ballroom refurb and a thousand other things to think about, but still, he was not about to dawdle.

Massey turned to the skinhead on his left, whose real name he had forgotten, but who he chose to call Pixie. Pixie and the second skinhead, who he called Dixie, *did* look remarkably alike, which was why Massey had been drawn to them in the first place, but Pixie was his favourite. There were, after all, key differences between them that were not immediately apparent.

'I'd be grateful if you could put the word out,' he said.

Pixie nodded, even though he was yet to discover what the word was.

Dixie nodded, too, because he thought he'd better.

'I'm keen to talk to our old friend Gary Pope. Sooner rather than later, if possible.' Massey picked up his phone, ready to shout at his interior designer again. 'Though someone *will* need to find him first.'

It was seriously scary, raising her voice to her mother-in-law, but Michelle couldn't help herself. Some people had the kinds of faces that, if you punched them once, you wouldn't be able to stop, and she guessed it was a bit like that. Once she'd started to shout, it was as if the floodgates had opened.

'Why don't you move? You need to *move*.'

'And you need to calm down.'

'I was perfectly calm until you interfered. Now, *please* . . .' Michelle took a breath and tried to sound more reasonable than she felt. It wasn't easy because she actually felt like kicking the old cow to death. '. . . get out of my way.'

'There's really no need to talk to me like that,' Jacqui said. 'I'm only thinking about you.'

'Good, well, you'll understand then.'

Jacqui was standing between Michelle and the front door, having moved into position as soon as she'd seen Michelle putting on her coat.

'You should be here,' Jacqui said. 'With the family.'

'I have been,' Michelle said. 'Apart from a lovely hour down at the mortuary, I've been here *all the time*, and now I just need to get out of the house for a while. Why is there a problem with that?'

'There's no problem, love. No problem at all.' The woman was all set to turn on the waterworks, Michelle could see that. A trick she'd seen many times. The quivering chin and the crinkly eyes, like it was all just too emotional to bear. 'I'm only thinking about what's best for you . . . and you're grieving, so maybe someone else needs to do that.'

'A couple of hours, that's all. Why is that such a big deal?'

'A couple of hours doing what?'

'Well, I'd quite like to go and see my kids. If that's OK.'

Jacqui smiled and cocked her head. 'That's a smashing idea . . . why don't we go together? Or get your mum to bring them here. I'm sure they're missing their grandma.'

The whole idea suddenly felt a lot less smashing. 'I don't know ... maybe I'll just do some shopping or something.'

'*Shopping?*' Mysteriously, those tears weren't coming after all. Now, Jacqui's voice dropped to something barely above a whisper, like it always did when she had something poisonous to say. 'What, get yourself a nice new handbag, while Adrian isn't even cold yet?'

'No, I don't mean—'

'Some of those lovely smellies you're so fond of?'

Michelle could feel the fight draining out of her, and she started to wonder if it was even worth it. There'd be a price to pay, whatever she ended up doing. 'Look, I might just grab a quick coffee or something. I just need a bit of air, Jacqui ...'

Michelle stopped, because she could see that Jacqui's attention was no longer on her. She turned to see Wayne coming slowly down the stairs. He'd been asleep and had obviously been woken by all the shouting, so now he'd probably be steaming. Michelle thought she might as well just take off her coat and offer to make everyone a drink, but instead of shouting even louder than *she* had, Wayne stepped across and began to gently stroke her arm. He looked at his wife and shook his head.

'Let her go out, love ... it'll do her good. She's just a bit over emotional and why shouldn't she be?' He turned to Michelle. 'All over the place, aren't you, lass?'

Michelle lowered her head and nodded.

'Course, same as we all are. I mean, grief hits people in different ways, and if you need to get out of the house and be somewhere on your own for a while, that doesn't sound ... unreasonable to me.' He turned back to his wife and winked. 'So, come on, Jac, let's not have a silly row, eh?'

Michelle said, 'Cheers, Wayne,' and moved towards the front door the moment she saw her mother-in-law step grudgingly aside. 'I mean, I said a couple of hours, but I probably won't even be that long.'

Jacqui Cutler was able to make even the simple act of quietly closing the front door seem like an act of war, but Michelle was beyond caring. Hearing it close behind her was enough. Being . . . out.

Had she not presumed she was being spied on from one of the windows, she might even have skipped to the Range Rover, and as soon as she was safely inside she screamed with relief. Sod it, she might buy herself that handbag anyway, because, aside from winding Jacqui up, it *would* probably make her feel better. It was called retail *therapy*, after all.

Pulling away as fast as she could without actually throwing up gravel, Michelle was already thinking about a purse to match the bag. Taking her time over the coffee afterwards. She was already in a more carefree headspace and, just as she hadn't clocked the long scratch that had been gouged into one side of the car, she failed to notice the figure watching her from beneath the trees.

TWENTY-FOUR

Cleaning out a ridiculously big rodents' cage (the cage, not the actual rodents) wasn't many people's idea of a good night in. It wasn't Miller's either. Given the choice, he'd rather have been washing a corpse, but it had to be done, so Miller spent twenty minutes sweeping their tiny turds into a dustpan, fishing out wet, smelly straw and wondering, as he always did on these occasions, why he and Alex hadn't just bought themselves a goldfish.

While he was getting busy with the rubber gloves and the Cif, he wondered if it was true that goldfish had no short-term memory. More to the point, if it was, how the hell anybody had discovered it?

'Hey, Splashy . . . how are you enjoying your sunken boat?'

Goldfish looks blankly.

'The sunken boat I put in your bowl like thirty seconds ago . . . ?'

Goldfish opens and closes mouth, swims around a bit.

'Aha!' *Writes scientific paper immediately.*

Miller thought that remembering things was over-rated anyway.

He tried listening to a phone-in on the radio as he washed out the bowls and water bottles. He was bang up for an argument. It was difficult to concentrate though, while Fred and Ginger were happily rolling around the living room in plastic globes, bouncing off the skirting board, bumping into furniture or engaging in what looked like a concerted effort to knock his guitar over.

'I'm sorry for the animal, obviously ... but what about my Mondeo?'

This particular genius had rung in after hitting a badger on a country road and writing his car off.

'So, there are these signs, right? I know, because I passed one right before I hit the bloody thing. They actually put up these signs with pictures of badgers on them ... like a badger-crossing area or whatever. My point is, why are they doing that? Why are they encouraging badgers to cross busy roads like that? I mean, it's asking for trouble, isn't it?'

It was not perhaps Miller's cleverest or best-articulated response.

'You ... brain dead ringpiece!'

By the time he'd returned Fred and Ginger to the cage (with two tiny turds strategically replaced in the litter to remind them where their toilet was) Miller decided that he couldn't be bothered to make himself anything to eat. He called Gemelli's and ordered a pizza for home delivery. Guessing that Pippa Shepherd had not yet managed to put a word in, he requested several extra toppings.

'Oh, and you might as well chuck in some garlic bread.'

Then Miller asked to speak to the manager because he had a few more questions that were not related to the menu.

As soon as he'd ended the call, he dialled another number.

'Hey, Finn . . .'

'Hey, Miller . . .'

Miller could hear music and chatter, the noise of traffic. 'What are you up to?'

'Just walking around,' Finn said. 'On the front.'

'OK.' Miller knew that by now she would be looking for somewhere to bed down for the night, and something to help her sleep. 'I was just wondering if you'd heard anything about the county lines boys. The shooting at the hotel, you remember?' Finn was a largely reliable source of information, but Miller understood that sometimes those things she took to help her sleep, on top of whatever else she took to get her through the day, could mess with her focus a little. It wasn't just goldfish that forgot stuff.

'Yeah, I talked to a couple of the local dealers.'

'Right.' Miller had guessed they would be her first port of call. He knew that most of them trusted her. Even the ones that didn't were usually happy to chat about stuff with a regular customer. The weather, the football, the recent double murder at a local hotel.

'So . . . it's highly unlikely that any of the boys you're thinking of had anything to do with what happened at that hotel.'

'I didn't think so,' Miller said. 'Worth checking, though.'

'I'm not saying they aren't happy about it, mind you. It's another little inroad, yeah? Anything that makes certain other parties fall out with each other is good for them.'

Miller knew exactly which parties Finn was talking about.

His recent conversations with each of them were still fresh in his mind.

'They probably *will* make a move at some point, but I don't think they'll want to draw quite so much attention to themselves.'

Miller laughed. 'Yeah, say what you like about the new breed of organised criminal, but they're not showy.'

Now Finn laughed, which was a sound Miller very much enjoyed hearing.

'What about the other thing?' he asked.

'What other thing?'

'Chesshead.'

'Like I told you, he's in London.'

'It's a big place,' Miller said. 'I was hoping you might be able to dig up something a bit more specific.'

'Well, I can't give you an actual address.'

'I should definitely have given you more than a tenner.'

'But I asked around and a couple of people mentioned somewhere called Hendon. *Is* there a place in London called Hendon?'

Miller knew there was. 'It's where Met Police cadets used to train. Might still be, for all I know.'

'Maybe Chesshead's turned over a new leaf and joined up,' Finn said.

'You think?'

'Stranger things have happened.'

Miller couldn't think of any off the top of his head. 'OK, well, that should be enough to get me started,' he said.

'You're welcome,' Finn said. 'And if you fancy bunging a little bonus my way, you know where I am.'

'Well, actually I don't. That's kind of what happens when someone's homeless.'

'You can always find me.'

Miller listened to the background noise for a few seconds. The chink of coins and the tinny melodies from arcade machines. 'So, how's it all . . . going? I mean—'

'It's fine,' she said, quickly. 'Listen, Miller, I need to crack on, all right?'

'No worries. Yeah, so . . . thanks. I was just—'

Finn had hung up.

'Sometimes she's just not in the mood to talk.' Miller looked up to see Alex standing at the window and she spoke without turning round. 'Not about herself, anyway and that's up to her, right? You shouldn't let it bother you.'

'I was only trying to find out how she was,' Miller said.

'She knows you care about her,' Alex said.

'That isn't what I'm worried about.'

'She seems to be doing OK.'

'Yeah,' Miller said. 'It's relative though, isn't it?'

Alex watched Miller eat without comment, and he reckoned he was lucky. He guessed that others in the – admittedly odd – situation of scoffing home delivery pizza next to an imaginary dead wife might well find themselves on the receiving end of some . . . snarky remarks. Something about standards having dropped now that their better halves were no longer around. The truth was that, as far as Miller and Alex were concerned, those standards hadn't exactly been sky-high to begin with. Alex had been no great shakes in the kitchen herself, so, despite his own limited skill set, Miller had always done the lion's share of the cooking anyway. They'd both liked a takeaway and less-than-regular working hours had meant they'd enjoyed them more often than most, but *she'd* been the one with Taste of the Raj and the Jade Garden on speed-dial.

The loyalty card from Nando's tucked in her purse.

'You did well with Ralph Massey today,' she said, when he'd finished eating.

'You think?'

'Well, no . . . you probably didn't make much headway as far as your case is concerned. I meant you did well not to smack him over the head with that stuffed weasel.'

'It wasn't easy.'

Alex followed Miller into the kitchen and watched him dump the pizza box in the recycling. She tutted when he threw most of the garlic bread away. 'Still over-ordering, then?'

Miller made himself tea, carried it back into the living room and flopped down on the sofa. 'So, you think Massey might have been involved?'

'With the killings at the hotel, you mean?'

'Well, there's at least *one* more I fancy him for, but yeah, let's start with those.'

'He's the obvious candidate, isn't he? Considering the bad blood. Not that he'd have killed Adrian Cutler himself.'

'Right, but he knows a man who can. As does the victim's widow.'

'You really think Michelle would hire a hitman?' Alex seemed dubious. 'She strikes me as the type who'd just have used those scissors on her old man herself.'

'. . . and the rest of his family, now I come to think about it.' Miller suddenly found himself wondering just how close Justin Cutler had been to his younger brother and how ambitious he was. Presumably, as far as the family firm went, the first son would now be due a promotion.

He'd talk to Xiu, get her take on it.

'Like I said before, you got lucky with her.'

'I'm not arguing,' Miller said. 'That *Carry On* routine, though? Wasted on her.'

'You should tell her the whole story, by the way. The night of the semi-final. Not telling her about your history with Massey might well compromise your case.'

'I know,' Miller said. 'I will. I just need to find the right time.' He looked at her. 'So, go on then. You think Massey was involved with what happened to you that night?'

Alex said nothing.

'Yeah, I know.' Miller lifted his feet up, cradled the mug of tea on his chest. 'Stupid question. Well, even if he wasn't, he seems to get a major kick out of letting me think that he was. That smug expression he had on his face today . . . same one he had up on the balcony that night.'

'You couldn't even see his face from that far away,' Alex said.

'I didn't need to see it.' Miller could feel himself starting to get angry. 'I mean, what was he even doing there?'

'It's his ballroom, he likes dancing . . . I don't know.'

'And when is Forgeham's joke investigation actually going to come up with anything? Or share what little they *have* got with *me*? They seem perfectly happy to talk to your friend Dominic Baxter.'

'Dom was a colleague,' Alex said. 'He wasn't my friend.'

'Whatever.'

'I think you need some sleep.'

'Of course I bloody do.' Miller sat up. 'And maybe I'd be able to get some if you were being a bit more helpful. If you didn't just lurk about having a go at me for not eating garlic bread. Hanging around and being . . . inscrutable.'

Alex turned away from him. 'Arguing with strangers on the radio who can't hear you is one thing, Miller.'

Miller closed his eyes and took a slurp of lukewarm tea.

'Arguing with someone who's not actually there – you know, because they're *dead* – is properly bonkers.'

Miller stood up in a huff and wandered towards the bedroom, muttering to himself. He stopped to pick up the cardboard 37, deciding that it probably was bonkers to keep it lying around like some kind of fetish. He carried it over to the dresser, to a drawer containing a disordered arrangement of takeaway menus, cards for local garages, taxis and decorating companies, old remotes, assorted batteries and yellowing receipts. The repository for all the stuff that didn't really belong anywhere else.

The 'drawer of all nonsense', that's what Alex had called it.

The bloody thing could live in there for a while . . .

Miller opened the drawer, saw the photograph and immediately forgot about putting the cardboard sign away. Instead, he reached in and lifted out an order of service.

TWENTY-FIVE

'I didn't know Alex as long as many of you . . .'

Miller looked up from his notes and out at the congregation. Alex's mum and dad – Janet and Mike – sat stony-faced. They were wearing black, of course, as were most of the others, but Miller was pleased to see that several had come in bright colours, or were sporting a loud accessory or two, because that's what he'd requested. He couldn't swear that's what Alex would have wanted, because they'd never discussed it, but it was what his gut had told him. Miller had chosen a grey suit and a green spotted tie and he couldn't help thinking that Alex's mother was looking up at him as though he was delivering his eulogy in a clown costume.

'I never knew her during the "wild" years.' There was muffled laughter from a few of Alex's friends. 'I've seen the pictures, though.' He looked across to the photo of Alex that lay propped on an easel in front of the dais. It wasn't one of the ones he was referring to, though he'd been sorely tempted.

'The serious goth phase, the grunge years . . . when I know she did quite a few things she never mentioned when she applied to join the police force.' A bit more laughter, from old friends *and* colleagues. 'I didn't know her when she was a geography student who could never find her way to lectures, or during her short-lived stint as a womenswear assistant. Short-lived because, by all accounts, she insisted on telling customers exactly what she thought of their outfits. I believe her use of the phrase "mutton dressed as mutton" was the final straw.' He smiled and looked up to see most of the mourners smiling back at him. Alex's mother and father were not smiling and Miller couldn't decide if it was grief or disapproval. He decided to give them the benefit of the doubt and to press on quickly before he fell to pieces altogether.

'I never knew Alex's grandparents, who she loved to bits and always missed, or the great many pets she adored as a kid – aside from Muffy the flatulent Jack Russell, who everyone I've spoken to seems to agree was a very unpleasant dog – and obviously I never knew her first husband . . . the late and largely unlamented Trevor.' There was a bark of laughter at that, or it might have been a gasp, as Miller looked down again and turned the page.

'Sometimes, I wished I *had* known Alex back when she was getting to know herself, but she always told me that the past was the past and most of the time we should let it stay there, because she and I had found each other and that was all that mattered . . .'

Miller faltered a little and reached for the plastic bottle of water that he really should have poured into a glass. He took a quick swig, aware of the bottle crackling loudly beneath his fingers.

154

'For anyone who doesn't know, we actually "found each other" one wet weekend at a Premier Inn just outside Preston, during a particularly tedious force-wide seminar on kidnapping. Seeing some of our fellow *Strictly* wannabes here, I should probably confess that, had I known then that she would one day drag me along to ballroom dancing classes, I might well have had second thoughts.' He glanced down to see Howard giving him a thumbs-up from the second row, Mary clinging to his arm. 'I should probably have paid a bit more attention in that kidnapping seminar, put it that way.

'What I *can* tell you, despite all the things I missed out on by not meeting her sooner, is that the ten years Alex and me had together were the best of my life by a country mile and I know she felt the same way.' He sniffed, leaving a beat. 'That they were the best years of my life, I mean. She told me that quite a lot . . .'

He almost laughed, remembering it. Then he remembered him and Alex dancing to 'You're the Best Thing' by the Style Council at their wedding, and the laugh became a sob, and he couldn't say a great deal that made sense after that.

Miller had expected the post-cremation get-together (which he thought of as a 'wake' but which everyone else called the 'do afterwards') to be a curling-ham-sandwich-and-quiche fest. As it was, the gathering – at a country pub near Alex's parents' house – turned out to be a somewhat swankier affair. He stood near the doorway accepting handshakes and muttered condolences, wondering if you could ever describe an event such as this as *swanky* and whether it was acceptable for the husband of the deceased to slope away and drink himself into oblivion before anyone so much as got a whiff of the coronation chicken.

Alex's mum and dad were on hand to ensure that didn't happen.

'I need to pop round at some point,' Janet said. 'To pick up a few of Alex's things. If that's OK with you.'

'Absolutely,' Miller said. 'What things?'

'Just some of her jewellery, a few bits and pieces. I think she'd want her sister to have them.'

'Yeah, of course. But can't she come round?'

'I enjoyed the eulogy,' Mike said, quickly.

'Oh good,' Miller said, thinking, *enjoyed*? 'I wasn't sure. It's so hard to get the tone right. Alex always said that lowering the tone was a speciality of mine, so . . .'

'It was fine.' Janet was staring at his tie. 'It was very you.'

Miller was rescued by Alex's sister Laura and, once her mum and dad had drifted away towards the buffet, she leaned close and said, 'I loved your speech.'

'Thanks, but I'm not sure your parents did.'

'Oh, they're just a bit all over the place. More to the point, Al would have loved it, too.'

Miller looked across and saw Janet picking out cutlery then cleaning each piece thoroughly with a napkin. 'Why don't they like me more?'

'They don't *dis*like you.'

'You know your dad stopped the car *on the way to the wedding*? Told the driver to pull over and asked Alex if she was sure she wanted to go through with it.'

Laura certainly did know and clearly still found it funny. 'Well, to be fair, Alex *could* be impulsive. I mean, that tattoo . . .'

Miller watched Mike ladling couscous on to his plate.

'Seriously, I know they always thought Alex could have done better, but I'll never quite understand it. I mean, the one before me was a premier league heroin addict and a full-on alcoholic who nicked her money on a regular basis and knocked her around when he was off his face. OK, so I wasn't in the top ten of the world's most eligible bachelors, but I was a step *up*, surely?'

'Shane MacGowan would have been a step up.' Laura downed a mouthful of beer. 'Oh wait, he's got money. But you do have better teeth.'

Miller grinned and touched his bottle to hers. 'It's generally frowned upon, right? To marry your dead wife's sister ... ?'

When Laura was waylaid by a pair of cousins she clearly didn't recognise, Miller thought he'd better do the rounds. He got the vicar out of the way first, telling him how much his words of comfort in the church had meant to everyone, even if the by-the-numbers remarks had sounded to Miller like a passage from *Funeral Sermons For Dummies*. It hadn't felt like he was talking about Alex at all. Certainly not any version of Alex that Miller recognised. He'd half expected the vicar to slip up and say, 'Today we gather together to remember *name of deceased* and to celebrate *name of deceased*'s life with those who loved *him/her/them*.'

Miller thanked the man anyway.

He was on his way to talk to the ballroom gang (the two older couples sitting together, while Nathan gamely schmoozed Ruth at the bar) but he was collared by one of Alex's oldest friends; a flash-suited homunculus who was proof that Alex hadn't always been a good judge of character. Dave, who Miller always called 'the cock', made comforting noises while Miller looked for an escape route. He chose not

157

to remind the man that they had not seen each other since his and Alex's wedding, when Dave had pushed Miller against a wall and said, 'You'd better look after her.' Miller wanted to slap him as much now as he did then, but contented himself with telling the cock how good his hair-weave was looking and urging him to try the coronation chicken.

He talked to Susan Akers and her girlfriend who were both gently sozzled and weepy, then to a couple of women who *had* known Alex in her student days. They shared several stories Miller hadn't heard before: the pub-crawl/bubble-wrap incident; the unconscious rugby player and the electric razor; the business with the kiwi fruit and the trouser-press.

Then, still reeling from the revelations about an Alex he *certainly* hadn't known, Miller spotted a familiar figure smoking in the beer garden and went out to try and cadge a cigarette.

'Hey, Finn . . .'

'Hey, Miller . . .'

She grudgingly gave him a roll-up and he leaned in for a light. 'I didn't see you in the church.'

'I was lurking at the back,' she said.

'OK . . .'

'I thought lurking would be best.'

He looked at her and it was clear that she'd been crying. She wore a dark brown hoodie over black jeans. There was a cross around her neck he'd never noticed before. 'I didn't know if you'd come.'

'To be fair, I wasn't invited.'

'Well, it is quite tricky to send an invitation to someone who doesn't actually live anywhere,' Miller said. 'Where do you address it to? *Care of the Doorway Opposite Argos*?'

Finn shrugged and tossed what was left of her roll-up away.

'Anyway, I'm glad you came.'

'I wasn't sure you'd want me to.'

'Why wouldn't I?'

'In case I robbed the collection plate or something.'

'Just try and be subtle about it,' Miller said.

They turned and stared back through the window at the people moving around inside. The friends and relatives Miller had met for the first time today and would almost certainly never see again. Alex's old student pals were laughing at another half-remembered story, while her mum and dad sat alone at a table in the corner, Mike pulling his wife close to him, their food untouched.

'Is it a free bar?' Finn asked.

'Well, there's a few hundred quid behind it,' Miller said. 'So we're good for a while. Or at least until my Auntie Bridget gets stuck in.'

She leaned in to him. 'Do you fancy getting absolutely battered?'

Miller looked down at her. 'Oh, I fancy that very much indeed.'

He opened the door for her, but before she stepped back inside, Finn turned and pulled Miller into a hug. He had been on the receiving end of a good few hugs already. They had been fierce or feeble, from friends and strangers alike, and there would certainly be plenty more before the day was out, but holding tight to this scrawny, stray girl – the bones of her shoulders sharp beneath her hoodie – Miller knew already that this one would mean the most.

TWENTY-SIX

Miller and Xiu pulled up outside the station within a few seconds of each other. Miller looked down at his moped, then across at Xiu's bike. Then he looked at Xiu, who was smirking when she took her helmet off.

'You're welcome to have a go,' she said. 'If you think you can handle it.'

'No, thanks. It's a bit flashy for my taste.' Miller took off his own helmet. 'Like men driving sports cars to compensate for their shortcomings elsewhere.'

'That's interesting. So, what am *I* compensating for?'

Miller thought about it. 'Have you got a really small penis?'

'I don't have any kind of penis.'

'OK, well, I'm sure I'll work it out.'

'Good luck with that,' Xiu said. 'The offer's there, though, if you want to take it for a spin.'

Miller shook his head and patted the moped's saddle. The grimy plastic had been patched up in several places with gaffer tape. 'This'll do me,' he said. 'Cheap and cheerful, like I am.'

Xiu nodded. 'It's also unreliable and makes strange noises.'

'Was that you making a joke?'

Xiu looked a little alarmed. 'It certainly wasn't intentional,' she said.

They swiped in with their warrant cards and Xiu turned towards the office. She stopped when she saw Miller heading the other way towards the stairs. 'The briefing starts in a few minutes,' she said.

'I know.' Miller kept going. He took the stairs two at a time, shouting down to her as he went. 'Make some excuse for me. Tell Sullivan I was savaged by a rat.'

'A *rat* . . . ?'

'Whatever. Use your imagination.'

Miller carried on up two flights and along a corridor until he came to a suite of offices laid out identically to the one in which his own team was based. He marched in, ignoring the apprehensive looks from fellow officers and firing out a volley of breezy greetings as he passed.

'Morning all, lovely day for it . . . cheer up, mate, it might never happen . . . mind you, looking at *him* it already has . . . but there you go, life's a bitch and then you die . . . and if you're really unlucky it'll be a team like this one that's trying to find out who was responsible, et cetera, et cetera . . .'

One youngish officer, clearly a candidate for the team's top kisser of senior backsides, stood up and moved to stand, a little awkwardly, in front of the door that Miller was barrelling towards. He raised a hand and cleared his throat.

Miller didn't break stride. 'Seriously?'

The officer finally got a good look at Miller's face and, at the last minute, stepped to one side, as though he hadn't actually meant to be standing in the way at all.

Miller patted him on the arm, said 'Good lad' and opened the door.

The woman seated behind the desk looked up and smiled. It wasn't a happy smile, but that would probably have been a little odd given the circumstances. 'Well, I'd say come in, but there doesn't seem much point now.'

'Sorry, ma'am,' Miller said.

'It's not a problem.'

If this particular visitor dropping in unannounced was making DCI Lindsey Forgeham anything like as uneasy as the rest of her team, she showed no signs of it.

'Thing is, I'm late for a briefing and my DI's ever so strict,' Miller said. 'I mean, that's probably fair enough, don't you think? When you're investigating a murder, every second counts, right?'

'Absolutely,' Forgeham said. She stood up and walked around to lean on the front of her desk. She was younger than Miller and dressed like she was a lot keener. She'd arrived a year or so before, with a reputation for not suffering fools – gladly or otherwise – and for getting the job done.

'Happy to hear that.' Miller could only assume that someone had seriously misunderstood the meaning of the word *job*. Their grasp of the word *fools* was iffy as well, as DCI Forgeham seemed to have surrounded herself with a team of officers who couldn't find their own backsides with a room full of mirrors and a sniffer dog.

'So, how are you, Declan?'

'I can't complain, ma'am.' *Well, actually, I can and you're about to find out that I'm spectacularly good at it.*

'That's good ... but you should probably have called if

162

there's something you want to discuss. Or I'm always happy to do this via email.'

'Oh, that's all such a faff,' Miller said. 'We're in the same building, aren't we? So, I thought it would be much easier if I just popped up, and anyway, I'm here now.'

Forgeham waited.

'So how's it going?'

'Yeah, all right, thanks. I'm—'

'The *case*,' Miller said. 'How's the case going?'

The DCI stiffened. 'You know you shouldn't even be here, right?'

'I do know that, but I am.'

'You can't have any part of this investigation. The regulations are quite clear about this. I shouldn't even be talking to you.'

'You're talking to other people though, aren't you?'

'We're asking questions, if that's what you mean.'

'That's not what I mean,' Miller said. 'How come some of the people my wife worked with know more about your progress on this than I do? I'm not asking to be part of it, I'm just asking to be kept informed.'

'Well—'

Miller laughed and clapped a hand to his mouth.

Forgeham stared at him. 'What?'

'Sorry, I just realised I used the word *progress*. It tickled me.'

Miller could see that the woman was irritated, but that she was keeping herself in check. If the simple fact that he'd barged into her office wasn't making his desire for answers obvious enough, the look on his face almost certainly was. The DCI might have been a bit fuzzy on *job* and *fools*, but she understood desperation well enough.

She knew it when she saw it.

'Look . . . we're working as hard as we can on this, I promise you. The fact remains that, as of now, we have no idea who Alex was going to meet that night. We've got a call that we're unable to trace, we've got a singular lack of witnesses and nobody seems very keen to talk to us. You know how it works with something like this . . . the kind of officer your wife was.' She took a step towards him, nodding, as though she'd recently attended a 'reassurance of relatives' seminar. 'I *can* tell you that we're looking for fresh leads.'

'So, look harder.'

'Now, hang on.' Forgeham stepped back. 'You can't talk to me like that, Detective Sergeant—'

'Look *harder* . . .'

On his way out, Miller stopped at the desk of the young officer who'd tried and failed to stand sentinel.

'A quick tip for you, you know, if you're still struggling to find it . . .'

The young officer looked up at him, but Miller loudly addressed himself to all the officers who appeared to have momentarily stopped what little they were doing.

'It's right *here*.' He reached behind himself and pointed. 'See? That big squidgy bit between the top of your legs and the bottom of your back?'

The officer stared at him, shaking his head.

'Your arse.' Miller marched towards the door, waving. 'You're welcome.'

TWENTY-SEVEN

In a perfect world, Miller would have been able to sneak into the briefing without drawing attention to himself. As it was, the things that tasted best were still bad for you, there continued to be far too many TV shows about people doing up houses and Sullivan looked up the moment Miller put his head around the door.

'Glad you could join us.'

Miller had no idea if Xiu had manufactured an excuse, so he simply grimaced and pointed to his nether regions. 'Sorry. Prostate . . .'

Nodding seriously, he walked gingerly to the table and sat down next to Xiu. He pulled across an information pack, well aware that she was staring at him, clearly desperate to know where he'd been. Miller nodded towards Sullivan. It was time to pay attention.

'Right, well, as I was saying . . . the good news is that we've now identified our mystery visitor to the Sands Hotel on the night of the murders.' Sullivan touched the screen of his iPad and the CCTV picture of the man they'd been looking for appeared on the Bluetooth-connected screen behind him. He swiped to show the appeal that had run in the local paper for the last two days.

Do You Know This Man?

Miller raised his hand. 'Is it Alan Titchmarsh?'

'*What?*'

'He looks bugger all like Alan Titchmarsh,' Clough said.

Carys Morgan was nodding. 'Actually, there's definitely a resemblance.'

'Thank you,' Miller said.

'The bad news,' Sullivan raised a hand, 'is that he's not our killer. He's actually a member of the town council called Geoffrey Phipps and the reason he took a little longer than might be expected to come forward is that he was there that night to visit a . . . gentleman friend.'

Clough smirked. Miller guessed *he* didn't have many friends of any sex or persuasion.

'Anyway, we should be grateful that Mr Phipps finally did the right thing.'

'Not sure Mrs Phipps would agree,' Clough said.

'So . . . as you can see from your packs, we've now got a full ballistics report.' Sullivan swiped again to display the relevant charts and images. 'It shows very clearly that the bullets taken from the bodies of Adrian Cutler and Barry Shepherd came from the same gun.'

Miller nodded, thoughtfully. 'Good to have that confirmed.' He looked around the table. 'Just out of interest, does anyone know what usually happens if two hitmen show up together at the same place? I presume there *is* some kind of protocol. Is it like two people turning up at a party wearing the same outfit?'

'DS Miller—'

'Does one of the hitmen have to nip home quickly and change?'

'I'm sure some people might think that your interjections are . . . good for morale.' Sullivan shook his head. 'Personally, I'm not convinced, but they certainly aren't a great deal of use.'

The DI turned his attention back to his beloved iPad. It wasn't a big surprise. Miller knew that, irritated as he was (and Miller was doing his very best), Sullivan wasn't the type to enter a battle of wits unarmed, certainly not in front of others. He was more likely to put something in writing to HR or go belly-aching to Susan Akers and Miller was fine with either of those.

'Right . . . so Tony, you've looked through all the financials?'

Clough glanced down at his notes. 'Yeah, and Adrian Cutler's look every bit as dodgy as you'd expect. Plenty of payments out and some major payments in, all of them untraceable. Nothing that suggests a particular motive, though '

Sullivan called up an image of Adrian Cutler. He then produced some sort of screen-pen and drew a circle around the picture, just in case anyone in the room remained unclear as to who they were discussing.

'Not very much to get excited about with Barry Shepherd,' Clough said. Another photo appeared on the screen, quickly followed by another circle for emphasis. 'Not unless he's got a secret stash we haven't found yet.'

Sullivan nodded. 'Well, we might know more about that when we've got the Digital Forensics report. Carys?'

Carys Morgan held up a sheaf of papers substantially

thicker than Clough's, though not quite as thick as Clough himself. 'We're still working on Barry Shepherd's computers, but as you'd imagine, there's a fair few of them. Five different laptops. Plus there's any number of external hard drives and there's even a whole bunch of floppy disks, believe it or not. I swear, the bloke had more kit than Curry's, but we're getting there.'

'Phones?'

'Well, we still don't know what happened to Shepherd's phone. His wife has confirmed that he definitely had one, because she was ringing it all night. So, we've got to presume that it was taken by whoever killed him.'

'Maybe it was a really fancy one,' Miller said.

'We're going through Adrian Cutler's phone, but honestly, it's like pulling teeth. No prizes for guessing that a lot of the numbers on there belong to burner phones.'

'Are you suggesting that Mr Cutler may have been keeping some unsavoury company?' Miller harrumphed. 'How very dare you?'

The Welshwoman's grin suggested that Miller was doing wonders for her morale, at least. 'On top of which, the phone company aren't exactly being helpful. As per bloody usual.'

'I'll get on to them,' Sullivan said.

Miller knew how trying the process could be, with network providers refusing to provide passwords and PINs until all manner of bureaucratic hoops had been jumped through, and then demanding that they be paid for the privilege. He had endured much the same pantomime with Alex's phone. Although he'd seen the call log himself and knew most of her passwords, he'd happily handed it over to the DFU for a deeper dive.

He might just as well not have bothered.

'We need the permission of the account holder.'

'The account holder's dead.'

Pause. 'We need the permission of the account holder ...'

Sullivan clapped his hands together. 'OK, come *on*, team. We need to keep working, keep digging. There are two grieving families out there, let's not lose sight of that. They won't rest until we bring whoever's responsible for that grief to justice, and neither will we.'

Sullivan clearly thought he was Jürgen Klopp giving a half-time pep talk, but the only thing Miller felt motivated to do was visit his house in the dead of night and pop a turd through his letterbox.

Sullivan said *'Neither will we'* again, like he was now channelling Martin Luther King.

Miller leaned close to Xiu. 'Thank God he reminded us. Otherwise I might have spent the day fishing, or gone to see a movie or something.'

Walking back to their desks, Xiu said, 'So where did you go?'

'I just needed to ask some questions about another case.'

'Your wife's?'

Miller stopped and looked at her. 'Blimey, you're good.'

'I know.'

'If I'm ever bumped off, promise me you'll lead the investigation.'

'How am I going to cope with that many suspects?'

'Now, that was definitely a joke.'

'I don't think it was.' Xiu pointed across to her desk. 'Right, I'm going to start chasing up Massey's employees.' She waited. 'What about you?'

'I've got a few calls to make.' Miller could see that she was waiting for him to elaborate, but he wanted to see how the calls went first. 'I'll fill you in later,' he said. 'A spot of lunch, perhaps?'

'Chips again?'

'No, let's go mad and dine in,' Miller said. 'The pub across the road does an overcooked lasagne to die for.'

TWENTY-EIGHT

Whatever Pippa Shepherd had told Miller, she *had* wanted to get out of the house and it was no different today. Fiona, the Family Liaison Officer, had looked every bit as dubious as she'd been the day before, but that was fine because Pippa knew the woman couldn't actually stop her. Pippa hadn't done anything, after all.

She was the one who'd had something done to her.

The worst thing.

So was it really any wonder she felt the need to spend some time away from the house? From all the things in it that reminded her of Barry; the smells and the memories? If the Family Liaison Officer didn't understand that, then she was obviously in the wrong job.

'It's your call,' Fiona said. 'I'll just wait here until you get back.'

'If you want.' Pippa heard herself being snappy, and however messed up her emotions might be, she didn't much like it. 'I mean ... thank you.' Fiona nodded. Pippa was already pulling on her coat, and nothing else was said before she closed the front door behind her, hurried down the front path and turned towards the sea.

She walked along the front and kept going until the crowds thinned out and the noise of people enjoying themselves had faded away behind her. It wasn't as cold as she'd thought, or perhaps it was just that walking as quickly as she was had made her sweat a little. She undid the buttons of her coat and sat down on a bench.

There was so much to think about.

All those 'arrangements' Miller had mentioned when he'd first been round to see her. The funeral for starters, which was ironic, because that was probably the easy bit. She knew there would be all manner of legal stuff to untangle – mortgages and insurance policies and whatever else she hadn't even considered yet – and Barry had always handled that side of things, so she had no idea where to begin.

If this was happening twenty or thirty years from now, when it might not have been unexpected, she knew that she'd be able to find some file with everything explained. Who to call, and when, and where all the necessary documents were. Barry would have thought ahead and taken care of everything, so she wouldn't have to worry.

Because that was the kind of man he was.

She remembered Miller pulling her into his arms that day. He'd talked to her about carrying on, about moving forward even when it felt impossible. If he'd been sitting on the bench next to her right that minute she might actually have given him a piece of her mind, because words like that were so easy to trot out when you didn't know what you were talking about.

'It's nice to see you,' the landlady said.

'Back at you . . . and thanks for sending flowers, by the way.'

'Our pleasure.' The landlady winked at Xiu. 'His wife was the nice one.'

Once the landlady had gone, Miller sat back and said, 'So, how was *your* morning at the crime-fighting coalface?'

'No joy with Massey,' Xiu said. 'Everyone on his payroll seems to have an alibi, which is then conveniently backed up by one of the others.'

'You can't buy that kind of loyalty.' Miller placed a beer mat on the edge of the table. 'Oh, wait, you absolutely can.' He flicked the beer mat up and failed to catch it with the same hand. 'I'm not sure it matters, though.'

'Because . . . ?'

'Because I'm not convinced it's one of Massey's lot we're after. Yes, I might be spectacularly wrong, and you'll be surprised to hear that it wouldn't be the first time.'

'I'm not surprised,' Xiu said.

'I don't see Ralph Massey being quite so . . . provocative, that's all. On top of which, I'm sure that in the course of his short, but glittering criminal career Adrian Cutler had managed to upset a lot of people.'

'His wife for a kick-off.'

'Absolutely, and there's probably plenty of others we haven't winkled out yet, but we will, because you and I are highly skilled winklers.'

Xiu seemed pleased; bemused, but pleased. 'Anyway, nothing to get excited about as far as Massey is concerned, but I did find out one very interesting thing.'

'Is it the fact that dolphins sleep with one eye open?'

'No, it isn't.'

'OK, that was a bit of a stab in the dark . . . let me have one more guess. Is it the fact that the man who invented Pringles had his ashes buried in a Pringles can? Original flavour, if you want to be precise.'

'I'd been thinking about Scarlett Ribbons,' Xiu said.

'Oh . . . I never had you down as the type.'

'What you said about not being able to rule her out quite yet?'

'I did say that, didn't I, and the pleased-with-yourself expression on your face tells me that was intuitive yet superb detective work on my part . . .'

Xiu's raised eyebrow would have put Roger Moore to shame.

'. . . and clearly there's now been some similarly brilliant detective work on *your* part.'

'I did a bit of digging,' Xiu said, 'and it turns out that Pauline Baker isn't Scarlett's real name either. She changed it eight years ago, after being released from a Young Offenders Institute.'

'Oh, please tell me she was inside for shooting someone in the head.'

'Stabbing them in the groin, actually.'

Miller winced. 'Shame.'

'Selina Carter, aka Pauline Baker, aka Scarlett Ribbons did three and a half years for wounding with intent. So, we've got a proven tendency towards violence.'

'Well, it's definitely a smidgen more serious than whacking someone on the buttocks with a spatula. Shall we pop in and say hello?'

'I've already got the address.'

'Of course you have.' Miller sat back. 'We should probably let our food go down first.'

'So, how was your morning?'

'Pretty good, as it happens.' Miller folded his arms and smiled. 'I've found Chesshead.'

'Finally! So, come on then, what's this story I won't believe?'

'OK, so ... *oh*, before I tell you, let's just say I can understand why you left the Met.'

'Well, I'm not sure you can—'

'The north London DI I had the misfortune to be dealing with on the phone this morning was a *massive* pain in the arse. Seriously grumpy, like he was doing me a favour just talking to me, you know—?'

'Are you going to tell me, or   ?'

'—mind you, he did eventually manage to track Chesshead down for me, and he's promised to pick him up and deliver him, so I might just find it in my heart to forgive and forget.'

'Just ... don't bother, OK?' Xiu looked away and folded her arms. 'I'm not sure I even want to know your stupid story now.'

Miller grinned and let her sulk for a few seconds, before he leaned across the table and told her.

THIRTY

If anyone deserved a plaque on the wall of most local police stations, or a Lancashire Prison System loyalty card, it was Gary David Pope. He'd been a well-known face – or more usually a photofit – on the criminal scene for as long as any serving officer could remember, and while he never really did anything that would merit serious jail time, and drink or drugs were almost always involved, there was rarely a crime committed anywhere within a twenty-mile radius that Gary didn't have some connection to. It was like 'Six Degrees of Kevin Bacon', only with stolen cars and cocaine.

Gary Pope wasn't the worst criminal Miller had ever encountered, not by a long chalk, but he was probably the most consistent.

He was a seriously committed wrong 'un.

About ten years earlier, on the day he turned thirty, Gary – who for some reason still lived at home – became involved in a family argument over a slice of birthday cake and was subsequently arrested for biting half his father's ear off. Despite the suspect's insistence that his slice had been notably smaller than everyone else's and that it was really good cake, he was charged and bailed to appear, after which his stupid/forgiving parents declined to pursue the matter and Gary failed to appear anywhere again for the best part of six months.

'He just disappeared?'

'Yeah, but he showed up again eventually,' Miller said. 'And that's the point. Oh, and it *was* really good cake, by the way. I nicked a bit at the crime scene.'

Nobody clapped eyes on Gary Pope again until he turned up one night at an ex-girlfriend's, bleeding profusely from a number of wounds to the top of his head. He was predictably upset. She, quite rightly, phoned the police who arrived to discover that person or persons unknown had carefully carved a series of deep and almost perfectly straight lines across the top of Gary's head; from the front of his skull to the back and from ear to ear, like the squares on a chessboard.

'Right,' Xiu said. 'Got it.'

'I never said it was an imaginative nickname, but it's accurate.'

The investigation into this serious assault was somewhat hampered by the fact that the victim could not remember where it had happened, or indeed why, and had no idea whatsoever who was responsible. The copious amounts of drink and drugs that were – unsurprisingly – involved had combined with the trauma of the assault itself to wipe his memory completely. The amnesia was not the strangest thing, however, because using CCTV cameras the police were subsequently able to establish that, following the assault, Gary had walked at least four miles to his ex-girlfriend's place, pouring with blood and even stopping to chat with alarmed passers-by.

'Chatting about *what*?'

'God knows,' Miller said. '"Why am I bleeding" ... ?'

Since no one knew quite what to do with the victim of a serious assault who couldn't remember anything about it, it was decided – once he'd been released from hospital – to remand Gary Pope to prison, for his own safety as much as anything else. With him now locked up and the investigation going nowhere, it was only down to the initiative of one smart-thinking officer that the crime was eventually solved. Having decided to check back through all the daily crime reports around the time of the incident, the officer came across a statement from a cleaner who had arrived at a council block to discover the floor and walls of one flat splattered with blood. Said blood was quickly matched to Gary Pope – now rechris-tened 'Chesshead' by all those on the case – and a search began for the individual named on the tenancy agreement. The toe-rag in question was a low-rent drug dealer known to his customers as 'Lidl', because he sold drugs that were almost but not quite the same as other drugs and a fraction of the price.

'That's quite clever,' Xiu said.

'It's *funny*.'

'If you say so.'

Police now had a prime suspect. The fact that they couldn't immediately locate him was finally explained when it emerged that Lidl had himself been arrested the week before for flog-ging iffy ketamine. Arrested, charged and – it was clear Miller was getting to the good bit – remanded ...

Miller was grinning and Xiu shook her head.

'Don't tell me ... remanded to the same prison as Gary Pope.'

'Even better,' Miller said. 'The same *cell* ...'

Had this been a meeting of minds between renowned scientists and not a pair of dodgy scrotes in a 12x8 cell staring at each other, the encounter might have been called a eureka moment. As it was, Lidl strolled into his new accommodation like Charlie Big-Potatoes, took one horror-struck look at his new cellmate and said, 'You won't tell anyone, will you?'

That was when it all came flooding back to Gary Pope. Hearing his attacker's voice, he instantly remembered everything: the row over a drug deal, the big knife Lidl had produced from behind a cushion and how much it had hurt. He was never able to recall exactly why Lidl had chosen to carve his head up quite as mathematically as he had, but to all intents and purposes Gary Pope's memory was back, justice was done and order (of a sort) had been restored.

'So, what happened next?' Xiu asked.

'I told you it was a good story, didn't I?'

'What *happened?*'

'Well, Lidl got sent down for attempted murder and, because Lidl was one of Wayne Cutler's boys, Chesshead immediately pledged his allegiance to Ralph Massey.' Miller reached for his jacket. 'I mean, I don't think it was formal or there was any kind of initiation ceremony ... he just turned up at the ballroom and asked if there were any jobs going.'

'Welcomed into the fold, I'm guessing,' Xiu said.

'Oh yes, with open arms. Massey was always going to be interested in someone who hated the Cutlers as much as he did.'

'So, you think Chesshead had something to do with what happened at the hotel?'

'I seriously doubt it,' Miller said. 'He was in London for a start.'

'Well, we don't know that. Because we don't know when he went to London, do we? He could have left straight after Cutler and Shepherd were killed.'

'Well, I suppose he could ... but Chesshead usually threatened violence rather than actually committing it, so an execution-style killing isn't really his kind of thing anyway. I think he might know whose kind of thing it is, though. He tends to know what's going on.'

'I thought that girl was your eyes and ears. Finn?'

Miller smiled. 'Finn doesn't miss much, but it's mostly street stuff. She doesn't really know the ins and outs of the gang world. Chesshead knows all the lovely people involved. Who's a bit miffed and threatening to get busy on someone's kneecaps with a Black and Decker.' He stood up and pulled his jacket on. 'Actually, I kind of like Gary. He's not really a bad lad.'

'He bit off his dad's *ear*.'

'Only half of it.'

Xiu stood up too. 'I can't wait to be introduced.'

'I'm sure you'll get on.'

'It's not like I'll have any trouble recognising him.'

'Don't bank on it,' Miller said. 'For obvious reasons, he does have an extensive collection of hats.'

They walked towards the door of the pub, but Xiu stopped before Miller could open it. 'Listen, I wanted to say ... you getting involved in the investigation of your wife's murder isn't the best idea you've ever had.'

'You don't know how bad some of my other ideas have been.'

'I'm serious,' Xiu said.

'I'm not "getting involved".'

'Of course you are.'

'All right then, I am. See what I mean? You're a natural winkler.'

'You need to be careful, that's all I'm saying. Because you not going anywhere near your wife's case is very much rule number one. You could find yourself in serious trouble and you might even end up jeopardising any future trial.'

'Hang on ...' Miller hurried over to the bar to collect the promised takeaway, then returned to the door and opened it. 'What can I say, Posh? I'm a glutton for punishment.' He used Xiu's complimentary baguette to wave the landlady goodbye and grinned when she waved back. 'I wouldn't have my lunch in here, otherwise.'

THIRTY-ONE

Pippa had downed two glasses of wine in fairly short order, but she was yet to stop shaking. It was not a Family Liaison Officer's job to interfere at such moments and it was obvious that the woman was seriously upset, so Fiona Mackie had merely sat there watching Pippa drink, making the necessary soothing noises and waiting for her to calm down a little. Or at least enough to give Fiona the chance to leave the room for a minute or two and call it in.

The wife of one victim being stalked and harassed by the family of another was not an insignificant development.

'Thanks for passing that on,' Sullivan had said. 'It might be significant.'

Fiona could see why Declan Miller thought he was an idiot.

She came back into the living room to find Pippa sitting exactly where she'd left her, on the edge of the sofa. She still hadn't taken her coat off and the wineglass had been topped up.

'I've let the team know,' Fiona said.

Pippa nodded and drank.

'Obviously, this should not have happened, and we want to be sure it won't happen again. So, I was thinking it might be best if maybe you don't leave the house again for a while.' She saw Pippa shaking her head, ready to object. 'Or at least not unaccompanied, if you do really want to go out. Maybe an officer could walk with you . . . at a distance.'

'I see.' Pippa turned suddenly, sloshing wine into her lap. 'So, I get harassed by some . . . gangster and now I'm the one who has to suffer.'

'Well, that might be putting it a bit strongly,' Fiona said. 'I'm just suggesting that someone would be keeping an eye on you.'

'I don't want someone keeping an eye on me.'

'I know it's not ideal, but—'

'It's not bloody fair. It's . . . infringing my civil liberties.' It might just have been her highly emotional state that had made the words tricky to say, but it was starting to sound like the alcohol was playing its part, too. 'It's not fair, because I'm the victim.'

'Nobody's disputing that,' Fiona said.

'Shouldn't *he* be the one who's being watched by the police?'

'Yes, and I'm sure he will be.'

'Good . . .'

'We won't let anything happen to you.'

Pippa stared, alarmed. 'You're saying something might happen to me?'

'No, of course not.' Fiona was aware that her effort at reassurance had been poorly phrased. 'Nothing is going to happen to you. I just want to do whatever's necessary to keep things as normal as possible.'

187

'*Normal?*'

Fiona cursed herself again, knowing she'd had better days at work. 'All I'm trying to say is that grieving is hard at the best of times, you know? It knocks you for six all by itself, so it's important to keep everything else on an even keel. Does that make sense?' She waited. 'Pippa … ?'

'He was scary.' Pippa looked up at her, pale suddenly and helpless as a child.

'I know he was,' Fiona said gently. 'They all are.'

'And the more he pretended that he wasn't, the scarier he actually was, you know? Same as when he was saying he wasn't trying to upset me, when that's exactly what he was doing. Asking me all about Barry being at the hotel that night … insinuating things. Nasty things …'

Fiona watched Pippa start to cry again, and moved across to sit next to her. 'Maybe you should go and lie down for a bit.'

Pippa shook her head.

'Or I could go and make you something to eat?'

'Why would I want to eat?' She said it like Fiona had suggested that she turn cartwheels or settle down to watch something funny on TV.

Fiona decided to try something a little more basic. 'OK, well, let's start with getting your coat off, shall we … ?'

She reached over to prise the wineglass from Pippa's hand, then eased her up and helped her out of her coat. She set the glass on a table and stepped out into the hall to hang the coat up. When she came back into the room, Pippa was staring at the wall, clenching and unclenching her fists.

'I'm just so … bloody angry all the time.'

'Course you are,' Fiona said, 'and that's perfectly natural. It's one of the stages—'

'It's not natural. It's the opposite of that, because it's turning me into something I'm not. I can stand here and kid myself I'm angry at that thug and his stupid dog, and yes I am, but that's not why I'm like ... *this*.'

'OK, let's not call it natural then, but it is very common for people suffering from grief to be angry. Angry at the situation they suddenly find themselves in. Angry at everyone around them and their silly attempts to make them feel better. Angry at God, even.'

'I'm not angry at God,' Pippa said.

'Well ... whoever.'

'I'm angry at Barry.' She turned to look at Fiona and quickly shook her head. 'Not because of what he might have been up to at that hotel ... that doesn't matter any more. I'm angry at him ... I'm completely bloody furious at him for leaving me. It just seems so incredibly ... selfish, and obviously I know that him being murdered wasn't actually selfish at all, so then I end up being angry at myself. Hating myself for feeling like that.' She was gritting her teeth, her fists now permanently clenched. 'I just want to scream *so* much.'

'In which case you should scream,' Fiona said.

'It seems so stupid, though.'

'It's always best to let the anger out.'

'I want to smash things.'

'Well, if you think it will help.'

'It'll definitely help.'

'Then that's exactly what you should do—'

Pippa did not need any further encouragement. She marched across to the bookshelves above the television, picked up the china seahorse then stepped back and hurled it against the wall. She stared down at the debris on the carpet.

'Feeling better?' Fiona asked.

Pippa nodded, breathing heavily. She pointed. 'What's that?'

Fiona walked across and they both stared down at the small metal object near the skirting board, so out of place among the colourful fragments of china.

A flash drive.

When Pippa bent to pick it up, Fiona moved quickly forward to take her arm. 'I think it's probably best if you don't touch it.'

'Right . . .'

Moving in opposite directions, Fiona reached for her phone as Pippa groped for her wineglass.

THIRTY-TWO

When calling upon a member of the public, for whatever reason, only a police officer with a phenomenal lack of self-awareness would expect a warm welcome. Nobody was ever thrilled to see you, that was a given. A copper (or even worse, two of them) on your doorstep was more or less guaranteed to put a crimp in anyone's day, but Scarlett Ribbons stared at Miller and Xiu as though they were a pair of leprous Jehovah's Witnesses who were demanding money with menaces while simultaneously urinating in her front garden.

'Oh, God . . . can you please be quick?'

Sighing theatrically, she spun on a seriously high heel and walked back into her flat. Miller stepped inside and followed her down the hall. 'Is that what you say to your clients?'

'No, but I'm thinking it.' She turned and sighed again, her arms stretched out in frustration. She was wearing extravagant glittery earrings and a matching necklace that Miller guessed had been less expensive than they looked. Blackpool Bling. 'Seriously, I'm trying to get dressed for work.'

Xiu closed the front door behind her. 'We'll try not to keep you, Selina.'

That stopped the woman in her tracks, for a moment or two at least.

Pauline – who had once been Selina and was now Scarlett – walked, rather more slowly than before, into her living room and dropped into a deep leather armchair. Miller entered the room a few seconds later and leaned against a wall, waiting for Xiu. The room was scrupulously neat and tidy, with a pair of furry slippers placed side by side near the door and a stack of interior design magazines on a low table, next to a collection of ceramic coasters. Miller was a little disappointed, having hoped there might be an interesting selection of whips and spiky rubber truncheons on display, or at the very least a couple of nipple-clamps to fiddle with.

'Nice place,' he said.

'Nicer than you expected, you mean.'

'Different.'

Xiu arrived and sat down on the sofa.

'This is my home.' Scarlett reached down for the handbag at the side of her chair. She took out make-up and a compact. 'I never entertain clients at home. It's strictly outcall only.'

'Very sensible,' Miller said. 'On top of which, I'm guessing that the average bloke in the market for no-strings sex doesn't make an ideal houseguest. No, you definitely don't want some randy herbert in here, messing the place up, leaving their pants lying around ... and I bet they never use a coaster ...'

Xiu raised a hand to cut the chit-chat short. 'Why did you lie to us, Scarlett?'

Scarlett began to apply foundation. 'I didn't lie.'

'All right then, why didn't you tell us what your real name was? Why did you fail to mention your conviction for a serious violent crime?'

'You never asked.' She glanced up. 'Is that too flippant?'

'Yeah, a bit,' Miller said.

'Fair enough, but you didn't ... plus I knew that if you looked hard enough you'd find out eventually.'

'Which we did.'

'Which is why we're here.' Miller walked across and sat down next to Xiu. 'Now, don't get me wrong, it's nice to catch up anyway, but knowing slightly more about you than we did before does prompt a few more questions.'

'Well, could you hurry up and ask them? I'm seeing a doctor in forty-five minutes.'

'Oh ...'

Scarlett smiled as she popped her foundation back in the bag and took out a mascara pencil. 'Seeing as in "a good seeing to".'

'Thank you for that information,' Xiu said. 'Now, why don't you start by telling us about the offence you were convicted for?'

Scarlett shrugged. 'I was fifteen and I wasn't working and this bloke got a bit handsy. So, I got handsy back.' She pointed with the pencil. 'Only *I* had a kitchen knife.'

'Sounds fair enough,' Miller said.

Xiu shot him a look. 'Well, whatever the circumstances, I hope you can understand, in the light of your criminal record, why we might want to re-examine the events at the Sands Hotel. Your visit to Adrian Cutler's room.'

'Not really, no.'

'Because we can now place, at the crime scene, an individual with a known history of violence.'

'I think she means you,' Miller said, pointing. 'Very nice eyebrow work by the way.'

'Fine ... whatever.' Scarlett put down the make-up and looked at them. 'I went to Adrian's room, I did what I was there for and I left. That's it.'

'How long were you in the room for?' Xiu asked.

'Half an hour, maybe. Adrian was usually pretty quick.'

'And he was definitely alive and well when you left?' Miller waited. 'I know you told us he was last time, but you know ... just in case you've since remembered that you shot him in the head right before you packed your spanking paddles away. I swear, you wouldn't believe what can suddenly come back to people.'

'Why the hell would I want to kill Adrian?'

'Maybe he got too handsy,' Xiu said.

'Well, first off, he was paying me to be handsy ... among other things.' She lifted up the handbag. 'On top of which, I don't normally carry a gun in my bag. I've got mace, because I'm not an idiot, but he wasn't maced to death, was he?'

Miller's look to Xiu was enough to let her know that, in his opinion, this particular avenue of enquiry had turned out to be a cul-de-sac. 'OK, let's go crazy and assume you didn't actually kill him,' he said. 'Did anyone else come into the room when you left?'

'Not that I saw.'

'Did you open the door to let anyone in?'

'No.'

'Did anybody, other than Adrian himself, pay you to be there that night?'

194

Scarlett considered the question. 'Was I in on it, you mean? Like . . . a distraction?'

'A sex-decoy, if you will.'

'So, what . . . my job was to go to that hotel room and soften the intended victim up doing you-know-what?'

'Well, I'm not sure *soften* is the right word.'

'To keep his mind on other things, so that when the actual killer turned up poor old Adrian would be lying there helpless in his boxer shorts with no chance of defending himself. Is that what you mean?'

'That's broadly what I'm driving at, yes,' Miller said.

'What do *you* think?'

Miller thought it was an unlikely but nonetheless conceivable scenario and that this woman might well be playing him and Xiu like copper-shaped fiddles. Stranger things had happened, plenty of them. What he *knew* was that they didn't have a shred of evidence to prove anything beyond the plain and probably irrelevant fact that she'd been in that hotel room.

Arresting her for that would definitely be a tad over-zealous.

'So, is there anything else?' Scarlett held up her make-up bag and rattled it. 'I've still got a lot of slap to get on.'

'Oh yes, don't miss your doctor's appointment.' Miller stood up, belched quietly and swallowed down the taste of burnt lasagne. 'If you do, it's a bugger to get another one.'

Walking back to the car, Xiu shook her head. 'A *sex-decoy*?'

'It's a perfectly acceptable description,' Miller said. 'Does exactly what it says on the tin—'

Xiu snatched at her phone when it rang, then stepped away to take the call.

Miller heard her say 'Sir' before she moved out of earshot.

The *sir* in question could, he knew, be any number of officers senior to Xiu. A boss from another team perhaps, or the Chief Constable calling for a chinwag. It might be an old teacher she was still too scared to address by name. There was always the remote possibility that Sir Tom Jones was calling, though Miller couldn't immediately come up with an explanation for why that might be.

Seeing Xiu's somewhat pained expression and having weighed it up, he guessed that, for whatever reason, she was getting an earful from the wankspangle.

Miller knew whose voice he'd rather be listening to, so instead of standing about waiting, he got into the car, took out his phone and gave his dead wife a quick bell.

THIRTY-THREE

His powers of deduction nicely oiled by Lancashire Bitter and with the Bull's Head as his own personal incident room, Howard was keen to share his take on the case. 'I reckon the prostitute was definitely in on it.'

'You can't say "prostitute" anymore,' Mary said.

'Why not?'

'I don't know. Because you can't.'

'Yeah, it's a possibility we've been considering,' Miller said. He'd told Howard as much only an hour or so earlier, before there'd been too much . . . oiling. 'I think it's unlikely, though.'

'Well, I wouldn't rule it out,' Howard said. 'However big and clever a bloke thinks he is, he can always get caught off-guard when there's nookie involved. So, this woman, who for reasons I still don't understand I can't call a prostitute, is very much the ideal candidate, I reckon.'

'I think Declan's considered all that,' Mary said.

'A sex-decoy!'

Miller smiled. 'Thanks, Howard.'

'Maybe that's not what she's lying about.' Mary had not drunk nearly as much as her husband, but she was equally keen to help. 'I mean she wasn't exactly honest the first time you interviewed her, was she? So what if she was lying about being there to see Adrian Cutler? I know you showed her a photo and everything, but what if she *was* there to see the other bloke? The computer man . . .'

'Barry Shepherd,' Miller said.

'Right. Him.'

'What's her motive for killing the computer bloke?' Ruth asked.

'Well, that's for Declan to find out, isn't it? I'm retired. Anyway, I never said she *killed* him, did I?'

'Again, it's a nice idea, Mary.' Miller had spent most of his time since the dance class had finished pointing out the enormous holes in whatever theory was being offered. He was trying to be as gentle as possible. 'But we only found Scarlett's DNA in Cutler's room. So we can be fairly certain she was never in Barry Shepherd's room.'

'Oh,' Mary said. 'Well, that's sorted then.'

'She was lucky when you think about it,' Nathan said.

Everyone turned to the youngest member of the group, who was happily necking a bottle of lager. He laid the bottle down and nodded.

'Scarlett was. I mean, presuming she's telling the truth, she could have come out of that hotel room and walked smack into the killer. He'd probably have killed her as well.'

Miller thought about that.

'Maybe the killer was there all the time,' Gloria said. 'Waiting for this young woman to finish her business and leave.'

'Waiting where?' Miller asked.

'In the room next door. In Mr Shepherd's room. I might not have been listening properly, but I don't think you know for certain that Mr Cutler was shot before Mr Shepherd or if it was the other way round . . . or have I got that wrong?'

'No.' Miller put his own beer down. 'You haven't.'

Miller knew that, whether or not Gloria was right about the killer hiding, she had inadvertently highlighted something important. All Prisha Acharya had been able to say for certain was that the victims had died within a few minutes of each other, but it had so far been impossible to establish the order in which that had happened. As far as this case went, Miller did not know very much. If he was being strictly accurate, he knew next to bugger all, but he was becoming convinced that knowing which of the victims was killed first would prove to be very important.

Would be the key to finding out why either of them had been killed at all.

'All right,' Mary said. 'I think we've talked about murder for long enough and we should let Declan have some time off.'

'I don't mind,' Miller said 'I asked, didn't I?' He thought Mary was slightly miffed that someone else's suggestion had gone down better than hers, but he knew it would all be forgotten in a gin or two. As it was, he genuinely didn't mind these boozy brainstorming sessions after class. The contributions being made by many of his esteemed colleagues – Xiu not included – were of the chocolate teapot variety, so he remained grateful for input from anywhere, not least a group that included two retired coppers.

'I tell you what, though,' Howard said. 'You were jiving like a professional in there tonight.'

'Like a professional darts player, maybe.' Miller tore open a bag of Mr Porky's finest. 'I'm still feeling a bit . . . clunky.'

'It'll all come back soon enough,' Mary said.

'Bang on, love.' Howard leaned over and helped himself to a scratching. 'Class is temporary but form is permanent.'

'Other way round,' Nathan said.

'Samba next week, I think,' Mary said. 'We haven't done that one in a while.' She looked round the table, waiting for nods of approval, then wriggled in her chair. 'Get those hips rolling a bit.'

'Fine with me,' Ruth said. 'I think that's actually my favourite.'

'I'll be your partner if you like.' Nathan was trying to sound casual, staring at his beer bottle. Miller could not fault the lad for trying, though he had a hunch that, romancewise, Ruth had other fish to fry.

'And we *will* have to give the paso doble a go at some point.' Mary looked at Miller. 'I know you might find that hard.'

'It's only a bloody dance, right?' Miller blinked away the memory; an empty spotlight and a band stuttering to a halt. 'Bring it on.'

Nobody said very much for a while after that, though Miller sensed that Howard, at least, had something he very much wanted to say. Eventually, the old ex-copper couldn't help himself.

'No news, I suppose? Alex . . .'

'I've been doing my best,' Miller said. 'Asking awkward questions, telling them they need to sort their ideas out. I'll probably get a spanking from the brass for sticking my nose in, and not the sort that Scarlett dishes out.'

'They can't blame you for wanting to know what's going on,' Mary said.

'It chuffing stinks if you ask me,' Howard said. 'This is one of their own we're talking about. Alex was a fellow officer and we know how that works, don't we?'

Mary nodded. 'How it's supposed to, certainly.'

'So, why does it feel like they're kicking the can down the road?'

'I wish I knew,' Miller said.

'You should let us help.' Howard was nodding, as though it was already a done deal. 'Me and Mary haven't been out of the game that long. We still know plenty of people and nobody can stop us asking awkward questions.'

'I'm not sure that's a good idea,' Miller said.

'It can't hurt, can it?' Mary looked at the others. 'I'm sure we'll all chip in to help however we can.'

There was a good deal of enthusiastic nodding. Miller smiled and took another handful of scratchings.

'I'm not sure I can be quite as useful as some of the others,' Ruth said. 'But if you need a place to meet up ... that isn't here, I mean ... like an HQ, you're welcome to use my house. I'll happily be the one who writes everything down, too. A plan of action or whatever.'

'You know I'm good with computers, right?' Nathan leaned forward. 'I can break into their system, check out all the files or whatever.'

Miller looked at him. 'You're going to hack the Police National Computer?'

'I'll give it a damn good go, mate.'

Ransford cleared his throat. 'Well, Gloria and I are just florists, as you know ...'

Miller smiled again and nodded at him. The couple had provided a glorious floral display for Alex's funeral and he still wasn't sure he'd ever really thanked them properly.

'. . . and I very much doubt that's remotely useful to you, but if anyone around this table comes up with anything that helps catch the person responsible for Alexandra's death, I can promise that they will never have to pay for flowers again.' Ransford was not a natural speechmaker and he looked a little embarrassed. He reached over and took his wife's hand. 'So, there you go.'

It wasn't that Miller had any issue with shedding a tear. How could he, when in the last few weeks he'd shed enough to fill . . . a shed. He just didn't want to, not at that moment . . . not sitting where he was and doing what he was doing.

He could shed a bucketful later on, when he got home.

He knew by the look on her face that Mary could see the effort he was making. It was the same expression she'd worn that first night back, after that first dance, when she'd told him that tears were nothing to be ashamed of.

Miller smiled at her and shook his head. Not this time . . .

Of course tears were nothing to be ashamed of, but nobody in their right mind wanted to eat soggy scratchings.

Climbing off his moped, Miller noticed that the security light had come on outside his front door. He took off his helmet and watched a figure move in and out of the shadows, like someone was pacing up and down.

Waiting for him.

A fearless, gung-ho kind of copper might have armed himself with the nearest big stick or gone looking for something even more useful. A sensible one would have reached for a phone and quietly called for back-up. Being neither of those, Miller walked towards his house until the figure revealed itself – much to his relief – to be a skinny-looking *she*.

Michelle Cutler was sweaty and out of breath.

'I've been running,' she said.

'Right.' It didn't quite explain what Adrian Cutler's wife was doing on his doorstep, but he guessed she would get to that in her own time. 'Do you want some water?'

'Have you got anything else?'

Miller walked past her and put his key in the front door. 'Fanta?'

THIRTY-FOUR

When Miller walked back into the living room with the wine, Michelle was on her haunches in front of Fred and Ginger's cage.

'*Rats?*'

He couldn't fault her powers of observation. 'They're relatively low maintenance, they're cleverer than a lot of the people I have to deal with on a daily basis and they almost never get sick. They're not smelly because they're incredibly clean and they love a cuddle. Oh, and they can actually giggle.'

Michelle leaned away as Fred and Ginger began to tart about, standing on their hind legs and pushing their noses through the bars of the cage. 'Yeah, but . . . rats?'

'They *could* probably do with a PR push,' Miller said. 'But, to be fair, that whole plague thing was a long time ago.'

'What are their names?'

Miller told her and saw that she didn't get the reference, but he felt no desire to explain.

'Don't they ... breed? I thought rats were at it like rabbits.'

'Well, they probably would if they weren't both female,' Miller said. 'Fred's short for Frederica.' He held up her glass and waited until she stood and moved across to join him. They sat down at opposite ends of the sofa. 'Should I be shocked that you know where I live?'

'Depends how easily shocked you are.' Michelle leaned across and touched her glass to Miller's.

'Cheers,' Miller said.

'Up your bum.' She took a drink then began to stretch; leaning back while pushing her lycra-clad legs out in front of her and flexing her feet. Her training shoes looked like they'd never been worn before.

'That some kind of warm-down?'

She looked at him, still stretching.

'If you've been doing exercise it's meant to be a good idea to warm down afterwards. Something to do with acid in the muscles? I mean, it's not really an issue with me as I never get warmed *up*, so ...'

She closed her eyes and let her head drop back. She rolled her neck a few times then sat up and had another drink. 'So, how's it going?'

'What ... me, or the investigation into your old man's murder?'

'Have a guess.'

'Well, to be fair there haven't been too many developments since I spoke to you ... yesterday. Unless you've come all the way here because there's something you want to tell me?'

Michelle smiled and downed the rest of her wine. 'I know you're amazed that I give a monkey's, but everything I told you at the house doesn't mean I don't care about what happened. That I'm not cut up.'

'Like Adrian's suit,' Miller said.

He'd been fairly sure that Michelle had seen him pocketing the contents of her kitchen bin the day before. So he wasn't surprised when she shrugged and nodded or that the smile she eventually managed was as empty as her glass. Miller reached down for the bottle and topped her up.

'Look, I get why you think I might have had something to do with it.'

'Did you?' She appeared to have no problem meeting his steely glare, so Miller held up his hands. 'OK, then. It's important to get that out of the way though, don't you reckon? I mean, I've got to ask . . . it's kind of in the job description.'

'I didn't,' she said. 'But you're not the only one who thinks I might have.'

'Killed Adrian?'

'Killed him . . . *had* him killed, whatever.'

Miller had a drink himself because he sensed that Michelle was keen to get something off her chest; that now would be a good time to shut up and let her talk. He watched her look towards the window. He watched her pull up her legs and hug her knees, keenly aware that Adrian Cutler's widow was no longer the cocky and entitled princess she'd been on her home turf. Miller could see how tense she really was. He'd only caught the faintest whiff of nervousness in that fancy kitchen, but suddenly it was stinking up his front room.

'A couple of the cousins have said things . . . the usual snide comments from Jacqui.' She talked quietly, staring at Miller's carpet. 'They're all watching me a bit too closely, you know what I mean? Keeping tabs.' She looked at the window again. 'Truth is, I bloody hate running. I just needed to get away for a bit.'

'I understand,' Miller said.

'Do you?'

'Yeah. I hate running as well.'

She flashed a smile and nodded, a little more sure of herself. With Miller, at least. 'Adrian's brother's been muttering stuff as well, which is a bit rich coming from him.'

'Why's that?'

'No reason really ... just that I don't think he's quite as upset about what happened as he's making out.' She glanced at Miller and saw that he was waiting for her to carry on. She was breathing nearly as heavily as she had been on the doorstep. 'Look, Justin's actually older than Adrian and he was a bit jealous, that's all. Because he thought Adrian was their dad's golden boy and *he'd* been overlooked.'

Miller nodded. 'So, he's like *Fredo*. Obviously I mean the character from *The Godfather* as opposed to the chocolate frog.' Seeing that Michelle didn't get the joke, Miller decided that Fred and Ginger would probably be a more receptive audience. He might get a giggle, at least. Then again, in light of Xiu's reactions, or lack of them, maybe he just wasn't as funny as he hoped he was.

Rather more important, what Michelle had told him confirmed Miller's notion that it was worth taking a closer look at Justin Cutler.

'It's all so stupid,' Michelle said. 'Thinking that I could have had anything to do with what happened to Adrian. I mean, yeah ... Adrian was a nightmare, but he was my nightmare. And I'd more or less got used to how he was, but lately ...' She took another sip of wine, but suddenly she didn't seem to like the taste.

'Lately, what?'

'It felt different. His ... messing around. Like maybe it wasn't just the tarts, or maybe there was one he'd actually fallen for. I was starting to think I might lose him.'

Miller could see that she was close to tears and that she was fighting it, much the same way he'd done himself a couple of hours earlier. A woman like Michelle Cutler would not want to cry in front of a copper. 'What about your own family? Couldn't you get them round if you need a bit of support?'

She shook her head. 'My lot don't tend to hang around with the Cutlers very much. They find them all a bit ...'

'Scary?'

'I was going to say intimidating, but I suppose it's much the same thing. Talking of which ...' She looked at her watch and quickly put away what little was left in her glass. 'I'd better get back.'

They both stood up and Miller walked her towards the door. Michelle stopped halfway there and stared at a framed photograph of Alex.

'Nice picture,' she said.

'Yeah ...'

'She looks ... kind.'

Half a minute later, Miller watched Michelle grimace then jog away towards the road. He waited until she'd disappeared from view but, just before he closed the door, he heard an engine start up and watched a car pull away and follow her. It was too dark to make out the model or see who was driving, but Miller caught just enough of the number plate.

THIRTY-FIVE

'I didn't have you down as a devotee of "the dance",' Massey said.

'Say again?'

'A fan of dancing.'

'I'm not.' Wayne Cutler stared down from the balcony at the pulsating throng below. 'I don't think I'd call that "dancing" anyway.'

'Rave night.' Massey sniffed, his fingers tapping against the dusty velvet-covered railing. 'Not my cup of Earl Grey either, but it gets the youngsters into the ballroom a couple of nights a week. Pays the bills.'

'Fair enough.'

'Pays a few of yours, too, judging by the state of some of them.' He stepped away and nodded. 'It's quieter in my office.'

'It's quieter anywhere,' Cutler said.

A few minutes later, once the door was closed and the unpleasantries were out of the way (insincere condolences dismissed, a drink offered and refused) they got down to business.

It had been a long time since the two businessmen had met face to face, but when Cutler had phoned saying he was keen to talk, Ralph Massey had seen no real reason to refuse. At any other time he might have demurred because *Death in Paradise* was on or explained that he was washing his hair, but silly excuses would have been a little churlish, given the circumstances. So he'd sent Pixie and Dixie off to amuse themselves for an hour and got the gin out.

Massey knew that Cutler hadn't come alone, of course: that several of his entourage would be downstairs, looking laughably incongruous as they tried to mingle with the ravers. It was fine, because there were plenty of his own boys down there too. It amused him to think they were probably propping up the bar together, telling war stories or showing each other scars.

A machete done that one.

That's a scratch, mate. Let me show you what two hedge trimmers and a nail gun can do . . .

'This doesn't have to take all night,' Cutler said.

'Shame.' Massey poured a G&T for himself. 'I thought we could have a good old catch-up.'

'Don't try and wind me up, Ralph.' Cutler shifted on one of Massey's bright red plastic chairs, uncomfortable in every sense. 'I'm really not in the mood.'

Cutler could not be doing with Massey's waspish carry-on at the best of times. It set his shiny new teeth on edge. It had taken a great deal of restraint not to toss the spidery sod off his own balcony.

'Let me just get it out of the way, then.' Massey leaned back, cradling his glass. 'What happened to Adrian was horrible, and I can see how much it's eating you up, but I can promise you it had nothing to do with me.'

210

Cutler nodded, unsurprised. 'Or nowt to do with anyone connected to you?'

'Are you referring to Gary Pope, perchance?'

Perchance? Why did the pretentious tosspot have to talk like he was in *Downton* bleeding *Abbey*? 'Yeah, that name crossed my mind.'

'It's really not Chesshead's style,' Massey said.

'You want someone dead badly enough, you don't care about the style.'

'Well, let's agree to disagree, but I am doing my very best to find him so I can make absolutely sure.'

'You and me both. In London, someone said.'

'I heard the same, but he'll be back soon enough. He's hardly Dick Whittington, is he?' Massey sighed and shook his head. 'Seriously though, Wayne, how could you think I was involved with this in any way? Why would I want you on the warpath and the police swarming all over the place?'

'Miller?'

'Oh yes ... he came by.'

'So, did *he* believe you?'

Massey smiled. 'I think it's safe to say that his head's not quite back in the game just yet.'

'The business with his wife, yeah?'

'Indeed. I think poor Detective Sergeant Miller's rather ... preoccupied with that.'

'Right, and now I know how he feels.'

'Well, of course you do.'

Cutler grunted as he repositioned his backside again. 'Sounds to me like they might never find out what happened that night.'

'A "seaside mystery".' Massey said it like it was the title of a marvellous new show he was promoting.

'Oh yeah. Definitely a mystery.'

They were like schoolboys in a staring competition, until Massey sat back and spread out his arms. 'Well, she was alive and well when she left my ballroom, I know that much.'

For a few seconds, there was only the insistent thud of the bass from the dance floor below and the chink of ice in Massey's glass.

'*Dick Whittington*,' Cutler said. 'That's a pantomime, right?'

'It certainly is,' Massey said. 'One in which I was delighted to star myself as it happens . . . many moons ago, at the Civic in Accrington.' He slapped his thigh and winked. 'Five miles to London and *still* no sign of Dick!'

'Leave it out, Ralph,' Cutler said.

Justin Cutler was playing games on his phone when his father returned to the car. He slipped the phone back into his pocket.

'It's not Massey.' Wayne was shaking his head as he started the big BMW. 'I never really thought it was, but I needed to hear him say it. To watch him while he was saying it.'

'Yeah, OK . . . I mean, whatever you think.'

Wayne turned the engine off. 'What does that mean?'

'Nothing.' Justin yanked his seat belt across and clicked it into place. 'Just that if it was him, he's hardly likely to come out and tell you, is he?'

Wayne laughed, but not because he thought anything was funny. 'You think I'm daft?'

'No, I didn't mean—'

'You think I don't know that? I can *read* people, son.' He looked long and hard at Justin. 'So, I always know if I'm being mugged off.'

'Yeah, course you do,' Justin said. 'Everyone knows that.'

'Right, good.' Wayne started the car again. 'Now let's get

home.' He nosed the car out and watched for a break in the traffic. 'If we're going to find out who *is* responsible for Adrian, there's a few more people I need to talk to.'

'All I meant was, it might be a mistake to rule Massey out completely, yeah?' Justin shrugged, like he was trying to be casual, because it rarely paid to be too pushy with his old man. 'Or at least wait until you're sure you can rule him out before you start looking elsewhere.'

'I'm sure,' Wayne said.

'Right. Well, it's your call, obviously.' Justin took out his phone again, turned away and went back to his game. 'Don't forget, you promised to bring a kebab back for Mum.'

Wayne grunted. 'Oh, Christ, yeah. Our lives wouldn't be worth living if we turned up without your mother's large doner ... come *on*, let me out, you muppet!' He pushed his way into a gap that wasn't really there, ignored the blast of a car horn and accelerated away.

A mile or so up the road, he double-parked in front of a parade of shops and fast food joints. He flicked on the hazards, then turned and dropped a meaty paw on to his son's knee. 'Listen, we've got to face the fact that your brother's not with us any more, may he rest in peace.'

'Yeah, rest in peace,' Justin said. 'Totally.'

'So, painful as it is to think about the future, we have to, because you're going to have to step up, all right, son? I'll need you there when I want some good advice or even ... a bit of guidance, who knows? I need to know I can count on you to do what's right for this family.'

Justin nodded, solemn. 'Extra chilli sauce and no salad. She'll go mental if there's salad.'

'Well, that's a start, I suppose,' Wayne said.

THIRTY-SIX

Miller lay in bed listening to the radio, but it failed to spark his interest because everyone was being far too sensible, so he turned it off and looked at Alex instead. She was sitting at the end of the bed, watching him. He folded back the duvet and patted the mattress.

'You can get in, you know?'

'Not right this minute,' she said.

'No funny business, I promise.'

'I should hope not, because that would be weird.'

'It doesn't seem fair.' He hauled the duvet back over himself. 'I'm the one doing the imagining . . . and I've imagined it a lot.'

She nodded, unsurprised, but she had her business face on. Her copper's face. 'Maybe if you stopped thinking about you-know-what and thought about this case a bit more, you might actually get somewhere.'

Miller sighed. 'Fine.'

'So . . . Barry Shepherd.'

'Yeah, I think we should look at him again.' Miller sat up. 'By which I mean we should actually look at him, because we really haven't. Not as anything other than a victim, anyway.'

'Which might be all he is.'

'Yeah, it might.'

Alex got to her feet and walked to the window. 'Pippa told you that her husband hadn't been behaving any differently before he was killed, and maybe he wasn't. Or perhaps he was and she didn't notice. Or she was lying.'

'Well, I know she's lied to me once already,' Miller said. 'The other day when I spoke to her in the street, she wasn't on her way to work. I talked to the restaurant and they confirmed that her shift wasn't due to start until hours after I saw her. Nobody's that keen, are they?'

'So talk to her again,' Alex said. 'Or maybe talk to some of Barry's workmates, see if they noticed anything.'

'Good idea,' Miller said. 'Thank you.'

'You're welcome.'

He was thinking about the conversation he'd had with Sullivan at the first briefing. That spiky exchange about making assumptions. From that point on, the team's enquiries had all been based on the theory that Adrian Cutler had been the killer's target and Miller had gone along with the consensus.

'Not like you,' Alex said. 'Not like you at all.'

'First day back.' Miller turned to punch his pillow into shape. 'I wasn't quite myself.'

'It's been nagging at you though, right?'

'Yeah, and now you are.'

Alex smiled and nodded. 'It's a good job I'm dead, because you know I wouldn't let you get away with that under normal circumstances.'

'Every cloud,' Miller said, smiling back.

The dance floor aside, Miller knew very well that he was usually out of step with everyone else. That was how he liked it. Clumsy and awkward as they were – stepping on toes and walking in the wrong direction as like as not – he was starting to feel as though he might finally be finding his feet again. The conversation he'd had with Michelle Cutler a couple of hours before had certainly altered his opinion of at least one suspect. It might even have revealed another one, and he'd be letting Sullivan know about that first thing in the morning. Telling, as opposed to suggesting, because some toes needed stepping on more than others.

'Well, we know that Shepherd was hiding *something*,' he said.

Alex walked back across the room and stood at the end of the bed, looking down at him. 'Maybe he was involved in something dodgy and upset the wrong person. Someone like him . . . good at using computers to hide money . . . maybe he decided to take some for himself.'

Miller knew that, without evidence, this was still just supposition, but it was as good a working theory as any other. Barry Shepherd had not been shot in the head because he'd looked at someone's girlfriend or spilled their pint. 'Hopefully we'll know a bit more once Carys has had a chance to look at that flash drive.'

'It could be that Cutler was the person Shepherd had stolen money from,' Alex said, 'and Shepherd didn't know he'd been rumbled yet. Maybe he went to that hotel for what he thought was going to be an amicable business meeting. He asked for a room next to his "friend", remember?'

'OK, but if Shepherd was the target, why kill Cutler?'

'Same question the other way round,' Alex said. 'If the killer was there for Cutler, why was Shepherd killed?'

'You're not helping any more,' Miller said. Then, he had another thought. 'Unless Shepherd was in bed with Cutler. I mean, not literally, obviously . . . but maybe someone was sent there to kill both of them.'

Alex looked unconvinced.

'This is doing my bloody head in.' Miller lay down again and stared at the ceiling. 'Let's wait and see what Chesshead makes of it all.'

'I never thought I'd say this, but I quite miss Gary Pope,' Alex said. 'I mean, *miss* is probably putting it a bit strongly . . .'

Miller closed his eyes, but he knew she was still there. 'What else do you miss?' He turned on to his side. 'Properly miss?'

'The lamb bhuna at the Raj, the chicken livers at Nando's, Marmite . . .'

'Apart from food.'

'I miss swimming in the sea. Fred and Ginger of course, and I really miss that long walk along the clifftops on a Sunday morning. Marching around the model village and pretending to be a giant—'

'People,' Miller said. 'What about people?' The two hours of dance practice and the beers afterwards had suddenly caught up with him. He was talking more slowly now, exhaustion taking hold. 'Which people . . . do you miss?'

'Well, my sister, obviously,' Alex said. 'And my mum. There's a few people from work and that nice bloke in the newsagent's.'

'Come on . . .'

'I'm trying to think. I know there's definitely one more person, but I'm struggling to remember the name.'

217

'I hate you.'

'Milton, is it? Or Mills . . . ?'

There was a smile on Miller's face when sleep finally took him.

STEP TWO

HAMMERLOCK POSITION

THIRTY-SEVEN

Having been told within sixty seconds of arriving at work that the DCI would like a word, Miller had known he was in trouble, and that the word in question was unlikely to be a nice one, like *bubbly* or *kerfuffle* . . .

This time, he thought it best to knock.

Akers did not even look up. 'Sit down, Detective Sergeant.'

Miller did as he was told.

'Three guesses why you're here.'

'Oh, right, we're starting with a quiz—'

'*Don't*. Just . . . don't.' The look on Akers's face made it abundantly clear that she was wearing her best bollocking trousers.

'Fair enough,' Miller said. 'I don't need to guess, anyway. I know very well that you've had Lindsey Forgeham in your ear, moaning about me interfering in her case.'

'Not *interfering*, no.'

'Not yet, anyway.'

'I'll pretend you didn't say that. She was just concerned at

221

you being there, because you aren't allowed to be. You can't go anywhere near the investigation into Alex's murder . . . God, why am I even bothering to tell you, when you know all this very well? It doesn't seem to be stopping you, though, so now I'm the one who's got to deal with it.'

'I wanted to see how they were getting on, that's all.'

'It sounded very much to me as if you were making accusations.'

'Well, I might have suggested they could at least consider pulling their fingers out.'

'Right, like that's really going to get them onside.'

'Why should I need to get them onside?' Miller felt the urge to jump up and stamp around the office a bit, but made do with squeezing the arms of the chair instead, imagining they were the scrawny necks of certain officers a few floors above him. 'I'm a copper, same as they are, and more to the point, she was my *wife*. It doesn't matter what I can and can't do, they should at the very least be keeping me up to speed. There's been a few hugely thoughtful cards and a pastoral visit to check I hadn't put my head in the oven and then . . . radio silence. Come on, Susan, don't you reckon they should be telling me what's happening, even if it's nothing? That's just common courtesy, don't you think? That's basic bloody humanity.'

Akers let out a long sigh and gave the smallest of nods. 'I'm not disagreeing, Dec, but all the same—'

'And by the way, why *have* they got nothing?' Miller waited, but Akers wouldn't look at him. 'It's been six weeks and Forgeham and her squad of numpties have got no more than they had in the first six hours. If I was the suspicious sort, I might be starting to think that they weren't actually trying very hard.'

'Now you *are* making accusations,' Akers said.

'Well, they're not exactly pulling out all the stops, are they?' Miller was ranting now and, though he knew it wouldn't cut any ice, he couldn't help himself. Being physically closer to the investigation into Alex's death had been one of the main reasons for coming back to work in the first place, but it clearly wasn't getting him anywhere. He was starting to think that, with the possible exception of hacking the Police National Computer (Nathan couldn't actually do it, could he?), maybe he should take Howard, Mary and the rest of them up on their generous offers to help. 'Or any stops at all, come to that. I know it, and you know it.'

Miller was pleased to see his boss look conflicted, for a few seconds at least, before she spoke.

'It would be wrong of me to make judgements on another team's investigation,' she said. 'So, if it's all right with you, DS Miller, I'm going to stop listening now.'

'Come on, Susan, you know I'm right.'

She shook her head, determined. 'No . . .'

'They're dragging their feet.'

'*I'm not hearing this.*' Akers raised her hands to the side of her head. 'I'm not hearing this.'

'Oh, really?' Miller shrugged, then said it again. Louder.

When Miller walked into the briefing room, Sullivan was ready with a withering comment that he'd clearly spent some time perfecting.

'Prostate playing up again, DS Miller?'

'Not at all,' Miller said. 'In terms of regularity and flow, everything in the urination department is tickety-boo, but thanks so much for asking. I'm late because I've just spent ten minutes being admonished, then threatened with suspension, for talking to the team investigating my wife's murder, but ... hey ho!' He ignored Xiu's *I told you so* expression and rubbed his hands together. 'So, what have I missed?'

'It's all there in your briefing document,' Sullivan said.

Miller sat down in the chair that Xiu appeared to have saved for him. 'We should have one of those helpful recaps like you get at the start of TV shows. *Previously on* Tim Sullivan Investigates ...'

Sullivan actually smiled, which was hugely disconcerting. Perhaps it was a simple reflex, like a dog wagging its tail when its name is mentioned. Or maybe he dared to dream that he might one day star in just such a TV show.

Either way, Miller didn't like it.

'We were discussing the contents of Shepherd's flash drive,' Sullivan said. 'Not quite as useful as we were hoping.'

Carys Morgan looked across at Miller. 'Well, not yet, anyway.'

'So, what's on it?' Miller asked.

'Two files, that's all. Neither of them named, unfortunately.'

'Shame,' Miller said. 'Always a bonus when there's a file called *Special Secret Clues*.'

'One is just a series of eight numbers.'

'Bank account?' Xiu said.

'Every chance, I reckon,' Carys said. 'The other file is enormous and looks to me like a self-contained operating system. The kind of thing you'd use if you wanted to go online for some reason and didn't want to leave a trace.'

'Looking for porn?' Clough asked.

Miller said nothing, because sometimes it was just too easy.

'Makes sense,' Clough said. 'Maybe his wife used to check his search history. I know mine does.'

Now, it was simply too tempting. 'And there I was thinking I couldn't have any more sympathy for Mrs Clough than I already do.'

'Knowing what the files are is all well and good,' Carys said. 'The problem is I can't get into them, because unlike the files on his other devices, they're password protected and the only person who knows the password happens to be dead.'

'That's probably taking your security a bit far,' Miller said.

'I've tried all the obvious ones – date of birth, wife's date of birth – but I'm not surprised he didn't want to make it easy.'

'OK, well keep working on it,' Sullivan said.

Miller raised a hand. 'It makes sense that we're finally considering Barry Shepherd as a possible primary target,' he said. 'But I'd like to throw someone else into the mix as a primary suspect. From what Michelle Cutler told me, Adrian's older brother Justin might well have had a half-decent motive.'

'We're all ears,' Sullivan said.

'Jealousy, basically. Thwarted ambition. Yeah, it's all a bit ... *Godfathery*, but it certainly sounds like Justin and Ade weren't what you'd call bestest mates.'

'Worth having a word with him?' Clough asked Sullivan.

'No reason why not,' Sullivan said. 'Worth having one with the father at the same time and making it very clear that he needs to stay well away from Pippa Shepherd.'

'Yeah, what was all that about, you reckon?' Miller asked.

'Could be perfectly innocent,' Xiu said. 'But from what Pippa told the FLO, it sounds like Mr Cutler was quite keen on finding out what Pippa had said to us.'

Miller thought about that, but if Wayne Cutler had an angle

or knew something about the murders they didn't, he had no idea, as yet, what that might be. 'Well, I'm sure young Justin will have a cast-iron alibi, same as Ralph Massey and everyone *he's* ever met, but that doesn't really matter. As of now, we're looking for whoever hired the shooter, so we should really be going through Justin Cutler's emails and phone records, finding out who he's been talking to.' He leaned across the table and smiled. 'Carys . . . ?'

'Right, like my team hasn't got enough to be getting on with. This flash drive's a full-time job on its own and we're still working on Cutler's phone, with no cooperation whatsoever from the service provider. They're certainly not providing a bloody service to *us*.'

'I thought we were getting that sorted.' Miller looked at Sullivan. 'You said you were chasing it up, sir.'

Sullivan muttered something which Miller heard perfectly well, but he couldn't be certain that everyone else had. 'Sorry, boss, I didn't quite catch that . . .'

The DCI spoke through teeth that were so firmly gritted, he might well have had a decent future as a ventriloquist. 'I'm still waiting for them to ring me back.'

'Ring you *gack*?' Miller said.

'That's ridiculous.' Xiu looked genuinely furious. 'This is a murder case. A double murder case.'

'You know when you get that recording that says *your call is really important to us*?' Miller shook his head sadly. 'Call me a cynic, but I'm starting to suspect that they might not actually mean it.'

THIRTY-EIGHT

Xiu set the satnav for an industrial estate on the outskirts of town and pulled out of the car park.

'Declan,' she said. 'That's Irish, right?'

Miller scowled at her. 'Oh, I see. Just because of my name, you're allowed to make ridiculous assumptions about what my background might be. To culturally stereotype me . . . put me in a convenient little box.'

'No, that's not what—'

'My name's Declan, so obviously I must be Irish. Would you like it if people did the same to you?'

'They do,' Xiu said. 'And no, I don't like it.'

'Well, there you go. So, what . . . because I'm called Declan I must neck Guinness constantly and talk about the *craic*? You think I might ask you to pull the car over so I could do a bit of Riverdance? Just because of my name?'

'I'm sorry,' Xiu said.

'Good.' Miller nodded, left a beat. 'Yeah, it's Irish.' He

turned, grinning, to stare out of the window. 'On my mother's side.' He turned back when he heard Xiu growl and watched her knuckles whiten around the steering wheel. 'So I only ever have *half* a Guinness.'

Xiu followed the satnav's instructions to the letter until they reached the main road out of town. 'Does your mother live locally? I'm sorry . . . she's still around, right?'

'Oh yeah, she's still around.' Miller took a few seconds, uncertain as to whether he should say any more. Aside from the . . . unconventional conversations he still had with a dead woman, he couldn't recall talking to anyone about anything that really mattered since Alex's death. He discussed police matters, of course; he interviewed witnesses and joked around with colleagues, but it had been a while since he'd talked about anything personal.

Xiu glanced across at him, open-faced and genuinely curious. It was far more than he deserved. He supposed it was high time he opened up a little, and besides, if he didn't take this opportunity to share *something* with her, he knew very well that he'd be getting it in the neck from Alex later on.

'I don't see very much of her,' he said. 'She's in a supported living place, just outside Manchester. She's fit as a flea, but she's got some serious mental health issues. So . . .'

'It's good that she's being looked after.'

'Oh, yeah, it's a great set-up. Costs an arm and a leg, but luckily my elder brother can afford to pay for all that.' Miller stared at the road ahead. 'As he never ceases to remind me.'

Xiu nodded. 'I've got a sister a bit like that. A doctor.'

'It's annoying, isn't it?'

'Never lets me forget how well she's doing.'

'I don't want to make it sound as if Ross and I are like Justin and Adrian Cutler or anything. I really wouldn't like you to think I'm horribly jealous of my big, successful brother. I mean, I *am*, obviously . . . but he does love to bang on about all the money he's making and exactly how much of it he splashes out on looking after our mum.' He turned away again, starting to wonder if he was doing the right thing. Opening up was all well and good, but you could rarely bank on what might come out. 'I need to get down and visit . . . haven't seen her since Alex's funeral.'

The satnav let them know that they would be turning off the main road in a mile's time, so Xiu moved immediately into the inside lane.

'I didn't see that much of her growing up, either,' Miller said. 'She was in and out of hospital, so I spent most of the time being ferried between my two mad aunties in Ireland. I say *mad*, but I don't mean mad like Mum was mad, just . . . eccentric. Like . . . Sally would sing constantly. I mean all the time, but she couldn't carry a tune in a bucket and she always got the words wrong. Not wrong because she'd misheard the lyrics, just as if she preferred to make up her own.' He shook his head. 'Actually, she was the sensible one. To this day, my Auntie Bridget rings me up and when I answer the phone she goes, "Yes, Declan?" like I'm the one who's called *her*. Every single time.' Miller found himself smiling and thoroughly enjoying it. 'They both still make me laugh . . .'

'What about your father?'

'Ah.' Miller stopped smiling.

'Where's he?'

'Right this minute, I couldn't tell you. He travels a lot with work. Don't get me wrong; there *have* been times when I've known exactly where he was.' He began counting off on his fingers. 'Six months in Pentonville, three in Parkhurst, a couple of stretches in Wormwood Scrubs ...'

'Seriously?' Xiu turned, taking her eyes off the road for far longer than she would normally consider acceptable.

'He's not a murderer or anything,' Miller said. 'I'd say he's more of a lovable rogue. To be clear, I'm using *lovable* the way you would to describe Vladimir Putin or a painful skin condition.'

'That must have been difficult for you. In the Job, I mean.'

'Not really. Yeah, I hear his name mentioned every so often, and we've run into one another a couple of times. Actually, I did have to arrest him once.'

'Oh my God ...'

Miller grunted. 'That was a fun afternoon. He was screaming about police brutality while I handcuffed him. Shouting his mouth off and saying I was only nicking him because he never bought me a bike.' He shook his head again, remembering. 'We're not ... close, but you'd probably worked that out already.'

Xiu nodded as she made another turn. 'I'm a good detective. Like you said, a winkler.'

'Yeah, but you didn't have to winkle it out, did you? I just ...'

Miller mimed throwing up. He'd *splurged* it out; the same way he'd tried, with very little success, to let the anger and the grief out in those first few weeks after Alex's murder. Everyone had told him that's what he needed to do. The counsellor he'd been to see twice. Susan Akers and Howard and Mary and even that newsagent of whom Alex was so mysteriously fond. It was presumably the same advice Pippa Shepherd had been following right before that flash drive had turned up.

Aside from the fact that Pippa Shepherd had got upset and smashed something, Miller didn't know exactly what the circumstances had been and he wasn't sure anyone who wasn't actually there knew either. Everyone had been so excited that what might turn out to be crucial evidence had been found that nobody had bothered to ask how.

He made a mental note to give Fiona Mackie a call.

A few minutes later, they turned into the industrial estate and parked in front of a grim, grey building that had clearly been the work of an architect with anger issues.

Miller looked up at the cheap sign: TECH THAT!

'See what they did?'

Xiu stared at the sign too and shrugged. She didn't.

THIRTY-NINE

The offices of the hilariously named Tech That! were in stark contrast to the building's utilitarian exterior. The place was bright and open-plan, with arty posters on the walls and the swampy wail of a guitar drifting down from speakers mounted in the ceiling. Though the furniture did not appear to have been designed for comfort – 'it's ergonomic,' Xiu said – a fluffy squadron of rather more cosy-looking beanbags had been arranged around indoor firepits, in what Miller guessed were probably called 'breakout wombs' or 'brainstorming nooks'. Half a dozen people sat staring at enormous monitors, while a few worked on the innards of dismantled computers and several others stood gathered in hushed conversation around a gleaming coffee machine.

There were two people playing table tennis.

'The work can get pretty intense, sometimes.' Ravi ('call me Rav') Varma nodded, like he spent his days defusing bombs or trying to cure cancer. 'The hours are long, too, so it's important to have a relaxing working environment and to have some fun. To even be a bit . . . wacky sometimes.'

Miller nodded towards the pair wackily playing table tennis. 'I'm guessing that Barry Shepherd wasn't the best ping-pong player in the office.'

'Well, you guess wrong,' Varma said. 'Barry was a demon, mate.'

'Are you pulling my leg, Rav?'

'I'm serious. Barry took a lot of money off us on that table.'

Miller was genuinely shocked, having presumed that the man he'd seen on that IT tutorial video was not even the type to *watch* sport, and certainly not someone who'd engage in anything more physically demanding than tiddlywinks. His business partner was not what Miller had been expecting, either. Varma was at least ten years Shepherd's junior and, based on Pippa Shepherd's description of her late husband, a lot more outgoing. There were tattoos and a piercing or two. His hair was shaved at the sides and floppy on top and even though, fashionwise, the look was what you might call don't-care-casual, he'd clearly gone to a great deal of effort putting it together.

He spun the silver bangle on his wrist as he studied Miller and Xiu. 'I have to say, I'm not altogether sure why you're here.'

'Well, you've already told us one thing we didn't know about Mr Shepherd,' Miller said. 'We're hoping you might have a few more surprises.'

Varma nodded, like he got it. 'So, you don't think Barry was an accidental victim.'

'That's interesting,' Xiu said. 'You're the first person we've spoken to who's even suggested that.'

'Well, only because you're here. When I heard about it, I didn't know what had happened, same as everyone else. We were all just so . . . shocked, you know? Then I read about it in the papers and found out who the other bloke was, so I assumed Barry was just in the wrong place at the wrong time.' He sat back, nodding as though he'd worked something out. 'But here you are asking questions about him, so it's obviously not quite that simple.'

Miller stared. *And neither are you . . .*

'So, what's the set-up at Tech That!?' Xiu asked. 'Or rather, what was it, before Mr Shepherd was killed?'

Miller was not surprised to hear Xiu asking exactly the right question. The teaching videos Shepherd had recorded were clearly only a small part of what the company did. The premises themselves had certainly not come cheap (Miller had checked) and looking around him, neither had the 'wacky' interior. With all that state-of-the-art computer equipment and at least a dozen people employed to use it, there was evidently a fair bit of money sloshing about.

'Basically we do anything and everything,' Varma said. 'Broadly speaking, I'm on the systems side of things. I design them, oversee the installation, all that. Big companies, small businesses, rich kids who want flashier gaming set-ups than their mates, whatever. It's bespoke, yeah?'

'What about Mr Shepherd?'

'Barry was more about the maintenance. His team looked after the contracts and sorted things out for our customers when they went wrong. That could be anything from a major system overhaul to one-to-one advice over the phone.'

'Does turning it off and on again ever really work?' Miller asked.

'Sometimes, but we can't really expect our customers to pay good money for advice like that, so we prefer to say things like "software reboot" or "hard restart".'

'I could do with one of those myself,' Miller said.

Varma smiled and spun his bracelet.

'Had you noticed any change in Mr Shepherd's behaviour recently?' Xiu asked.

'No. Not *really* . . .'

'What does that mean?'

'Well, everyone can be a bit moody now and again, can't they? Not themselves for one reason or another.'

'We're not talking about a bad day at the office,' Miller said.

'No . . . yeah, right.' Varma thought, or pretended to think. 'I suppose he *had* been a bit . . . guarded, the last month or so. Keeping himself to himself more than he normally did.'

'Like there was something on his mind?' Xiu asked.

'I suppose so, yeah.' Varma inched his ergonomic chair a little closer to the table. 'One day I needed to talk to him about something and he clicked off his screen really fast, you know? Like there was something he didn't want me to see. I never said anything, but it was kind of obvious.'

'Any problems moneywise?' Miller asked. 'The company, I mean. Is there any possibility that Barry was taking money out that he shouldn't have been?'

Varma shrugged. 'Look, he certainly had the computer skills to do something like that, but why would he? Barry could probably have hidden any kind of fraud, but if he had, me and most of the people working here have got the skills to have found it.'

'I can see why that wouldn't make a lot of sense,' Xiu said.

'He'd have been stupid to do anything like that at work, and

Barry certainly wasn't stupid. If he was doing something he shouldn't, it would be far easier to do it at home.'

'Did you check?' Miller asked.

Varma said 'No' a little too quickly, but even if the man was lying, Miller wasn't sure there was much he could read into it. Varma would have been being no more suspicious than *they* were, after all. A business partner gets murdered in the room next door to a major gangland figure and it's probably only natural that you'd want to have a quick look to make sure there weren't any financial discrepancies and check that no fluffy beanbags had gone missing.

Varma got to his feet and waved a colleague across. 'You should probably talk to Jonah Nixon. Jonah spent as much time with Barry as I did. More, actually . . .'

The man in question was one of those chatting by the coffee machine. He nodded, then walked somewhat tentatively over to join them.

'These detectives are asking about Barry,' Varma said.

Nixon was thirtyish; tall and balding, with watery eyes behind thick glasses. He was dressed rather more soberly than his boss, in black trousers and a black sweater, and he sported a flashy-looking toolbelt stocked with tiny screwdrivers, a variety of pliers and a large vape.

Miller and Xiu introduced themselves.

Nixon looked at Varma. 'What do they want to know about Barry?'

'If you'd noticed any strange behaviour, maybe,' Xiu said.

'Like what?'

'Anything out of the ordinary.'

'Like keeping a deadly weapon in his briefcase,' Miller said. 'Whispered phone conversations or furtive meetings with mysterious visitors. Notes left lying around saying "Remember to hide money". We're just asking if anything struck you as odd or out of character.'

'Not that I can think of.'

'Nothing at all? Just bowling along being completely normal until he was shot in the head, that right?'

Nixon just stared. 'Barry was Barry.'

Pippa Shepherd had said much the same thing, but coming from her, the emotion it expressed encompassed a decade or more of marriage and the memories that went with it. It had been loaded with love and pain and a blinding incomprehension at what had been done to her husband. Trotted out now by this screwdriver-festooned SAS wannabe, the same observation made Miller want to chuck a wireless mouse at him.

'Sorry,' Nixon said. 'It's just ... I still can't get over what's happened.'

'None of us can,' Varma said.

On the way out, Xiu said, 'Anything?'

'Yeah ... *something*,' Miller said. 'Something about Barry Shepherd that we're not seeing.'

'What, just because he played table tennis?'

'Maybe it's all about the table tennis.' Miller took out his phone and began to dial. 'Some of these ping-pong players can be vicious bastards.'

Xiu struggled to find a response, then gave up when she saw Miller raise a finger.

'Hey, Dec,' Mackie said, when she answered the call.

Miller pushed through the door. 'Fiona ... can you talk me through what happened when you found that flash drive?'

'I already told Sullivan.'

237

'You might just as well have told the station cat.'

'I didn't know there was a station cat.'

'*Please* ...'

Five minutes later, once Miller had ended the call, he fired off a text message to Carys Morgan. He knew that she would be sitting at her desk, swearing quietly and drinking more coffee than was good for her as she sweated over the password to Shepherd's flash drive.

Miller texted:

Try SEAHORSE

Thirty seconds later, Morgan texted back:

BINGO.

Miller replied immediately:

No, not BINGO. SEAHORSE!

FORTY

The station was crowded with tourists heading home. Knackered-looking men and women were hanging about, carrying bags a lot heavier and wallets significantly lighter than when they'd arrived. Kids full of sugar ran around in cardboard hats and plastic sunglasses, a few brandishing giant sticks of rock that, in a different situation, might well be classified as deadly weapons. Moving to avoid a young lad waving one around like a stripy lightsaber, Miller found himself wondering why more people weren't beaten to death with them, because it was always handy if you could eat the evidence afterwards.

Carys Morgan called as Miller and Xiu were walking down on to the platform. The train they were there to meet was only a minute away.

'Tell Xiu she was right about that file on the flash drive being a bank account.'

'I don't want her to get big-headed,' Miller said.

Xiu mouthed a 'What?' and Miller waved it away.

'Just working through all the transactions now,' Carys said. 'Lots of medium-sized deposits . . . a hundred and fifty here, two hundred there, then a withdrawal of three grand, two days before Shepherd was killed.'

'Interesting.' Miller saw the train come slowly around the corner and approach the platform. 'What about the bigger file?'

'Yeah, it's an operating system. I've started digging around, but there's nothing as straightforward as a conventional search history.'

'He was too smart for that,' Miller said. 'Very good at table tennis too, if that helps.'

'What?'

'Doesn't matter. So, what's your best guess?'

'Well, put it this way, I don't think Shepherd set all this up just so he could spend time on Google.'

'Somewhere a bit . . . darker?'

'Every bloody chance.' Carys sighed. 'Always a treat to head down that rabbit hole.'

'You know you love it,' Miller said. The train had stopped and the doors were opening. 'I need to go, Carys. I'll talk to you later . . .'

They watched as the passengers spilled from the train; a flock of fresh holidaymakers or stag- and hen-nighters, over-excited and bang up for it. New blood. Once the crowd had thinned out a bit, the people Miller and Xiu had come to meet were easy enough to spot.

Miller pointed and waved. 'There he is . . .'

Xiu stared at the two men walking towards them. She had already worked out who the one wearing the hat was. 'That bloke with him . . . the Met officer, right? Is he really tall?'

'Not especially,' Miller said. 'It's just that Chesshead . . . isn't.'

'Why didn't you mention that?'

'I don't think being a bit on the short side is his most distinguishing feature, do you?'

The officer escorting their witness introduced himself as DS David Holland and announced that he'd be spending the day in town. Miller told him the model village was not only way cheaper than the pleasure beach but a lot more fun, recommended two chippies and a kebab shop, then introduced Xiu to Gary Pope.

'Oh, right,' Pope said. 'Like that fancy gravy in posh restaurants.'

'It's good to have you back,' Miller said.

'I'm not here for long, Mr Miller.'

'Talking of which.' Holland announced that he and Pope were booked on the nine o'clock train back to London and that he fully expected Miller or someone else to make sure Pope was at the station in good time. Miller assured the man from the Met that it wouldn't be a problem, and as Holland walked away, clearly looking forward to spending the day as a tourist, he shouted after him, 'Tell your boss he's a miserable bugger.'

Holland shouted back. 'He knows.'

They left the station and sat down on a bench in the park opposite.

'You didn't need to have me *arrested*, Mr Miller.' Pope looked a little hurt. 'If I'd known you wanted to speak to me I'd have come anyway.'

Miller liked the fact that Pope always called him *Mr* Miller. It was endearing, in spite of everything. 'It wasn't my doing, Gary. What did they arrest you for, anyway?'

'Receiving stolen goods.'

'Did you?'

'Yes, but that's not the point I'm making.'

Pope reached beneath his battered trilby to scratch his head and Miller clocked Xiu trying to sneak a peek. He hadn't seen this particular hat before (it was usually a baseball cap or something woolly or, on one notable occasion, a pith helmet), but otherwise Gary Pope looked much the same as he had the last time Miller had seen him. A long coat over a tracksuit, worn somewhat bizarrely with highly polished shoes. The face was as uniquely ... striking as ever. It was one of which not even Pope's own mother could be awfully fond (especially now that her husband only had half an ear), and even without showing off those famous scars or waving a claw hammer around, it was easy to see how the man had made a tidy living out of frightening people. Diminutive though he was, Chesshead could look scary if he was asking you the time and carrying a slice of Battenberg.

'Come on then,' Pope said. 'I'm not here very long and there's a few people I'd like to catch up with.'

'We were hoping you might be able to help us with a case.' Xiu took out a notebook. 'We're investigating—'

'I know what case it is, miss. London isn't that far away. People have phones.'

'So, what exactly have you heard?'

'Well, I know who you've been talking to.'

'So, are any of them the people we *should* be talking to?' Miller waited, but Pope seemed hesitant. 'How about if I reel off the names and you just touch your nose when I say the right one?'

'I'm not sure Ralph Massey would have got much out of

having Adrian killed, except maybe getting himself killed. You know he's not daft as well as I do.'

'What about Adrian's wife and brother?' Xiu asked.

'Well, everyone knew that Adrian liked to play away and Michelle's certainly got a temper on her,' Pope said. 'Some woman cut her up once when she was dropping her kids off at school, so Michelle followed her home. I'm not sure exactly what happened, but I know there was an "incident" on the doorstep and that Wayne had to give the woman five hundred quid to keep her quiet afterwards.' Pope shook his head 'It strikes me that if Michelle had wanted to hurt Adrian for messing her about ... kill him, even ... she'd have done it herself. She'd have enjoyed doing it.'

It was much the same conclusion Miller had come to.

It was also what Alex had said.

'Justin I don't know so much about. I do know him and Adrian weren't close, but that's how it goes with brothers sometimes, isn't it?'

Miller was aware that Xiu was looking at him.

'He was definitely a bit less flashy than Adrian was ... but it's the quiet ones you have to watch out for, isn't it? So yeah, it's possible I suppose, but I haven't heard anything to back that up.' Pope looked at them both. 'I *have* heard that you're looking into the other bloke that was killed at the same time ...'

'We're exploring all possible avenues of enquiry,' Xiu said.

'I think you might have to.'

'What does that mean?' Miller asked.

'Nothing, really.' Pope waved at a little girl who was walking past with her mother. He stopped waving when the little girl started to scream and the woman drew her daughter quickly away. 'I just heard a whisper that what happened at that hotel might not be ... straightforward. It's probably rubbish, because criminals are worse than hairdressers when it comes to gossip, so ...'

'Would you be willing to tell us who was doing the whispering?' Xiu asked.

'I'm struggling to remember, I'm afraid. To be honest, it was probably just some stupid remark I heard in a bar.' Pope sniffed and stretched his shoulders. 'Opinions are no problem, I've got loads of them, but I'm not so good with names.'

'Seriously?' Xiu was looking at Miller as she thrust her notebook back into her bag. 'You think that's why we brought you all the way up here? Just so we could ask your opinion?'

'Oh, I know exactly why I'm here, miss,' Pope said. 'Yeah, I'm happy to tell you what I think about the hotel thing, but I know there's at least one more case we'll probably end up talking about. Isn't that right, Mr Miller?'

Miller stared at his feet until he hoped Xiu wasn't glaring at him any more, then looked up at her. 'Could you give us half an hour? Is that all right?'

Xiu said nothing, making it all too clear that it very much wasn't.

'I just need to have a word about ... something else.'

Xiu stood up and snatched at her bag. 'Twenty minutes.' She pointed back across the road at a coffee shop next to the station. 'I'll wait for you in there.'

'Get yourself a *really* fancy coffee,' Miller said. 'And a big cake. They're on me.' He could see that Xiu was hovering still, staring down at Pope, or more specifically at the top of his head. Miller slid across the bench and gave Pope a nudge. 'Go on, Gary, just give her a quick flash.'

'Bloody hell, I should start charging for this.'

'I've given it such a big build-up.'

Xiu said, 'I'm honestly not that interested,' but she didn't go anywhere.

Pope sighed, then looked up at Xiu and politely raised his trilby, just for a second or two, as though he was simply wishing her 'good afternoon'.

Xiu nodded, then turned and walked away.

Miller watched her go, shaking her head as she marched across the road. He could not be sure if it was in exasperation at him or amazement at what she'd seen underneath Gary Pope's hat.

FORTY-ONE

'So, are you just broadening your horizons down in that there London?' Miller asked. 'Or were you chased out of town?'

'Just wanted to get out of the game,' Pope said.

'How's that working out for you?'

'Well—'

'I'm being sarcastic, obviously, considering you've just been arrested.'

'I wouldn't expect anything else, Mr Miller, but I'm talking about the gangland stuff. I'm trying to leave all that nonsense behind. I say *leave*, but something like this happens – Adrian Cutler getting topped – and I'm well aware that people are going to come looking for me. Cutler's old man's trying to find me, naturally, and I know my erstwhile employer's been putting feelers out.' Pope saw Miller's reaction. 'Are you surprised?'

To be fair, Miller was as taken aback at Pope's casual use of the word 'erstwhile' as anything, but he was surprised to hear that Ralph Massey was on his trail. Either Massey believed that Chesshead himself was responsible for the murders at the hotel – which was a stretch – or thought that he might know who had been.

All of which suggested that Massey himself had not been involved.

Unless, of course, that was precisely the impression that a slippery sod like Ralph Massey was trying to create.

'Why the major lifestyle change then, Gary?'

'Something happened the last time I was inside.'

'You got religion?'

'Not religion, Mr Miller. *Chess*.'

'Say *what* now?'

'Look, I know what everyone calls me, so I thought it was high time I found out how you actually play the game. And bugger me if I didn't love it, right from the off. It concentrates the mind, because you have to think three or four moves ahead and that calms me down. I started ... re-evaluating things, you know? I apologised to as many people as I could about the bad things I'd done to them. I even said "sorry" to my dad ... you know, for the ear-biting business. He didn't deserve that.'

'Well, it was your birthday and he *did* eat Colin the Caterpillar's face.'

'Right, but I've got to let all that stuff go, Mr Miller. I'm a different person now and I swear, these days, it's all about the chess. All day long it's chess, chess, chess ... and maybe the occasional something that's fallen off the back of a lorry.' Pope leaned in and lowered his voice. 'Talking of which, I don't suppose you're in the market for some seriously cheap plumbing supplies?' He saw Miller start to shake his head. 'Luxury men's fragrances?'

'I'm all good for ballcocks and aftershave,' Miller said. 'Thanks for thinking of me, though.'

'Well, you were always fair with me, Mr Miller, which is why I'm keen to help. I know I didn't have much choice about coming in the end, but it's worked out well, I reckon. Now I've got the chance to do a bit of good.'

'We're not talking about the hotel case any more, are we?'

Pope shuffled along the bench. 'I'm sorry about what happened to your wife. I know you'll have heard plenty of people saying that, but I haven't seen you, have I?'

For reasons Miller couldn't quite fathom, the sincere condolences from this career criminal meant rather more than the empty words of shock and sympathy he'd heard trotted out by plenty of people he worked with. He swallowed hard and nodded. 'Cheers, Gary.'

'It's a disgrace that they still haven't nicked anyone for it.'

'Tell me about it,' Miller said.

'Maybe I can do better than that.' Pope nodded. 'Something, anyway.'

'What?'

Pope turned to watch two young men in baseball caps and Puffa jackets who were approaching on e-scooters. He waited until they had passed the bench.

'I've got something for you,' he said.

Xiu had asked for whipped cream on her coffee and ordered *two* cakes, but it hadn't stopped her being irritated with Miller. Feeling like she was being used. It was obvious that this Chesshead bloke hadn't been brought up from London because Miller honestly believed he could help with the Cutler and Shepherd case. So Pope knew all the main players and he'd shared a few opinions about suspects, but none of it got them anywhere, did it?

It had always been about Miller's wife.

She bit into the second of her cakes and the irritation eased a little. It was odd how a brownie could do that. If Chesshead knew anything that might move the investigation into Alex Miller's murder forward, could she really blame Miller for overstating his importance as a witness on the case they were *supposed* to be working? Yes, she was meant to be his partner and yes, he'd conned her, but then again ... chocolate.

It was only twenty minutes.

The truth was, she had been to the King's Arms again the previous evening and she was never at her most tolerant the following day. She always woke up with her ears still ringing, feeling irrationally angry with whoever she woke up next to. Angry with most people, if the truth were told, even though it was herself that she needed a serious word with.

Her phone buzzed on the table and, glancing down, she saw that it was Sullivan calling. There wasn't a brownie big enough to make that any better. She reached for a serviette in case there was chocolate around her mouth and even though she knew it was ridiculous, because Sullivan wouldn't be able to see her, she used it anyway.

Xiu was only grateful that Miller wasn't there to take the piss.

'Any time you like, Gary.' Miller was keeping it light, trying to disguise his impatience. If Chesshead really had something that might help identify Alex's killer, he was just about ready to turn the man upside down and shake it out of him. 'I like a bit of suspense as much as anyone, but we're not voting someone off *The X-Factor*.'

Pope shook his head. 'I haven't got them with me.'

'*Them?* Could you at least tell me what they are?'

'I've made arrangements, OK, Mr Miller? You'll get them soon enough and that's the best I can do.'

'Is it, though? I really hope you're not messing me about, Gary.'

'I swear, Mr Miller. I'm honestly trying to help.'

Miller stood up. He didn't want to keep Xiu hanging about any longer than he had to. 'OK, well, I'm still none the wiser as to what we're actually talking about, but I suppose I'll have to trust you.' When it came to finding out who was responsible for Alex's death, Miller was starting to realise that there weren't too many people he *could* trust. A reformed gangland enforcer seemed as good a bet as any. 'Where are you going to be later on?'

'I'm not sure.' Pope stood up too, and looked around. 'Like I said, there's a few people I'd rather not run into, which is why it's only a flying visit.'

'Fine,' Miller said. 'But I'll need a contact number, in case I need to call you.'

Pope gave Miller a number which he immediately rang. A tinny melody which Miller didn't recognise rang out from Pope's pocket. Miller stared at him.

'It's a song called "Chess",' Pope said. 'From the musical *Chess*.'

'Blimey, you really love chess, don't you?'

'Do you play, Mr Miller?'

'I know *how* to.'

'Maybe we should have a game,' Pope said.

Miller nodded, considering it 'Want to make it … interesting?'

Pope looked happy enough with the idea. 'How do we do that?'

'By not playing chess,' Miller said.

'Eight pounds and sixty pence.' Xiu handed Miller the receipt as soon as he'd sat down. 'Thanks for that.'

'*How* much?' Miller studied the receipt and shook his head. 'Was the brownie coated with gold leaf?'

'If you're going to get coffee for yourself, I'll have another one.'

Miller raised an eyebrow. 'Was someone overdoing it last night?'

'Just a small one, but with extra whipped cream . . .'

As soon as Miller was back with the coffees, and a pastry for himself, Xiu said, 'So, was that useful, then?'

'Well, I think we can probably discount Ralph Massey and I tend to agree with what Pope said about Michelle Cutler, so . . .' Miller saw Xiu shaking her head and stopped. 'What?'

'I'm talking about your wife's case,' Xiu said. 'We both know that as far as this case goes – you know . . . the one we're supposed to be working – your friend was never going to contribute anything particularly useful.'

'Oh, you figured that out, then?'

'You need to be straight with me.'

Miller scooped the froth from his coffee with a spoon.

'*You should tell her the whole story, by the way . . .*'

So – because it was usually the right thing to do – Miller did what his dead wife had suggested and told Xiu exactly what had happened on the night Alex had been killed. He decided to skip some of the more esoteric details (the key differences between a tango and a samba) but all the important elements

251

were there. The empty spotlight, the deserted dressing room, the abandoned phone and Ralph Massey looking down from the balcony.

All of it, from the band striking up to the death knock.

'That must have been terrible,' Xiu said, when Miller had finished.

'It really was,' Miller said. 'What with one thing and another, I didn't get round to taking my tuxedo back to the hire shop for a week and those buggers charge by the day.'

'You don't have to do that,' Xiu said.

'Do what?'

'Make a joke of it, like you usually do. You're allowed to be . . . normal.'

Miller smiled and dabbed at the crumbs on his plate. He turned to stare out at the comings and goings for a minute or so. People moving a little faster than they otherwise might past the window, then umbrellas going up as it began to rain.

'So, you think it was Massey or Cutler?'

'Got to be,' Miller said. 'Alex was hurting both their businesses. She was really good at what she did. Too bloody good, as it turned out.'

'Was Chesshead any help?'

'He says he's going to be.' Miller was still thinking about those 'arrangements' that Gary Pope had mentioned. 'Something he's sending me, but your guess is as good as mine.' He grinned. 'Sorry, it's hard to take you seriously when there's whipped cream around your gob.'

Xiu snatched at a serviette. 'That reminds me, Sullivan called.'

'Oh, zippidee-doo-dah.'

'They've finally got somewhere with Adrian Cutler's

mobile. Lots of calls to and from burner phones, like you'd expect, but now they know when and where some of them were bought.'

'Let me guess,' Miller said. 'Sullivan has very generously tasked you and me with the plum job of visiting assorted mobile phone shops and wading through their CCTV footage.'

'Just one phone shop.' Xiu gathered her things together, ready to move on. 'There was a lot of traffic between Cutler and one number in particular in the weeks leading up to the murder. So shouldn't be too much wading.'

Miller looked at his watch as they stepped away from the table. 'Well it'll be shut soon anyway, so why don't we put off this particular treat until first thing in the morning?'

He stopped at the door and held it open for Xiu.

'What you said about being normal? I've done that and it's definitely overrated.'

FORTY-TWO

After almost a minute of deliberation, having decided on speed and trajectory, Imran Mirza rose slowly from his haunches and stood over his putt. His breathing was nice and shallow. The late afternoon sun bounced off his high-vis jacket as he settled his shoulders and wiggled his backside. He took a slow and steady practice stroke. He took another, then, after one final glance towards the hole, he eased his putter back . . .

Miller coughed.

Imran straightened up and turned. 'You cheating git!'

'What?' Miller stared, outraged; his own putter dangling from his outstretched hand. 'I had something stuck in my throat.'

'You'll have my fist stuck down there if you do that again.'

'Oh, just get on with it,' Miller muttered as he watched his opponent turn back to refocus and begin his irritating routine once again. The bum-wiggling and the practice strokes. 'It's not St Andrews . . .'

254

Imran sank the putt, punched the air and turned round, beaming in triumph. 'Right, that's one up with one hole to go. I hope you've got cash.'

A few minutes later, once Imran had won the final hole and pocketed the scrunched-up fiver Miller had reluctantly handed over, they settled down on their usual bench. The one with YOUR NAN IS A SLAG carved into it. It was freshly painted and birdshit-free, because Imran Mirza was one of the council's more diligent groundskeepers.

'You are so jammy,' Miller said.

'Pure skill, mate.'

'Skill? You know all the breaks.'

'Not really.'

'What d'you mean, *not really*? You mow the bloody thing.'

'Always the same excuses.' Imran sighed and took out his cigarettes 'It's sad, really.' He lit up and sat back to survey his kingdom. The paths down which he steered his motorised sweeper, the playground from which he regularly chased weed-smokers, the nine-hole putting green which was his pride and joy.

'I'm not making excuses,' Miller said. 'I just wish you didn't gloat so much when you win.'

Imran turned, shaking his head. 'Remember the time *you* won? I say *time*, because it *has* only happened once. You danced around like you'd won the sodding Masters. You ran over and hugged that woman who was walking her dog, remember?'

'I only scared her a bit.'

'She was about ready to call the police, until you told her you were the police. I think that actually scared her more.'

'I'm just saying . . . you've got advantages. Maybe we should play in a park you're not actually in charge of. That would be a more equal contest.'

'Yeah, but then we'd have to pay for the putters and the balls.'

'Good point,' Miller said.

Miller and Imran had known each other since they were eleven, when they'd found themselves seated next to one another in class. There'd been plenty of Asian kids at the school, but for reasons Miller had never understood, Imran had been singled out and picked on by some of the bigger, stupider kids; called all the predictable names by the likes of Graham Trotter and Danny Finch. To this day, Miller wished he'd done something. Said something. He hadn't joined in, which he told himself was the main thing, and by the time he and Imran were in the sixth form and Graham Trotter was flipping burgers, Miller and Imran were inseparable. The glorious day – many years later – when Miller nicked Danny Finch for driving drunk in an untaxed and decidedly unroad-worthy Ford Fiesta remained one of his proudest on the job.

'So, how's it going then?' Imran asked. 'Being back at work.'

'You know, up and down.' Miller considered telling his friend about the case he'd come back to, but not for very long. They talked about work if Miller had a funny story to tell, but rarely otherwise, and that went both ways. Imran was about as interested in casefile preparation and prosecution thresholds as Miller was in fence maintenance and the bulk-buying of fungicide. That said, Imran had some fantastic stories about the things people got up to in his park at night, and on one occasion – when human remains had been discovered behind the public toilets – his knowledge of what was and wasn't bio-degradable mulch had proved invaluable.

Hanging around with Imran meant that Miller did not have to think about the likes of Wayne Cutler and Ralph Massey. It was time generally spent laughing and talking nonsense; as precious in its way as the dancing, even if it usually ended up costing him rather more.

Miller reckoned that losing a fiver every couple of weeks was a price well worth paying.

'Long as you haven't gone back too soon.' Imran ground out his cigarette beneath his boot. He bent down for the butt and tucked it carefully into the pocket of his overalls. 'I'm probably not the first person to say that.'

Miller mimed a theatrical yawn.

'Only sometimes your judgement's as rubbish as your putting.'

They said nothing for a while, watching a couple being walked by a pair of French bulldogs near the playground. A man rolled slowly past the bench on a skateboard. Miller desperately wanted to shout 'Grow up', but the man looked a bit useful, so Miller kept his opinion to himself.

'Grow up,' Imran shouted.

Miller enjoyed being reminded just why he and Imran got on so well.

'There might be something happening with Alex,' he said.

Imran turned to look at him. This was the only case he was keen to hear about. Alex had been Imran's friend too. He had been one of those carrying her coffin into the church.

'Might also be nothing, but you never know.' Miller told him about Chesshead (with whom Imran was familiar) and his promise of help. The mysterious 'arrangements'.

'Let me know what comes of it, yeah?'

Miller promised that he would and looked away just in time

to see the man fall off his skateboard at the bottom of the hill. He couldn't help but admire the man's attempt to style it out, like a gymnast who's cocked up on the asymmetric bars but strikes a pose anyway.

'Why do people hang bags of dogshit in trees?' Imran asked.

Miller looked up, half expecting to see one dangling above him. Imran's complaint, though it was one he had heard several times before, had come somewhat out of the blue. 'I don't know ... because they can?'

'Because they're selfish morons.'

'Oh, right, it was a rhetorical question.'

'Do you know how many bins specifically for the disposal of canine faeces there are in this park?'

'No, but I'm longing to find out.'

'Twelve.' Imran held up eight fingers and two thumbs. Then two more fingers. '*Twelve*, and I know that because not only did I install most of them bins, I'm the mug who empties them. I'm also the idiot who has to clamber up stepladders on a daily basis because certain people have chosen not to use those bins, but rather to leave their poxy poo-bags suspended from branches like they're ... decorations or something.'

'Maybe it's some kind of statement about the commercialisation of Christmas.'

'If it was up to me, I'd hang *them* from the bloody trees.'

'That might be going a bit far.'

Imran grunted, but his expression made it clear he didn't think the summary execution of the offending dog owners should necessarily be off the table. 'Your lot should do something about it.'

'What, some kind of dedicated arboreal dog-shit squad?'

'Yeah, or just a copper with a big stick.'

It was at this point that Miller remembered that he *did* have something to do, having neglected to follow up on the vehicle he had seen outside his house the night before. He got up and stepped away, called the office and asked Andrea Fuller to run the partial number plate through the system.

He walked back across to the bench and gave Imran a thumbs-up.

'I've put a call in to the Chief Constable,' he said.

FORTY-THREE

Using some leftover vegetables, two cold sausages and a packet of microwavable rice, Miller knocked up what he liked to call 'a can't-be-arsed paella'. He fed Fred and Ginger before sitting down with his own meal, so that they could all eat together. With one ear on the radio and watching the rats make short work of what had been put in front of them, he thought about what Xiu had said in the coffee shop.

You don't have to do that . . .

His new partner clearly saw right through him and Miller couldn't decide if he liked it or not. It was . . . unnerving. Seeing as she'd already given Xiu a resounding seal of approval, it would be helpful to get Alex's take on things, but for whatever reason she wasn't 'around' right then to share her thoughts on the matter.

Busy being dead, Miller thought, which was certainly a decent excuse.

It didn't seem altogether fair though, considering that she

was only ever 'around' inside his own head, so maybe their face-to-face conversations were entirely dependent on what else was clattering about in there. On having sufficient head-space. He could usually imagine what Alex might say in any given situation (because she had never been shy about telling him) but seeing her seemed rather more . . . arbitrary.

It was as if, even though *she* was dead and *he* was imagining her, Alex was somehow the one who decided when she was going to show up.

Like she was still in charge.

It was just after eight o'clock, and Miller was washing up, when he heard the rattle of the letterbox. He opened the door, and beyond the security light he could see a figure on a bike pedalling furiously away. The hoodie-wearing cyclist could have been male or female, fourteen or forty. Miller closed the door and bent to pick up the large brown envelope with his name on that was sitting on the doormat. He carried it through to the living room, sat down and tore it open.

Five minutes later, he was on the phone to Chesshead.

'So, what am I looking at, Gary . . . ?'

He knew *what* he was looking at, obviously. Two large black and white photographs of Alex on some unidentifiable semi-dark street, deep in conversation with an equally uniden-tifiable man who could have come straight from the 'Shadowy Figures' department at Central Casting

What Miller wanted to know was *where* and *when* and *who*.

'I can't really talk, Mr Miller.'

'Where did you get these?'

'I've had them for a while.'

'You're not answering my question, Gary.'

'Sorry, Mr Miller, but—'

261

'Who took these bloody photographs?'

'I did,' Pope said. 'Someone asked me to take them ...'

Miller stared down at the photographs. One thing he was sure about was that they had not been taken on the night of Alex's murder. She was not wearing the same clothes. He knew he was almost certainly looking at a snapshot of an ordinary work-related encounter. A Serious and Organised officer working undercover and gathering intelligence from a suspect or perhaps an informant. A woman doing her job. If that was the case, though, why did he feel so uneasy and why had Gary Pope been asked to take the pictures in the first place?

Why did Chesshead think these photos could help?

He knew that Alex would not have been able to answer his questions, but Miller glanced around just in case, hoping desperately to see her watching him from the doorway or staring out of the window.

There was only an absence.

'Who asked you to take these?' he asked.

There was silence for a few seconds, what sounded very much like pub noise in the background. 'Come on, Mr Miller ... that's as much as I can tell you.'

'Was it Ralph Massey?'

'I think I've done my bit,' Pope said. 'Shouldn't even have done this much, probably.'

'So, you've no idea who the man in the photos is?'

This time there was nearly half a minute of breathing and noise before Pope said, 'Look, I took those pictures about a month before your wife was killed, OK? Now, I really need to go ...'

Though Miller wasn't altogether sure what he was thanking Pope for, he did it anyway. He reminded him that he needed to present himself at the smaller of the town's two stations in good time to make his train back to London.

'Don't you worry about that, Mr Miller. Sooner I'm out of here, the better.'

'Call me tomorrow.' Miller felt confident that Pope would be rather more forthcoming when he was somewhere he felt safer.

'I'll do my best,' Pope said.

Once Chesshead had hung up, Miller could do little but sit and study the two photographs, in the vain hope that he had missed some crucial detail which might suddenly reveal itself. When the heating turned itself off and the room began to feel cold, he grabbed the duvet from his bed and wrapped it around himself. He made some tea. After that, there was just the burble of the radio in the background and the squeak of the wheel as Fred and Ginger worked off their dinner.

Miller jumped slightly when his mobile began to ring.

'Blimey. I thought you'd be tucked up in bed with a hot milky drink by now.'

'No,' Xiu said. 'I'm not.'

'OK.' Miller pulled his feet up on to the sofa and lay back. 'If you're calling to remind me about our hot date at the phone shop tomorrow, I've put a Post-it note on my fridge.' He waited for a reaction, but there wasn't one. 'You all right, Posh?'

'I wanted to say thank you, that's all. For today.'

'It was only a couple of cakes,' Miller said. 'Yes, they were ridiculously expensive, but I'm an exceedingly generous man. Also, I'm going to claim them on expenses.'

'Not the cakes.'

'Oh.'

'Thank you for being honest. For trusting me. What you told me about that night at the ballroom, your wife . . .'

'Right.' Now Miller felt slightly more unnerved than he had done before, but also oddly comforted. 'You're welcome.'

Xiu said nothing. Miller was on the verge of asking if she was still there when she finally spoke again. *Very* quickly.

'Once or twice a week, I get dressed up and go to this Heavy Metal night in the room above the King's Arms. The big pub on Thornton Road, near the roundabout? It's very loud and very crowded and I drink and dance until I find someone I like the look of. By that time I've usually drunk enough to like the look of anyone in there who isn't absolutely hideous, but anyway ... as soon as I've found someone who'll do, I take them home with me.' She paused. 'For sex.'

It was Miller's turn to say nothing for a while.

'You're shocked, aren't you?' Xiu asked.

'Too bloody right I am,' Miller said. *'Heavy metal?'*

FORTY-FOUR

Staring across at the man who was half on, half off and half asleep on her sofa, Michelle might well have asked herself what she'd done to deserve this. But the answer was pretty obvious, so she didn't bother. He'd been several sheets to the wind when he'd shown up at her door an hour earlier, and, after the two glasses of wine he'd insisted on, he was now on the verge of passing out. That might well have been the best outcome, all things considered, but right then she simply wanted him out of her house.

She walked across, stood over him and raised her voice.

'Justin.' She put a hand on his shoulder and shook it. 'You need to go home ... I'm calling you a cab, all right?'

He opened his eyes and smiled up at her. 'Is there any more wine?'

'No there isn't,' she said. 'Please, Justin ... I need to go to bed.'

The smile widened and became wolfish. 'Now we're talking ...'

Her day hadn't been half bad up to then. Wayne and Jacqui had finally decided she didn't need babysitting any more and gone home. Michelle had immediately driven round to her mum's place to pick up her kids and, once she'd dealt with the awkward questions about where Daddy was ('dealt with' as in 'lied' because she didn't know what else to do), they'd had a brilliant few hours together. Teatime had been predictably chaotic and getting them bathed and ready for bed had all but wiped her out, but it had been the first time Michelle had felt genuinely happy since Adrian had died.

No, the first time she had felt happy in months.

She had just got the kids settled and opened a bottle when the doorbell had rung and Uncle Justin had bowled in.

'Come on, Justin. For God's sake ... you need to get up.' She grabbed his hand and tugged; then, before she realised her mistake, he'd pulled her down on to the sofa next to him.

'That's better,' he said. 'Cosier.'

'What do you think you're doing?' Michelle stared at her brother-in-law, hard. 'Seriously? You think this is a good idea?'

'Well, you seemed to think it was a pretty great idea last time.'

'There wasn't a *last* time,' Michelle said. 'Because there isn't going to be a *next* time.' She stared at his red, ridiculous face and reminded herself just how much of an idiot she'd been. 'It was *one* time, Justin.'

One night when she was a lot drunker than Justin was now. One night when Adrian was away and up to no good. One night when cutting up a shirt or smashing one of his toy trains had not been enough and a rather more basic way of getting her own back had presented itself.

Three months before, on the very same sofa.

266

'My baby brother's let himself go a bit,' he'd said, then. 'And I know you've always fancied me.'

She hadn't. She *didn't*.

'Adrian's not around any more,' Justin said, now. 'So, it's not a problem.'

'Not for you, maybe, because you're clearly even more of a psycho than I thought you were.' Michelle snatched her hand away and got to her feet. 'Sorry to spoil your sad little party, but I have no interest whatsoever in swapping one Cutler for another, least of all when the one I was married to is lying in a steel drawer.' She picked up her mobile from the table. 'Now, here's a thought ... why don't I call your old man and ask if he'll come and pick you up? You can tell him exactly why you came over on your way home, see if *he* thinks it's a problem.'

Justin seemed to sober up very quickly. Michelle watched as he hauled himself off the sofa and began to swear at her. She took a step away and waited patiently until he'd finished.

'It's your choice,' she said. 'I can call a cab company or, if you want to save yourself a few quid, I could just as easily give Wayne a quick bell. So, what's it to be, Justin?' Her finger hovered over the keypad. 'Taxi or Dad?'

'It's pretty standard in murder cases, I'm afraid.' Fiona Mackie leaned back against the worktop in Pippa Shepherd's kitchen. 'These things drag on and it's always horrible for the families, because how are you supposed to make plans or move on? I am doing my best, and I promise to keep you informed, but as of right this minute they still can't tell me when they plan to release Barry's body.'

Pippa nodded, but she couldn't remember why she was being told this or how the conversation had started or even

267

if she'd asked Mackie a specific question. Because she hadn't been sleeping much and she was tired, but mostly because her mind was elsewhere.

She was thinking about that flash drive.

The police would know what was on there by now, what Barry had wanted kept secret, and she was trying not to worry too much about why she hadn't been told. Maybe it was just the way they did things, or at least the way that strange detective Miller did things. Pippa knew he'd already found out she'd been lying when they'd spoken on the street two days before. Her boss had told her all about the bloke who'd rung to order pizza and then asked questions about her working hours, and she could only presume that Miller hadn't confronted her about it because he was biding his time. Or more likely because he'd already worked out that it wasn't important.

Which it wasn't. Not really . . .

'Sometimes there are . . . stipulations,' Mackie said. 'I don't know what Barry's wishes were or how you were planning to do things, but even when they do release the body, they may insist on burial instead of cremation. Just in case there's a trial and the defence ask for a second post-mortem. I know, it's horrible to have that option taken away, and I really can't see it happening in this instance, but just so as you're prepared.'

Pippa said thank you and that it was all useful information. 'Have you heard anything about the actual case? About any progress, I mean?'

'If there was anything I could tell you, I would.' Mackie could see that Pippa was upset and stepped across to comfort her. 'It's awful being kept in the dark, I know. I will tell you one thing, though. We are doing everything we can to catch whoever killed Barry. I can promise you that much.'

Pippa nodded and stared into the blackness beyond her kitchen window. The FLO's arm felt good around her shoulder, though it wasn't going to stop her shaking. She was grateful too for the reassurance, but right then, though there were a good many things she was desperate to know, the identity of her husband's killer wasn't top of the list.

The middle-aged man (shaggy mullet, too much jewellery) flicked over his king to resign the game and sat back, scowling. 'Made me look like a right pillock.'

'It wasn't very hard.' Gary Pope leaned across the table to shake his opponent's hand. 'I'll have another Glenlivet, ta very much . . .'

As the man stood up and stalked away to the bar, Pope began to reset the board. He'd meant every word he'd said to Miller; he bloody loved chess. He loved playing it, loved the fact that he'd finally found something he was good at that wasn't illegal, and he especially loved the fact that, in the three hours he'd been taking on all-comers in the corner of the pub, he hadn't paid for a single drink. It was an arrangement with diminishing returns, though, Pope knew that. The more he won, the more he drank and the more he drank, the more likely he was to get sloppy and start losing.

All the same, free booze was free booze.

Another game or two couldn't hurt.

He moved the last pawn into position and checked his watch. He'd need to be on his way pretty sharpish after that if he was going to meet that copper and make the nine o'clock train. Much as he'd enjoyed himself, Pope wouldn't be sorry to be heading out of town again. He guessed that most of the people he was trying to avoid would know he was here, so lying low had felt like the sensible thing to do once he'd got the business with Miller out of the way. It was a shame, because there *were* people he would have liked to see – not least of all his mum – but he wasn't going to take chances. If he popped round to see an old mate, he could get spotted by someone who might tell someone else and suddenly things wouldn't be looking too clever. It was like he told Miller: he had to think ahead, same as when he was playing chess.

Still scowling, the man with the mullet delivered his whisky and, by the time he'd wandered away, there was already a fresh challenger standing by and keen to take Pope on. The young bloke looked more like a football hooligan than a chess player, so Pope reckoned he'd earn himself another drink before he'd had a chance to finish this one.

He took a sip of whisky then pointed to the empty chair.

'Help yourself. You're black and you get to make the first move . . .'

The bloke casually slid a pawn forward without bothering to sit. Pope sat up a little straighter. It might have been random, but it might also have been the first move of someone who knew exactly what they were doing.

'Queenside bishop's pawn to C5,' Pope said. 'Sicilian defence, right?'

The young man shrugged.

While Pope considered his response, he glanced across and saw another young bloke dressed almost identically to his new challenger and watching them carefully from the bar. Pope caught his opponent's eye and nodded towards the man at the bar.

'Oh, there's two of you . . .'

FORTY-FIVE

Miller woke to a somewhat terse text message from Tim Sullivan, demanding his urgent attendance in Susan Akers's office. Reading the phrase *upon your arrival at the station*, Miller had nearly choked on his corn flakes, but while the message served perfectly to confirm that Sullivan was a pompous arse-nugget, it also suggested, rather more worryingly, that Miller was not being invited in for teacakes and Scrabble.

'So, why am I getting called by the Metropolitan Police in the early hours?' Sullivan asked, upon Miller's arrival.

Miller guessed from Sullivan's 'I know something you don't' expression that it was a rhetorical question, but thought he'd have a bash at answering anyway. 'Ooh . . . I don't know, are you getting transferred? When? I mean . . . is it *soon*? It goes without saying that we'll all miss you horribly, but huge congratulations.'

Sullivan and Akers just stared, as though waiting to be sure that Miller had finished.

'I am of course familiar with Gary Pope,' Sullivan said.

'I think we all are,' Akers said.

'And I'm well aware of his criminal connections.'

'Ah, right.' Now Miller understood why he was in trouble, but he didn't think that talking himself out of it would present much of a challenge.

'What I *wasn't* aware of, however, was that you'd arranged to have him brought up from London.'

'Yes, because I thought he'd be a useful source of intelligence on the Sands Hotel murders.' It wasn't strictly true, of course, but as lies went it was every bit as little and white as 'my phone died' or 'no really, that was delicious' or 'honestly, I'm a Canadian'. 'I could have sworn I'd told you,' Miller said. That was another favourite.

'No,' Sullivan said. 'You didn't.'

Akers was looking serious. 'The explanation had better be good, DS Miller.'

'Understood.' Miller wandered over to see how Akers's potted plant was getting on. He was pleased to see that the grey mould was clearing up. 'I was using my initiative.' The bark of derisory laughter from Sullivan and the stare from Akers was a fairly solid indication that it hadn't been quite good enough.

'Why didn't you keep DI Sullivan in the loop?'

'Well, I *did* . . . sort of.' Miller turned to Sullivan. 'I mean, I gave the Met your details, what with you being the senior investigating officer and everything. Which is probably why they called you.' The effort not to smirk was positively Herculean. 'Was it *very* early?'

Sullivan shook his head, dismissive, making it clear that having his much-needed beauty sleep disturbed was not the

272

reason they were here. 'I'm sorry to say that Mr Pope failed to catch his train back to London.'

Miller sighed. 'You just can't trust these criminals, can you?'

'It wasn't entirely his fault.'

Miller was not greatly surprised, but doubted that the ramifications would be hugely serious. 'Look, the Met did us a favour, I get that, but they only nicked him for receiving stolen goods and *that* was only to make sure he got here, so it's not like "Britain's Most Wanted" has done a runner, is it? To be honest, they're probably chuffed to have got Chesshead off their hands for a bit, and anyway, there's no need to panic, because I'll find him.' Miller shrugged. 'I'll find him and put him on the train back to London myself.'

'Well, that shouldn't be too difficult,' Sullivan said. 'Because we know exactly where he is.' He looked across, giving Akers her cue.

'Gary Pope was found dead just after two o'clock this morning,' Akers said. 'A gunshot wound to the head.'

Sullivan looked as content as he had since Miller had walked into the office. Perfectly happy to watch Miller absorbing the information and reacting to it. Relishing the fact that, for once, Miller had nothing to say, and the emotions that he guessed Miller was now wrestling with as he struggled to respond.

Shock, alarm, guilt. Oh yes, definitely guilt.

'Well, it *must* be connected to what happened at the Sands,' Miller said, eventually. He looked somewhat desperately at Akers. 'I mean, it's got to be, right?'

'Let's find out,' Akers said. 'Clough and Fuller are at the PM, so why don't you and Xiu get down to the crime scene, dig around a bit.'

Miller nodded, but he was finding it hard to focus. 'Right . . .

but we're supposed to be reviewing the CCTV at the phone shop. That number on Cutler's phone.'

'I think this takes priority,' Akers said.

Miller knew that she was right, of course. He moved towards the door, still working it through, thinking out loud. 'Maybe we're looking for the same killer,' he said. 'Maybe whoever killed Cutler and Shepherd was worried that Chesshead *did* know something. That makes sense, right? I bring Chesshead up from London to talk to him about the murders and he's killed almost immediately.'

'That's certainly one way of looking at it.' Sullivan sat down in front of Akers's desk, the two of them clearly set to carry on talking about Miller after he had left.

Miller waited, because it was obvious that Sullivan wanted to tell him what the other way was.

'You bring Chesshead up from London and you *get* him killed.'

Miller and Xiu stood together halfway along a stinky alleyway behind the football ground. The forensic team had already packed up and left and now the only clues to what had happened there ten or so hours earlier were the bored-looking uniformed officer standing guard, the fluttering scraps of crime scene tape and the bloodstain.

They both stared down at it.

'Checkmate,' Miller said.

Xiu nodded sadly, then wandered slowly off along the alleyway. Miller watched her, uncertain as to what she was looking for. What either of them was looking for. The forensic team would have taken away anything that might be physical evidence, there were no CCTV cameras and, although the house-to-house had already begun, the crime scene was not overlooked by any windows. Whoever had killed Gary Pope had chosen the spot very carefully.

Xiu turned at the end of the alleyway and wandered back.

'It's not your fault,' she said.

'Oh, cheers.'

'Seriously.'

'He wouldn't be dead if I hadn't brought him back.'

'You didn't kill him, though.'

'Once again, peerless detective work,' Miller said.

'So, who did?'

They turned together and began walking back towards the road. There were still several police vehicles parked there and more uniformed officers hanging around. A couple of lads with BMX bikes were loitering as Miller and Xiu emerged, and one of them pointed back into the alleyway.

'What's gone on down there, then?'

'Fatal dogging incident,' Miller said.

'For real?'

'Some of them get carried away.'

Miller and Xiu left the wide-eyed teenagers behind and kept on walking.

'It can't be *unconnected* to what happened at the Sands. Don't you think?' Miller thought he sounded less convinced and less convincing than he had when he was talking to Akers and Sullivan, but he was clinging to the possibility. 'Shot in the head same as Cutler and Shepherd, on top of which nobody's reported hearing a gunshot, so probably a silencer.'

'Maybe,' Xiu said. 'From what Pope was saying, there were quite a few people he didn't want to run into. I think we know a couple of them.'

275

'Right . . .'

'Why kill him, though? I can understand them wanting to find out what he knew, same as we did, but they must have known he wasn't in town when it happened. Nobody could seriously think he was responsible.'

Miller stopped. 'There is another possibility.'

Xiu stopped a pace or two later, came back and waited.

'I think he might have been killed because he was talking to me. Because of what we were talking about yesterday, after you left.'

'While I was having cake.'

'While you were having two cakes,' Miller said. 'He sent me something.'

'What—?' She jumped slightly when her mobile rang, checked the caller ID then stepped away, same as she always did when Tim Sullivan was calling.

Miller watched her listening, then muttering considered responses. He presumed, because Xiu wasn't brain-dead or a psychopath, that she was actually no fonder of their boss than he was, but he understood that she was not quite as free to express her dislike as him.

Free in the sense of not giving a tuppenny toss.

It made him feel quite sorry for her.

You've told her most of it already, so it can't hurt to tell her about the photographs . . .

He guessed that's what Alex would say. Only a guess, because, for whatever reason, he hadn't talked to her in a couple of days. When Xiu ended her call and walked back, Miller was all set to tell her exactly what had been delivered to him at home the night before, but he wasn't given the chance.

'Sullivan,' she said, all business. 'Apparently there's a

witness who claims to have seen Gary Pope in the Black Pug at around eight o'clock yesterday.'

'Yeah, I phoned him and he sounded like he was in a pub.'

If Xiu was curious as to why Miller had called their murder victim a few hours before he was killed, she made a good job of hiding it. 'The witness claims that he saw Pope leave with a pair of skinheads.'

Miller nodded. 'Well, one skinhead can look a lot like another.'

'*Identical* skinheads,' Xiu said.

FORTY-SIX

There was a small photoshoot taking place in front of the Majestic Ballroom when they arrived. Something for the local papers, Miller reckoned, or perhaps a website. He presumed there was a website ... www.dodgydancehall.com

While the photographer set up a couple of standing lights and umbrellas, Ralph Massey – decked out in an electric blue suit with his hair tied back in a ponytail – was busy arranging a group of four dancers, fussing at two women wearing dresses so short that Miller could have worn them as glittery T-shirts and purring instructions at their male counterparts, whose suits were tight enough to give traditionalists like Howard and Mary heart attacks. Once he was happy, Massey took up his own position in the middle and stood with arms outstretched and thumbs aloft.

'OK, lads and lasses ... tits and teeth.'

Suddenly the cheesy grin Massey had plastered on vanished and he glared at the photographer. 'It might help if you took the bloody lens cap off.' The grin was replastered, but disappeared again just as quickly when he spotted Miller and Xiu waving from the other side of the road.

Waiting for Massey to join them, Miller stared up at the sign that had been draped across the ballroom's entrance.

The Majestic: Eat, Drink, Dance!

'Presumably they didn't have room for "do iffy drugs, catch an STD and put money in a gangster's pocket".'

Xiu grunted, still watching the dancers, who were now standing around looking bored; lighting fags and grumbling as Massey ambled across the road. 'Those poor girls must be bloody freezing,' she said.

With his photoshoot held up, Massey had every right to be impatient, but despite the money he'd shelled out for a photographer who was now being kept waiting he appeared more than happy to answer Miller and Xiu's questions.

'I invited Mr Pope over for a chat,' he said. 'He accepted the invitation.'

'Sounds like he didn't have much choice,' Xiu said.

Massey brushed lint from his shiny lapel. 'I sent my nephews along to collect him and make sure he got here safely, that was all. This can be a very dangerous town.' He looked at Miller. 'Well, you know.'

Miller said nothing.

I know because I'm a police officer?

Or *I know because my wife was murdered?*

'Would you mind telling us what your chat with Mr Pope was about?' Xiu asked.

'Absolutely not,' Massey said. 'I wanted to be sure he'd

had nothing whatsoever to do with Adrian Cutler's murder, because that would have been putting me in a very difficult position. He assured me that he hadn't and that was good enough for me. We talked for a little while longer after that because I was interested to know why he'd left in the first place. Why he didn't want to work for me any more.'

'Chess,' Miller said. 'Obviously he was sick to death of being part of an organisation that launders dirty money and uses violence or threats of violence to gain an advantage over business rivals. But also, chess.'

'Yes, he explained about the chess.' Massey shrugged. 'I shook his hand and wished him well.'

'What time was this?' Xiu asked.

'He left the Majestic just after nine o'clock, I think.' Massey nodded back towards the ballroom. 'There's cameras everywhere, so it's easy enough to confirm that.'

'Thank you,' Xiu said. 'We'll check the footage.'

'I'm surprised to hear that Gary willingly stayed that long,' Miller said. 'I'm sure you're a very generous host, Ralph, but he was due to catch a train back to London at nine and I know how keen he was to be on it.'

'Yes, he *was* a bit upset that he'd missed it.'

'Upset?'

'Miffed. He was ... miffed. These things happen though, don't they? He said he'd stay over and get the train first thing this morning instead. I actually offered to give him the money for a ticket.'

'You're all heart,' Miller said.

'Well, he wouldn't have missed it if it wasn't for me.' There was the hint of a smile when he looked at Miller. 'If he hadn't been talking to me, I mean.'

'Right.'

'All academic now though, isn't it?' Massey sighed and shook his head. 'No more chess for poor old Chesshead. Like I said though, it's a dangerous town.' He turned to look back at the ballroom and waved at the waiting photographer. 'Can I ... ?'

'Fill your boots,' Miller said. 'And don't worry, they can do amazing things with Photoshop these days.'

They watched Massey jog back across the road and strike a pose.

'When he shook his head to show us how desperately sad he was, did you see his ponytail swinging?' Miller looked at Xiu. 'Stupid bloody thing just ... swinging from side to side. I was tempted to grab hold of it.'

'And then what?'

'I hadn't thought that far ahead.' Miller heard the ping of a message arriving and reached into his pocket for his phone.

if you've got 5 minutes could you pop over for a chat?

something I need to tell you

On seeing that the sender had used his initials to sign off, Miller could not help but smile. 'We've been summoned,' he said, putting his phone away.

'Sullivan?'

'Oh God no, not *that* bad,' Miller said. 'Just another gangster.'

As they walked back towards the car, he said, 'If you're unfortunate enough to have embarrassing initials like WC, why the hell would you draw attention to them? I bet you Vin Diesel never does that.'

FORTY-SEVEN

The metal gates at the end of Wayne Cutler's drive slid open as Miller and Xiu approached and half a minute later they parked in front of an open garage that was big enough to contain Miller's house. Cutler, wearing a pair of oil-stained overalls, was already stepping out to greet them. He wiped his hands and watched as Xiu took in the assortment of vehicles in the garage behind him: a Range Rover, a Hummer, a couple of quad bikes and something old and sporty raised up on a ramp.

'Nice, right?' Cutler turned and nodded towards the sports car. 'It's a Mark One MG Midget.'

Xiu took a step closer, still looking. 'Sixty-three?'

'Sixty-two, actually.' Cutler looked impressed. 'I'm restoring it.'

'Is that the original shell?'

'Yeah, as good as, but the engine needed a total rebuild.'

Miller raised his hands. 'Don't get me wrong, this is absolutely fascinating, and much as I could happily stand here all day listening to you two wanging on about greasy crankshafts and big ends that need replacing I don't think that's why you asked us to drop in, is it, Wayne?'

'I heard about Chesshead,' Cutler said.

'Oh, you *heard*?'

'People talk, don't they? News travels.'

'So what, is there some kind of ... gangland WhatsApp group or something? Do you send each other cute little messages and pics? "Here's what happened to the thieving little shitehawk who tried to stiff me on that coke deal? LOLZ!" I presume there are baseball bat and knuckle-duster emojis ...'

Cutler actually seemed to find Miller's routine quite funny. 'Look, I knew that because of the history, you'd be knocking on my door eventually. I know you were busy enough *before* what happened last night, so I thought I'd save you the trouble.'

'I'm touched.' Miller turned to Xiu. 'Are you touched?' He wiped away a non-existent tear. 'I think I might actually be filling up.'

'Take the mickey all you like,' Cutler said. 'I just wanted you to know that Chesshead came to see me last night.'

'He came to see *you*?' Xiu asked.

'Trust me, I was as surprised as you are.'

'I seriously doubt that,' Miller said. 'So, what time was this?'

'I don't know ... around nine-thirty.'

'And what time did he leave?' Miller was trying to work out what the hell Chesshead had been up to, if, having been delivered to the Majestic Ballroom by Massey's twin goons, he had then voluntarily trotted along to visit Cutler. How many moves ahead had he been thinking? 'I presume he *did* leave, as opposed to ... for instance ... being bundled into the back of one of your cars and driven to an alleyway behind the football ground.'

'He was here about an hour, so ten-ish. It's easy enough to check.'

'Let me guess.' Miller nodded up to the security camera above the garage door; one of three he'd seen since arriving at Cutler's gates. 'It's all on film, right? Handy, that.'

'Why did he want to see you?' Xiu asked.

Cutler looked like he was thinking about it.

'It's a reasonable question,' Miller said. 'I mean, mice don't tend to chuck themselves on to traps, do they?'

'He said he wanted to set things straight. He knew I'd been looking for him.'

'Because of what happened to Adrian?'

'Yeah. I knew he hadn't actually done it, but he might have had a hand in the arrangements, mightn't he? Or known who had. He wanted to let me know in person he'd had nothing to do with it.'

'Did you believe him?'

'I did, actually,' Cutler said. 'I'm pretty good at reading people.'

'Really?' Miller looked at him, doubtful that Cutler could read anything much beyond a pop-up book. 'Can you read me, Wayne?'

'Well . . .'

'Am I thinking, "Fair enough, thanks so much for bringing this information to our attention, all very helpful et cetera, et cetera"? Or am I thinking, "What the hell, I might just bring in a forensic unit to be on the safe side and let them spend the rest of the day crawling all over your fancy garage"?'

'Hold on—'

'I refer the dishonourable gentleman to my previous comments about cars and bundling and alleyways behind football grounds.' Miller smiled. 'So, what do you reckon?'

Cutler shrugged and rolled his eyes at Xiu, as if in sympathy. 'Do what you like, Miller.'

Miller caught the look from Xiu, who was ready to move on. He almost certainly wouldn't be bringing in a forensic unit and he'd actually been thinking that he should get his moped checked over because it was making that funny whiny noise again and that he quite fancied pasta for dinner. He wasn't done with Cutler yet, though. 'Did Pope say where he was going when he left?' He used his fingers to put 'left' in quote marks.

'He'd missed a train, hadn't he? Told me he was going to see his mum and probably stay the night there. Maybe you should be talking to *her*, because I don't think they were exactly close.'

'We will be,' Xiu said.

Cutler took a step away. 'Right, I've got stuff to do ...'

Miller said nothing for just long enough to let Cutler think they were finished, then shouted after him. 'Oh, while I've got you ...' He waited for Cutler to come back. 'Why were you harassing Pippa Shepherd the other day?'

'I wasn't harassing anybody,' Cutler said. 'I just ran into her while I was walking the dog, so I stopped to say hello.'

'You asked her what she'd told the police.'

'Well, I'm still quite keen to find out why my son was killed, and I'm not getting any answers from you, am I? That's not what it was about, though. I just wanted to talk about it to someone who was going through the same thing as me. Someone who's grieving.'

'Right,' Miller said. 'Whatever. You need to stay away from her.'

285

'That's why they have bereavement support groups, because it helps.' Cutler took a few more steps back towards his garage, then turned. 'You should try it yourself.'

Miller could not ever imagine a day when he'd take advice from the likes of Wayne Cutler, but immediately found himself thinking about Howard, Mary, Gloria and the others.

'I've got one of my own,' he said.

As the gates slid back to allow the car out again, Miller glanced up at yet another security camera. He leaned out of the window to give it a wave. 'A bit odd how Massey and Cutler are both so keen to distance themselves from Chesshead's murder.'

Xiu glanced over at him. 'Is it, though?'

'*Super* keen.'

'Isn't that what you'd expect them to do?'

'Not when you're as cocky as those two. Normally they don't give a monkey's if we think they're guilty or not. It's all about whether we can prove it.'

'Do you think there's anything to prove?'

Miller groped for the handle to tilt his seat back. 'Obviously it's still possible that either of them could have had Chesshead killed after he left Cutler's, but I'm not convinced. Even if that's the case, I don't think it's got a lot to do with the murders at the Sands.' He slid down in his seat and closed his eyes, as though he was trying to catch forty winks. 'Whoever killed Chesshead, it wasn't because of that.'

'So . . . something else.'

Miller grunted, knowing exactly which *something* Xiu was cautiously suggesting. He'd told her about the photographs Pope had sent him on the journey to Cutler's place. She hadn't said very much then and didn't say anything more now for several minutes.

Miller wasn't asleep, but wondered if Xiu thought he was.

'Briefing's in an hour,' she said, eventually. 'Enough time to go and ask Pope's mother a few questions.'

'*I've* got a question,' Miller said. 'First there's the whole heavy metal slash casual nookie business, and now it transpires that you're some kind of tragic classic car nerd.'

'I prefer "expert",' Xiu said.

'Which is exactly what a nerd would say. So . . . any other dirty secrets I should know about, Posh?'

'No . . .'

'Promise?'

Miller opened his eyes in time to catch Xiu reddening.

FORTY-EIGHT

Tim Sullivan was on fire.

Not in the way Miller would have liked, obviously, but he had to admit that the DI was certainly 'giving good briefing'. Another murder could do that, could raise a person's game, even if said person didn't have much game to begin with. Sullivan talked about the crime scene forensics like he was about to reveal who had really killed JFK, but in the end there wasn't a fat lot to get excited about. Whoever had been responsible for killing Gary Pope had not only been careful in their choice of location but had left nothing behind in the way of helpful physical evidence. The forensic team had taken plenty of stuff away, he said, and tests were, of course, ongoing—

'So, nothing with a name and address on?' Miller asked.

'There's a boot-print that looks quite promising,' Sullivan said.

'Bloody inconsiderate, if you ask me.'

It was Miller's first and only contribution to the initial

288

stage of the briefing. Xiu had volunteered to talk the team through the interviews she and Miller had conducted with Ralph Massey (he had seen the victim and would happily supply footage of him leaving alive and well), Wayne Cutler (ditto) and Veronica Pope (she *hadn't* seen her son the previous evening and didn't appear hugely bothered about the fact that she was never going to see him again). So, knowing that he was unlikely to hear anything he didn't already know, Miller tuned out for a while.

He still nodded occasionally and managed to look interested. He even scribbled a few notes when Sullivan talked about the likely time of death before running through the postmortem notes in unnecessary detail.

Gunshot to the head?? NO WAY!!

This ability to appear engaged while actually being – mentally and emotionally – entirely absent, was one that Miller also put to good use in a variety of social situations. It came in very handy at boring dinner parties (they were always boring) or if anybody was describing a dream they'd had. It was a veritable godsend if someone was talking about cryptocurrency or wild swimming, but zoning out on such occasions usually meant he was compiling a list of things he needed from the supermarket or running through dance steps in his head.

Mundane stuff, *harmless* stuff.

He wasn't thinking about a growing tally of gunshot victims or about lethal chess games. He wasn't telling himself not to panic about a series of mysterious photographs that posed a great many more questions than they answered.

Who's the bloke in the pictures, Alex . . .?

It had to have been Ralph Massey who had asked Chesshead to take the photographs. He was working for Massey at the time, so it couldn't really be anyone else. If Massey knew that Alex was investigating him (and it wasn't like she'd made any secret of the fact) then it made sense that he would want her followed and to have her movements recorded. If anyone believed in knowing their enemy it was Massey, and Alex was certainly that.

Would anyone on your team know? Should I show the photos to Dominic Baxter?

But if that's all the photos were, why had Chesshead been so reluctant to talk about them? Why had he arranged for someone to deliver them rather than handing them over to Miller himself, and why (rightfully, as it had turned out) had he been so scared?

If I show them to anyone, it should probably be Lindsey Forgeham . . .

Miller tuned in again very suddenly when he heard Sullivan say, 'So, until we have evidence that suggests otherwise, we're working on the assumption that Gary Pope's murder is connected to the murders at the Sands Hotel. Everyone agreed?'

Without needing to look, Miller knew that Xiu was staring, waiting for him to speak up. Having had time to consider the matter, he had already made it very clear – to Xiu at least – that he did not agree, on top of which she knew that he was in possession of evidence that might do exactly what Sullivan was talking about. If *she* wanted to say something, there was nothing Miller could do to stop her. He wouldn't *try* to stop her.

Miller said nothing.

Xiu said nothing.

'Right then ... Carys.' Sullivan nodded at the Digital Forensics team leader. 'Where are we on Cutler's brother?'

'So, he was very happy to cooperate and unsurprisingly he was keen to hand over a phone that places him miles away from the hotel on the night of the murders.' Morgan shrugged. 'Doesn't prove a great deal, though, as we're not thinking Justin was the one who actually pulled the trigger. The financials we've been able to examine so far suggest that he's doing pretty well for himself, so there's no obvious motive there.'

'If it *was* the brother, it's more of a personal thing,' Clough said. 'Sibling rivalry can get very nasty.'

'I just used to pull the head off my brother's Action Man,' Miller said. 'Besides which, the jealous brother, the pissed-off wife, the business rival ... none of them explain Barry Shepherd.'

'Well, we just need to keep working the case until we *can* explain it,' Sullivan said. 'Keep working harder.' He turned to Xiu. 'Sara, you and DS Miller go back and talk to Gary Pope's mother again. Find out if anyone else came to see her yesterday, asking about her son's whereabouts. Unless you think she's too distraught to talk to us again so soon.'

Miller was annoyed that he hadn't asked that question himself and amazed that Sullivan had actually made a sensible suggestion. 'I've seen people more distraught at missing a bus,' he said. 'I think we're good.'

'What about that phone shop?' Xiu asked. 'We haven't checked their CCTV yet.'

'Tony and Andrea can do that,' Sullivan said.

Clough and Fuller nodded.

'I want you two to keep working the Pope murder.' Sullivan looked at Miller. 'I'm sure that's what DS Miller would prefer anyway. After all, he was the one who used his initiative and brought Gary Pope into the picture to begin with.' He began to gather up his notes, pleased with himself. 'I know he feels a certain ... responsibility.'

In the incident room, Miller walked a little sheepishly across to Xiu's desk. She spoke without looking up.

'Don't put me in that position again.'

'You sound like a stroppy contortionist.' Miller knew she wouldn't react, so didn't bother waiting. 'I'm sorry.'

'You should have said something about the photographs.'

'Said what?'

Now, Xiu looked up at him. 'Oh, I don't know ... that they were sent to you by our murder victim? That they may well be the reason he was murdered?'

'We don't know that.'

'Which is precisely the reason why we need to find out.' Xiu's voice was raised. 'We, as in the team you're supposed to be a part of.'

Miller knew that actually shushing his partner was likely to end badly for him, but he glanced around to make sure that nobody was eavesdropping, which was when he became aware of the gathering near the door.

Sullivan and Akers were deep in conversation with DCI Lindsey Forgeham and another of her officers. The youngish one who had tried to prevent Miller from barging into his boss's office two days earlier.

Xiu was saying something about integrity being compromised, but Miller wasn't really listening. She was saying something else about him not walking away when he began doing precisely that.

The group by the door were huddled and muttering, but moved quickly apart when Sullivan noticed Miller coming across.

'Call me paranoid,' Miller said. 'Actually don't bother, because I know you're talking about me.'

'Forget what I said at the briefing,' Sullivan said.

'I usually do.'

'Declan.' Akers raised a hand.

'Forget what I said about you talking to Pope's mother.'

Forgeham took half a step in Miller's direction. 'The Gary Pope case is now ours.'

Miller looked to Akers. 'But it's part of our investigation into the murders at the Sands Hotel. DI Sullivan made that very clear.'

Akers said nothing.

'I do understand that and obviously there will still be liaison,' Forgeham said. 'I'm not saying that other members of DI Sullivan's team aren't free to pursue leads on the Pope murder where it relates to the other two. You, however, are not.'

'Because I got in your face the other day?' Miller scoffed and shook his head. 'Because I came into your office without knocking?'

'Because it's protocol.'

'A word you should probably look up,' the youngish officer said.

'There's been a significant development,' Forgeham said. 'And I'm telling you this as a courtesy.'

Miller bowed. 'God bless you, ma'am.'

'Declan,' Akers said again.

Forgeham's expression was icy, businesslike. 'We're expecting the full ballistics report by the end of the day, but from what we know so far, we're almost certain that Gary Pope was shot with the same gun that was used to murder your wife.'

STEP THREE

SHADOW POSITION

FORTY-NINE

Miller was in no mood to dance, but he arrived in time to provide piano accompaniment for a last chaotic rumba before joining the group as they wandered over to the Bull's Head. He was in the mood for a pint or two and to talk through developments with his ad hoc advisory team. With a leg of lamb waiting in their slow cooker, Gloria and Ransford had gone straight home, so Miller sat with Howard, Mary, Nathan and Ruth at a small table in the corner.

Miller got the first round in: beers for himself, Howard and Nathan; gin for Mary and wine for Ruth. As well as the obligatory pork scratchings, there were two sorts of nuts and three different flavours of crisp on the table, because no two members of the team shared a snack of choice.

And because there was a lot to talk about.

'It's good news,' Howard said.

'Being taken off the case?' Miller was already half a pint and half a pack of scratchings to the good. 'You think so?'

'Well, it's hardly the first time, is it?'

Miller would have liked to argue, but couldn't.

'Howard's right,' Mary said. 'It's progress on the investigation into Alex's murder and that's the most important thing.'

'It's a break in the case.' Nathan sounded enthusiastic. He nodded to Ruth. 'That's what they call it.'

'Thanks,' Ruth said.

'I get what you're saying, obviously,' Miller said. 'But it's a break I can't follow up. It would be frustrating enough anyway, because I do feel partly responsible for what happened to Chesshead.'

'Well, you shouldn't,' Mary said. 'That's the kind of world he chose to get mixed up in.'

Howard nodded. 'If you lie down with dogs . . .'

'You'll get shot!' Nathan used his thumb and finger to illustrate the point.

'That isn't actually the expression,' Mary said. 'But in this instance, yes.'

'Even if you're not officially working the Pope murder, you're close to the people who are, right?' Howard emptied nuts into his palm and threw them into his mouth. 'They'll tip you the wink.'

'Course they will,' Mary said.

'Yeah . . . in theory.' Miller hoped that Xiu would be one of those Howard was talking about but, having 'compromised her integrity' once already, he couldn't count on it. 'It was hard enough before,' he said. 'Forgeham and her lot wanting me at a distance. Now they've actually got something to work with, I'm not sure I can deal with being cut out any more.' He downed what was left of his drink. 'I feel like telling them all to stuff it and going back on leave.'

'All the more reason why you shouldn't hand over those photographs,' Ruth said. She took a fast glug of wine when all eyes turned to her. 'If you do, Forgeham's team will swallow them up as evidence and you'll be lucky if you ever hear about them again. They'll be gone and so will your only chance to do anything about Alex's murder yourself.'

Everyone at the table was staring, and not just because Ruth was the one who usually had the least to say. There was a good deal of nodding as the remaining drinks were finished up, and Mary leaned across to touch Ruth's arm.

'Well said, love,' she said. 'Well said.'

Howard stood up and volunteered to get another round in. A few minutes later, he sat down again, lifted a fresh pint from the tray and passed it across to Miller. 'You're spot on about Massey, I reckon.'

Mary nodded, taking her gin. 'Spot on.'

'It's just like him to want Alex followed and photographed. He's the sort who likes to keep an eye on the people he's dealing with. I wouldn't be surprised if he'd got people taking pictures of you on the sly.' Howard nodded slowly then looked around, just to be sure there wasn't someone surreptitiously snapping away from the bar or lurking in the doorway to the Gents.

'Yeah, it was probably Massey,' Miller said. 'But I'm far more concerned about who the bloke in the photos is and what he's up to.'

'He's probably just one of Alex's contacts,' Mary said. 'She'd have had plenty of those, one or two of them inside Massey's operation.'

'And Cutler's,' Howard said.

'Definitely. Alex had cultivated all manner of sources like this bloke.'

'He's a snout.' Nathan nodded at Ruth again, clearly hoping she'd be impressed with his knowledge of underworld slang. 'Or a JIZZ. I saw that on TV. Not sure why they're called that, but . . .'

'It's CHIS,' Miller said. 'It stands for Covert Human Intelligence Source.'

'So what does SNOUT stand for?'

'It doesn't stand for anything,' Howard said.

'It looks to me like the bloke knows he's being photographed,' Miller said. 'Or at the very least he thinks it might be a possibility. He's got his head down and he's hunched over. He's keeping out of the light.'

'Send the photos to me,' Nathan said. 'I can do a bit of jiggery-pokery on the computer. Blow them up, zoom in and stuff.'

'Can you do that?'

'I can learn,' Nathan said. 'How hard can it be?'

Miller smiled, thanked Nathan for the offer then looked across at Mary who had her hand on her husband's arm. 'What?'

Howard nodded towards the bar and lowered his voice. 'Bloke over there's up to something. I think he might be taking photos or filming you.'

'He's just on his phone,' Mary said.

'That's what he wants us to think.' Howard pushed his chair back. 'He looks like a wrong 'un.'

'You're being daft, Howard.' Mary looked pleadingly at Miller. 'Tell him not to be daft, Declan.'

'Since when did he listen to me?' Miller said.

Howard got to his feet, squeezed from behind the table and began walking purposefully towards the bar.

Miller shouted after him. 'If he *is* taking pictures, tell him it's twenty quid for topless. Or I'll do full frontal for twenty-five.'

'Ruth was right,' Alex said. 'About hanging on to the photographs.'

Miller was brushing his teeth. In the mirror he could see Alex sitting on the edge of the bath, watching him. He grunted, dribbling toothpaste.

'Are you angry with me, Miller?'

'No, because that would be stupid.' He wiped away the minty mess that was running down his chest.

'It's fine if you are. It's one of the stages anyway, isn't it?'

'That's all rubbish.' Miller put down the brush and spat out the toothpaste in his mouth. 'I read up on it and apparently the five so-called stages of grief were originally meant for people who were dying, not people who were grieving. I mean ... *denial*? I could hardly deny you were dead, could I? I saw you laid out on Prisha Acharya's shiny table. Bargaining? Who exactly am I supposed to bargain with? Besides, I was angry before.'

'Not really,' Alex said. 'You were never an angry man. I don't think you can count getting worked up because the next door neighbour puts his recycling in the wrong colour bin.'

'He's still bloody doing it,' Miller said.

'Tetchy, that's what you are.' Alex grinned. 'You're a tetchy man.'

'Who's the man in the photographs, Alex?' Miller waited and watched as Alex lowered her head. 'Stupid question, right?'

She took a few seconds, then looked up again. 'You need to stop obsessing about those photographs and you should really stop worrying about being taken off Chesshead's murder.'

301

'The murder that's very probably connected to your murder, you mean? That murder? It's all got a bit . . . *murder*y, so I want to be clear.'

Alex sighed and shook her head. 'Yes, *that* murder.'

'Right . . . cheers. I'll bear it in mind.'

'I'm serious. Why don't you do your job and focus on working the murders in that hotel? On a case you can actually solve.'

'So you think I can solve it?'

'Well, if anyone can, it's the man I was married to. He was almost as good a copper as he was a dancer and he was one hell of a dancer.' Alex stood up, smiling as she moved across to stand close behind Miller. She leaned in to him and whispered. 'So, yeah . . . the dancing detective can definitely solve this case. The whingeing widower . . . I'm not so sure.'

Miller cupped his hands under the cold water. 'Nice pep talk,' he said. He leaned down to rinse and spit, and when he straightened up again, Alex had gone. Reaching for a towel to wipe his mouth and dry his eyes, he could swear that her breath was still drifting across his neck.

FIFTY

When it came to his abilities as a detective, Miller was not lacking in confidence – not usually, at any rate – but, if pushed, he might eventually concede that he was not always brilliant at reading the room. Or more specifically, the people in the room. That said, he required only a fraction more sensitivity than the average tree stump or doctor's receptionist to work out – eventually – that Xiu was still angry with him.

There was a muscle working overtime in her jaw and a slight twitch at the corner of one eye. The first time Miller had noticed it (as they were getting into the car outside the station) he'd thought she was winking and had reflexively winked back. The ferocity with which she'd yanked the car door shut however, had quickly disabused him of any notion that Xiu was flirting (highly unlikely), being playful (never in a million years) or – best-case scenario – letting him know secretly that, despite everything, she was still on his side.

She *did* say, 'I'm sorry you got taken off the Pope case ...'

though she didn't sound particularly sorry and left a significant, if unspoken, *but* hanging in the air.

. . . but it's procedure, so get over yourself.

. . . but it's probably no more than you deserve considering that you're withholding evidence.

. . . but that doesn't mean I'm not still very pissed off with you.

Their conversation en route was limited to say the least. There were a few muttered swearwords which Miller hoped were aimed at other morning road users and, other than a few long-suffering sighs and the occasional grunt, Xiu waited until they had arrived at their destination before reminding Miller why they were going to the phone shop in the first place.

'We're here to examine CCTV footage.' She pulled carefully into the kerb. She turned off the engine and undid her seatbelt. 'In the hope that we can identify the person who purchased the pay as you go phone that made several calls to and received a number of calls *from* Adrian Cutler's mobile in the weeks leading up to his murder.'

Miller looked at her. 'Did you think I'd forgotten?'

'I think it's entirely possible.'

'Oh, it definitely is,' Miller said. 'But I hadn't. So, do you think I'm an idiot?'

'Sometimes,' Xiu said. 'No . . . a lot of the time.'

'At least it's not *all* the time.' He raised his hand for a high-five. 'I'll take that as a win.'

Xiu turned to stare at him, struggling for words. 'Were you . . . like this *before* your wife died?'

'You'll need to be more specific,' Miller said.

'Annoying.' Xiu paused, but only to take a deep breath. She'd obviously compiled a healthy list. 'Bloody-minded. Childish . . .'

'Are you actually doing them *alphabetically*?'

'Insensitive, inappropriate, pig-headed, rude ... stupidly over-confident and completely dismissive of authority.' Miller tried to interrupt, but Xiu was not struggling to find the words any more and quickly began counting off some of Miller's remaining character flaws on her fingers. 'Inattentive, flippant, sarcastic, annoying, erratic, unreliable, flaky—'

'You've said "annoying" once already and those last three all basically mean the same thing.'

'*Well* ... ?'

'Can I take them one at a time?'

Xiu looked like she was about ready to slam her head against the steering wheel. She took a few moments to steady herself and asked again, nice and slowly. 'Were you like that before?'

Miller thought about it, then shrugged. 'Probably,' he said. 'If I'm honest, I think I just get away with it a bit more since Alex died.' He opened the car door. 'Come on, there's got to be *some* perks.'

Inside the shop and without consultation, it was Xiu who took the lead; producing the warrant card and asking to speak to the manager. Miller hung back, resigned to his place on the naughty step, and when Xiu was escorted through a side door he mooched around the shop whistling and looking bemused. He looked out of the window for a while. He examined a shiny new iPad and decided that the phrase 'keep taking the tablets' was only encouraging shoplifters. He leafed through a pamphlet about 5G connectivity and briefly engaged a fellow browser in an inane conversation about dongles.

'I like dongles. Do you like dongles?'

'Well, if you need broadband on the move they're certainly useful.'

'To be honest, I just like the name,' Miller said.

He couldn't blame Xiu for being angry with him or feeling let down. Despite her impressive catalogue of complaints, he was reasonably sure that she'd come round, but he wondered if there was anything he could do to speed that process up. He would say sorry again, certainly, but it felt as if going that extra yard couldn't hurt.

He should probably buy her something as a peace offering.

They had worked together less than a week, though, and finding the ideal gift for Xiu, based upon what little he actually knew about her, was going to be a tall order. He knew she liked heavy metal ... or was it just that she liked heavy metal as a short-cut to casual sex? Either way, Miller didn't think she'd appreciate a quickie with Ozzy Osbourne even if such a thing could be arranged and paid for.

Maybe he could buy her a joke book.

As a joke.

Which she wouldn't get.

Maybe he should just apologise several more times ...

An assistant who clearly had not seen Miller and Xiu come in approached as Miller was staring at a wall of mobiles.

'Anything I can help you with?'

'Possibly.' Miller took down one of the phones and inspected it. 'This one's got four cameras, right?'

The assistant nodded and smiled, as though Miller had made an excellent choice. 'Yes, indeed. Three at the back, one at the front. There's 5G connectivity—'

'I read the pamphlet.' Miller pointed.

'Right, yes. So, it's got a pixel density of 441 ppi, and—'

Miller raised a hand to stop him. 'I'm looking for something that makes and receives calls.'

The salesman chuckled. 'Well, obviously.'

'No, that's it.' Miller gently led the young man towards the centre of the shop and they both sat down. 'OK, the recorder thingy's quite useful for work, but I don't need any other stuff. Cameras and apps and Uncle Tom Cobley. I don't want to play games and I don't need it to measure my heart rate or tell me how many steps I'm taking. I just want something I can use to call people and that they can call me on, yes? Something ... nice and chunky.' He held two fingers up, six inches apart. 'Like ... *this* size, and something that, when it rings, actually sounds like a phone ringing and not like some tiny robot being sick.'

The salesman just stared, blinking.

'Basically,' Miller said, 'I'm looking to downgrade.'

It was very clear that the shop assistant had no idea how to deal with such a request. He looked helplessly around for his manager, but was saved any further difficulty when the side door opened and Xiu stuck her head round.

'You need to come and see this,' she said.

Miller stood up, took a step towards the door then turned back to the salesman. 'Oh, and I don't mind if it's one of those flippy ones. I like pretending I'm in *Star Trek* ...'

When Miller walked into the office, Xiu was already back at the computer scrolling through the CCTV; rewinding to the point from which she needed Miller to watch. 'We knew what time the phone was purchased, so it wasn't very tricky ... here we go.'

Miller watched as the customer they were looking for entered the shop and stood looking, rather nervously, around.

Xiu froze the image and zoomed in, but there was really no need because Miller could see immediately who it was.

'Bugger me,' he said.

307

FIFTY-ONE

'So, just to confirm that even though you are not under caution, this interview is being recorded.' Xiu looked to make sure that the woman opposite understood and saw her glance up towards the large camera mounted in the corner of the room. 'And that you've chosen to do without the legal representation that you've been offered.'

'Why would I need it?' Pippa Shepherd asked. 'I don't even know why I'm here.' She shook her head and looked at Miller. 'How am I supposed to start moving on? Like you told me.'

'I know it's not ideal, Mrs Shepherd,' Miller said. 'But we've just got a couple more questions. A few things that need clearing up, that's all.'

'Well, anything I can do to help, obviously.'

'Thank you, that's much appreciated. Oh ... before we get stuck in, would you mind telling me where you were three nights ago? Around ten o'clock?'

'I was at home, I think.'

'You sure about that? Where was your car?' Miller knew exactly where her car had been, having run that partial number plate he'd seen on the vehicle driving away from outside his house, but he waited for Pippa to answer.

'Oh ... that's right, I went for a drive. I was trying to clear my head a bit.'

'By driving to my house?'

Pippa looked horrified. '*What*? I don't even know where your house is. How could I know that?'

'I'm not saying you did, I'm just telling you that's where you happened to end up. Small world, isn't it?'

'I was   driving around,' Pippa stammered, and worried at the rings on her fingers. 'I can't remember where I was.'

'Let me try to help, then. Can you remember that you were following a woman named Michelle Cutler? There's a good reason why the name might sound familiar, by the way. As a matter of fact you bumped into her at the mortuary.'

It was the least relaxed shrug Miller had ever seen. 'Like I said, I was just driving around.'

Xiu leaned forward. 'And I don't suppose you'd know anything about damage caused to Mrs Cutler's car around the same time. A white Range Rover? She called the police to report that someone had keyed it.'

Miller thought that Pippa looked like a deer caught in the headlights. Or maybe a soon-to-be flattened badger, like the one that moron on the radio had been talking about. 'OK, let's park that one for a while and talk about why you lied to us when we ran into you. Remember? When you were on your way to work, five hours before your shift actually started. I mean, Gemelli's was only round the corner from where we saw you and you could have walked to Preston in that time.'

'I was just out for a walk,' Pippa said. 'I didn't want you to think I was out . . . enjoying myself, when I should have been at home grieving for my husband. That's all. I'm sorry, it was stupid of me.'

'Yeah, it was a bit,' Miller said. 'So, just to clarify, you weren't walking to Michelle Cutler's house with your keys in your fist?' The doomed badger expression returned to Pippa's face. 'OK, well, as porky-pies go, I suppose it's a fairly small one. It's like one of those mini ones you can get from M&S, which I highly recommend, by the way.' He sat back and stretched out his arms. 'Right then . . . quickfire round. Have you any idea why your husband withdrew three thousand pounds from a secret account, two days before he died?'

'*What*?' Pippa looked genuinely stunned.

'I'll take that as a no then, shall I?'

'Three thousand pounds?'

Xiu leaned forward again. 'Or what about the hidden operating system he was using to access the Dark Web? Do you know what he might have been doing on there?'

'Dark Web?'

'It's kind of like Amazon,' Miller said. 'But with drugs and guns and kiddie porn.'

'I don't . . .' Pippa lowered her head and shook it. 'Was that what was on the flash drive thing?'

'Everyone has secrets, Mrs Shepherd.'

Xiu took a sheet of paper from her file. 'Now it's time to talk about yours.'

Miller waited until Pippa was looking at him. 'We need to move on to a porky-pie that's considerably bigger than the last one. You know the biggest pork pie in the world weighed over twenty-three thousand pounds and was nearly eight feet wide?

We're talking about something that kind of size, you know . . . relative to the seriousness of this investigation. A properly *massive* porky-pie, Mrs Shepherd.'

Xiu slid the sheet of paper across the desk. 'Can you take a look at that list of phone numbers, please?'

Pippa reached into her bag for glasses. She put them on and stared down at the list in front of her.

'See the ones that have been highlighted?' Miller reached across to stab at several of the numbers. 'All the same number. Do you recognise that number?'

Pippa removed her glasses and slid the sheet back to Xiu. 'It's mine.'

'Would you mind speaking up a little, Mrs Shepherd?' Xiu nodded towards the twin cassette deck on the table. 'For the recording.'

'It's my number.'

'It's *one* of your numbers,' Miller said. 'You know, if we're being picky. A pay as you go phone, which you bought several months ago and which I'm guessing you don't use very much. That list is the call log from a handset belonging to Adrian Cutler. Remember him? He was the man whose body was found in the room next to your husband's. The man you told us you'd never heard of.'

Pippa swallowed hard and glanced up at the camera again.

'How did you know Adrian Cutler, Mrs Shepherd?' Miller gave her a few seconds, but she'd lowered her head again and didn't appear hugely keen to answer. 'I mean, it's probably just my blinkered worldview, but Adrian Cutler wasn't exactly the sort of bloke I'd expect someone like you to be . . . friendly with.' He gave her another chance to respond, but she didn't take it. 'It's a surprise, that's all I'm saying. I'm not sure how

311

much you knew about him, or about his business – and I'm using the word "business" rather loosely there – but . . .'

Pippa looked up at him suddenly, sad yet oddly defiant. 'Adrian came into Gemelli's one night with a few of his friends.'

'When was this?' Xiu asked.

'A few months ago.'

'Don't tell me,' Miller said. 'He complained about the stinginess of the pizza toppings, you bunged him a bit of extra pepperoni on the sly and one thing led to another.'

'He was . . . flirting a bit and being Jack the Lad and he wrote his number on a napkin. Just showing off for his mates, I thought. So, a few days later, I was sitting at home and Barry was working late and . . . I rang it.' She saw Xiu glance at Miller and the defiance ratcheted up a notch. 'I can tell you think I should be ashamed, or that I'm just a stupid old slapper who was kidding herself that a younger man would be interested.' She leaned forward. 'But he *was* interested. He really was . . . and it was exciting. Barry was all sorts of things . . . all sorts of wonderful things, but he was never that.'

'So, to be clear,' Xiu said. 'You and Adrian Cutler were having an affair?'

Miller turned to stare at her. 'You're just getting that?'

'It was half a dozen times,' Pippa said. 'That's all. I'm not daft; I knew it wasn't going anywhere. It was just—'

'Did Barry know?' Miller asked.

'No, I don't think so.' She looked from Miller to Xiu and back. 'I mean, God . . . I hope not. But he wasn't a stupid man. I swear, that's all I've been able to think about ever since . . .' Now the defiance had gone and she looked horrorstruck. 'Is that why Barry was *there*?'

'We don't know yet,' Miller said.

'At the hotel?'

'The investigation is still ongoing.'

'Is that why he's dead?' Pippa was beginning to panic, breathing heavily and clutching at the arms of her chair. 'Him *and* Adrian? I don't understand . . .' She began to cry, pressing the heels of her hands against tears of grief or guilt or both.

Miller gently nudged a box of tissues across the table.

Ten minutes later, Miller and Xiu stood in reception and watched Pippa Shepherd leave. She looked broken.

'Hard to imagine,' Xiu said. 'Losing two people you care about at the same time. Like *that*.'

Miller watched Pippa Shepherd step out of the revolving door and walk slowly away across the car park. Yes, she had been stalking her lover's widow because she was nosy or jealous or perhaps because she suspected Michelle Cutler of killing Adrian. She had taken those feelings out on her rival's shiny new Range Rover and by lying she had quite possibly hampered a police investigation. Though Miller couldn't swear his superiors would see things in the same way, he was in no great hurry to nick her for any of that.

In the end she was guilty of nothing worse than being stupid and scared.

'She needed that hug even more than I thought,' he said.

FIFTY-TWO

Miller was pacing rapidly around Susan Akers's office. 'OK, go with me on this . . .'

While she did not appear to be exactly champing at the bit, Akers shrugged like she had nothing better to do, while Sullivan, who was sitting in the chair nearest her desk, pulled a face which strongly suggested his unwillingness to follow Miller anywhere. Xiu watched from the corner of the room, having already agreed, with a degree of reluctance and one or two serious reservations, to go along for the ride.

Ten minutes earlier, Miller had led her into the corridor outside the incident room and talked her through the theory.

'It makes a . . . kind of sense,' Xiu had said when he'd finished. 'I do have some *buts*, though.'

'I'd be disappointed if you didn't.'

'Some big buts.'

'I like big buts,' Miller said. 'And I cannot lie.'

'What?'

'It doesn't matter . . .'

Now, it was all about convincing those higher up, even if some of them were considerably lower down the food chain.

'So . . .' Miller waited until he was sure he had everyone's attention. 'We were right in our initial assumption that Adrian Cutler was the primary target.'

Sullivan raised a hand. 'Let me stop you there.'

'Do you need the toilet?' Miller asked.

'What do you mean *our* assumption? You've been the one who's been challenging that all along.'

'Someone has to ask the difficult questions,' Miller said.

'Agreed,' Akers said. 'But that's not the same as being difficult.'

Sullivan nodded, like he was about to clap. Miller was just hoping he would catch it. 'Look . . . I'm more than happy to admit that I've not always been on the right track with this, but sometimes the answers aren't where you expect them to be and you need to go off road a bit.' He looked at Akers and held out his hands. 'Am I right?'

'Ask me again when you've finished,' the DCI said.

'Making the odd mistake along the way is all part of the journey and I think we can all agree that getting there in the end is what counts.' He turned to Akers again. 'Slow and steady wins the race.'

'Not if it's a sprint,' Xiu said.

'*What?*'

'If it's like . . . the hundred metres or something, slow and steady's rubbish.'

Miller tried to ignore the smirk from Sullivan and flashed Xiu a look to let her know that she very much wasn't helping.

'Fine,' Miller said. 'I still think my point stands, because we were looking in the wrong place when it comes to the identity of the person who took out the contract on Cutler.'

'Shepherd.' Akers had been observing the interview with Pippa Shepherd and was, unsurprisingly, a little ahead of him.

'Give the woman a coconut,' Miller said. 'I mean, presuming you want a coconut. I was going to say cigar, and it's not like I don't think you could carry that look off, but in the end I decided that you'd probably go for the coconut.'

'Please get on with it, DS Miller.'

Miller nodded and resumed his pacing. 'So ... Barry Shepherd finds out that his wife is having an affair with Adrian Cutler and decides to do something about it. He takes out the money from his secret account and goes shopping on the dark web.'

'He was an IT expert,' Xiu said.

'Right.' Miller's look made it clear that this was more like the kind of support he'd been expecting. 'He could do that stuff in his sleep.'

'So, he goes looking for someone who can do something about it,' Akers said. 'He hires a hitman.'

'Correct,' Miller said.

Sullivan scoffed. 'For three grand?'

'Something of a Poundland hitman, admittedly,' Miller said. 'But basically, yes. Chances are, Shepherd's watching Cutler, so he quickly finds out about the weekly spanking sessions with Scarlett Ribbons at the Sands. So now he's got the perfect location.'

Sullivan garnished the scoff with a derisory snort. 'Well, that might ... I say *might* explain Cutler, but how does Barry Shepherd end up dead?'

Miller nodded thoughtfully, as if he had been expecting

exactly that question. It had been the biggest of Xiu's buts. 'Because our hitman doesn't like to leave loose ends ... ?'

'Is that the best you've got?'

'It's a fair question,' Akers said.

Much as he would have liked to, Miller couldn't disagree. 'Look, I don't know exactly what happened that night and I'm still trying to work out what Shepherd was doing there in the first place. We do know that the same shooter killed both of them.'

Xiu stepped forward, nodding. 'The ballistic report confirms it was the same gun.'

Akers looked at Sullivan. Miller grinned at Xiu.

'So, we're *there*, pretty much.' Miller stared around, expectantly. A round of applause or perhaps a small confetti cannon would have been nice, but at the very least he thought that long overdue cake should be putting in an appearance quite soon.

'Tim ... ?' Akers looked to her DI.

Sullivan stood up and leaned against the desk. He gave another small nod and Miller had to fight the urge to punch the air. He winked at Akers, who pretended not to notice.

'I don't want to rain on your parade ...' Sullivan said.

Miller waited, his jaw aching from keeping the smile fixed in place. *Oh yes you do. You'd happily rain hot stale donkey piss all over it and dance a jubilant, if uncoordinated jig while you were doing it.*

'It's just that I do think "pretty much" is putting it a bit strongly. Don't you, DS Miller? Because, if we actually want to see someone prosecuted for these murders, there's just the small matter of catching your mystery hitman.'

317

FIFTY-THREE

The white Range Rover was nowhere to be seen. Pippa could only assume that it was being repaired and she was wondering how much something like that might cost as she rang the door-bell. She was also doing all she could to control her breathing, to keep the nerves in check so that she could get her words out when the time came.

Not that she had a very clear idea what those words might be.

The woman who answered the door was wearing one of those fancy tracksuits like the one she'd had on at the mortuary. She'd been wearing full make-up that day, too, but now her face was scrubbed and pale and she would probably say she looked rough, even though Pippa still reckoned she looked amazing. Pippa had taken over an hour to get ready and redone her own make-up twice.

Michelle Cutler peered around the door and narrowed her eyes, like she recognised the face of her visitor, but couldn't quite place it.

'Sorry,' Pippa said. She took a sharp breath and shook her

head. She tried to smile. Even though she *was* sorry – for all sorts of things – it didn't feel like a good start. 'My name's Pippa Shepherd. My husband Barry was killed on the same night ...' She stopped when she saw Michelle Cutler start to nod.

'Yeah, I've got you now,' Michelle said. 'I know who you are.'

'Right, yeah ...'

Michelle studied her.

'Can I come in?' Pippa asked. 'I won't take up too much of your time, I promise.'

'I've only just put my kids to bed.' Michelle seemed unsure, but eventually opened the door. 'OK, if you're quiet ...'

Pippa wondered why the woman might think she *wouldn't* be quiet, but said 'thank you' anyway.

Downstairs, in the biggest kitchen Pippa had ever seen, Michelle fetched wine from the fridge and poured Pippa a glass. 'I've already got one on the go,' she said.

'I've had a bottle open ever since it happened,' Pippa said. 'I mean, I like a glass now and again anyway, but the last few days ...'

'I know what you mean.' Michelle held her glass up and leaned across the island to touch it to Pippa's. 'You don't know what to do with yourself, right?'

They drank in silence for a while. Pippa was wondering if Michelle was wondering why the hell Pippa was there, and what she would say if she was actually asked.

'Have you thought about what you're going to do with all your husband's ... sorry, I can't remember ...'

'Barry,' Pippa said.

'Right. With all Barry's stuff. His clothes and what have you.'

'Not really. This copper told me it would be a good idea to deal with all that, though, so I could "move on".'

319

'Miller?'

Pippa nodded.

Michelle nodded in return. 'He's an oddball, don't you reckon?'

'I mean ... how can I even think about moving on when they won't release my husband's body? I'm not going to start giving his clothes away until I've decided what to bury him in.'

'Yeah, right,' Michelle said. 'It's ridiculous.'

'Have you heard anything about that? When they might release your husband's body, I mean.'

'Not a dicky bird.'

Pippa sipped her wine. 'So, what about all Adrian's things?'

'Yeah, Adrian had a lot of nice stuff ... expensive suits and all that. Well, apart from the ones I cut up.'

'Sorry?'

Michelle smiled and waved Pippa's question away. 'There's a place in town that does pre-loved designer clothes. I thought I might try them. They sell them for you, then they take a small commission.' She shrugged. 'Might as well make a few quid, eh?'

'Why not?' Pippa said. She turned and nodded towards the door down to the basement. 'What are you going to do with his trains?'

'God knows. They're a pain in the—' Michelle stopped and cocked her head. 'How did you know about Adrian's trains?'

'Oh ... I'm not really sure.' Pippa tried to remain calm. 'Maybe Adrian's dad mentioned them.'

'You've met Wayne?'

'Yeah, I ... ran into him. He must have said something.'

Michelle considered this then shook her head. 'No, that's not it.' An icy smile broke across her face. 'It was *you*, wasn't it?'

Pippa lowered her head. She hadn't come here with the

intention of telling Michelle Cutler that she'd been having an affair with her husband, but part of her had wanted the woman to know. She needed to feel ... acknowledged. In the end, she had decided against saying anything, because whatever else she was, she had never been cruel, but now it was out in the open there seemed little point in denying it.

'I knew that something was different,' Michelle said. 'That it wasn't just another Bootylicious Babe.' She necked what was left in her wineglass. 'I knew he'd actually fallen for someone.'

Pippa had no idea what to do. Adrian had told her some fairly scary stories about his wife, about her temper. She sat frozen, wondering if she should at least try to run, half-expecting the woman to come flying across the island at her with the empty glass.

Instead, Michelle just shook her head and the icy expression thawed a little. 'But I never expected   I mean, you're so *old*.'

Pippa looked up, horrified. 'I'm *forty-three*.'

'Like I said.'

'It was a stupid fling,' Pippa said. 'That's all. I know it probably won't count for anything ... but I'm sorry.'

'Don't be.' Michelle stood up. 'I only wish I was more bothered.' She walked across to the fridge, looking for a new bottle. 'He could never keep it in his pants, that was my old man's trouble. He was a decent dad and he always took care of everything financially, but he was *always* unfaithful to me.' She turned and pointed. 'And you can be damn sure he was unfaithful to you, too.'

Pippa was stung. Despite the somewhat unusual circumstances and irony notwithstanding, the woman's comment felt unnecessarily harsh. 'I scratched your car, too.' She sat up straight. 'That was me.'

'Now that I *am* bothered about,' Michelle said.

Pippa blanched. The woman looked like she meant it and now she had a bottle in her hand. She didn't take her eyes off Michelle as she walked slowly back to the island and sat down again.

'Have you got any idea what happened that night?' Michelle opened the wine and poured herself a new glass.

'Not the foggiest,' Pippa said.

'I mean, I know why *Adrian* was there.' She raised her hand and mimed a slap. She made a surprisingly accurate *whiplash* noise to go with it.

'Oh, really?'

'He had to pay for it, because I'd never do that kinky stuff for him.'

'Why on earth should you?' Pippa decided that now was not the appropriate time to admit that she *had* done. Or that she'd enjoyed it rather more than she'd expected to.

'Don't get me wrong,' Michelle said. 'I wanted to slap him loads of times, but not in a way he'd have enjoyed.'

There had been moments when Pippa had wanted to slap Barry, too. To slap a little life into him. She felt terrible about that, now; ungrateful and profoundly wicked. She watched Michelle Cutler conjuring images of the things she wished she'd done to let Adrian know how she felt and, more than anything, Pippa hoped that her own husband had not been thinking badly about her at the end. She would never know of course, but all she could do was cling on to that hope.

'I'll pay for the damage to your car,' she said.

Michelle leaned across to top her up. 'Too bloody right you will.'

FIFTY-FOUR

As soon as Miller had fed himself and the rats – his own 'finest' microwaved risotto looking only marginally more appetising than Fred and Ginger's rodent muesli – he'd set to work. He'd spread out all the case paperwork on the kitchen table, downloaded all the voice recordings from his phone to his laptop and got stuck in. That felt like a long time ago, largely because it was. Now, somewhere between stupid o'clock and sparrow-fart, even the rats had thrown in the towel, but Miller was not ready to call it a day/night/whatever just yet.

He glanced across at Alex, who was leaning against the worktop looking bored. She opened her mouth to speak, but Miller raised a hand.

'I know, I know . . . it's in here somewhere. It always is. You really don't need to tell me.'

'I don't know why I'm even here,' Alex said.

'Because I quite like having you around.'

'Good, because I like being around.'

'What, even if I *whinge*?'

He stood up and flicked the kettle on to make himself another coffee, then dropped back into his chair and began to sort through the case notes and statements, having already lost count of the number of times he'd done so already.

'A break wouldn't hurt,' Alex said. 'Do something else for a while and the answer might just pop into your head. Like when you're doing a crossword.'

'This isn't a crossword.'

'Like you said, it's in there somewhere. Chances are you've seen it by now and it just hasn't registered.'

'Do *what* else?'

'Anything.'

'What, flick idly through a magazine? Make a start on *War and Peace*? Maybe I should go next door and sit scrolling through your phone like I usually do in the middle of the night . . . clutching that stupid bit of cardboard like it's Gollum's bloody *precious*.'

'How is that going to help with this?'

'It might help *me*,' Miller said.

'I was thinking more like putting the radio on for a bit and trying to relax. Taking the mickey out of a few phone-in nut-jobs.'

'I could always spend an hour or two looking at those photographs again.' Miller turned to stare at her as the kettle began to grumble. He knew that poring over Chesshead's pictures was exactly what he would have been doing, were it not for the fact that a solution to the hotel murders felt so tantalisingly close.

'I don't think that's a good idea,' Alex said.

'Because?'

'Because you need to focus on one case at a time, and the solution to the hotel murders is—'

'So tantalisingly close, I know.' He groaned and tried to shake away the fatigue. 'Well, of course I know, because it's me that's thinking it. I'm the idiot who's rattling away to himself in an empty house, like that's going to help me crack a murder case. *I'm* the nut-job . . .'

He stood up again because the kettle had boiled and popped a coffee pod into the machine. He stood next to Alex. He could see the soft hairs on the back of her neck and smell the fancy coconut soap she used. 'I'm the one imagining you in that dress you never wore much, but which I always really liked.' He pointed. 'And with your hair a bit shorter than you normally had it, because even though I never said anything, I always preferred it that way.'

Alex ran fingers through her neat bob. 'It's hugely selfish of you.'

'I know . . . it's basically me, me, me, but you've got to admit that's kind of understandable, given the circumstances. Given the fact that there *is* no you, you, you.'

'It's fine,' Alex said. 'I hear what you're saying and I really don't mind about the dress or—'

'*What?*'

Alex stared back at him. 'What?'

'What did you just say? No . . . what did I just say you said? *I hear what you're saying.*' Miller moved quickly back to the kitchen table. He had forgotten about the coffee. '"Seen it by now", that's what you said before.' He pulled back the chair and sat down. 'Not seen it . . . *heard* it.'

He snatched up the headphones that were plugged into his laptop and began playing through the voice recordings. He'd used his phone's record function every time he'd spoken to someone and there were dozens of conversations that he'd listened to at least once already.

325

Ten minutes later, Miller was grinning as he set the head-phones down again. 'I think I've found our hired killer.' He got to his feet and began walking around the kitchen.

'Well, they'll definitely get you that cake now.'

'But I need someone to help me prove it.' He looked at his watch. 'As soon as, preferably.'

'Like who?'

'Well, on a magic island . . . *you*.' Miller was still pacing, thinking it through. 'That's probably not a goer. Posh'll be fast asleep and dreaming about vintage cars by now or shacked up with some metalhead. So . . .'

'She'll still be awake,' Alex said.

Miller knew who she was talking about. 'You think?'

'I can't vouch for what state she'll be in, mind you.'

Miller grabbed his mobile and dialled. When the call was eventually answered there was just breath and rustling, then something between a grunt and a growl.

'Hey, Finn . . .'

'Christ, Miller.'

Perhaps Finn's greeting had not been quite as jaunty as usual, but that was understandable, given how late/early it was. Miller knew that homeless drug addicts tended to keep somewhat . . . unusual hours, but even so. He also knew that her mood could be easily improved.

'Listen, Finn . . . are you busy?' He pressed on before she had the chance to tell him what a phenomenally stupid question it was. 'I need your help with something and there's twenty quid in it for you.' He waited, looking at Alex who was ready with a tentative thumbs-up.

'Have you any bloody idea what time it is?'

'Fair enough,' Miller said. 'Make it twenty-five.'

FIFTY-FIVE

'Were the boxer shorts really necessary?' Finn's voice dripped with something that was closer to genuine horror than simple distaste.

Stretched out face-down on the bare mattress and naked apart from the undercrackers to which Finn was referring, Miller reached instinctively back to the off-white boxers. 'Absolutely,' he said. Had he been able to procure a pair with penguins on, he most certainly would have been sporting them, but he'd been pushed for time.

'What can't be cured must be endured, Declan ... so make do and mend.'

It was an expression both his Irish aunties had been fond of trotting out, when they weren't calling him to ask what he wanted or changing the words to classic showtunes. It was fairly anodyne compared to a few of Sally's favourites like 'May the cat eat you and the devil eat the cat', which Miller had never understood. Or when Bridget was moaning about her late husband's philandering and saying, 'The cute hoor was lobbing the gob with that wagon next door, so I told him to go and bollox,' the gist of which he'd eventually picked up.

Standing in the doorway, Finn looked up from the crime-scene photos again and shook her head at Miller's display. 'So much . . . *flesh*, though.'

'Accuracy is crucial,' Miller said.

'If you say so.'

'We're recreating a scene.'

Finn grimaced. 'It's all . . . mottled.'

Miller tried not to sound quite as outraged as he felt. 'Mottled?'

'OK, then . . . pale. Looks like you're recreating a sack of boiled potatoes.'

At least the boxers were clean . . .

Miller assumed a provisional opening position. He wasn't altogether surprised that Finn was far more disturbed by his own semi-clad form than she was by the photographs of a dead man. He guessed that she'd probably seen worse, which was one of the reasons why she was the ideal choice for the job. That, and being reasonably cheap.

'Are you ready?' he asked.

'All I'm saying is, how am I ever supposed to *unsee* that?'

'Finn!'

'Fine, let's get it over with . . .'

The room in which the body of Adrian Cutler had been discovered six days earlier was much the same as it had been left, after the forensic team had been about their business. The bed had been stripped. The thin carpet was lined where evidence markers had been placed and the few pieces of furniture that remained were stained with the residue of fingerprint dust. Miller imagined that the room next door was in a similar state and, grateful as he was that the crime scene remained virtually intact, he could not understand why hotel management had not set about refurbishing them as soon as they'd been allowed the chance.

Maybe they had no intention of doing so. There was never any shortage of ghouls, Miller knew that, so perhaps they were planning on leaving the rooms exactly as they were, in the hope of attracting guests with . . . particular tastes.

The Sands Hotel presents: The Murder Rooms.

£75 per person/per night (inc bloodstains and breakfast).

'Right,' Miller said. 'Just tell me where my arms and legs need to go.'

Looking back and forth between the various photographs of Wayne Cutler's body and Miller's boiled potato-ish re-creation of it, Finn began to issue instructions. 'OK . . . the legs are good, but your right arm should be a bit more stretched out.'

Miller stretched out his arm. 'Straight or bent?'

'Straight,' Finn said.

'Good.'

'And your hand should be flopping over the edge.'

'Like that?'

'Hang on.' Finn looked at the pictures again.

Miller waited. 'A bit more . . . or is that enough floppage?'

'Yeah, but you need to turn your head more . . . no, right over, so your face is hard against the mattress.'

'Like this?' Miller's voice was muffled by the mattress and he was struggling to breathe. 'Finn . . . ?'

'Yeah, close enough.'

Miller lifted his head, irritated. 'No, "close enough" is not good enough, certainly not when it's costing me twenty-five quid. It's got to be identical.' He put his head down again and shouted into a mattress that smelled of things he didn't want to think about for very long. 'Now then . . . are we there?'

After a few more minor adjustments, Finn announced that they were.

'Right, good,' Miller said. 'Now, go outside and close the door. Then come in again and tell me what you can see. *Exactly* what you can see . . .'

Twenty minutes later, Miller and Finn were walking across the hotel lobby towards the exit. The place was just coming to life. Miller saw the concierge gossiping with one of the reception staff, while a cleaner gave the bell a cursory wipe before spraying polish on the front desk. He turned to see another cleaner half-heartedly moving a vacuum cleaner around and a third pushing her trolley into the lift, as he knew Sofia Hadzic had done the morning the bodies were discovered. The same morning Miller had gone back to work.

He was finally starting to think it had been a good idea.

When he turned around again, he saw the hotel manager coming in through the revolving door. He watched him straighten his tie as he exchanged nods with the concierge. Miller waved, then watched the confusion spread across Paul Mullinger's ruddy features as he crossed the lobby to meet him.

'Detective Sergeant Miller . . . what are you doing back here?'

Mullinger glanced at Finn with undisguised distaste, as if her very presence was lowering the tone of the place, though

330

Miller reckoned it would take an awful lot of doing. Finn smiled, pretending not to notice, then ambled across to one of the sofas, turning to give Mullinger the finger once she was out of his eyeline.

'It's a random biscuit check,' Miller said. 'Nothing to worry about. I just wanted to see if you'd addressed the shortbread-slash-ginger snap disparity.' He wasn't sure if Mullinger's blank stare was because he'd forgotten their previous conversation or had simply neglected to address the issue. 'I'm only kidding ... there's actually been another murder. I'm afraid this place is getting *quite* the reputation.'

Now, Mullinger laughed, albeit a little nervously.

They talked rather more seriously for another few minutes after that and the hotel manager was very helpful, if a little taken aback by the matter Miller wanted to discuss.

'I asked you the wrong question,' Miller said, when he'd got the information he needed.

'Pardon me?'

Miller began walking across to join Finn then turned and called back. 'That first morning. I asked you the wrong question ...' He didn't bother to finish because it really didn't matter any more and he was already composing a triumphant text to Xiu.

I know who our 'hitman' is. I am king of the winklers! I am expecting cake ...

Finn had occupied herself rolling a cigarette and now she looked up at Miller, smiling as she licked the edge of her Rizla. 'Twenty-five quid I think we said.'

Miller reached for his wallet and counted out the cash.

Finn snatched it and tucked it into her bag. 'You can buy me breakfast as well, if you want.'

'How about I make you breakfast?'

Finn made a show of thinking about it, like she wasn't starving, then stood up. 'Better not be muesli.'

'Are you *high*?' Miller asked.

FIFTY-SIX

Miller cleared away the remains of a hearty breakfast to which the description 'full English' did not even begin do justice. He carried the dirty plates and cutlery through to the kitchen, put away the sauce bottles (ketchup for him, brown for Finn) and flicked the kettle on.

Leaning against the worktop, he could all but hear his arteries screaming for mercy.

Much as he'd enjoyed the bacon and eggs – and the sausages and the beans and the mushrooms and the fried bread – watching Finn eat had been even better. It had not been pretty and he'd tried not to stare, but he couldn't recall the last time he'd seen someone take such pleasure in devouring what was put in front of them. It made him wonder how long it had been since she'd eaten anything. It made him want to cook for her again, to do all he could to put some meat on her bones.

When he carried the mugs of tea through to the living room, Finn was just emerging from the small toilet near the front door.

Miller pointed to her tea and sat down. 'Better?'

'Oh yeah.' Finn dropped down next to him on the sofa and nodded towards the toilet. 'You might want to give it a minute.'

'I meant the breakfast.'

Finn slurped her tea and grinned. There was a small blob of brown sauce at the corner of her mouth. 'Well, the bacon wasn't *quite* as crispy as I like it . . .'

'Everyone's a critic.'

'But otherwise it was awesome.'

Yes, Miller definitely wanted to feed her again.

They said nothing for a minute or two and, though the silence wasn't exactly comfortable, it wasn't awkward either. Miller waited and watched Finn rolling another cigarette, wanting the moment to be right.

'This doesn't have to be a one-off, you know,' he said.

Finn turned to stare at him.

'I mean, I'm sure I can get the bacon right next time and apart from anything else, it's going to start turning a lot colder out there soon.' Miller was trying his very best to sound casual. 'So I was wondering if you fancied staying here for a while.'

Finn's eyes narrowed across the rim of her mug.

'Just for a couple of nights, you know. See how it goes.'

'We doing this again, are we?' Finn said.

'How can I not ask?'

'Because my answer's always going to be the same.'

Miller had run out of road. He felt gutted, helpless, but he was determined not to let those feelings show on his face. He obviously didn't manage it.

'Look, I'm sorry, OK?' Finn put her completed roll-up into her tobacco tin and closed the lid. 'I'm sorry you miss her so much.'

'Don't you miss her at all?'

Finn looked away, spoke to the floor. 'The last few years . . . no, *more* than that, she was just someone who stopped to give me money every day. That's about it.' She swallowed and sniffed. 'I miss the money.'

'I'm not sure I believe you,' Miller said.

Finn shrugged, half-hearted. She gnawed at her nails for a few seconds then began tugging at her hair.

'Christ, this is hard.' Miller was staring at the photograph of Alex next to the TV.

'I know,' Finn said, well aware where this was going. 'Because—'

'You look so much like her.'

Now, they were both staring at the picture of Alex and this time the silence was very awkward. Miller knew it was his job to try to ease the tension. 'I mean, with a few less piercings obviously, and I think she washed her hair a bit more often than you do.'

Miller looked at her, but his smile was not returned and, seeing her shove her tobacco tin into her backpack and get quickly to her feet, Miller could see that she was in no mood for jokes, however tenderly they were meant.

'Finn . . .'

She stomped across to the front door. 'Thanks for breakfast.'

'God, you're every bit as stubborn as she was.'

'I wouldn't have come if I'd known there'd be strings attached.'

'Come on, that's not fair.' Now Miller stood up too, and held out a hand. He called her name again but, in the end, he could do nothing but watch Finn storm out and slam the door behind her.

Fred and Ginger crept to the bars of their cage and watched, like they could sense Miller's mood as he stood there for a minute or more, frustrated and furious. Finally, he cursed loudly enough to send the rats scurrying back to their bed and marched into the kitchen. He tossed what was left of the tea away, slammed the mugs down on the draining-board and stood trying to calm himself, his knuckles whitening around the edge of the sink.

Every bit as stubborn . . .

How *dare* she eat a lovingly prepared breakfast, then stomp out of there in high dudgeon? In any kind of dudgeon come to that? And what the hell was dudgeon, anyway? For crying out loud, he'd only been doing what he knew was right. What Alex would have wanted him to do if she was around. Miller turned to make sure she wasn't, which was when he glanced out of the window and caught sight of the figure on the other side of the road.

Watching the house.

The anger was immediately replaced by something else. It gave way to incomprehension and bewilderment and then horribly quickly – because how didn't matter – to fear.

How didn't matter, because Miller knew *why*.

He moved slowly to the kitchen door and peered round it. He'd have a better view through the living room window. He was hoping that he'd imagined the whole thing; that he'd see nothing out there but trees and sea and sky, or a harmless passer-by who by now would be fussing over a dog or been joined by the friend they'd been innocently waiting for.

The figure was still there, stock-still in a long dark coat.

Miller could not make out the face, shadowed by the peak of a baseball cap, but he didn't need to, because he *knew*. He knew who was out there and why they had come. When he saw a hand reach into the pocket of that long dark coat he knew exactly what was in there, too.

It wasn't a dog-treat or a packet of Polo mints.

He bolted into the living room and grabbed his mobile, thanking God and anyone else who might be listening that Finn *had* left. Stabbing at the screen while trying to keep out of sight, he thought how ridiculous it was that the quickest way to send for help was to simply dial 999, the same as someone might if their cat was stuck up a tree or if they had their head trapped in some railings.

When he'd identified himself and been put through to the control room, he said all the things he needed to say, even if they might not have come out in an altogether comprehensible order.

Firearm . . . real and credible threat . . . yes, now would be good.

As soon as Miller had hung up, still with one eye on the figure across the road, he sent much the same message to Xiu, hoping that she was awake and that caps would stress the urgency of the situation.

KILLER IS HERE.

SERIOUSLY.

HOW FAST IS THAT MOTORBIKE . . .?

He laid his phone down on the table and stood desperately trying to decide what to do, his mind racing through his options, such as they were. He watched the figure look left then right, before stepping into the road and starting to walk calmly towards the house.

There was only one thing he *could* do.

Miller ran across the room and charged up the stairs.

FIFTY-SEVEN

Xiu could not have been any more pumped up than she was, but the crowd pressed up against the cage – baying for blood and punching the air as they chanted her name – was certainly not harming her cause.

XIU, XIU, XIU . . .

When she turned to give her fans a clenched fist salute, the noise only got louder.

XIUUUUUUUU . . .

She was starting to perspire more than a little in the black leather one-piece, but only because it was so hot in the arena. She slapped her thighs and grunted aggressively, her palms slipping against the oil she'd lathered over every inch of exposed flesh. That was when she realised it was actually cooking oil, which would account for the sizzling noise and explain why she smelled like a roast chicken.

It didn't matter. She had a job to do.

Xiu glared across at her opponent, who was hopping

gingerly from one foot to another in the opposite corner of the cage. Justin Bieber looked nervous and he had every right to be. The screams and roars of Xiu's fans were far louder than the pitiful squeaks coming from his, because the Beliebers knew what was coming.

She smiled, baring her teeth as the countdown began.

J-Beebz tried to smile back, but the Canadian teen-idol-turned-rapper couldn't quite manage it. The only thing ready to rumble was his perfectly toned tummy, bless him.

The bell rang and Xiu rushed across the ring, ready to do some serious damage . . .

. . . and opened her eyes.

The room was lit only by her phone-screen on the bedside table and Xiu realised that the *ding* in her dream had been an alert; the sound of a text arriving. She looked at the clock. It wasn't even seven-thirty yet and a message this early could only be work-related and was likely to be important. She inched across the bed, nervous, yet excited and also a little annoyed because she knew she could have taken Bieber inside the first round.

Still not fully awake, she reached for the phone.

There was a soft moan from the other side of the bed and an arm slid across Xiu's chest to draw her back. Xiu glanced down at the tattoo on the inside of the wrist; the rose, inked delicately in red and green that she had first noticed the night before. A not-so-shy wave after their eyes had met, which was when Xiu had begun moving through the crowd in the packed room above the King's Arms, neither she nor the tattoo's owner paying much attention to the heavy metal any more.

DoomToilet, rocking like monsters.

Xiu had seen and touched all the other tattoos since, of

course – the mermaids and the birds and the pierced heart in a very saucy location – along with everything else she'd imagined beneath the leather and the denim. The softness, the smoothness; those curves she'd noticed moving in time to the music the night before. It was exactly what Xiu had been looking for. Mostly, the choices she made depended on her mood, but sometimes she just wasn't in the market for a hairy chest and all the bits and pieces that (usually) went with it.

Her phone dinged again, the text message still unread.

That arm across her chest tightened a little and the young woman pressing herself into Xiu's back, whispered, 'Leave it . . .'

Xiu *really* wanted to.

Several miles away, what Finn really wanted was to punch something, or better yet, somebody. The next unlucky sod she ran into. She stopped at the end of the road, swore at a seagull perched on a parked car, then stamped out the roll-up on which she'd been furiously dragging since she'd slammed Miller's front door behind her.

God, she *hated* feeling angry and it was always worse when she couldn't decide who she was angriest with.

She was angry with her mother (no change there and not just because she was dead) and she was especially angry with Miller, even if she couldn't quite work out why. Probably because in his own daft and unmeaning way he'd managed to push all her buttons. Because he'd made her feel pig-headed and ungrateful.

Which wasn't fair.

Not really . . .

Worst of all, she was annoyed with herself, for letting Miller get to her, and as she watched the seagull squawk, every bit as ill-tempered as she was, before flapping grudgingly down into the road, she began to feel guilty.

It was even worse than being angry.

Maybe she should go back and at least thank Miller properly for the breakfast, which to be fair *was* amazing. She wasn't going to back down on the other stuff, the moving in business, but it couldn't hurt to let him know that she appreciated the effort. Because obviously she did. She didn't want him to think that he was only around to provide handouts and that she didn't *feel* anything.

She turned to walk back, having made up her mind, then stopped when she saw the figure in the baseball cap crossing the road towards Miller's house. Walking nice and calmly, like it was just an early morning stroll, but with weird little looks to check there was nobody around.

Instinctively, Finn moved to conceal herself behind a tree and kept watching.

She saw a hand come out of a pocket carrying what was quite clearly a gun – *WTF?* – then clamped her hand across her mouth to stifle a shout when the figure stepped calmly up to Miller's front door, pointed the gun and blew the lock off. There was no sound, but it was obvious enough; there was a ... *recoil* or whatever it was called. Finn watched, shaking her head when a foot was casually lifted to push the door open before the figure disappeared inside.

WTAF ...?

She stepped from behind the tree, fighting to catch her breath, then pulled out her phone to dial 999, taking three goes to punch in the numbers correctly because her hand was shaking so much.

She blurted out the address, said there was a gun, told them to come.

Finn had spent most of her life ignoring stuff. She'd ignored her mother when Alex had said that living with one addict had been bad enough and there was no way she was living with another. She'd ignored Miller and the advice he'd given her more times than she could remember. Now she ignored the voice in her head telling her very clearly that she was being phenomenally stupid as she began walking back towards the house.

FIFTY-EIGHT

The silenced pistol sweeping the space ahead of them, the killer-for-hire – whose name was only the latest in a long line of aliases – moved swiftly through the downstairs rooms of Miller's house. They pointed the gun into the small toilet by the front door, before walking through the living room (pausing momentarily to shudder after spotting the rats) and checking the kitchen.

Empty.

It was mildly annoying, because getting in and out quickly was always best, but not the end of the world.

Because hunting would be fun.

Back in the living room, the gun was laid down and the cap and the overcoat quickly removed. The coat was good for masking appearance, but might inhibit movement if there was a need to move or get a shot off quickly. Picking up the gun again, the uninvited visitor noticed a familiar mobile sitting there on the table. The policeman was obviously still in the

343

house somewhere – the kitchen still smelled of fried food, the girl had left alone and the moped was parked outside – and it was a delightful irony that, wherever Miller was hiding, he did not have his phone with him.

That phone would be the undoing of him, after all.

The sudden noise from directly above made the target's whereabouts very obvious. The muffled cursing and the clattering. It was looking like the job would be relatively quick, which was actually a shame, because anyone who chose to keep . . . *vermin* in their house deserved to suffer at least a little. On cue, one of the rats squeaked indignantly and the decision was made that, once Miller was out of the way, his pets would be dealt with, too.

The killer crept to the foot of the stairs, listened for a few more seconds, then began to climb.

Miller winced a little as he dropped down, knackered and breathless behind his makeshift barricade. He'd done himself a minor mischief dragging the chest of drawers across the bedroom, but it was a small price to pay. A mischief of any sort was preferable to what would almost certainly happen if he found himself staring down the barrel of what ballistics had identified as a suppressed Ruger Mark IV Hunter (presuming the killer was carrying the same weapon used to kill Barry Shepherd and Adrian Cutler).

Did hired assassins have a favourite gun?

Was this one superstitious about those things?

Maybe they had a lucky pair of killing socks . . .

Miller reminded himself that he had rather more important things to think about.

He looked up at the ad hoc fortifications he'd assembled and stacked up against the bedroom door, wondering if it would do the trick. The chest of drawers, an old armchair, the pine box that Alex had kept shoes in and two unsteady-looking bedside tables. He seriously doubted that the wicker litter basket perched precariously at the top of the pile would make much difference one way or another, but to be fair, he *had* been in a hurry and hadn't been thinking very clearly.

Would it be enough to keep a smart and ruthless killer at bay? He thought there was a fair chance because, as he remembered—

Miller heard a creak on the stair and knew he was about to find out.

A few seconds later there were two gentle taps on the door. The metal of a silencer against the wood. Then a voice he'd last heard on a phone recording the night before.

'Knock, knock . . .'

Miller remembered a conversation he'd had with Xiu, five days earlier at the Majestic Ballroom.

I just want to open the door . . .

He could only hope Posh Gravy was on her way, though he couldn't even be sure she'd received his message.

'Who's there?' Miller asked.

The killer sighed and leaned close. 'Unfortunately, this is not a joke.'

'Oh, that's a shame,' Miller said.

Sofia Hadzic stepped back, raised the gun and fired through the door.

Inside the bedroom, Miller flinched at the *pffft* of the silenced shot and the far from silent smashing of the full-length mirror on the wall opposite the door. He sank as low as he could to the floor, instinctively folded his arms across his head and tried to keep the terror from his voice.

'OK ... so you won't be surprised to hear that I have questions.'

'Of course you do.' Sofia sounded perfectly reasonable, pleased even; right before she fired through the bedroom door again.

Miller gasped as the bullet flew over his head. When he'd started breathing again, he looked up to see that the panel in the door was already starting to splinter. 'I mean, you're obviously here because somehow you saw that text I sent this morning. Come on, I've *got* to ask ...'

'It's not complicated,' Sofia said. 'When you interviewed me in the manager's office, you went out of the room for a few minutes and left your phone behind. The same phone which is sitting on the table downstairs, which is how I know you're not cowering in there calling for back-up.'

'Oh, I'm definitely cowering,' Miller said.

'Good.'

'But how do you know I haven't *already* called for back-up.'

'Well, let's listen, shall we?' Sofia waited. 'No, I don't hear any sirens.'

Sofia believing that he hadn't sent for help was the best weapon Miller had. The only weapon. Now it was just a question of keeping her there – on the other side of that door – until that help arrived. 'So ... what about my phone?'

'When you left it, it was easy enough for me to get your email address and then I just sent you a spam email with a keystroke logger attached. You were foolish enough to open it.'

'OK, now I feel like an idiot,' Miller said. 'Because I was

warned about that. But when you saw the text, how come you weren't in Venezuela or something? A fancy contract killer like you, I would have thought you'd be miles away by now.'

'Normally, I would be,' Sofia said. 'But another job came in which is not too far from here. Pontefract?'

'Very nice,' Miller said. 'You should visit the castle if you've got time.'

'So, lucky for me. Not so lucky for the businessman I will be shooting later today in Pontefract, and *definitely* not lucky for you.'

'No, I get that—'

Sofia fired again, leaving a bullet hole next to the bedroom window and, rather more worryingly, another large crack in the door. Miller could see that his barricade – even taking the wicker basket into account – was going to be worthless if she fired enough shots to create a hole in the door big enough to lean through. Could a Ruger Mark IV Hunter *do* that? How many more shots would it take? That ballistics seminar was another one Miller wished he'd paid a bit more attention to.

'I'm serious about that castle,' he said. 'It's where Richard II died apparently. Oh, and in case you're interested, during the English Civil War, it was the site of some really famous sieges. Ironically . . .'

FIFTY-NINE

The voice in Finn's head was far louder and getting distinctly sweary as she poked her head around the front door.

What the f**k is wrong with you? You saw the gun. Are you completely f***ing mental?

She eased the front door open as quietly as she could and crept into Miller's living room. The only signs of life were small and furry, peering up at her through the bars of their cage. She took out a phone and sent Miller a text.

where r u?

A second later she heard a *ding* and turned to see Miller's phone on the table. Maybe he had seen whoever was coming and legged it through the back door before the front door was blown open. If so, then the intruder had almost certainly followed him. She walked into the kitchen, only to discover that the back door was locked.

Miller and the gunman were both still in the house.

Now the voice in her head was really giving her a talking to, screaming and dropping more F-bombs than a Tarantino movie, but Finn took a breath and shouted over it.

'Miller ... !'

Sofia had heard the message alert from the phone downstairs and stepped away from the bedroom door. She was standing at the top of the stairs, her finger still caressing the trigger of her gun, when she heard the girl shout from below.

She had trained herself to remain calm when situations altered, when a change of plan was called for. Hadn't that been exactly what had happened at that hotel almost a week before? Sometimes, you just had to adapt and think on your feet. If anything, at moments such as these she became even more relaxed. It was like a Zen mind control thing, or maybe she was just a stone-cold psychopath; she wasn't much bothered either way.

Clearly though, *someone* in the house was getting a little jumpy, because suddenly there was an awful lot of noise from the other side of that bedroom door.

Sofia moved back to the door and leaned close to it

'Don't go away. I won't be a minute ...'

Miller had heard Finn calling his name and the jolt of panic and horror had pulled him instantly to his feet. He was dizzy with adrenalin. Suddenly he was no longer concerned about the bullets that might be coming through the door and all that mattered was clearing away the barricade so that he could reach Finn as quickly as possible.

Now, he needed to get out.

Sweating and shouting with the effort, he threw that stupid litter bin across the room, pushed the bedside tables aside and lifted away the pine box.

Why the hell had she come back?

Why had they had that stupid argument?

He grabbed the edge of the chest of drawers and began to heave. He had certainly done himself some damage when he'd dragged it into position five minutes before, but the pain didn't matter. All that mattered was keeping Finn safe and now he could sense Alex just behind him, willing him on, and he knew how very much it mattered to her.

Miller heaved again, and yelled.

'Finn! Get out . . .'

Sofia moved slowly down the stairs, ignoring the thumps and the shouting behind her. She held the gun ahead of her, ready to use it at the slightest movement. She paused on the bottom stair, then stepped quickly out into the living room, two hands wrapped around the pistol.

There was no sign of the girl.

She moved into the kitchen, saw it was empty and checked the back door. It was still locked. She walked back through the living room then slowly across to the toilet by the front door.

The door was closed.

Was that the way she'd left it . . .?

'Wait . . .'

She heard the footsteps crashing down the stairs and turned to see Miller come charging into the room. He was panting and looking around the room desperately. The relief on his face was clear enough when he did not see the girl, but quickly changed when it dawned on him that the situation wasn't quite as rosy as it seemed. He raised his arms.

Then he shrugged.

'Go on then.'

Sofia trained the gun on him.

'The girl knows nothing,' Miller said. 'She's no threat to you, so you should really just shoot me and leave.'

'I shoot you, *then* I shoot the girl,' Sofia said. 'Or the girl then you, it doesn't matter. Then I shoot your stupid rats.'

Miller could see that she meant it and he knew that, if he did see Alex again, when the two of them were in the same boat deathwise, she would almost certainly tell him what an idiot he'd been.

There was nothing to do other than close his eyes and wait for the gunshot, but before he could do so he saw the door of the toilet swing open and watched as Finn crept out carrying the heavy porcelain cistern lid.

Dry-mouthed and desperate, he tried not to let Sofia know that he'd seen *anything*, but she caught the change of focus and the flare of panic in his eyes.

'Oh, right,' Sofia said, smiling. 'You want me to think there is somebody behind me, yes?'

'Believe me, I'd very much rather you didn't,' Miller said. 'But there is, and she's armed.'

He watched, horrified, as Sofia's smile slowly evaporated and she began to turn. Now he closed his eyes, which is why he didn't see Finn charging forward, swinging the cistern lid. He *did* hear the *clunk* when she smashed Sofia across the back of the head with it.

Miller opened his eyes just in time to see the hitwoman hit the floor, spark out.

The pair of them stared down at the body.

'Is she . . . ?'

Miller stepped forward, kicked away the gun and then, because he thought he'd better, he bent to check for a pulse. 'Sadly not.' He looked up to see Finn staring into space, wide-eyed, as though she couldn't quite believe what she'd done. He watched as she let the cistern lid slip from her grasp on to the carpet. He said, 'I hope you flushed.'

Before Finn could respond, the door was kicked open and a scrum of armed officers burst into the room, shouting and screaming like over-enthusiastic extras from *Line of Duty*.

'Armed police!'

'Down on the floor. Oh . . .'

As the weapons were lowered and confused looks exchanged, Xiu appeared behind them and pushed her way through. She quickly took in the scene, but was clearly every bit as bewildered.

Miller looked up at her and shook his head. 'Honestly, I've had pizzas get here quicker.'

SIXTY

'It was quite a bizarre conversation actually,' Miller said. 'Though I did feel like a bit of an idiot when it clicked. The whole "asking the wrong question" thing.'

'You weren't to know.' Xiu glanced down at the woman in the bed. 'He wasn't to know.'

Miller shrugged then stared, looking for any sign of a reaction. He pressed on. 'Anyway ... when I saw him in the hotel lobby I mentioned your name to Paul Mullinger ... remember him?' Miller waited a few seconds, but again there was nothing. 'And after he'd very helpfully given me the address of your flat—'

'Which we forensicated thoroughly,' Xiu said.

'Yes, thoroughly ... he told me that you'd left for good. I can't say I was very surprised, *obviously*, but *he* said – because he didn't know then *why* you'd scarpered – that he couldn't really blame you. Because of the trauma you'd been through. Because nobody expects to open a hotel room door and find a body, do they? I said, "Well, I suppose not … not even in a Travelodge." Then he said something like, "Certainly not on your second day" and *that's* when it clicked. That's when I remembered asking him on that first morning if any members of hotel staff had left unexpectedly. I mean … d'uh! What I should have asked him, of course, was if any members of staff had just *started*.' He leaned a little closer. 'Which you had, of course, because you're very clever.'

'Or think you are,' Xiu said.

Sofia Hadzic's eyes were closed, but Miller knew she could hear every word – that she was well aware he and Xiu were sitting at her bedside – because he'd seen her close them. He could see her eyeballs moving behind the lids and her fingers clutching at the edge of her blanket. The fingers on the hand that wasn't handcuffed to the bedframe.

To be fair, it was understandable that the woman might not be in the chattiest of moods. Her injury had not been life-threatening, but there was a neck-brace and a thick bandage around her skull. There were wires and tubes and assorted machines beeping every few seconds.

All the same, Miller had been hoping for a *bit* more back and forth.

'"I could see the blood where he'd been shot in the head".' Xiu inched her chair a little closer to the bed. 'That's what you told Detective Sergeant Miller when he first spoke to you in the manager's office.'

'You were *ever* so upset,' Miller said.

'He recorded your conversation,' Xiu said. 'Remember?'

Miller held up his phone and waggled it. 'Handy little trick, if you forget things. You should try it, Sofia, because you've obviously forgotten quite a few things.'

'Like what you could see when you opened that hotel room door.'

'So, you could see that Adrian Cutler had been shot, could you?'

Xiu nodded. 'That's what she said.'

'Well, that's more than I could, until they turned him over. Cutler was lying face down and he was shot from the front.' He leaned towards Sofia Hadzic and tapped his forehead. '*Here*, see? I actually checked all this out for myself with the help of a ... friend of mine. We staged a re-creation of the scene that I would say was ninety-nine point nine per cent accurate.'

Xiu looked at him across the bed, her face asking the question.

Miller looked back at her. 'I'm knocking point one of a per cent off due to the absence of penguins on my boxer shorts, but I really don't believe that made any material difference.' He turned back to Sofia. 'So, unless there's some X-ray vision thing you haven't mentioned, how did you know he'd been *shot* at all?'

'It's a mystery, don't you think?' Xiu asked.

After a few more beeps, some moaning and a slight shifting on the bed, Sofia slowly opened her eyes. 'No comment.'

Miller sighed. 'Oh, we're not doing *that*, are we?'

'This isn't even a formal interview,' Xiu said.

'Plus, we brought you some fruit!' Miller pointed to the bowl beside the bed. 'Detective Sergeant Xiu wanted to get grapes, but I told her they were boring, so we opted for something a bit more tropical instead.'

'You can stick your fruit,' Sofia hissed.

'Well, that's charming,' Miller said. 'You got any idea what a mango costs?'

The door opened and a nurse poked her head around the door. She tapped her watch. 'Time's up, I'm afraid. The patient needs to rest.'

'Oh, that's a shame,' Miller said. 'We were having such a great chat.'

Xiu stood up. 'Perhaps you'll feel more like talking when you're feeling a bit better.'

'Absolutely.' Miller stood up too. He moved to the end of the bed and reached down to give Sofia's foot, or what he estimated to be her foot, a squeeze through the blankets. 'You look after yourself.'

Sofia glared up at him, steaming.

'No, I mean it, because the sooner you're on the mend, the sooner we can get the whole silly interview/charge/trial/prison business out of the way, and then you'll never have to see me again. I mean, it's not like I'll be visiting, is it?'

Sofia tried to raise her head and spit, but the neck-brace meant it ended up dribbling down her chin.

'I need you to leave now,' the nurse said.

Miller turned to look at her. 'You're quite ... fierce, aren't you?'

'I haven't even started,' she said.

Miller and Xiu walked towards the door. 'You will look after her, won't you?'

'Of course, if we're given the chance.'

Miller turned to give Sofia Hadzic a final wave, then nodded to the woman who was still waiting impatiently for them to leave. 'Carry on, nurse.' The nurse sighed, long-suffering, then moved to close the door, but Miller nipped back in and hurried across the room. 'Sorry, I forgot my fruit.'

356

SIXTY-ONE

'Concussion can be a nasty business . . .'

Miller knew that the Force doctor was right. He'd once seen Ransford and Nathan clash heads during an over-exuberant group routine, after which the older man had not been himself for several days. He doubted that the possibility of Sofia Hadzic's being unable to carry off a decent cha-cha-cha would be a major legal issue, but Miller well understood that a decent defence brief might call into question any statement given in evidence, if proper recovery time was not allowed.

'If she claims later on that she'd felt a bit dizzy or confused in the interview room,' the doctor had said, 'the whole case could get thrown out. Ridiculous, but what are you going to do?'

The bottom line was that Miller would not be able to further question the woman who'd tried to kill him for another fortnight. Two weeks during which he found himself extremely busy, not least because Blackpool's criminal fraternity was working overtime.

A cousin of Wayne Cutler was found washed up near the pier, with injuries unlikely to have been caused by a fish, unless that fish had been armed with a lump-hammer. Three days later, a senior member of Ralph Massey's staff at the Majestic Ballroom was trampled to death after a hoax bomb threat had started a stampede of mashed-up ravers. Perhaps most challenging of all was an incident during which an intoxicated holidaymaker from Chorley, who'd got lippy with a bingo caller, was almost beaten to death with a giant stick of rock.

Miller triumphantly announced that it had been an 'accident waiting to happen'.

Murders, attempted murders, assaults ... marking out the days.

Miller and Xiu worked the majority of cases together. Miller was happy with the arrangement and his suspicion that Sullivan wasn't thrilled about it made him even happier. Though Xiu would never be one to 'bring the bantz', her tolerance for Miller's jokes had seemingly reached a level where she didn't simply stare at him quite so often. For his part, Miller became a far better judge of when was and when was definitely *not* the right time to tell his partner what was on his mind. He grew to respect and even to be afraid of that slight twitch around Xiu's eye. He learned when it was time to shut the hell up and back off.

Though it nearly killed him, Miller didn't mention the heavy metal/sex thing again for almost thirty-six hours, before frustration got the better of him and he asked her innocently if men who were into AC/DC could do it 'all night long'. He was inordinately pleased with himself, but equally relieved that he did not elicit a twitch.

There were also several funerals to attend.

358

Barry Shepherd's was a quiet affair; a small church and a couple of dozen mourners. Miller had talked to Barry's parents and brother, then been studiously ignored by Ravi Varma who was the only representative of Tech That! The Cutler funeral was predictably a little more lavish, with plumed horses, top-hatted undertakers and Adrian's name spelled out in flowers. Miller did not get the chance to speak to Michelle, who was ushered from place to place by a phalanx of protective family members, but they exchanged nods outside the church. He thought she looked a little less fearful than she'd seemed that night at his house. He hoped she found the strength to get as far away from them all as possible.

Chesshead's send-off was basically a massive piss-up. Miller thought that the chess set on the coffin was a nice touch, but from that point on it was just an excuse for every housebreaker, car thief, forger and extortionist within a ten-mile radius to descend on a local pub and do their utmost to drink it dry. Which they did. There were a good few fancy watches on display (even if most of them were fake) and more ankle-tags than you could shake a blunt instrument at. Ralph Massey brought Coco Popz out of retirement for the occasion and, though Miller didn't hang around, he heard afterwards that Wayne Cutler was seen tearfully joining in with Miss Popz's moving rendition of 'Wind Beneath My Wings'.

Taking advantage of a brief but convenient lull between stab-bings, Miller seized the opportunity to go up to Manchester and visit his mother. She spent most of the time ignoring him and the rest of it believing him to be someone called Colin.

Miller had had better days.

His father – who was certainly *not* called Colin – predictably failed to get in touch, though Miller was able to stay abreast of his whereabouts via the Computer Aided Dispatch system. It was quite handy, really. His old man had been done for disorderly conduct in Warrington, nicked in Glossop for driving without due care and attention, and was currently on bail having been arrested in Huddersfield for stealing a car and *then* driving without due care and attention.

The days went by.

And Miller danced . . .

He waltzed with Gloria. He got through a somewhat unorthodox bolero alongside Howard and even managed to get back on the horse that Mary was always banging on about by nailing a paso doble. He loved every minute of it. The rest of the crew were ticking along, even if some ticked a little more sporadically than others. Ransford took a week off for a cataract operation and Mary's angina inhibited some of her bolder moves, though it didn't keep her away from the pub. The younger members of the team were in fine fettle though and Nathan had even modified his preposterous stance on the Beatles a little ('I don't mind that one about the submarine'). Miller was not surprised to see that Nathan still fancied his chances with Ruth and, while taking care not to encourage the lad, he didn't quite have the heart to tell him she was seeing a carpet-fitter from Lytham St Annes.

Miller was well aware that, at home alone, he still spent more time than was good for him on Alex's phone or staring at the number 37 scrawled on a tatty bit of cardboard. When he wasn't doing that, and if Fred and Ginger didn't need attending to, he studied the photos Chesshead had sent. By now, Forgeham and her team knew for certain that the weapon used to kill Alex had also been used on Chesshead, but even though they were now hunting the individual responsible for *two* murders, they didn't seem to be in any more of a hurry than before. Miller reckoned he'd made a good decision in keeping the photographs to himself.

He still asked Alex questions about them, of course, even if he knew she was no more likely to answer him than the idiots he continued to shout at on the radio. The two of them discussed everything. Cases old and new, rodent welfare, Miller's habit of dragging his right foot a little too much during the *legato* sections of his tango.

Picky. She was always so bloody picky.

Finally, sixteen days after having been brained by a blunt if somewhat unorthodox instrument (courtesy of Armitage Shanks), Sofia Hadzic was pronounced fit for interview. However dizzy she might later try and claim to be, Miller was raring to go. There were still several questions he knew he could get answers to.

SIXTY-TWO

'Now this *is* a formal interview,' Xiu said.

Miller guessed Sofia Hadzic had worked that much out already. That the reading to her of her rights, the presence of recording equipment, the duty solicitor next to her and the fact that they were sitting in an *interview* room had provided all the clues she needed. He could only presume that Xiu had said it simply because she felt like needling their suspect a little, which pleased him enormously.

He was all for a spot of needling.

Xiu withdrew two sheets of paper from her file and passed them across the table; one for Sofia and one for the solicitor. 'Could you look at this please?' she said. 'It's a DNA profile based on samples taken from your flat. It matches an existing profile on the DNA database of the European Crime Agency. How do you explain that?'

Sofia looked at her solicitor, who nodded. 'No comment.'

'Specifically, DNA associated with a murder last year

in Poland and two murders the year before in Germany and Croatia.'

'No comment.'

Xiu looked down at her notes. 'Oh ... and *another* couple the year before *that*, in Spain. Sorry ... don't know how I forgot those. That was actually two in the same week, which is very impressive.'

'Do you do discounts?' Miller asked. 'Sort of a two-for-one thing?'

There was another glance at the solicitor.

'No comm—'

'It's money for jam basically, isn't it?' Now, Miller was staring at the solicitor, a ruddy old soak named Escott. 'You roll up, cast a weary eye over the evidence, tell your client to say nothing, then just sit there looking smug while you're thinking about when the pubs open. Job done. What are you on ... two hundred quid an hour?'

Escott sat up straight and opened his mouth, but Miller turned back to Sofia. 'Did you get a chance to do any sightseeing while you were there?'

Sofia said nothing.

'Spain, I mean. I've always fancied going to Barcelona.'

'Me too,' Xiu said. 'All that amazing Gaudi stuff.'

Miller looked at her. 'You mean the cheese?'

'That's Gouda, which is Dutch. Gaudi's Spanish.'

'Is it like Manchego?'

Escott looked ready to interrupt, most probably to enquire as to the relevance of cheese to the crime for which his client had been arrested, but Miller and Xiu were not about to let him.

'He was an architect,' Xiu said.

'Oh, right.'

'There's loads of his buildings in Barcelona.'

'You live and learn.' Miller and Xiu were now talking to each other as though Sofia wasn't even there. 'Now, here's the thing I don't get. Even though she's . . . how can I put this? . . . at the *cheaper* end of the market, she's obviously good at what she does.'

'Better than good, I'd say.'

Miller pointed to Xiu's notes. 'I mean, just look at that CV. She's highly efficient, she can do all sorts of fancy technical surveillance, she's clearly been super-inventive with her various "jobs" and disguises and she's always nice and neat—'

'Oh, no question,' Xiu said.

'Until *now*.' Miller shook his head. 'Until that unholy cock-up at the Sands Hotel.'

'Yeah, that was messy.'

'*Messy*. That's exactly what it was.'

Sofia was getting fidgety, breathing a little more heavily.

'You think she just got careless?' Miller asked. 'Took her eye off the ball or whatever?'

'It happens,' Xiu said.

'Happens to the best of us.'

Sofia grunted and grabbed the edge of the table. Suddenly, she was looking every bit as irritated as Miller and Xiu wanted her to be.

'Or maybe she's just lost her mojo, you know?' Xiu nodded. 'That can happen, too.'

'Well, of course it can,' Miller said. 'One day you're all fired up, swanning round Europe with your guidebook in your backpack and a gun in your bum-bag, then suddenly, for no good reason, you're not . . . feeling it any more. You turn up, ready to do the business, and the old magic just isn't there.

You go through the motions because you're a professional, but now you're sloppy and you end up making a mess of things, because—'

Sofia sat forward. '*He* was the one that made a mess of it. *Shepherd.*'

Miller and Xiu turned to look at her. Escott sighed and shook his head.

'I do the job I was paid to do and then he ruins everything. Makes things very difficult for me.'

'Oh, dear,' Miller said.

'He told me to call when the job was done, to let him know when Cutler was dead. He told me he'd be close by.'

Now Miller had a clearer picture of it. Barry Shepherd had been there because, for whatever reason, he'd wanted to be close to the action; on the spot when the man who was sleeping with his wife got what was coming to him. Miller imagined Sofia Hadzic coming out of Cutler's room that night after she'd shot him, calling the client to let him know that the job was done, then being horrified to hear his phone ringing in the very next room. Perhaps she'd simply knocked on the door and forced her way in or maybe Shepherd had opened it and stepped out into the corridor. Either way . . .

'I'm betting you didn't think he'd be *that* close,' Miller said.

'No, that was a . . . surprise.'

'So, you killed him because he could identify you?'

'It was his fault. He should not have been there.'

'I'll pass that on to his widow,' Miller said. 'I'm sure it will be a great comfort.'

Xiu was gathering her notes together and Escott was doing the same. His client's confession meant that the solicitor was going to be in the pub a little sooner than he expected. But Miller wasn't going anywhere just yet.

'Obviously there are days when I wish I'd stayed in bed,' he said. 'Spent the day messing about on my guitar instead, or playing with the rats.' He glanced at Xiu and Escott. 'I play the guitar and I have pet rats ... but most of the time I enjoy my job, so I'm always interested in whether other people feel the same about theirs.' He leaned across the table. 'What about you, Sofia ... ?'

She shrugged and sneered. 'It's about the money. It's *always* about the money. I don't think you get that.'

'Ah, right.' Miller sat back. 'Thank God you've cleared that up. I wouldn't have slept otherwise.'

'I don't kill anyone because I *enjoy* it.' She shook her head. 'That's stupid. Why does anyone work if not for the money? Money they can save.'

'It's a fair point,' Miller said. 'And I do admire the long-term financial planning, even if your nest egg won't be a fat lot of use where you're going.'

'You still don't understand.' Sofia lowered her head and shook it slowly. 'I need every single penny. Why do you think I empty their wallets? Every penny! I save because I have to, so I can send money back to my family in Serbia. What is *left* of my family ...'

Miller waited. The young woman swallowed hard and grimaced with a pain that did not seem physical.

'These things I've done, these killings, they are like *horrors* for you ... but it's different when you have seen your mother and father shot dead in front of you. When you were made to clean up the blood and then dig their graves.' Her face was a grim mask, as the terrible memories resurfaced. 'When you were made to do ... all sorts of things.'

Miller was transfixed.

'I grew up with death, like you grow up with toys and teddy bears and jigsaw puzzles.' There were tears now, but she made no attempt to wipe them away. 'Death all around me and the fear of death every moment of every day, until you learn to do whatever it takes to stay alive. Whatever it takes, do you understand? I was one of the lucky ones . . .'

Xiu stared at Miller. She could see that he was hanging on every word.

'Seriously? You're *buying* that?'

Miller watched Sofia wink, then start to smile. 'No.' He cleared his throat and looked at Xiu as though she was mad. 'Obviously not . . .'

For the recording, Xiu announced that the interview was terminated, before she and Miller got to their feet. The solicitor was muttering something about cheese as he reached for his coat.

Miller stopped at the door. 'Well, thanks,' he announced. 'It's been a hoot.' He looked across at Sofia Hadzic. 'Oh . . . and on behalf of myself and the team, and most especially the widows of Adrian Cutler and Barry Shepherd, I'd just like to say . . . may the cat cat you and the devil eat the cat.'

As they walked back into the incident room, they clocked Tim Sullivan talking to Akers. They had both been watching the interview via camera, and while Akers and the rest of the team beamed and applauded, Sullivan threw them a small nod as though to congratulate them on a job well done.

A job done, at any rate.

'I've been meaning to tell you.' Xiu looked a little nervous. 'For a while actually . . .'

'Oh yes?'

'Back when we were first teamed up. Sullivan was using me as a kind of . . . informant. Wanting me to report back to him, you know?'

'Really?' Miller sighed, sadly. 'That is peak wankspangle.'

'He specifically asked me to keep an eye on you.'

Miller chose not to let Xiu know he'd been well aware of Sullivan's sneaky surveillance job since day one. That it would be a way for Miller to find out one way or another what his new partner was made of. 'So, how's that been working out?'

'What can I tell you?' Xiu said. 'My eyesight's not very good.'

THE FINAL STEP

FALLAWAY

SIXTY-THREE

While Fred and Ginger skittered and squeaked and tossed hay around like furry little maniacs, Miller sat noodling on his guitar, picking out some tune he couldn't remember the name of. It was laid-back and lilting and it suited his mood.

It had been a good day.

He thought about the look of pride and pleasure on Xiu's face when she had formally charged Sofia Hadzic. The go-ahead from the Crown Prosecution Service had come almost immediately and Miller had invited Xiu to do the honours.

'Why me?' They were approaching the desk sergeant.

'Why not?'

'Don't *you* want to . . . ?'

'No, you should do it.' Miller hung back. 'You've had a lot to put up with these last few weeks.'

Xiu stared at him, then got it. 'Oh, you mean *you*.' She stepped forward and raised the charge sheet. 'Right . . . yeah, I'm not going to argue.'

He remembered how thrilled Howard had sounded when Miller had called to tell him it was done and dusted. Yes, the pride in *his* voice, too; the sort of pride a father might feel, if they weren't mooching around looking for someone to take advantage of or banged up somewhere. Howard said he couldn't wait to tell Mary and the rest of the gang and promised a big celebration in the Bull after the next practice session.

'I might even swing for an extra bag of pork scratchings,' he said.

Miller played on and thought about Alex. She hadn't shown up for a day or two, but something about the music he was playing – was it a tune she'd used to hum? – prompted a deluge of memories and images. Happy moments and daft ones ...

Alex with a glass of wine in her hand and a rat perched on her head.

Alex working wonders with a monkey-wrench, her face streaked with motor oil as she tried to fix Miller's moped.

Alex trying on that dress her sister had made, twirling in front of the mirror.

Miller looked up and his gaze settled on the envelope that contained the photographs he'd been sent. He stopped playing. Suddenly, there were very different pictures in his head.

Less pleasant memories.

Ralph Massey whistling that tune and Wayne Cutler telling him he was the *perfect man for the job* and the colour of Alex's face when that sheet was peeled back ...

... and before Miller knew what he was doing, he was asking Alexa to play 'My Generation' by the Who and he was on his feet and throwing himself around the living room like Pete Townshend. He pulled off his guitar and began smashing it viciously against the floor, the wall, the furniture. By the time the song had finished, he was wide-eyed and panting like a knackered dog, holding half the neck of his guitar with what little there was left of its body attached by two strings.

He looked up to see Alex in the kitchen doorway.

'You twat,' she said.

Miller stared down at the rather extensive damage and could see little point in arguing. There were pieces of his shattered guitar all over the place, dozens of them. The pickguard was over by the curtains, half the saddle was just visible under the sofa and he counted five bridge pins dotted around the carpet.

Alex was wearing a look of disapproval he knew all too well.

Miller plucked the remaining bridge pin from his hair and tried to summon all the dignity he could muster.

'I can *fix* it,' he said.

The following morning, Miller emerged from the music shop with a brand new guitar in a bag slung over his shoulder and spotted Finn begging on the other side of the road. She was sitting outside a branch of Greggs, though Miller reckoned there were so many branches in town it was almost impossible not to be.

He crossed over.

'Hey, Finn ...'

'Hey, Miller ...'

It didn't look like she was having much success and there were barely enough coins in her scruffy hat to buy a steak bake. Or even any proper food. Miller squatted down next to her.

'I was wondering how you were doing. After ... you know.'

Finn lowered her head and shook it slowly. 'Not great, if I'm honest. I've been having a few nightmares.' A passer-by stopped to chuck a coin into Finn's hat. She mumbled a thank-you without looking up.

'I'm really sorry you had to go through that,' Miller said. 'I can find someone to talk to if you like.'

Finn raised her head and looked at him. 'You do know I'm talking about you in those boxer shorts?'

'Oh, right. Fair enough.'

Finn fiddled with her backpack. 'By the way, I reckon you probably still owe me a couple of quid. Bearing in mind that I, you know . . . *saved your life.*'

Miller pretended to think about it, then reached for his wallet. 'Yeah, I suppose that's got to be worth a tenner.'

'Come on, Miller, you're worth a bit more than that.'

'I'm deeply touched, but let's not forget what it's going to cost me to replace the lid of that cistern. You actually managed to crack it.'

Finn shrugged. 'Call it twenty, then.'

Miller pulled out a banknote and was about to hand it over when he remembered what was strapped across his back. 'Wouldn't it be more fun if we *earned* it . . . ?'

Finn looked at him . . .

It was a thoughtfully curated selection of songs, which managed to draw a small crowd. Well, a handful; the majority clutching freshly purchased sausage rolls. Miller more than did justice to 'Watching the Detectives' and 'I Fought the Law' and chucked in a passable rendering of 'The Laughing Policeman' because he was in such a good mood. The set was rounded off in fine style with a jaunty version of 'Police and Thieves' which saw Finn joining in on backing vocals and even prompted a couple of drunks to dance, if the definition of that word was expanded to include jigging about a bit before falling into a bush.

'Elvis has left the building!' Miller shouted, when they were done.

To a smattering of applause, Miller shoved his guitar back into its bag, waving away the demands for an encore from one of the men in the bush. Finn happily counted up the donations and announced that they could consider themselves square.

Until the next time Miller wanted information.

Miller pointed out that he didn't only call her when he wanted something and asked her to think again about his offer of temporary accommodation.

'You know, if it really starts to get nippy outdoors—'

He reached into a pocket when his phone began to ring and instantly forgot whatever else he was about to say when he saw the caller ID. Finn was saying something as she gathered up her things, but Miller wasn't listening. He couldn't hear anyway, over the rushing noise in his ears and the screaming in his head.

The call was coming from Alex's phone.

SIXTY-FOUR

Miller had not been surprised when the caller had hung up as soon as the call had been answered and he wasn't surprised when he opened his front door and saw what had been done to the place.

Chairs turned over, stuff tossed around. A mess.

Miller hurried straight to the cage to check that Fred and Ginger had not been harmed. He reached inside, moved straw out of the way and was relieved to see them huddled together, looking back at him. They'd been frightened by the noise, but were otherwise all right.

'It's OK,' he said. 'It's all fine ...'

He'd known where Alex's phone was of course, so it had been obvious immediately where the call had been coming from. Miller had left Finn and rushed home, all too aware that he'd had ... visitors.

Now, he moved around the room, taking it all in.

He saw immediately that any straightening up would have to wait.

As far as he could tell, nothing significant had been taken. The envelope containing the photographs was still there and so was his laptop, though it wasn't where he'd left it. To Miller's trained eye, whoever had broken in had not been looking for anything. Stuff had been chucked about to make a point, that was all, to let him know they meant business, though the message wasn't quite as obvious as the one that had been left on the wall.

The number 37 had been spray-painted in huge characters. Miller guessed that they'd chosen the colour deliberately, so that the drips and spatters of red would look like blood. It was heavy-handed but effective, and the wonky red arrow that had been added underneath made it very clear what it was they wanted Miller to see next.

He sat down at the table.

His laptop had been opened, waiting for him. Miller nudged the trackpad to reveal the opening frame of a video, a *play* symbol pulsing in the middle of the screen.

On the other side of the room, the rats had ventured from their hiding place. They were probably just hungry. Ginger was on her hind legs, nosing at the bars of the cage.

Miller looked across. 'What do you reckon?' He was trying to sound casual, but there was a catch in his voice. 'Shall we . . . ?'

He clicked *play* and sat back to watch.

It lasted no more than fifteen seconds; a clip from something longer, Miller guessed, but it was enough. Alex and the man from the photographs. Whoever the man was, he'd done just as good a job at keeping his face out of shot and staying in the shadows as far as possible, but Miller was certain it was him. The film was a little shaky, but the action wasn't hard to follow.

The man handing Alex an envelope.

Alex looking inside.

Counting . . .

The moment it was finished, Miller watched the clip again. There was no way to identify the man in the footage, who once again appeared to know he was being filmed, but something about him rang the most distant of bells and not just because of the photographs. Miller leaned close to the screen, paused then played, paused then played. Perhaps it was just the . . . shape of the figure or the way he moved, but he suddenly seemed familiar.

Something . . .

Miller turned and noticed Alex. She was sitting on the floor, squeezed into a small gap between the wall and the edge of the sofa. She looked like she was hiding, same as the rats had done.

He said her name, nice and quietly, but she would not look up at him.

Miller turned back to watch the film again.

ACKNOWLEDGEMENTS

Changing direction can be a tricky business (check out Dolly Parton's thrash metal album) and when that means embarking on your first new series in more than twenty years and writing something very different in tone (see Marilyn Manson's folk musical about squirrels) the support of those you work with is going to be even more important than usual. I am enormously lucky. Not only have these individuals shown unfailing support for this foolhardy venture, but they've actually encouraged me.

I know, right?

So, I am even more grateful than usual to all sorts of people.

Thank you to George Faber, whose crazy idea got this ball rolling in the first place, and to George Ormond and Anna Price at The Forge for their help in bringing Miller to life.

Team Tom at Little, Brown has morphed brilliantly into the Miller Mob and thanks, as always, are due to: David Shelley, Charlie King, Catherine Burke, Robert Manser,

Callum Kenny, Tamsin Kitson, Jon Appleton, Tom Webster, Sean Garrehy, Hannah Methuen, Gemma Shelley and Sarah Shrubb.

Thank you to my brilliant and brave editor Ed Wood, to my tireless agent Sarah Lutyens and to my endlessly patient publicist Laura Sherlock, who not only tells me what I'm supposed to be doing and where, but makes sure I get there in time.

I'm once again grateful to Graham Bartlett (seriously, you just ring 999?), to Wendy Lee for plugging the holes and to Nancy Webber for another bacon-saving copy-edit.

The biggest thank you of all, goes – of course – to the readers who have supported me for twenty-odd years and who I hope will join the dance and embrace Declan Miller as warmly as they have Tom Thorne. Oh, and those who are wondering when they'll encounter Tom again need not worry. He's not gone far. In fact, he's just outside the door whistling country tunes already, and Declan Miller can't dance to them.

DS MILLER WILL BE BACK IN 2024 IN . . .

THE WRONG HANDS

Read on for an exclusive look at the first chapter

ONE

He was a stone cold mechanic out of Miami with a job to do. Just a regular killing. Just some punk who was going to get what was coming to him. It would be a snip.

'The train now standing at platform two is the 8.37 to York calling at Poulton-le-Fylde, Preston, Blackburn, Accrington . . .'

He downed two fingers of Beam and checked the Glock strapped beneath his left arm. The weight of it felt good. Like an old friend.

'. . . Burnley Manchester Road, Hebden Bridge, Mytholmroyd, Sowerby Bridge . . .'

He slapped a five on a ten for the bartender and slid off the barstool. It was time for work.

'Travellers are reminded that there is no buffet service available on this train. We apologise again—'

'Oi . . . Andy!'

'Oh . . . sorry, Keith, I was . . .'

'Yeah, miles away, course you were. Where the heck have

you been? I said half-eight under the clock. It's nearly twenty to!' Doody stared and shook his head. 'Bloody hell, what have you come as?'

Andy Bagnall self-consciously pulled his shirt down over his beer gut and adjusted his ponytail.

'We're supposed to be inconspicuous, you dozy twonk.'

'I am inconspicuous.'

'In a Hawaiian shirt? You look like you've puked up on it.'

'This is from Florida. My auntie got it for me when she went to Disney World last Christmas.'

Doody wasn't listening. He was staring across the busy station concourse towards the public toilets. Bagnall watched him and, for want of anything better to do, he stared as well.

Keith Doody thought this was probably his best plan ever. Businessmen carried all sorts of valuables in their brief-cases. Laptop computers, mobile phones, wallets, iFags. Businessmen had to pee. Businessmen had to pee with two hands. Nobody kept one hand on their briefcase and tried to wrestle out their old fella with the other. And no businessman wanted wee on the bottom of their briefcase, so they put it down a reasonable distance away from the urinal. Doody knew all this because he'd done the research.

Create a diversion. Away with the briefcase. Piece of piss.

'So, you know what you're doing, Andy?'

'When?'

'In the toilets, mate.' Doody tried to stay calm. 'In the bloody bogs.'

'Oh, yeah. I'm creating a diversion.'

Doody saw the worrying glint in Bagnall's eye and the flaw in his otherwise perfect plan became glaringly obvious.

'Now, when I say "diversion" I don't mean throw a bleedin'

fit or anything. When you see somebody put their bag down, just talk to them. Ask them to help you find a contact lens or summat.'

'I don't wear contact lenses, Keith.'

Doody sighed and rubbed his tired eyes.

'I could ask them to help me find me sunglasses.'

'It was just an example, Andy. Oh, and make sure it's a decent briefcase or summat like that. I'm not doing this for some poxy Adidas bag full of rancid football socks, OK? OK, Andy?'

'Yeah, got it. No socks . . .'

'Right, off you go. Just hang about and wash your hands or whatever. I'll be in in a bit.'

Bagnall ran his fingers through his bleached blond hair and strode off across the concourse, the heels of his cowboy boots clack-clacking on the polished stone. He stopped at the entrance to the toilets and after a moment turned back to look at Doody.

Doody held out his hands and mouthed at him.

'What?'

Bagnall mouthed back.

'Can you lend me 20p?'

Doody knew he was the brains of the outfit, but didn't that at least *imply* the other bloke was the muscle? The only muscle Andy Bagnall had was between his ears. He was pondlife and that was all there was to it. They'd do a few more stations after this and then Doody would tell Bagnall he was branching out on his own. OK, so they'd been mates at school, but playing footie and dicking around with Bunsen burners was one thing, when it came to basic thieving, Bagnall was a liability. If he hadn't actually got his head stuck in some stupid thriller and pretending he was American, he was staring off into space with a gormless expression like someone had sprinkled Mogadon on his cornflakes. Well, sod him, because Keith Doody was moving up. Bagnall could go back to cut-and-shutting Ford Sierras.

Doody ambled towards the toilets. It was time to go and see just how much of a balls-up Bagnall had made of his beautiful plan.

He'd spotted the mark straight away. It was all going down like the Man said. Time to make his play. He was cool, like always. Look nobody in the eye. Mr Invisible. After the hits went down, it was like he'd never been there. Ice cold and no bad dreams. Waste 'em, then go look for the nearest cold beer or hot woman.

Time to roll the dice.

Bagnall reached for his weapon . . .

Bloody Nora, thought Doody, he's talking to some bloke at the pisser.

Bagnall was indeed calmly urinating while chatting amiably to a tall, dark-haired man who was standing next to him, similarly engaged. Doody saw the abandoned briefcase and strolled towards it, taking in every detail in a matter of seconds.

Nice and chunky, good quality leather.

He began to pick up speed.

Combination locks, he'd have those off with a decent screwdriver.

As he picked up the case, Doody became aware that Bagnall's new chum was turning towards him. He started to run. As he vaulted the turnstile, the swinging briefcase laid out a middle-aged bloke blithely inserting his 20p on the way in. A hideous scream came from the toilets behind him and rang across the concourse as Doody sprinted away.

Its echo was hot on his heels as he legged it towards the exit and away into Blackpool town centre.

Detective Chief Inspector Bob Perks nursed half a shandy in the Station Hotel and sat wishing he was more interesting. He didn't want to be a cliché, like all those coppers on the telly, with broken marriages and drink problems, he just fancied . . . livening his lot up a little. He'd given quirks a go, but the truth was, he just wasn't cut out for them. He wasn't religious, he didn't have any strange hobbies (or normal ones, come to that) and with the exception of Michael Bublé (who he adored) he thought most music was rubbish.

He wasn't like . . . some coppers he could mention. Rats and ballroom dancing, for pity's sake.

Bob Perks's life was comfortable and ordered.

An unemployed good-for-nothing from Woodplumpton and an over-imaginative grease monkey from Mereside were about to change things.

When his mobile phone rang, Perks froze. He kept meaning to change the Bublé ringtone ('Everything' – his signature song), but could never bring himself to, because Bublé was the business. He shrugged at the pinched faces of the lunchtime regulars as if to say, I'm not an idiot, I'm a high-ranking police officer, so get over it.

'Sir?'

DS Dominic Baxter was trying to sound efficient, but Perks could hear laughter in the background.

'Better be good, Dom, I'm having my lunch.'

'There's been a robbery at the station, sir.'

'So? Let robbery handle it. We're watching Draper.'

'That's just it, sir. It was Draper that got robbed.'

Perks put down his drink 'I'm listening, DS Baxter ...'

'Well, Draper was talking to some bloke in the toilets.'

'Of course he was.'

'He puts the case down and a second bloke grabs it and legs it out the bogs. This other bloke hurdles over the turnstile, whacks somebody in the face with the briefcase while he's at it and ...' Baxter hesitated.

Perks took another sip of beer. At least things were livening up. 'Sounds like our luck's in, Dominic. Now we can have a look in the case without blowing the surveillance. Not that we don't have a pretty good idea what's in it.'

'We haven't got the case, sir. The bloke who nicked it got away.'

There was more laughter in the background. Perks hissed into the phone. 'What about Draper? Lost him as well?'

'No, sir, we know exactly where he is. Fact is he had a little accident ... zipped up in a bit of a hurry. He's in Victoria hospital.'

'Let me get this straight, Baxter. Draper is about to meet Wayne Cutler and hand over the briefcase. After a three-month operation, we're about to tie the Cutlers to Tony Panaides' murder and you watch some tuppeny ha'penny tealeaf waltz off with the evidence while Draper's eyeing up some bloke's todger?'

'That's about the size of it.'

'Are you trying to be funny, Baxter?'

'We didn't want to blow our cover, sir.'

Perks took a deep breath. He *seriously* needed that quirk. A decent amphetamine habit, say.

'This bloke that Draper was trying to pick up ... you *did* work out that he might have been in on the briefcase snatch?'

'We didn't actually work that out, no, sir.'

'Right.'

'He sort of melted away in the melee.'

'*Melee?*'

'It means a confused fight or a scuffle—'

'I know what it means, Baxter.'

'Yes, sir.'

'And Cutler never showed?'

'Oh yeah, he showed.'

'That's something. You get pictures?'

'Well, no. Actually it was him who got whacked in the face with the briefcase.'

Better make that a crack habit, Perks decided. A serious one.

'He's on his way to the Vic as well,' Baxter said. 'Concussion and a suspected broken collar bone.'

Perks recognised the laughter in the background now. DC Stuart Knight. He'd have the jumped-up little tit for breakfast. He stood and wedged the phone between ear and shoulder as he struggled to put on his coat.

'Nobody move. I'm coming in. And tell Knight to start ironing his uniform.'

'We've got Draper, sir!'

'Got him, *how* exactly?'

'I mean, we know where he is, at least.'

Perks was gobsmacked at the note of triumph in the DI's voice.

'And what do you propose to hold him on, Baxter? Indecent exposure?'

'It's a thought, sir.'

'He was in a public toilet, you idiot.'

Perks's growl rendered the entire saloon bar silent. He couldn't be arsed with more apologetic shrugging because he had work to do. He had to find the poor bugger who'd stolen that briefcase before Wayne Cutler did.

Within half an hour they were back at Doody's place. Bagnall sat slurping Fanta, as Doody set about the briefcase with a rusty screwdriver.

'I have to say, Andy, that was cracking. You did really well, mate.'

The Man wasn't telling him anything he didn't know. The Mechanic shrugged and took another hit of bourbon. He knew he was the best.

'Oh ... cheers, Keith. I didn't actually do anything, really. I was just a bit nervous, you know ... so I went for a wazz and this bloke just came up and started talking to me. He was dead friendly.'

Doody smirked at him. 'Probably your shirt, mate.'

Bagnall smiled. He'd known the shirt was a good idea. Then he got it. 'I don't think I like your intimations there, Keith—'

And the briefcase flew open.

He'd seen dough before. Lots of it. And it always looked great. It looked like freedom. It looked like—

'Jesus H Christ on a bike, Keith!'

There were rings; four *massive* signet rings. Two gold sovereigns, one that looked like it had a ruby set into it and one huge square one embossed with the letter A. But it wasn't so much the rings that caught Andy Bagnall's attention, as the fact that they were still in place on the waxy, swollen fingers of two neatly severed hands.

'I swore by Elvis and all the saints that this last teenage year of mine was going to be a real Rave... Yes, man, come whatever, this last year of the teenage dream I was out for......

FANTASY

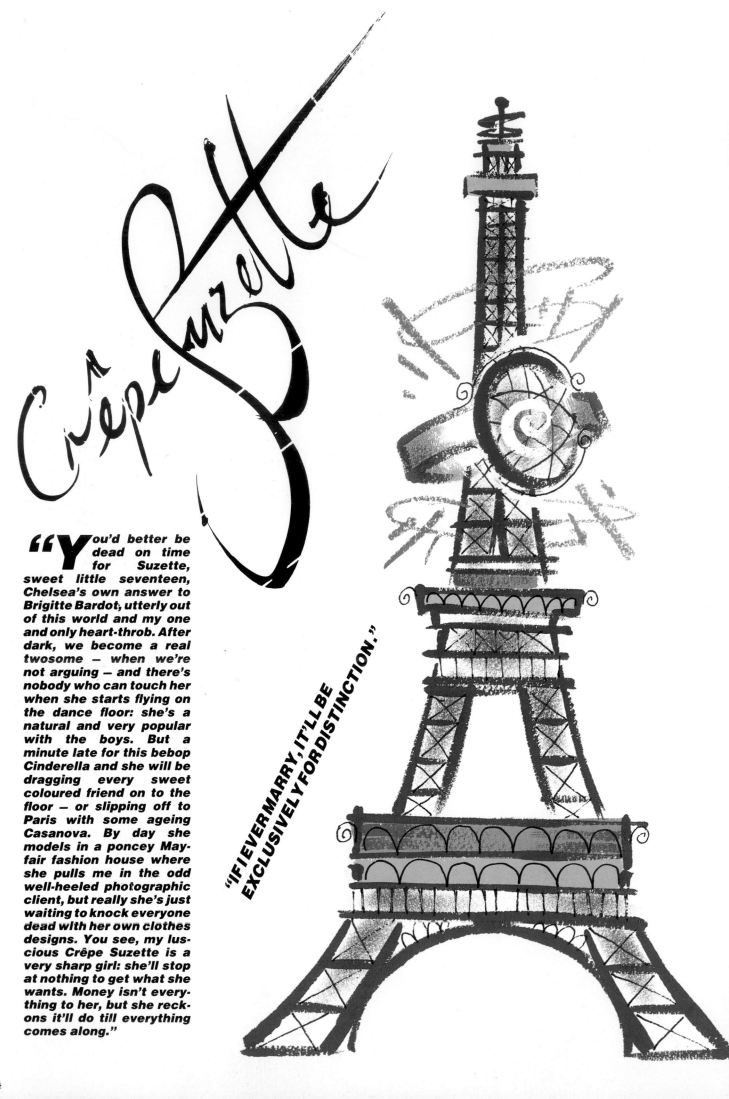

Crêpe Suzette

"You'd better be dead on time for Suzette, sweet little seventeen, Chelsea's own answer to Brigitte Bardot, utterly out of this world and my one and only heart-throb. After dark, we become a real twosome — when we're not arguing — and there's nobody who can touch her when she starts flying on the dance floor: she's a natural and very popular with the boys. But a minute late for this bebop Cinderella and she will be dragging every sweet coloured friend on to the floor — or slipping off to Paris with some ageing Casanova. By day she models in a poncey Mayfair fashion house where she pulls me in the odd well-heeled photographic client, but really she's just waiting to knock everyone dead with her own clothes designs. You see, my luscious Crêpe Suzette is a very sharp girl: she'll stop at nothing to get what she wants. Money isn't everything to her, but she reckons it'll do till everything comes along."

"IF I EVER MARRY, IT'LL BE EXCLUSIVELY FOR DISTINCTION."

4

...A pair of grey, pointed, mock-crocodile casuals hit the street: pink neon ankle crêpe, nylon-stretch socks, sky-blue glove-fit jeans, Roman-cut short-tail jacket, vertical-striped happy shirt, wrist identity jewel, lucky neck charm and a Rolleiflex camera permanently slung round his neck. This is Colin, eighteen years old and as sharp as the music.

Crêpe Suzette

"You'd better be dead on time for Suzette, sweet little seventeen, Chelsea's own answer to Brigitte Bardot, utterly out of this world and my one and only heart-throb. After dark, we become a real twosome — when we're not arguing — and there's nobody who can touch her when she starts flying on the dance floor: she's a natural and very popular with the boys. But a minute late for this bebop Cinderella and she will be dragging every sweet coloured friend on to the floor — or slipping off to Paris with some ageing Casanova. By day she models in a poncey Mayfair fashion house where she pulls me in the odd well-heeled photographic client, but really she's just waiting to knock everyone dead with her own clothes designs. You see, my luscious Crêpe Suzette is a very sharp girl: she'll stop at nothing to get what she wants. Money isn't everything to her, but she reckons it'll do till everything comes along."

"IF I EVER MARRY, IT'LL BE EXCLUSIVELY FOR DISTINCTION."

'I swore by Elvis and all the saints that this last teenage year of mine was going to be a real Rave... Yes, man, come whatever, this last year of the teenage dream I was out for.......

FANTASY'

...A pair of grey, pointed, mock-crocodile casuals hit the street: pink neon ankle crêpe, nylon-stretch socks, sky-blue glove-fit jeans, Roman-cut short-tail jacket, vertical-striped happy shirt, wrist identity jewel, lucky neck charm and a Rolleiflex camera permanently slung round his neck. This is Colin, eighteen years old and as sharp as the music.

THE NAKED

"I love this city – and I want the whole damn lot of it. From the south, where the Thames bends round Battersea's fairy lights, up to the northern slopes of Hampstead Heath, where on a clear day the whole glorious panorama of spires and skyscrapers offers itself like a feast; from the east, where Tower Bridge still stands like a couple of stiff-backed sentries at attention, all the way west to our ramshackle villas in sunny Notting Hill. At the heart of it all, the proverbial pulsating heart of the city, Soho's neon beats out a life into its veins, pumping it into a bebop hosannah that soars and swells over the rooftops until all its natives have to admit they want to join the party.

Don't get me wrong. I'm not including those dormitory suburbs where the carbon-copies-of-The-Times-and-a-furled-umbrella chaps go to recharge their batteries, or those garden gnomes gaze out over the new motorway routes. Nor all the unnecessary evils of those grandiose, stuck-up British institutions with their doormen and bank clerks who treat you like a moron because you're sporting pale-blue casuals instead of their serge and tweed uniforms. There's just a buzz to olde London town that makes

it somewhere I never want to leave, and that even goes for the oldsters as well. Think of all those toffee-nosed dowagers in minks outside Harrods when it's done up like a Christmas tree, the busbies and the beefeaters, the coppers and the cabbies in their black Hitchcock taxis, the waitresses in frilly white aprons serving afternoon tea at Joe Lyons, the porters in Covent Garden and the pickled preserves at Fortnum's, the buskers round the cinema queues, even the Yank tourists with their checked pants and cameras, and the millionaires in their Rollses on the way to penguin-suited dinners and soirées – they're all, although they may not know it, part of the feast.

You only have to wander down the Serpentine or look up at those gleaming white mansions like something from a Cary Grant picture, or get lost round the dinky mews with cobbled streets and window-boxes and vintage Bentleys to realise that London in this year-of-our-lord nineteen-hundred-and-fifty-eight has been truly blessed with the faculty to please someone who doesn't have to punch the clock at nine every morning to earn a crust.

And what the days have recently brought has been a

CITY

surprise: namely, sun, and more sun, and then some more. It's been a glorious heatwave lasting right through the days, turning some citizens into varieties of broiled lobster, radioactive, bright pink creatures who try and fend off the enemy with hankies on head and tweed garb, and transforming others into bronzed continentals who lie back and give the sun a come-hither look through squinted eyes. It's a thoroughly crazy and wholly welcome heat that makes the nights so warm you could swear blind you were swimming through the streets, all glistening with water.

It could be Cairo or Naples or New York for all I care. But of course, it isn't. It just happens to be the place where the Romans once were, and Queen Victoria ruled an empire, and where the empire has turned up on its doorstep another fifty years later to take a look for itself, and added a whole new reason to wake up of a morning and hear the quaint early morning overture of church bells and cars screeching round in search of a parking meter. Because in this topsy-turvy, phew-what-a-scorcher, thoroughly un-English summer, you know for sure that anything crazy could happen. In fact, it almost certainly will."

Checking his watch, Colin cuts through the teeming neon night on a wave of bebop adrenalin, his eyes scanning the human swarm, for scenes to snap. A BUSKER serenades a CINEMA QUEUE, HOOKERS cruise past in the opposite direction pulling TRICKS into waiting taxis. A CHINESE CHEF tries to entice a cat into his restaurant, a frying pan in his other hand. SPIVS, CARD SHARPS, TRAMPS sashay back and forth on the pavements trying to waylay PASSERS-BY. SHOWGIRLS walk past in G-strings and feathers and a BLIND MUSICIAN takes off his glasses and catcalls.

'The legend is that Soho is cosmopolitan, a centre of good eating, and London's "square mile of vice". The first it remains . . . it offers certainly greater variety of cuisine than any other locality. As for the "vice", it does remain an area of criminal congregation largely because it is central, informal, and houses a great variety of private clubs in which persons of various racial, sexual and professional peculiarities can conveniently foregather. I think Soho's most attractive feature, though, is none of these: it is that there, as is rare elsewhere in London, the denizens live in the streets, and do not merely use them — as is the custom elsewhere in English cities — as places to get from here to there, but never to linger in chatting, lazing, or doing some business or other.'

COLIN MACINNES — *London — city of any dream*, 1963

Soho's Neon Night

WIZARD

"Not-so-sweet-sixteen and London's number-one teenage hustler, the Wiz is a baby-faced shark whose Italian-style jacket is always stuffed with fivers and whose eyes beam out a come-and-kill-me look that frightens even his best friends. It's fine when he's on your side, but just watch out that you're not going to be on next week's hit list. Whenever you see him he's got some new kind of racket. Maybe it's the old staple of clawing the poor tax-payers on the raw and whizzing a few wallets from some mugs' pockets, avoiding attention with an immaculately tailored pair of arms, or maybe it's one of his more recent kiddo brainstorms like his Cut-Your-Own Disc booth into which all those brylcreemed tiny tots swim like so many minnows. As a pimp, of course, he's a natural talent, since it kills two birds with one stone — raking in bundles of loot and practising his hatred for the toupéed oldsters who slip up the stairway to secretly purchase that precious commodity, namely — youth."

"DON'T KNOCK IT, COLIN. MILK IT, SHAKE IT, RAKE IT, MAKE IT, TAKE IT FOR ALL IT'S GOT."

"The hippest black cat in town, Mr Cool is a local British product who survives on a strict diet of cool jazz. Moving against the flow of the crowd, he'll suddenly raise his trumpet to the stars and blow a string of heavenly notes from his horn. But quite how he keeps himself in Miles Davis LPs I don't know. On the quiet he rolls dice, but his Dad — a strictly conformist number — disapproves so much that even if he was to win, which he never does, the loot would turn out to be trouble at home as well as round the corner. So he's always skint, with just the bare essentials — his one black suit and no other furniture other than his hi-fi and hammock. There's only one time when you really notice the sadness and fierceness in his face — when he stares straight into your eyes and asks which side you'd be on if the trouble started."

"SOME ARE MORE FREE THAN OTHERS."

Mr. Cool

11

Big Jill xx

"With more curves than Jayne Mansfield, the strength of an orang-utang and a proverbial heart of gold, it's a miracle she can squeeze herself into that pink bubble car of hers. But the impossible is achieved twice daily when she rolls into Soho to describe the voluptuous charms of the Parisian dancers in her strip joint to the passing trade with a stream of come-and-get-it patter. In short, the biggest thing on Jill's mind is sex. A lovelorn lady killer, she can sit for hours swooning over some sexy chick singer, like Miss Athene Duncannon, and she keeps a string of idiotic les chicklets in tow wherever she goes. She's forever nosing in about my sex life like others would ask you about the weather, and always at the wrong moments. But though she won't let on, she's very wise for her years."

"I DON'T KNOW WHAT YOU SEE IN THAT CHICK. YOU'RE A ROMANTIC, KID. A SECOND-FEATURE ROMEO."

The Fabulous Hopfote

"MY GOD, WE'RE SO FREE. I'M SO FREE IT HURTS. WILL SOMEBODY FREE ME FROM THIS INTERMINABLE FREEDOM?"

"Don't scoff at the Fabulous Hoplite because he's a shameless glamour puss. He's very good-looking in a curious way and extremely waggish-tongued, but he is also a most sensitive and dignified character: a star in his own firmament, definitively his own irresistibly stylish creation. He can float serenely past jeering bouncers and dustmen, sporting his skin-tight, rubber-glove-thin, almost-transparent pastel cotton slacks, with a cravat and a powder-blue maternity jacket, fielding catcalls with royal disdain. Formerly in business with some of the capital's top poof raves, Hop is now hitched up to the Knightsbridge-Chelsea circuit as a contact man for gossip columnists, with whom, needless to say, he is very popular. It's not just that he's very friendly — I mean he really does like all these people he falls in love with."

S D eAn wiFt

↓

"DOESN'T THIS SCENE STINK!

BUTTERFLIES!
PUSH-CHAIR PRODUCTS!
MINDLESS INSECTS!
JUVENILES!
SINGERS?
DON'T MAKE ME LAUGH!"

"**T**his solemn modern jazz creation never takes off his shades. His eyes gaze out from behind them at the teenage fish-owl like those of a con-entration camp exter-minator, knifing through  his biggest hates: namely teenagers, coppers and trad jazz fascists who have yet to appreciate the gospel according to John Coltrane. You see, aided by several varieties of blue pills the Dean manages to live in a twenty-four-hour world, at least twenty-three of which are filled by cool modernist sounds. The spare moments in between were once spent reading Sartre's Nausea in the original, but that was before the Dean became a junkie. Now he is more interested in nicking a pack of syringes from the local chemist's than debating existentialism and he has distilled his philosophy down to just one logical proposition: ALL LIFE IS FOR KICKS. Nevertheless, the Dean still manages to sermonize to his Soho parishioners from the modernist pulpit."

THE MISERY KID

"THEY'RE PLAYING MY SONG . . . THE ONE I SOLD FOR A TENNER. IT'S ON THE HIT PARADE!"

"**E**nemy number one on the Dean's hit list — that's the Misery Kid, leader of the rival jazz faction. You know the type — a proud keeper of the trad flame, such as it is, since the day King Oliver kicked it, an authentic-bohemian-Soho-teen who earns a spare crust hawking a sandwich-board advertising the Macabre coffee bar round the Soho streets — all so he can concentrate on his call-ing in life as tireless organizer of the duffle-coat and open-toed sandal brigade, whipping them into wild enthusiasm for any jazz blown before the days of Charlie Parker. All he ever listens to is hot, rooting-tooting New Orleans sounds of the variety usually impersonated by groups of stripey-shirted and bowler-hatted suburban bank clerks on their days off. Of course, there are plenty of suckers for fol-lowers — all those Universities and Left-Review kids hiding behind their tastefully low-key tweeds and beards, and beatnik girls in sloppy sweaters slum-ming it before hightailing  back to college to read Politics, Polite Behaviour and the Post-Suez-crisis Situation. Well, in a way, I suppose, he is the real McCoy, a true bohemian; the eternal deadbeat."

NAPOLI

The first rays of sunlight filter through a gap between the crumbling buildings of Napoli, which is like a London Harlem. Crescents that were meant to twist elegantly now seem to lurch. Huge Victorian mansions too tall for their width, built with the spoils of Empire, are now cut up to house its refugees, rented out by every stinking square foot. Once shining white façades are peeling, unpainted and black. Broken milk bottles scatter the cracked streets like snow. Cars abandoned and stripped, stray sofas thrown from the sky, red curtains everywhere, you've only got to be there for a moment to know there's something RADICALLY WRONG.

"Welcome to my manor, a territory known on your maps as Notting Hill W10, or W11, but known to both its inmates and the readers of the *Police Gazette* as Napoli, Little Harlem, or even just 'Jungle W11'.

What a place! If you ever want to see the difference between the haves and the have-nots, then just step down to Napoli. Down to the south are those gleaming white mansions of w10, with their jewelled candelabra twinkling in the windows and the Bentleys and Bristols parked outside, all that'll-do-nicely-James, the upstairs-downstairs world of the Hooray Henries who occasionally lose their way, turn north and roar round our streets, racked with *nostalgie de la boue* and swilling champagne.

Those same tottering mansions slowly turn to grey and black as you cross the border and move north. The paint begins to peel, washing gets draped like coronation bunting over the graffitied walls, and instead of candelabra you get

one 40-watt bulb and some burnt-out wreck of a Ford Popular adorning the driveway. This is the home of all the Irish who couldn't afford Kilburn, the Spanish who hate Franco, the Italians who work in the West End *trattorias*, and the English who've been decanted from Bermondsey, Poplar, Shadwell and the docks. No upstairs-downstairs here: two families on each floor, six to a room, and three sleeping shifts a day. It's home to whoever's passing through, though judging by the notices that have started to pop up outside the net curtains, saying 'NO BLACKS', some are more welcome than others.

Now the best way to see this exotic home-sweet-and-sour-home is to stroll back after a Chez Nobody all-nighter in that pure dawn light when the sun is clambering over all those ramshackle towers and let that crazy Napoli symphony hit your ears. Forget the twittering birdsongs you might hear over in Kensington Park. I'm talking about the dice from the twenty-four-hour crap game click-clacking on the paving stones, the flies buzzing over the crammed dustbins, the blast of a favourite Puccini *aria* from Mario in his café, and the rhythmic percussion of the Spanish housewife over the road sweeping her step in a cool 4/4 beat. Yes, you can tell from the crunching milk-bottle glass beneath

your feet that Napoli has a sound all of its own.

By midday it's soaring into a real racket. Trader Horn, juggling his yams and sweet potatoes, leads the fruitsellers' cries against the wide-boys trading boxes of oranges fresh from the back of a lorry, while a few sharp-suited individuals with a dozen watches up each sleeve, mutter the virtues of their wares more quietly — and suddenly fall silent when one of the boys in blue rounds the corner.

By early afternoon the whores start waking up and parade down the streets with their pimps, turning the other cheek to the catcalls and whistles from upstairs windows and the disapproving looks from the local peasantry.

And yours truly, refreshed and bathed, begins to surface and prepare for the night to come, ready to take to the streets in the cool evening air. Maybe it's a night for the Santa Lucia, the local blues club where wild Afro-cubop or hi-life pumps out to the early hours of the morning, or maybe it's a balmy evening to be saved for a rickety old balcony with monster speakers blasting out some hot new Prince Buster platter. Sitting up there on the rooftops, the hubbub below drops to a murmur as the loping, shuffling rhythm and honking horns float out, as free and loose as could be, into the aether.''

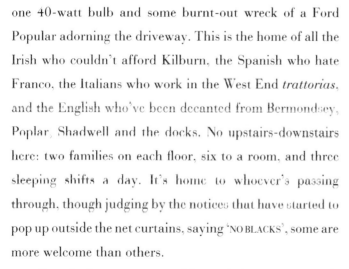

'The Sunday morning, four of the boys was looking for place. They walk all the way from Paddington station reading notice board, until they land up in the Grove. The boys was Fiji, Algernon, Winky and Buttards, and all of them come from Jamaica.

Winky take a second look at the notice.

"That don't look so bad," he say.

"It always have a catch when they say coloured people welcome," Fiji say.

Now, the latest rake when them English landlord and landlady want to sell house, is to get the tenants out, because the more empty room they have the more money they could ask for the place. And to get the tenants out, what some of them was doing was to let out rooms to spades, and when the white tenants see that they say: "Gracious me! I can't stay in this house any longer!" and they hustle to get another room while the landlord laughing. Next thing, he give the spades notice, and by the time he ready to sell house bam! the whole house empty.

In fact, this rake was so successful that if any landlord have undesirable white tenants, the best thing was to let out couple of rooms to coloured people, and one by one the Nordics would evacuate. They used to do that, especially in them houses what have tenants from long before the war, who paying ten-twelve shillings for two-three rooms, because these days, you only have to put a put-you-up and a table and two chairs in a room and hit somebody three-four guineas a week for it.'

SAMUEL SELVON — *Ways of Sunlight,* 1952

'It was impossible to believe you were in twentieth century England: terraced houses with shabby, crumbling stonework and the last traces of discoloured paint peeling from their doors, windows broken, garbage and dirt strewn all over the road, derelict cars . . . every second house deserted, with doors nailed up and rusty, corrugated iron across the window spaces, a legion of filthy white children swarming everywhere and people lying drunk across the pavement so that we had to walk around them.

We came to the house which was to be our home and the African owner led us up the decrepit stairway to a room practically filled with ugly furniture and the noise of trains passing on the adjacent railway tracks. The floor was covered with worn linoleum, the single gas ring for cooking was outside on the dismal landing, there was no bath in the house – and he wanted £2 15s a week. We were desperate and we moved straight in. By the time we'd installed a cot for the child and piled up our suitcases there was hardly room to turn around, but we were still better off than most others in the area.'

MICHAEL MALIK – *From Michael de Freitas to Michael X.*, 1968

'A district of horrid fascination . . . save for a few bourgeois enclaves a rotting slum of a sharp, horrible vivacity. It is the Christie country round Rillington Place – now renamed Rustin Close . . . the whole mess bisected into squalid segments by a railway running high above the slumscape like the old New York L, and by the dank, stagnant, boatless Grand Union Canal. This complex has a marked Anglo-Sicilian flavour. The citizens, among whom a criminal element is traditional, live on the streets, in a way rare even in prosperous working-class areas. Teds tailed by their mute birds, tough unforthcoming adults, gnarled, wry old people, and infant Arabs and Lolitas, all create a hard, animated Northern Casbah. This is a place the Welfare State and the Property-owning Democracy equally passed by.'

COLIN MACINNES – *The Observer*, 1962

If you're looking for action well after dark
And you're tired of the Wild West End,
Why not check out the wrong side of the park
For a groove I can recommend?

If you're looking for a mix of black and white,
If you're looking for smoke or jazz –
Or just the glow of a warm red light –
You'll find people that hasn't and has.

Napoli, Napoli, not the one in Italy –
We live happily in Napoli beside the Wormwood Scrubs.
Napoli, Napoli, in London it's gotta be,
Napoli, Napoli, non-stop hubbub . . . .

Julien Temple

SOMETHING'S ILL – IN NOTTING HILL

A coloured man was brutally beaten up by racialists and today lies in a West London hospital, the *West Indian Gazette* reported yesterday. His attackers have not yet been apprehended.

The same issue of the *Gazette* contained a report on the appointment of the first West Indian shop assistant in the Notting Hill area. A spokesman for the employment agency said, 'Many colonials work in hotels as kitchen porters, washing dishes, cleaning and assisting the cellarman, and on the buses as drivers and conductors, but it is very difficult to place coloured staff with shop employers. They claim it puts business at risk.'

NOTTING HILL FAMILY 'THREATENED'

Hearings at a West London Rent Tribunal were adjourned yesterday after coloured tenants repeated allegations of 'threats and harrassment' from a local landlord.

Mr and Mrs Vernon Powell of 248 Powis Square W11 were appealing against the actions of a Mr Harry Saltzman, who, it was claimed, had been acquiring increasing amounts of property in Powis Square and surrounding streets and raised rents from £3 to £10 per week within six months.

When Mr Powell had complained to Mr Saltzman about the increase, they were allegedly offered a sum of £25 to 'f—— off and never come back' and verbally abused. When they declined, the Powells and their four children were visited the next day by a gang of six white youths who smashed their windows and dumped furniture on the street.

The area, known as 'the Dale', has recently become a haven for West Indian and African immigrants who mix with existing Irish, Italian and Spanish communities. Because of its advanced delapidation, property developers have recently put forward new schemes for rebuilding. But most of the large Victorian terraced houses have been split into short-lease flats with whole families sharing a single room. As many as fifty companies are estimated to be letting such rooms without restrictions on overcrowding. According to local sources, white families can expect to pay 15s. for a room, but black families usually pay 30s to £2.

'Lots of the blacks are taking over leases themselves,' said a landlady in the same square, 'But they let them at such high rents that it's only the prostitutes or the pimps that can afford them.' Cases are also known of landlords bringing in West Indian tenants to try and get rid of sitting tenants so higher rents can be charged.

Mr Powell explained that he and his family had been refused rooms at several adjacent premises, even though there had been a sign with 'Vacancies' in the window. 'This flat was one of the only ones without a sign in the window saying "No dogs. No Irish. No coloureds", or "Colour Tax".'

Mr Saltzman was unavailable for comment yesterday, either at his agent's office or that of an affiliated company, White City Properties Ltd.

23

ED the TED

"**O**ne of the newcomers to our W10 manor is this hangover from the prehistoric Edwardian era known as Ed the Ted, the pasty-eyed, scabies-ridden, rancid face of rock 'n' roll, complete with axle-greased quiff, blocked drainpipe trousers, scratch 'n' sniff socks and purple beetle-crushers. Now Ed, who is as proud of his brethren's record for seat-slashing and brick-throwing as he is of his British bulldog ancestry, devotes a fair amount of his brainpower to doing up his shoelaces in the morning. But he was recently picked out as something of a Great Ted Mind the other month in a telly prog on the juvenile delinquency problem. He strung together a couple of words about his 'broken home' and moistened a few saps' eyes with tears. I had to chuckle — but remember that Ed's idea of a constructive dialogue is being the only one in possession of a cosh, a cut-throat razor or a chopper. Sad, very sad."

"ARVE MOVED DARN EAR WIV ME MA."

TED AIN'T DED

There's trouble on the rubble, the bombsite is the hop
I know you don't like it, but Ted ain't gonna stop
Like it or lump it, you can't show us the door
We licked Hitler in 1944.

We don't wanna buy the things you're tryin' to flog
We're British as a bacon roll and spotted dog
Flikker's at the pictures, he's slashin' up the seats
Teds are on the prowl and the bobby's on the beat.
Ted ain't ded, gonna kick you in the head

They keep forgetting Ted ain't gonna stop
Stab-U the Elephant Boy is comin' round the block
Give him one good reason why you say we're through
That'll be the last thing that you ever do.
Since I was a young boy, only 'bout thirteen
I knew rockin' Ted would out live any passing scene

TED AIN'T DED, get it in your head

Here or there it comes to much the same

TED AIN'T DED, it's alive and kickin' boy

TED AIN'T DED, gonna kick you in the head —

WHO YOU SCREWIN'? WHO YOU SCREWIN'?

Written by Edward Tudorpole and Julien Temple
By kind permission of Warner Bros. Music Ltd. copyright 1985

Up West

For today's deb or duchess – what could be more perfect for floating across the lawns and through the ballrooms of the long, hot summer than this delicious jus d'orange shantung suit? With this year's unfitted, hip-length jacket, puff-ball skirt and daring on-the-knee hemline, teamed with a matching apricot Breton hat and new-look stiletto heels, it'll keep you in touch with la mode Parisienne for at least five months – and for only 800 guineas. Available in all good Knightsbridge stores.

"**Y**ou'll dig Henley right away if I describe him as a cold queer, a smooth, collected, let's-talk-this-one-over type from the banks of the stockbroker Thames. He's Mayfair's swankiest fashion designer, catering exclusively for the old fur-clad bats in silly hats who like to fill in a morning perched on a little gold chair and throw away their spouses' money on tasteless pastel and diamanté. I am not saying that Henley isn't clever – he makes a lot of money and he keeps bright young Suzette gainfully underpaid and over-employed in case she produces any ideas worth getting his hands on. Effortlessly debonair and cold with just a hint of camp, he's charming as only a devil-may-care Brit aristocrat from the James Mason mould can be. The French have a word for his sort, but disgusting is close enough for me."

Henley of Mayfair
By Appointment
Dressmaker to the Queen

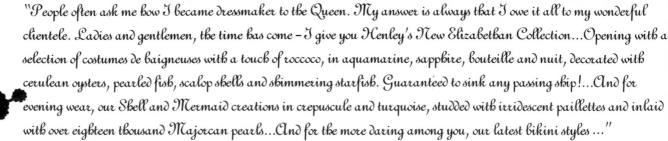

"People often ask me how I became dressmaker to the Queen. My answer is always that I owe it all to my wonderful clientele. Ladies and gentlemen, the time has come – I give you Henley's New Elizabethan Collection...Opening with a selection of costumes de baigneuses with a touch of roccoco, in aquamarine, sapphire, bouteille and nuit, decorated with cerulean oysters, pearled fish, scalop shells and shimmering starfish. Guaranteed to sink any passing ship!...And for evening wear, our Shell and Mermaid creations in crepuscule and turquoise, studded with irridescent paillettes and inlaid with over eighteen thousand Majorcan pearls...And for the more daring among you, our latest bikini styles ..."

"Really, Dido, there's nothing worse than the back of a woman's knees. They remind me of under-done rock-cakes."

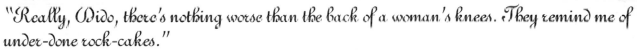

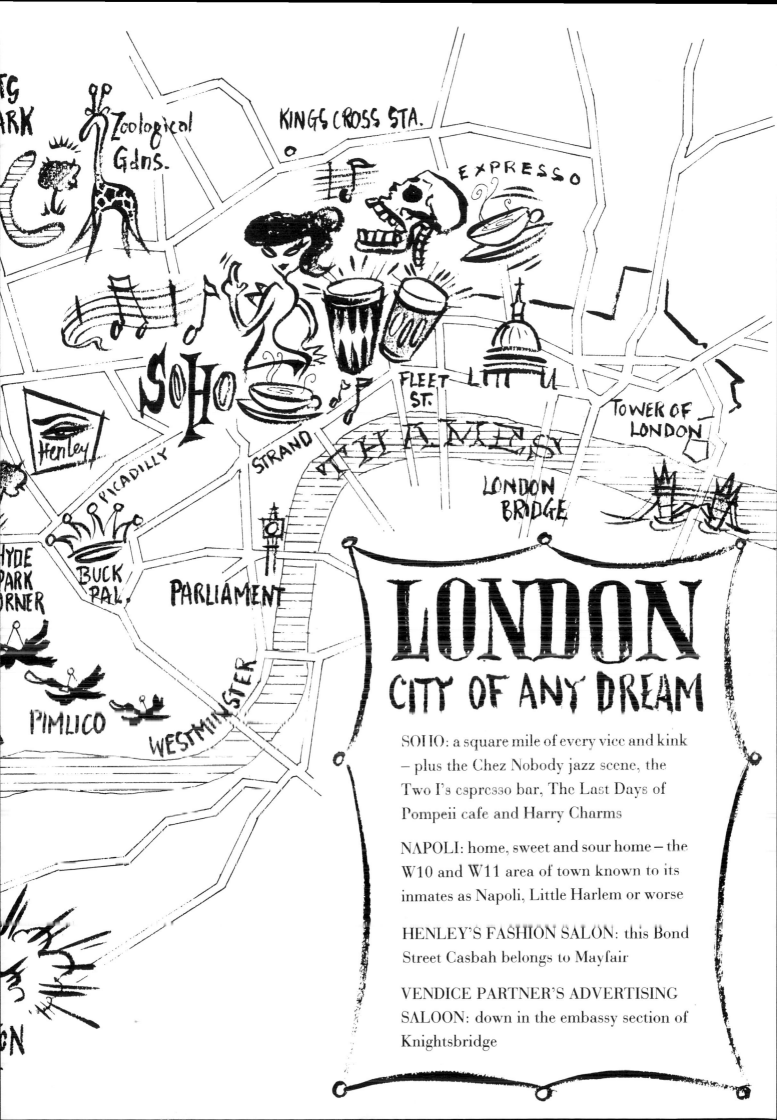

LONDON
CITY OF ANY DREAM

SOHO: a square mile of every vice and kink – plus the Chez Nobody jazz scene, the Two I's espresso bar, The Last Days of Pompeii cafe and Harry Charms

NAPOLI: home, sweet and sour home – the W10 and W11 area of town known to its inmates as Napoli, Little Harlem or worse

HENLEY'S FASHION SALON: this Bond Street Casbah belongs to Mayfair

VENDICE PARTNER'S ADVERTISING SALOON: down in the embassy section of Knightsbridge

"IT'SA

-WAY 1

TWIST

THIS

AGE P

ARTY."

   "It seems only yesterday when being a teenager meant doffing your cap and listening to all that don't-rock-the-boat-sonny-Jim from some tuppenny colonel who won the war single-handed with a couple of Victoria Crosses to boot. And now you wake up in living Technicolor to see all these sucklings in their latest bri-nylon drip-dries with a sherbert dip and a fizzy pop, a duck's-arse haircut like their elder bro and Italian strides — millions of them clutching their latest 45s and begging Mum and Dad to get them a hi-fi. And on the telly you see that smug smile from Mr Macmillan that just says 'good for business', and you read that these oh-so-cute babes-in-arms are cashing £830,000,000 — I'll repeat it, eight-hundred-and-thirty-million-bloody-quid — every year on all this vinyl, plastic, formica, dacron, crimplene stuff. So then you think, JUST HOLD IT, this is the time for yours truly to get smart. You gotta stay two steps ahead of the crowd — keep your eyes peeled for a brand new racket — and keep the oldsters out of your party, or the game is up. And let me tell you, it nearly *is*. I certainly won't regret it when the teenage label is torn off my drip-dry, sky-blue jeans.**"**

Let's speak teen!

Teenspeak for Bods from Squareville

Introduced by Call-me-Cobber, host of the Searchlight chat show.

'If you're an old square like me, I'll bet you need this groovy dekko at the jivetalk of the in-crowd – at least, that's how I think they'd say it. So let's get stuck in!'

A

ACID-DROP: *sharp-tasting sweetie – but I've also heard it used by teens when their other half's playing hard to get.*

ALL-NIGHTER: *when there's a lot of blue, a white circle and a tiny red dot like* the RAF insignia in a teenager's eyes, then you know they've been to an all-nighter club (aka frolic pad), 'grooving' to this so-called music.

B

BEATSVILLE: *a hang-out for these beatniks. Definitely no squares like you or me allowed on the premises.*

BLAST: *supposed to mean a good time, but the only time I was asked to have a 'blast', by some sleazy jerk in a club, he wanted me to share his ciggy – disgusting!*

BLOW OUT: *teenspeak for cancelling – usually just because they cannot be bothered to turn up for job appointments, interviews with me, that kind of thing.*

BLITZ BABY: *a teen hatched in these parts in 1940 when Hitler was bombing the shit out of London. Those pram traumas were responsible for a lot, I'd say.*

BLUES: *I used to think that blues were just that wailing Yank music, but now it seems to mean anything from pep-pills to an unlicensed club.*

BRETHREN: *gang or a clique. So you and I are elder brethren – see? You're getting the hang of this now.*

BUZZ OFF: *teen-talk for 'Scram!' Cheeky little brats use it a lot – even to me.*

C

CAFF: *you may think this is just an Eyetie word for a coffee bar, but you gotta crack it a bit more than that. It seems to be the centre of a crucial teen-ritual, something to do with abstract expressoism. It's all to do with this 'Gaggia' – pronounced Gadjah – machine on the bar, which produces more steam than Victoria Station and a slimy black liquid or cotton-woolly-milky-goo (called espresso and cappuccino). Cut the fancy names and let me crack a cold tinny any time – but those in the know regard the stuff as teenage ambrosia and sit there mooning over it for hours on end. All pretty pointless you'd think, but I reckon it might have something to do with the mad look in their eyes.*

CAT: *a keen male groover.*

CLOBBER (aka **DRAG** aka **SCHMUTTER):** *what we call togs, although I'd also call them eyestrain-outfits.*

CLOBBO (aka **DUNCE** aka **HALFWIT** aka **MUG** aka **PRONK** aka **THIKKO):** *This one's quite different – a teen who's IQ is the same as his age.*

COSH BOY: *spotty, leather-jacketed delinquent like a gutter version of Adam Faith who skulks in alleyways with unidentified weapons. Nasty, eh? Good telly, though; my prog about them got really high ratings.*

COWBOY: *policeman (aka Mr Plod, bobby, copper, filth).*

CLUE ME IN: *wise me up – even if it goes in one ear and out the other!*

COOL: *beats me, this one – seems to mean almost anything from 'OK' to 'great, mate' – and a lot else besides. Certainly very positive, though – you cannot go wrong with this one if you want to sound hip.*

CUBE: *a three-dimensional square, so – geddit? – a super-dullo who couldn't even make squaresville.*

CURVESVILLE: *where the beatiful (sorry, beautiful) chicks hang out. (This teenspeak thing can be useful too – give us oldies a fair suck at the sauce-bottle!)*

D

DADDY-O: *greetings for anyone over twenty-one.*

DARK SEVEN: *a bad week.*

DEADBEAT: *straight from the morgue – so completely unhip (cf. cube).*

DEKKO: *taking a dekko is getting a good sneak – it's a tip that something's worth getting your eyes on.*

DIG THIS: *if a hipster (q.v.) mumbles this at you, they want you to understand.*

E

ENDSVILLE (aka **CLOUD 9** aka **REAL RAVE):** *teen bliss describing anything from a new Miles Davis platter to a pair of winklepickers.*

ESTABLISHMENT: *everything you'd think these kids should respect – and don't: royalty, Ascot, their elders and betters etc.*

F

FLIP YOUR LID: *go wild. Dig this!*

FORM-FILLER (aka **CONSCRIPT** aka **TAXPAYER** aka **OLDSTER):** *you've guessed it – another slag at decent, hard-working citizens.*

FREAP: *a cross between a freak and a creep.*

G

GIVE GLOOM THE GO-BY: *get happy.*

GIVE ME FIVE: *shake hands.*

H

HIPSTER: *a cat (q.v.) – a smartie who's in the know and ahead of the crowd (learnt about this one when I did a prog on Norman Mailer – he's a hero with the teens who can read).*

I

IN-CROWD: *the lot who think they're fashionable and hang round together like a bunch of sheep.*

J

JELLY BOWL: *fat person – who's enjoyed a few too many free lunches.*

JEWISH PIANO: *cash register. Geddit?*

JIVE: *how hipsters (q.v.) dance. It's also what they think non-teens talk – ie rubbish. They should talk!*

K

KIDLET (aka **SPERMLET** aka **STUDLET):** *honorary title for pre-teen 'short pant products'.*

L

LES: *watch out if you're on a date with a girl they call Les because in these days – it isn't short for Leslie.*

LESSONSVILLE: *school.*

LIVEWIRE: *when these teens get jumpy, they get known as* livewires *– and there's drugs involved, unless I'm very much mistaken. Had a dose of that white powder they call* speed *once, and felt like the proverbial wild man of Borneo.*

LOOSE GOOSE: *yet another insult someone with an ill-connected fusebox, not too quick on the up-take.*

LOOT aka **BREAD** aka **DINERO** aka **LOLLY:** *money. They've got more words for the crunchy buckola than they have the real thing!*

M

MANE-RAKE: *comb.*

MOCK-CROCS: *the ultimate in hip footwear: imitation crocodile-skin shoes.*

N

NANCY BOY (aka **POOF** aka **QUEER):** *one of those lads you and I would call less than a man – effeminate chaps.*

NUMBER: *very confusing. If you really want to* parler *teen, you call a person a* number *– I'd be an 'Oz number'. Yeah?*

O

ORBIT: *out-of-this-world (coined by all those sputnik fans).*

P

PLATTER (aka **VINYL):** *gramophone record, described as either a cool platter or a piece of red-hot vinyl.*

PRE-MODERN: *anything before 1955. I know that's most of your and my lives, but try not to think about it.*

R

RAVE: *a teen-style tabbo party – what I'd call a bender, and bugger the consequences.*

S

SELLING OUT: *some of them get into a real hot-dog temper on this one – it's even applied to someone passing a friendly word with someone like me.*

SHARP (aka **SNAZZY):** *neat dresser (well, what* they *call neat).*

SNOG: *teen for a bit of the other – in their case usually cuddling in the corner like ferrets in the proverbial sack.*

SOLO: *alone, so ON THE SOLO LIST, without a date.*

SPIELER: *gambler, good bullshitter.*

STEAM: *'on the steam' is just on the radio – where teen addicts get their shot of rock 'n' roll.*

T

TED: *a hooligan who nicked his fancy frock-coats and brocaded waistcoats from the toffs (q.v.) who revived the Edwardian style. Usually looks like a gorilla done up for a wedding. I did a really great prog on this bunch, so you probably know the full moronic story.*

TOFFS: *stuck-up (toffee-nosed – geddit?) idiots with plums in their mouths and pokers up their arses.*

TON-UP: *young tearaways on motorbikes who 'do the ton' in their leathers, zooming along at 100 mph. Always breaking their necks – but they're popular. Good viewing, and some vicar's even getting in on the act now. That'd be really great television!*

U

UTOPIA MANOR: *where ton up vicars go after a nasty skid, aka heaven.*

V

VESPA: *the scooter. There's another Eyetie brand, but you wouldn't need to know, would you?*

W

WINKED OUT: *kicked the bucket – the prelim to utopia manor.*

WITH IT: *in fashion. Of course, some people like myself, are beyond all that – we're without it, apparently.*

Y

YOBBO: *Young 'Orrible Boy.*

Z

ZOOTY: *modern.*

Z's: *sleep aka Dreamsville – so piling up the Z's is getting forty winks after an all-nighter. Well, they're welcome to it!*

The Power of Youth

'. . . Exploitation of the kiddos by the conscripts, and exploitation of themselves by the crafty little absolute beginners. The net result? "Teenager" 's become a dirty word or, at any rate, a square one.'

COLIN MACINNES – *Absolute Beginners*, 1959

'We are in the presence, here, of an entirely new phenomenon in human history: that youth is rich. Once, the jeunesse dorée were a minute minority; now, all the young have gold. Earning good wages, and living for little, or even for free, like billeted troops on poor, harrassed Dad and Mum, the kids have more "spending money" than any other age group of the population. Farewell the classic, century-old pattern of Youth the industrious apprentice, penniless, nose glued to grindstone, and Age, prosperous, authoritative, in fair round belly with good chump-chop

lined. Today, age is needy and, as its powers decline, so does its income; but full-blooded youth has wealth as well as vigour. In this decade, we witness the second Children's Crusade, armed with strength and booty, against all "squares", all adult nay-sayers. An international movement, be it noted, that blithely penetrates the political curtains draped by senile seniors, as yet unconscious of the rising might of this new classless class.'

COLIN MACINNES – *Pop Songs And Teenagers*, 1958

Rrrrrrrr!!

Meeaaaoow!

Well, there's gonna be some changes
Around the garbage cans,
Goodbye all you old faces – here I am – oh yeah!
I may look like a little kitten inside a tiger skin – Rrrrrrrr!
Look out KING CAT, LITTLE CAT'S movin' in.

Well, you Siamese and Persians
And you big old ginger tom,
Must all be missing persons when I come along.
I may look like a little kitten
Until I start to roar – Rrrrrrrr!!
Look out KING CAT, LITTLE CAT'S cut his claws.

Oh-oh you chase that cat around
And you get misunderstood!
But if you are in this town
You never had it so good
Well, the GIRL CATS here all know it,
You should hear them all – Meeaaaoow!!
Look out BIG CAT, LITTLE CAT'S king cat now.

LOOK OUT BIG CAT, LITTLE CAT'S MOVIN'
LOOK OUT BIG CAT, LITTLE CAT'S GROOVIN'
LOOK OUT BIG CAT, LITTLE CAT'S KING CAT NOW – RRRRRRRRR!!
YOU NEVER HAD IT SO GOOD!

Written by Nick Lowe
By kind permission of Plangent Visions Music Ltd., 1985

Magic Charms

Pop Mogul Harry Charms, the toast of Tin Pan Alley, gives his philosophy of teen.

I'm often stopped outside my office and asked, "Harry, just what is the secret of your success? How did you find all your fabulous teenage discoveries?" Well, I will tell you.

CREEPING

Before I formed the HARRY CHARMS STABLE OF STARS, I was called many names: the TITAN OF TEEN, SOHO'S SVENGALI, the CREEPING CZAR OF THE COFFEE BARS. But believe me, my secret lies in a little bit of hard work — and *a lot* of the Charms magic.

BORING

I was the first manager in Britain to see that boring old Blighty needed fresh faces for the fifties to blow away the blues. Now that teenagers call the tune they want their own idols. So roll over Denis Lotis! And forget all those Yank stars like ELVIS with their slick showbiz schmaltz and incomprehensible southern drawls! I wanted my British boys to become TROUBADOURS OF TEEN so that boys and girls could understand them. They wanted one of their own. And where did I find them, I hear you ask?

SNIFFING

I devoted many lonely nights to sniffing them out. I loitered in the dingy cafés of SOHO, the boys' clubs of DAGENHAM, the milk bars of PENGE, the sweaty gymnasia and boxing halls of the ELEPHANT & CASTLE and BERMONDSEY — in fact, wherever the boys were!

QUIVERING

I was searching for CRAZY YOUNG CATS with that vocal twang, those pouting lips, quivering thighs and a wiggle in the hips that declared these recruits ROUGH 'N' RAW BUT READY-TO-ROCK!

FAMOUSING

But it wasn't just their talent, you see. It was MINE as well. I took them all from NOWHERESVILLE. I tamed them, named them, famoused them. Who gave ZESTY-BOY SIFT his DA haircut? Who made sure SOFT-SOX GRANITE got 2,000 fan letters every week? Who bought them their BRYLCREEM, showed EDDY SEX how to cartwheel and sing at the same time? Yes, it was Harry who added that MAGIC CHARMS TOUCH!

GRINDING

My publisher tells me I may have to explain why my boys 'GRIND'. With pleasure! I know some people call their acts 'VULGAR'. Let me say that my boys move their hips *in time* to the music — it's all young and fun, and if TV still won't show them below the waist it's a real shame. Goodness only knows what they might get up to if they didn't GRIND on stage! I am also often asked why there aren't any 'girls'. Well, I can only say that my eyes have not lighted on any little nightingales yet. Maybe a female Soft-Sox or a Zesty-Girl Sift will come along, who knows?

SELLING

But I'm sure when all you fans see my latest discovery, fourteen-year-old BABY BOOM in full, you'll agree with the words of his latest fabulous 45 (AVAILABLE ON THE STABLE OF STARS LABEL, PRICE 5/4D, and selling like hot cakes!) — "YOU NEVER HAD IT SO GOOD!!"

© **Harry Charms Promotions/Stable of Stars Inc.**

49

"Listening to jazz is ultimate heavenly bliss. And it's also a way of saying you're different to all those form-fillers and time-wasters, whose heads are so filled with foxtrots and waltzes and soapsy-sudsy-tunes to do the dishes by that they are mentally unable to do anything more than accept whatever's thrown at them. *AND* that you couldn't give a monkey's fart for this conveyor belt of tousled young louts in tight lamé pants who are whisked from the espresso bar at the Two I's to the pink and purple backdrops of the *Six Five Special* within the time it takes to peel a zipper. You see, all that plinkety-plonk-pizzicato-stringed saccharine pap and treble warblings is nothing to do with 'music'. You bet not! You see, there's only one thing that really makes these oldsters' eyes light up, and that's the easy moolah to be made. In a word, MONEY.

As far as I can see it might just be another wicked ruse for greaseball oldsters to hoodwink a whole generation of sucklings out of hard-scrounged pocket money. Let me explain. If young Baby Boom sells a million and gets to number one in the Hit Parade, he gets to double his pocket money from 2/6d to 5/- a week and thinks of it as a gain of 100%. But that leaves the proceeds from the other 999,999 records for the oldsters and their cronies, whose heads squander their ill-gotten gains on monogrammed cufflinks, two-way mirrors, cocktail cabinets for their jags and other essentials. Simple, isn't it? Like taking candy from a baby.

So when I discover some haunt has just become the latest scouting ground for another Laurie London, I steal down Wardour Street to a club where, courtesy of imports by our G.I. friends, the latest Basie, Lady Day and Ella plays next to new platters by Ray Charles, Jimmy Reed and Jimmy Smith; where the music swells through to the early

hours and the sweat runs down the walls and the dancers who faint are passed out through a grille up on to the pavement; where weird John Coltrane sounds blow in, leaving a trail of notes that just don't quit you for days, or Tubby Hayes shakes the walls with his flattened 13ths when he blows his alto up on stage in some sweaty little basement. Heaven!

Usually, these clubs get hot for a few months and the G.I.s get into some rough stuff with blades and a stabbing puts them off limits for a few months and the sources dry up. But a few weeks later you're all back in action. You see, jazz is something quite different. It's a way of resisting from within all that stuff they want you to learn, and a sweeter way you couldn't hope for. And you get to know the strangest folk: fans and buffs, bluffers and drifters, mockers and moochers, downbeats and deadbeats, all glorying

in jive about Coltrane's melodic curves or Gil Evans's dynamics of structure or how Miles Davis came to be the black Picasso of sound. But who cares in the end, as long as at three in the morning you're still flying."

Jazz is a thing so wonderful that if anybody doesn't rave about it, all you can feel for them is pity: not that I'm making out I really understand it all – I mean, certain LPs leave me speechless. But the great thing about the jazz world, and all the kids that enter into it, is that no one, not a soul, cares what your class is, or what your race is, or what your income is, or if you're boy, or girl, or bent, or versatile, or what you are – so long as you dig the scene and can behave yourself, and have left all that crap behind you, too, when you come in the jazz club door. The result of all this is that, in the jazz world, you meet all kind of cats, on absolutely equal terms, who can clue you up in all kinds of directions – in social directions, in culture directions, in sexual directions, and in racial directions . . . in fact, almost anywhere, really, you want to go to learn.

COLIN MACINNES – *Absolute Beginners*, 1959

Killer Blow

Pretty little thing –
She held all the magic that's so hard
*   to believe,*
Never too far away. It's hard to
*   conceive.*
Never thought she'd have to go.
Never thought she'd leave.
It came as a killer blow.

Funny isn't it –
That a little girl can make the world
*   seem small.*
Hard to believe a little girl can seem
*   so tall.*
And the thing that he calls love
Isn't big enough – she had to go.
And that's the way it goes.

Her love had wings
That took her to the things he
*   couldn't give.*
She's got the kiss of life,
Kiss of life.
She's gone where it's so easy to live.
It's so easy to leave,
Searching for the scent of content.

Get along without me, boy.
Get along without me. You see,
Things aren't quite what they
*   seemed.*
Get along without me,
Wipe me out of your dream.
I'm no angel, I know.

KILLER BLOW
KILLER BLOW
KILLER BLOW

Written by Sade Adu/Working Week
By kind permission of Angel Music Ltd. © 1985

ABSTRACT EXPRE

SSOISM

'Come this night we take the locomotive to the jazz club. We not dragged too crazy, 'cos the chance is the management not going to admit bare feet and nightshirts. The leader who call himself "Big Chief Jive," got a scraggy mane, sort of flicking his shoulders and all. He always wear these black corduroy pants and a black leather jacket. He got a handsome face on him and several of they pseudo-witches, with pale lipstick, and masses of eye make-up, give him some wide come-on signs. He plainly different from the usual mob and this excite them.

We grabs a seat near the band, which were a fair trad effort. Most the witches about the floor seem mighty young, and evidently dig not the finer points of trad. They even prefers these madmen platters which come on in the interval. Them hip-wriggling guys with graty voiceboxes and such.

The modernists come in their mobs and plainly dominate the pad. I keen on some of their drag. It strike me as far out, but this not mean I going to become a convert. I reckon them little skirts with frills at the bottom, and they balloon-bursting boots with them fancy buckles. Some he studs got zooty-type manes and all, but it blacken me to know they done sat in some mane-scraggers plenty long in order to achieve the effect.

Big Chief and I swings clearly trad much times and even gets a fair proportion of the mob eyeballing our effort. We gets some loud belly-racks from them Teddy types in they crepe-sole boots and flashy shirts. Big deal! They done had their time mainly about five years ago. It surprise me there still be some living. They as old-fashioned as the struggle-buggy.'

FENELLA – *Through Beatnik Eyeballs*, **R. A. Norton**

'You may wander into a coffee bar: the juke box is blaring, and the mods and rockers are having a ball, they give you a suspicious glance but that is all, you are still alone. A staggeringly beautiful young girl comes in with her boyfriend and they put some money in the juke box and begin to dance together. You cannot take your eyes off the young girl's backside as it jerks wildly from one side to another. After a time she notices that you are watching her but pretends that she has not. She starts to get even more brazen in her movements and you get up and rush out, wiping beads of sweat from your brow.'

FRANK NORMAN – *Soho Night and Day*, 1966

'It seems that at about the age of sixteen the boys . . . tend to lose interest in athletic games, and although they sometimes recover it later, for a few years they concentrate on rock 'n' roll. But that is not the worst. They do not even tire themselves out by rocking 'n' rolling: they leave that to the girls, while they sit against the walls, like elderly sultans. And you will not be surprised to hear, my Lords, that on occasions the police have had to be called in and the club cleared with police dogs.'

LORD PAKENHAM – *House of Lords debate*, **November 1958**

"Large parts of the night can be spent in dark and smoky cellars, cavernous basements with slimy walls – no bigger than your aunt's living room, some low-key with a few open bottles and dusty glasses to pass as a bar, and others dominated by the gleaming chrome gaggia perched on the counter – but all have low lights, a few Spanish sherry-bottle lamps, a small stage up-front and art-school expressoism on the walls. Friends, enemies, long losts and uncommitted teens all swim in the heat and get lost in the music, and as the evening moves on and the music changes gear, there's only one question that counts. Are you a deadbeat or a livewire? The dance floor becomes a frantic jazz battleground . . . two tribes, the hot and the cool, their fingers clicking like sniper fire.

The **cool**, lit and dressed in icy blues, greens and whites, are the cool jazz brigade. They dance, of course, but existentially – is it worth the effort? Either way, they don't raise a sweat: their breath hangs in the air. The **hot** are the trad jazz merchants, wrapped in russets, reds, browns and black, whose God is Louis Armstrong, or anybody in the pre-modern style. Glistening with perspiration, they have grubby, white stiff-starched collars, striped shirts, all-one-colour ties, old tweed jackets, flannel pants and suede shoes. The dance number climaxes as the **drummer** hoovers up a line of sulphate from along his drumstick and launches into a scorching solo. . . ."

"ARE YOU WITH IT OR WITHOUT IT?"

asks Miss Dido Lament

I thought I'd seen everything five years ago in the
US of A: Presley, Dean, Brando, all those sexy
hunks moaning and mumbling in T-shirts and blue
jeans. But tho' the teen scene has started later on
this side of the Atlantic, it's **FULL OF
SURPRISES**! It's the most, to say the least!!
The Teenage Revolution has hit little ol' England –
and make no mistake. Forget that olde picture-
postcard Englande of beefeaters and bowler hats, of
stuffy city gents and strait-laced ladies. My teenage
pals tell me that's all ancient history – look out! Get
WITH IT!! In 1958 England is about to **SWING**!!!
And yours truly was the first to discover the new
youngsters who are dragging England into the age of
the sputnik!

It's just so much fun visiting all those teenage
hangouts in bustling Soho where the Angry Young
Men sit and preen. All those coffee bars on Old
Compton Street are packed with boys wearing the
latest smart Italian look – cute bum-freezer jackets
and dee-vine winklepicker shoes – and the girls, well,
they are sporting just **CRAZY** neon numbers with
hems way above the knee, I'm happy to say.
It may not suit the old Mayfair fuddy-duddies – at
least that's what they pretend – but it certainly has
what I'd call credibility. Once only the rich set the
trends. Now it's time for the Young Idea to show the
way, to show who's alive and looking, listening,
ready to try anything new. The youngsters call the
rich greybeards who used to set the trends 'The
Establishment'. And the Henleys, Hartwells and
Amies of this world are definitely without it.

It's that questioning attitude which makes these
youngsters so young and fresh, so **ZIPP-ZAP-
POW!** Now take sex for example. Everybody talks
about it – and about anything from puberty to
homosexuality to who-knows-what. But they're not
hung up about it. Some of them don't even seem to
care! Boyfriends and girlfriends are all old hat
nowadays in the permissive scene. So do these
teenagers all have active sex lives? I'm not sure yet.
They're very romantic, you know, and a little bit
secretive. But one thing's for sure watch this space,
because – 'with it' or 'without it', I'm going to find
out what they're hungering for!

© Miss Dido Lament

You never had it so good

"**Yes, it was a terrible time to be young, son, the 1930s.** Poverty, unemployment, fascism, no sunlight at the end of the corridor, just a lot of frightened, rich old men sitting on top of the dustbin lid to keep the muck from spilling over. They hated us and they hated life. It's better now, even with the bomb. . . . And then there was another thing . . . the venereal. It was a scourge – a blight hanging over all young men. It cast a great shadow over love and made it hateful. No modern drugs and quick relief like now. . . . I should have had my youth today along with all the drip-dry clothes and sputniks like you have.

Mind you, we found our own ways of having fun – dressed to the nines, with a girl on each arm and a smart suit – no vents, always double-breasted. I would take your ma out in the cab, and we'd go jitterbugging at the Hammersmith Palais or head for a bit of Arthur English or Max Miller's cheeky stuff at the Holborn Empire. Then of course, the petrol began to run short, and I got a bad back and things went from bad to worse. But as long as I've got my Old Holborn, the H.P. sauce and Peter May's batting average in the *Mirror*, I'll be happy enough, son. We're really quite alright up in my room, my budgie and me."

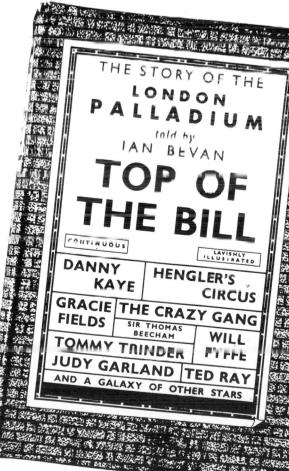

THE STORY OF THE
**LONDON
PALLADIUM**
told by
IAN BEVAN
**TOP OF
THE BILL**

CONTINUOUS

LAVISHLY
ILLUSTRATED

DANNY KAYE	HENGLER'S CIRCUS
GRACIE FIELDS	THE CRAZY GANG
	SIR THOMAS BEECHAM
TOMMY TRINDER	WILL FYFFE
JUDY GARLAND	TED RAY
AND A GALAXY OF OTHER STARS	

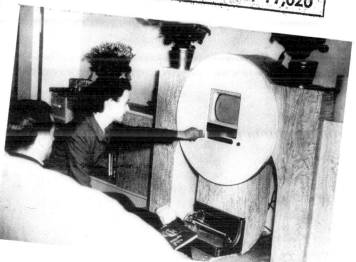

Daily Mirror

WED
SEPT 3
1958

2½ FORWARD WITH THE PEOPLE
No. 17,020

"Ugh!

My brother Colin, he's just one of these namby-pamby teenagers with their nasty poofy haircuts. Juvenile delinquents, you can tell 'em a mile off, none of 'em ever picked up a shovel in their bleedin' lives. A load of nancy boys, 'in't they? And what's more, they got no social conshunz neither. Traitors to the working class, the whole rotten bunch. You know what? They've spoilt it all. Too much free orange juice on the Welfare, thanks to Mr Attlee, that's their problem. And they don't even know the word thankyou. What they need's a spot of national service to sort them out — a short back and sides, a rifle and a bit of khaki, and they'll soon change their tune. After all, it's done that Elvis a power of good . . . ."

"**Has Arthur been going on again
about the good old days?** It's all in
the mind, you know. I'd go mad if I ate
another plate of spam. Today, of
course, there's plenty of jam to go
round. The more the better, I say.
Soon have this place looking brand
new. If you could see some of the
things you can get on the never-never
from that mail-order catalogue:
pop-up toasters, Nite-Lite curlers —
oh, and there's a lovely ice-cube
maker in walnut veneer. I might just
have to get one of those to go with the
new cocktail bar. Well, it's an invest-
ment really, isn't it? And I'll be
needing another lodger if I want that
holiday I promised myself. Arthur
only ever wants to go to Butlin's, but I
fancy *le continent* – maybe a fortnight
in Malta – I've seen a special offer on
the new jumbo-packets of Daz. And
then it'll be a new fridge . . . ."

COCKTAI

Why not be tempted by a **Goat's Delight** – the gruff little drink with a real kick! Kirsch topped up with brandy, a dash of Pernod, a splash of orgeat syrup and a yummy teaspoonful of cream. Shake well and down it in one! Or for the very daring, how about a spicy **Between the Sheets?** It's a wild mix of cointreau, brandy and light rum with just a twist of lemon or lime and a cocktail cherry to give you instant sex appeal! And if there's still something missing in your life try **Terminal Boredom**, our new atomic cocktail with the sting in its tail: just a giant-sized slug of whisky, a whiff of tequila, a tot of gin, a dash of bitters, crème de menthe, cherry brandy, sweet martini, a small bottle of brandy . . . in fact, just empty the cocktail cabinet.

You'll be blown sky-high! You may not think straight or walk straight, but who gives a damn. anyway . . .

"Ah, you're the one, Harry's told me all about you. I'd love to delve into your portfolio. . ."

L TIME!

"I hear you've got integrity, Colin. Just the thing my agency stands for. I could use someone like you. Bell me sometime, teenager, on Mayfair Double O-Double O."

THAT'S
MOTIVATION

"Welcome to the world of your dreams.
Where you can do what you want,
Commit horrible sins...

And get away with it."

"I don't sell things, Colin, never things. I sell dreams."

LUST
GLUTTONY
PRIDE * ANGER
SLOTH * AVARICE
Jealousy

Efficient! Economical!
Well designed!

Get up to date

Do you hear what I hear – do you see what I see?
I want you to use your imagination....You wake up one
morning. You'll ask yourself......

"Why am I so exciting – what makes me so dramatic?"
You're trying to say something about yourself –
This dazzling crime of wisdom
You fall for reality. You're bruised and bewildered.
Then you learn to fall in love with yourself.
THAT'S MOTIVATION.

You raise yourself high, presenting your soul
You step from the shadows. You hear the command,
An image to dream, and you tremble permission.
Tomorrow's rewards blur the skies of today.

You're swept by the tide on to life's every dream
A life of such powerful meaning.
Now you has class, now you has flash,
Now you has Mass Motivation.

"I don't sell things, Colin, never things. I sell dreams."

Here's an image I can recommend,
Here's a product you will die for –
Here's a nightmare that will never end
It gets you fired up and running till you go-go-go....

You know you got something – you know you got style –
We don't take much – just a little bit.
THAT'S MOTIVATION.

No more false illusion – goodbye to confusion.
Stand out from the madding crowd –
Motivation in symphony.

SYMPHONY IN STYLE, Mass Motivation
BRILLIANT – ORIGINAL – Mass Motivation
SCINTILLATING – CHARISMATIC – Mass Motivation
AS FRESH AS TOMORROW – Mass Motivation
Sell what – MOTIVATION
Say what – MOTIVATION
New Motive
Sole Motive
Now you has CRASS MOTIVE
NOW YOU HAS MASS MOTIVATION

Written by David Bowie. By kind permission of
EMI Music Publishing Ltd. © 1985

DREAMS COME TRUE

go electric !

This is it !

INTERLUDE

DIDO LAMENT · COLIN YOUNG · HAROLD CHARMS · AMBERLEY DROVE

SEARCHLIGHT

Proudly Presenting..

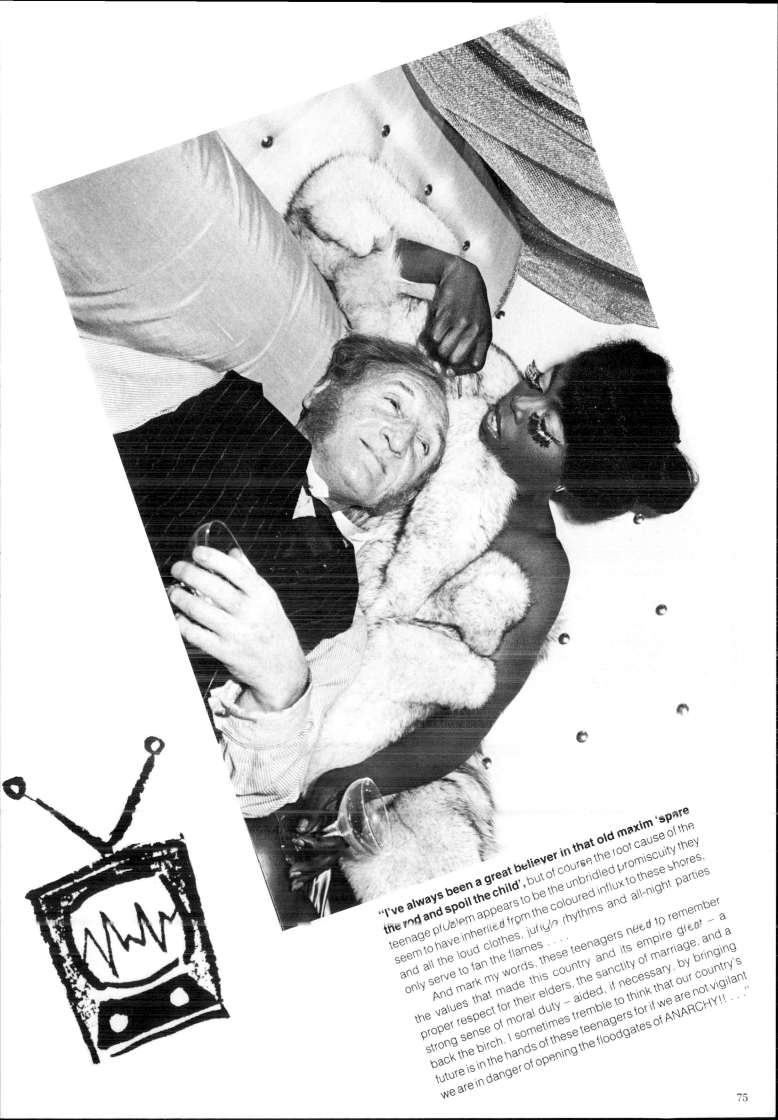

"I've always been a great believer in that old maxim 'spare the rod and spoil the child', but of course the root cause of the teenage problem appears to be the unbridled promiscuity they seem to have inherited from the coloured influx to these shores, and all the loud clothes, jungle rhythms and all-night parties only serve to fan the flames . . . .

And mark my words, these teenagers need to remember the values that made this country and its empire great – a proper respect for their elders, the sanctity of marriage, and a strong sense of moral duty – aided, if necessary, by bringing back the birch. I sometimes tremble to think that our country's future is in the hands of these teenagers for if we are not vigilant we are in danger of opening the floodgates of ANARCHY!! . . ."

"I'VE GOT A MESSAGE FOR YOU, AND YOU, AND YOU, AND ALL THE TELLY WITCH-DOCTORS AND ADVERTISING PIMPS . . . and all the old sordids with your toupées and falsies. This teenage ball had a real splendour in the beginning, when we found out that no-one could sit on our faces anymore because we had loot to spend at last, and our world was to be our world, the one we wanted and not standing on the doorstep of somebody else's waiting for honey, perhaps.

Well, it's over now, it's finished, you choked it. This teenage fishbowl of yours is as real as nothing, so much smaller than life . . ."

BLACK TOWN
WHITE CITY

'From the time you start to live in England, it is as if a sea of white faces is always around you. . . . Some people will go out of their way to try to make you feel comfortable. Many may believe that you have never gone to a real church before. . . . Do not insult them for this ignorance. They will learn better in time. . . . If they smile with you in church and look away from your direction in the bus, it is just one of those things . . .'

Going to Britain, BBC Publication, 1959

'It does have certain times in London, when a kind of blight descend on the boys. Everybody hard-up, and you can't get an ease-up from your best friend. And the point is, it don't happen in summer, when at least you have a little sunshine and a daffodil or tulip to console you, but in them grim days of winter when night fall on the city from three o'clock in the afternoon, and you looking all about in the fog for a friend to borrow a shilling for the gas meter. But everybody cagey-cagey, men looking at you with suspicion from the time you appear to the distance, and some fellars, as if they have radar, could sense when a hard-up test on the horizon, and right away they begin to limp and cry big water, so that by the time you get near you realise it have a situation here that far worse than yours.'

SAMUEL SELVON – *Ways of Sunlight*, 1952

'I was at the Labour Exchange, I'd just been demobbed, and I saw that my file was marked *Coloured* and I went mad. I got out my Air Force Pay Book and threw it at the clerk. "This isn't marked coloured", I shouted. "No one in the Air Force cared whether I was coloured or not, why should you?" That sort of thing kept on happening. I went for a job once at a factory, and when I walked towards the personnel office I heard some music, *Ole Man River*. I remember humming it, because I thought I'd get the job. But I didn't, and later I heard that when coloured people came for jobs they'd play that tune to warn everybody.'

A TRINIDADIAN in Notting Hill, 1958

'No, well, you see, I come in September last year but I have no work for six months. I live on National Assistance, £2 10s. My room costs £2, but I have money with me, from home, Antigua. The National Assistance people are good. I do ordinary work. I work in a hospital. Now I work in a hotel. I get my food there, but the money is not good. I am forty-four and not married. All my friends here are from Dominica and Grenada. I never go out after seven; too many fights. I listen to the news, and read. You have to take what you can find, cannot pick friends, all black men together. If I have the money I go home now.'

A MAN FROM ANTIGUA interviewed in Edgware Road, 1958

'One-third is tolerant of coloured people, one-third is mildly prejudiced, and one-third is extremely prejudiced.'

DR CLARENCE SENIOR on the population of Great Britain in *Report on Jamaican Migration to Britain*, November 1955

'I should like to have here a city like Florence or Venice. I should like to have in this country some of the restaurants one finds abroad, and some of their food. We are trying to get those things by encouraging immigration of French and Italian chefs. They have been a very helpful standby. I should like to see some of these coloured people coming in, in the same way, and doing the same kind of work; and I imagine that in time that will come.'

LORD OILKIN *House of Lords debate*, November 1958

'It is widely said that the coloured men undercut the white men in the labour market; that more than their proportion live on immoral earnings; that a high proportion of them suffer from unpleasant diseases, and that they do not know how to use lavatories. Those are things which are being widely said. There is very little truth in them, although there may be in some cases, of course, just an element of what is not altogether incorrect.'

LORD WINSTER – *House of Lords debate*, November 1958

"This summer can't last?"   *"Oh yes it can Daddio, it can last until the calendar says stop."*

GIVE ME YOUR HATE

We must keep Britain white. That is our theme tonight.

We don't want the Blacks or Jews, Yellow, Red, Brown or Blue . . .
and let's kick out the Homos too.

Hitler had the right ideas – don't knock him, son, you need him here.

Jack-boots smashing up your ear.

Fascism is here to stay: trains on time, regular pay
– jobs for all the Christian Whites.

Hate's the way to win our fight.
Hate's the way we must unite.

Hate in church and hate in school
Hate at home, hate in your hand.
Hate's the way to clean the land.
Hate in a strong white, curled up fist.

We'll give you the black shirt, the boots and the stick.

Give me your hands to make us free
Give me your fists to crush the beast
Give me your pain and misery . . .
Give me your votes for victory!

KEEP BRITAIN WHITE
KEEP BRITAIN WHITE

'The tribesman Teds staring, in tensed, dead-pan groups, with blank, meaningless hostility. The girls showing their paces and bursting youth with a real glamour that transcends their fierce determination to be glamorous.'

COLIN MACINNES – *The Observer*, 1962

'. . . it would be equally possible to see, in the teen-age neutralism and indifference to politics, and self-sufficiency, and instinct for enjoyment – in short, their kind of happy mindlessness – the raw material for crypto-fascisms of the worst kind.'

COLIN MACINNES – *Pop Songs and Teenagers*, 1962

"Now though he may have been hatched somewhere humble, like the Elephant or Bow or Bermondsey, you can tell by his sartorial garb and royal disposition that this Flikker gentleman regards himself as something of a rajah among the Ted rabble. You only have to get one look from those piercing blue eyes to know why he's king of the castle. He'll get you to bow down if he wants you to. And you won't be getting up in a hurry."

"What we have to do is form ourselves into committees. We must elect officers and make representatives to the Police Commissioners and our Members of Parliament.

This is England remember . . ."

"You've got the accent and you've got the words and the authority, but you're talking a whole load of shit. We don't need committees and representations. What we need is a few pieces of iron and a bit of organization so that when they come in here tonight we can defend ourselves . . ."

' I was talking to some English friends who lived nearby when a police car pulled up across the street and a police officer got out and came over to us. He look at me and said: "You – off the streets!" I said: "What do you mean – me or us?" He replied: "I'll give you two minutes to get off the streets."

It didn't make any sense to me. I continued to ignore him and went on talking with my friends.

"All right," he said and he crossed the street and drove off. Three minutes later a car came screeching up and three policemen burst out and bundled me inside.

They took me to the nearby police station where the charge room was a very strange sight. One side of the room was full of West Indians looking bewildered. On the other side were three or four white guys. And in the middle were a line of policemen and a police sergeant sitting at a desk covered with broken bottles, knives, pieces of iron, razors . . . .

I joined the West Indian side and we waited in silence for some twenty minutes. It was quite a mystery. There was no riot – and yet there we were inside.

Then the ritual began with the West Indians. A young policeman took the first man to the desk and the sergeant said: "What's he charged with?" The policeman picked up a piece of iron off the desk and replied: "Armed with this weapon to commit a felony." The sergeant took the iron, put a tag on it and sent the West Indian off for fingerprinting as a prelude to a night in the cells. "Next!" the sergeant called and the performance was repeated with the next in line.

At one point one of the West Indians said: "That's not mine, sir. I'm not signing for that."

The sergeant looked him up and down and said: "You're one of those, are you? All right – take him upstairs."

Two policemen grabbed him on either side and took him away. All this had a very funny effect on me. By the time I reached the desk I was crying, not from fear or concern for myself, but because the whole scene was so terribly sad. Before the sergeant could speak, I said, "Which one is mine?"

MICHAEL MALIK — *From Michael de Freitas to Michael X,* 1968

'In the small hours of the morning, a gang of nine white youths aged between 17 and 20, most of whom came from Shepherd's Bush, toured their district and the adjacent ones in a car. They were, as they said, "nigger-hunting"; and they were armed with iron bars, torn from street railings, starting handles, table legs, pieces of wood and a knife. Once in a while, when they saw a coloured man walking on his own, or no more than a couple, they stopped to attack. Five coloured men whom they had assaulted were taken to hospital; three of them were seriously injured. One was wheeled into the Magistrate's Court to give evidence. Another, with a chest wound, was carried in on a stretcher.'

RUTH GLASS — *Newcomers. The West Indians in London,* 1960

"Welcome to Little Rock West 10 – these are the streets of Notting Hill in torment, rent asunder by the passions of a colour riot...."

'It comes as a shock to hear the ugly phrase "Lynch him!" on English lips in an English city. But it must be reported that these words were used not once but a dozen times yesterday afternoon.

The object of this venom, a young West African student, was running for his life down Bramley Road, followed by a gang of young toughs who had set upon him, kicked him and twisted his leg before he could escape. Dashing into a greengrocer's shop, he persuaded the owner's wife to bolt the door and hid himself in a back room until the police came and rescued him. By that time a crowd of two hundred white people had gathered on the pavements and in the roadway, and it took the combined efforts of police on horseback, in radio squad cars and twenty constables on foot to disperse them . . . .

Mr Seymour Manning is a 26-year-old African student who is at present living in Derby. He had come down for the day to see friends in Notting Hill, and though he did not know it he was under close observation from hostile eyes from the moment he stepped out of the Latimer Road Underground Station.

In the four hours that I had been in this area he was only the third coloured person that I had seen venture out of doors. I watched him disappear up Bramley Road. A few minutes later there was an outburst of screams and jeering and I saw Mr Manning sprinting back towards the underground, his tie and blazer streaming out behind him. As his three pursuers closed in, he turned in desperation and flung himself into the doorway of a greengrocer's shop, turned, and slammed it shut. A moment later the shopkeeper's wife . . . appeared in the doorway, locked the door behind her, and turned to face the trio of toughs. She had two friends with her – a housewife of her own age and a boy in his teens.

She kept them at bay until the police arrived a few minutes later. Soon after the first two constables came to her rescue, a radio car arrived, and after that came full reinforcements. It was during the interim period, before it was clear that the police were on their way in force, that people on the opposite pavement called out for a lynching. I went up to one of the young men, who looked to be about 25, and asked him what he had against the African in the shop. "Just tell your readers that Little Rock learned us a lesson," was the reply . . . .

Half an hour after he had taken refuge in the store, Mr Manning was rescued by a squad of policemen who held back the crowd and escorted him to a car. He was taken off to the home of his friends, where he was treated for bruises and shock.'

The Manchester Guardian,
2 September 1958

Absolute Beginners

But we're absolute beginners.
But if my love is your love
We're certain to succeed.
If a love song could fly over mountains,
Sail over heartache just like the films,
If there's a reason to feel all the hard times—
To lay down the hard lines—
It's absolutely true.

Written by David Bowie. By kind permission of EMI Music Publishing Ltd. © 1985

Flashback: 1958

"Then suddenly, from 1956 onwards, there came a crack in the social-political situation that released old allegiances and left conventional parties frozen into postures that ignored these changes. There came Poland, Hungary, Suez, death of Stalin, rise of Africa, the New Left, the teenage phenomenon, the race riots, the teacher strikes, Osborne and the new-wave writers, and, for what is it worth, CND . . ."

COLIN MACINNES in *Queen*, 22 May 1962

'58: MacInnes writes *Absolute Beginners*.

'58, when in Britain the population topped 50 million, unemployment reached an all-time high of 500,000, and 10-year-old Prince Charles became Prince of Wales
. . .when post-war coal rationing and price controls finally ended, when Jerry Lee Lewis flew into London with his 13-year-old bride and a vicar banned Teddy Boys from church for wearing luminous socks . . .

'58, the year in which Kruschev became Soviet premier and referred to 'the catastrophe on a colossal scale' that war between the USA and the USSR would bring . . .

. . . when Greek-Turkish fighting raged in Cyprus and the British Embassy in Baghdad went up in flames . . .

. . . when Castro emerged as a Cuban rebel leader, De Gaulle was elected President of France and Pope John XXIII was elected.

'85, when Ronald Reagan and Mikhail Gorbachov met to discuss the new 'Star Wars' defence program.

'58, when the defence budget reached £1,000 million and Macmillan's Conservative government was celebrating the British H-Bomb . . .

. . . when 25,000 citizens joined the newly founded Campaign for Nuclear Disarmament and the first Aldermaston march, held on Good Friday, was a huge success.

'85, when in Britain the population reached 55 million, unemployment topped 3.4 million, and the 37-year-old Prince of Wales and wife Lady Di gave their first intimate TV interview
. . . when Britain celebrated the fortieth anniversary of VE-Day, when Wham! flew into China, and the first television advertisements were shown against British youth's heroin 'epidemic' . . .

'58, the year tights began to replace stockings to become 'the first fashionable draught excluder' . . .

. . . when new fads included water-skiing, hula-hoop, pet chimpanzees, the dogs in space, an aerial moto-scooter called the 'Rotocycle,' Beatniks, parking meters, the new French franc and electronic computers.

'85, when a quarter of British households owned a video, nearly a tenth a home computer and the nation was glued to *Dallas* and *Dynasty.*

'58, a year that saw auto tail-fins getting longer in the US and a boom in bubble-cars in Britain owing to petrol shortages after Suez . . .

. . . during which a design team was starting work on the new Mini . . .

. . . when a gold-plated Daimler with zebra-skin seats hit the headlines. "Mink" explained the owner, Lady Docker, "is too hot to sit on."

'85, when the government pressed on with plans to privatise the telephone and water systems, British oil and British aerospace.

'58, a year when Britain's 4 million waged teenagers took home an average of £8.00 per week . . .

. . . when teenagers spent over £50 million on records, buying 80% of the record industry's output . . .

. . . when Britons had been trying their luck with ERNIE's premium bonds for three years, despite the Archbishop of Canterbury's fear that a monthly cash lottery would debauch the country.

'58, when Harold Macmillan opened Britain's first motorway and work started on the M1, 'a symbol of a new era in motor travel' . . .

. . . when BOAC started the first transatlantic jet passenger service with the new Comet airplane, and the Boeing crash at Munich airport killed 21 people, including 7 players of the Manchester United football team.

'58, when Brigitte Bardot was at the height of her fame as the devil's favourite 'sex kitten' and Vincente Minelli made *Gigi* . . .

. . . when film audiences were down to half their post-war level, but audiences flocked to see Hitchcock's *Vertigo*, Elvis in *Kid Creole* and Alec Guinness in *Bridge Over the River Kwai*.

'58, Mary Quant's third year in her clothes shop *Bazaar* on the King's Road.

"The party went Z-O-O-M from the start. So did Bazaar. People literally rushed in . . . We were mad; the whole thing was hysterical. But people loved it . . ."
Mary Quant

. . . when 23-year-old Yves St Laurent became heir to Christian Dior and, with the success of his 'trapeze' line and skirts rising above the knee, newspaper headlines announced 'St Laurent has saved France' . . .

. . . when with-it English girls wore 'the sack' and stilettos, and waists went high under the bust, while smart guys went for the 'Italian look' with round-collar shirts, bum-freezer jackets and winklepickers . . .

'85, when schoolkids aged 7 to 17 had a joint disposable income of nearly £2,000 m.

'58, when the novel *Saturday Night and Sunday Morning* shocked British taste with its earthy portrayal of adulterous sex and the play *A Taste of Honey*, showing a black-and-white love affair, raised eyebrows . . .

. . . when parliament debated the Wolfenden Report of 1957: its recommendations on prostitution led to stiffer penalties for soliciting on the streets, but its proposals that homosexuality between consenting adults should no longer be a criminal offence were not enacted as law.

'58, when the last debutantes were presented at court and the House of Lords admitted its first life peers, including women. . .

. . . the year when stereo gramophones arrived in England and Tommy Steele was put in Madame Tussaud's waxworks, but both were overshadowed by the news that Elvis Presley had joined the US army and cut his hair.

'58, when the British Hit Parade was only four years old and rocking to Elvis Presley's *Jailhouse Rock* and Little Richard's *Good Golly, Miss Molly*, as well as skiffle and Cliff Richard's first hit . . .
. . . when the Royal Variety Performance, compèred by Max Bygraves, featured The Beverley Sisters, Mantovani and his New Music, and songs from the hit musical *My Fair Lady* . . .

. . . when the Marquee Jazz Club opened and the Soho jazz spots featured Ken Colyer and Chris Barber for the trads and Ronnie Scott with Tubby Hayes in the Jazz Couriers for modernists but the self-respecting hipster still had a hard time.

'85, when Rock Hudson died of AIDS and Nicaragua defended its borders against US-backed troops.

'58, when Britain was emerging as a nation of telly addicts: 60% of adults reckoned they spent at least 4 hours in front of the box every day, the opening of parliament was televised for the first time and new series included *Panorama* and *Your Life in Their Hands*.

'58, a year of record strikes, headed by the London bus strike, which lasted 7 weeks.

. . . when an American submarine successfully passed beneath the North Pole ice-cap, taking some of the limelight from the Soviet sputniks which had been in orbit since the previous year.

'58, when Norman Mailer was being interviewed about 'The Religion of Hip', Jack Kerouac's *On The Road* hit Britain and *West Side Story* hit Broadway . . .

. . . "wishing I were a negro, feeling that the best the White World has offered me was not enough ecstasy for me, not enough life, joy, kick, darkness, music."
Jack Kerouac

'58, the year when restrictions on hire purchase were finally abolished and four out of five families started to live-now-pay-later on installment plans . . .

. . . when you could own a Ford Popular car for a down payment of £4 8s 5d and a refrigerator for 3 guineas; or buy a pint of beer for 7p, twenty cigarettes for 19½p, a gallon of petrol for 20.4 p, a 'package holiday' to Spain for £53.00, and a new house for £2,300.

'85, when over £5,000 million was spent on home furnishings and nearly two-thirds of British households owned a home freezer.

'58, when Ronald Reagan was still a liberal and Alaska became the 49th state of America.

. . . when Mies van der Rohe did the Seagram Building in Manhattan, Pablo Picasso was painting *The Bay of Cannes* in the South of France, and Richard Hamilton and Eduardo Paolozzi were celebrating the consumerist era in a new style dubbed 'Pop Art' . . .

'58, when the West Indies Federation was inaugurated and the total West Indian population in the United Kingdom was estimated at 107,000, of whom 40,000 lived in London . . .

. . . when the fascist organisations The White Defence League and the Union Movement were active in Notting Dale, their newspapers boasting headlines like 'America Pouring Black Troops into Britain' and 'Reds Count on Blacks' . . .

"It's all the . . . Queen's fault. She goes to all the black countries and they do their war-dances for her and they think they can come over here and take our jobs." *The Observer*, 7 September 1958 (interview with 'Teddy Boys')

. . . when landlords like Peter Rachman were purchasing properties in Notting Hill and dividing them into high-rent flats aimed at the immigrant market who found little housing available elsewhere in London . . .

'58, the year Sir Edmund Hilary reached the South Pole overland and the last steam locomotive was built in Britain . . .

. . . when riots against blacks began in the St Ann's area of Nottingham on August 23. A week later, trouble flared again: 3,000 white people gathered after a newsreel cameraman, one of 35 press present, set off a magnesium flare.

In the same week, the rioting in Notting Hill hit the headlines.

'85, when the Queen toured the Caribbean, and the West Indian labour force in the United Kingdom was estimated at 510,000 of whom 300,000 lived in London . . .

"Although no-one was killed, the actual violence and, even more, the cumulative threat of violence, produced an atmosphere of menace and fear which clearly resembled that of a text-book race riot.' Ruth Glass in *Newcomers*, 1958

'85, the year when riots started in the streets of Handsworth, Brixton, Tottenham and other British inner city areas. On his arrival in the streets to survey the damage, the new Home Secretary was greeted by a barrage of stones. He denounced the events as criminal activities, as if oblivious to the most recent and forgotten lessons of his country's history.

'85: cameras roll for *Absolute Beginners*.

Daily Mirror

2d · FORWARD WITH THE PEOPLE · No. 17,018 · MON SEPT 1 1958

Police squads rush to Notting Hill

400 CLASH IN 'COLOUR' RIOT

This picture was taken by a Daily Mirror reader in a Notting Hill street at 11 o'clock last night. A policeman's helmet lies in the gutter. Another dramatic picture is on the Back Page.

M.P. sends SOS to Yard

By GEORGE MORTON-SMITH

POLICE reinforcements were rushed to Notting Hill Gate last night as "colour" riots flared FOR THE SECOND TIME IN TWENTY-FOUR HOURS.

EACH TIME the riots began after gangs of white youths had jeered at coloured people.

EACH TIME the incidents developed into

Daily Mirror

2d · FORWARD WITH THE PEOPLE · No. 17,020 · WED SEPT 3 1958

BLACK v WHITE

THE PROBLEM ... in one picture

Cyprus: Briton and wife shot SEE PAGE THREE

What we must do..

EVERY decent person in this country is ashamed of the outbreak of race rioting and hooliganism in British streets.

It has come like a kick in the pants to all of us. We have lectured other countries, but failed to prevent the stinking explosion in our own backyard.

The Mirror is probably more guilty than any other British newspaper in assuming that it couldn't happen here. It has. The events of the past few days have brought our smug satisfaction to an abrupt end.

Let's cut out the moralising. Here is the Daily Mirror's plan for ACTION NOW.

1 COMMONWEALTH CITIZENS—whatever the colour of their skin should not be allowed to enter Britain as immigrants unless they have a job AND a home to come to.

Mr. Maurice Edelman, Labour M.P., had the courage to

Continued on Page 20

58 arrests in last night's colour riots

POLICE made fifty-eight arrests in colour clashes with gangs at Notting Hill last night.

Daily Mirror

2d · FORWARD WITH THE PEOPLE · No. 17,031 · TUES SEPT 16 1958

FOUR YEARS' PRISON FOR NINE WHITE THUGS

SENTENCING NINE LONDON YOUTHS TO FOUR YEARS' IMPRISONMENT EACH FOR ATTACKING COLOURED PEOPLE, MR. JUSTICE SALMON SAID AT THE OLD BAILEY YESTERDAY:

RACE RIOTS: BY A JUDGE

MR. JUSTICE SALMON

"YOU are a minute and insignificant section of the population, but you have brought shame upon the district in which you live and have filled the whole nation with horror, indignation and disgust.

Everyone, irrespective of the colour of their skins, is entitled to walk through our streets in peace, with their heads erect, and free from fear. That is a right which these courts will always unfailingly uphold.

I am determined that you and anyone, anywhere, who may be tempted to follow your evil example, shall clearly understand that crimes such as these will not be tolerated in this country, but will inevitably meet in these courts with the punishment that they so justly deserve."

THE CASE IS REPORTED ON PAGE 7

A Musical fo

Absolute Beginners, the musical: cast and crew at Shepperton

r the 1980's

CAST OF CHARACTERS

COLIN	*Eddie O'Connell*
SUZETTE	*Patsy Kensit*
VENDICE PARTNERS	*David Bowie*
HENLEY	*James Fox*
ARTHUR	*Ray Davies*
BIG JILL	*Eve Ferret*
THE FANATIC	*Steven Berkoff*
ATHENE DUNCANNON	*Sade*
DIDO LAMENT	*Anita Morris*
HARRY CHARMS	*Lionel Blair*
THE WIZARD	*Graham Fletcher Cook*
MA	*Mandy Rice Davies*
FLIKKER	*Bruce Payne*
ED TED	*Tenpole Tudor*
COOL	*Tony Hippolyte*
CALL ME COBBER	*Alan Freeman*
BABY BOOM	*Chris Pitt*
DEAN SWIFT	*Paul Rhys*
MISERY KID	*Julian Firth*
HOPLITE	*Joe McKenna*
AMBERLEY DROVE	*Ronald Fraser*
MRS LARKIN	*Irene Handl*
CYNTHIA EVE	*Sylvia Syms*
SALT BEEF MAN	*Eric Sykes*
VERN	*Peter Hugo Daly*
SALTZMAN	*Johnny Shannon*
DORITA	*Amanda Jane Powell*
MARIO	*Robbie Coltrane*
SANTA LUCIA CLUB OWNER	*Ekow Abban*
JOHNNY WONDER	*Gary Beadle*
CAPPUCCINO MAN	*Jess Conrad*
SMILEY CULTURE	*Smiley Culture*
SLIM BROTHER	*Robert Austin*
TON-UP VICAR	*Gerry Alexander*
SLIM BROTHER	*Jim Dunk*
CARMEN	*Carmen Ejogo*
EDDY SEX	*Paul Fairminer*
SLIM GAILLARD	*Slim Gaillard*
MRS COOL	*Pat Hartley*
MR COOL SNR	*Astley Harvey*
IRON LEG JACK	*Johnny Hutch*
PAMPHLETEER	*Colin Jeavons*
BERT THE TAILOR	*Alfred Maron*
CHEZ NOBODY BARMAN	*G B (Zoot) Money*
MALTESE LODGER no. 1	*Hugo First*
MALTESE LODGER no. 2	*Bruno Tonioli*
DANCERS IN 'KILLER BLOW' SEQUENCE	*Jazz Defektors*
DANCERS IN SANTA LUCIA CLUB	*IDJ*

Londres 1958,
Les Teenagers Attaquent!

'Look, I give you my word: Mr Bowie is *not* filming this week and Sade is giving absolutely *no* interviews.' The publicity girl repeats the words wearily, then hangs up. 'They're spitting mad. And you know what I have to look forward to in a couple of weeks? A coachload of Japanese journalists. What am I supposed to do with *them?*'

She does not seem to realise that there is, in fact, a far more fundamental problem. It is one thing to cope with the excited frenzy of globetrotting journalists literally quivering with anticipation as they jet in to London in the hope of catching a glimpse of Sade, the sexy Sadie of the eighties, or the lead singer of the Kinks, Ray Davies, both making their screen debuts. It is quite another to success fully explain what the film is about.

For *Absolute Beginners* is absolutely unlike any other film. On the one hand it is a huge, multi-million dollar production – $8 million to be precise – which is enormous by English standards. On the other hand, nearly everyone involved in the movie is either very young or unknown: the actor and the actress in the lead roles are both newcomers, the director is under thirty and the producer is just twenty-seven. In fact, it is very doubtful that anyone would have heard of the film, let alone be talking about it, if it was not for the sensational rock 'n' roll names on the cast list.

As it is, the film is roller-coasting along on a mammoth wave of advance publicity – in England, it is already so talked about that some people think shooting finished months ago. But, for all that, there seem to be very few others than those directly involved with the film who have any notion of what kind of animal it is, or who understand that it is one of the most genuinely adventurous films to have come out of Britain for many years: a musical comedy, freely adapted from the cult novel by Colin MacInnes, a writer rather fondly looked on by the English as their answer to Jack Kerouac. It has nothing in common with the rock films currently flooding the market. Far, far more ambitious than that, it is an attempt to recreate the wild follies, the extravagant panache and, above all, the *style* of the great Hollywood musical. The storyline? A guy and a girl fall in love, break up and come back together again – all against the background of a sizzling summer and race riots. I know what you're thinking: nothing very original in that. But just hold on.

Enter producer Steve Woolley, aged twenty-seven, ponytail trailing down his back and dressed – in the loosest sense of the term – in a cardigan and shorts hanging off his stocky legs. His appearance alone is enough to guarantee any sceptic that the film is going to be a blast – and that is before he has deposited his pushbike in a corner and started firing off information and ideas at a hundred miles an hour. Woolley is one of the founders of Palace Productions, the young film and video distribution company which first struck gold with *Diva* and *Merry Christmas, Mr Lawrence*, and then went into production with *Company of Wolves*.

'This hasn't been an easy film to get off the ground. We had to start hustling in Hollywood months ago to get an American deal simply because it is so hard to get over to people exactly what the film is about. It is an explosion of colour, music, style – a romantic film in the tradition of *Guys and Dolls* or one of Gene Kelly's movies, with characters who are larger than life. Yet, at the same time, it's also very hip. And it is more of a collage than a narrative. But there's something even more fundamental: in 1958, for the first time, the kids had money. Until then, it had been Mum, Dad and the family. Then, very suddenly, they had the chance to look beyond all that.'

Don Macpherson, ex-cinema critic who co-wrote the script and co-ordinated the music for the film, makes the same point. 'The war was still being felt in everyday terms as late as 1958. Britain was 'Grey' rather than 'Great':

there were necessities rather than luxuries, and no clothes or music to speak of – nothing. Then, at long last, everything came at once: kids who had been craving change, freedom, the kick of being young, suddenly woke up one day to find that they had it all, right there on a plate.' At exactly the same time, too, came the first wave of immigrants from the West Indies bringing with them a whole new set of rhythms to rival those of rock and jazz. And in the middle of all this is our hero, England's very first teenager – Colin. Not just England's first teenager, but also its only one: the total teenager. An absolute beginner, but with the whole world waiting for him.

Julien Temple never shouts. That is the job of his assistant director, a rough-and-ready type with an electrifyingly stentorian voice: just one word and every technician is rooted on the spot. An absolute sergeant-major. Temple, meanwhile, is conscientiously delegating a hundred and one sub-responsibilities to assistants, and to his scriptwriter, cameraman and choreographer, making full use of the film unit's hyper-hierarchy to take care of every little detail and so leave himself surrounded by an oasis of calm. He seems relatively little affected by his jump from wonderboy of the rock-video world – with a track record which includes the Kinks, Culture Club and the Stones – to director of a Cinemascope song-and-dance blockbluster. It is clearly a pose: Julian Temple is a dandy.

Sitting near a playback monitor, he is watching a scene being set up. His clothes are baggy and gathered: harem pants and a jacket with padded shoulders. Most distinctive of all are his shoes: exotic, new-wave, Turkish slippers with a finely textured Vasarely-like patchwork the like of which haven't graced a film set since Vincente Minnelli's extravagant lemon-yellow footwear. The parallel fits well. Minnelli is Temple's favourite director.

The scene is a crucial one – the opening of the race riots in Notting Hill, during which our innocent teenager, Colin, is caught up in a sudden wave of social violence.

The scene takes place in Big Jill's basement flat. Temple is talking. 'Colin's like a madman. Outside, they're fighting in the street yet meanwhile, on the telly, there's some politician making unbelievably reactionary statements. He is dumbfounded. How can the two things be going on at once? Just as Colin starts moving towards the telly to smash it in, Big Jill stops him. 'No, it's my telly!' And *she* kicks it in herself. I have wanted to get that scene into one of my films ever since *The Great Rock 'n' Roll Swindle*. In those days, though, I could not afford to break a screen. So here I finally got my chance – let myself go. Actually, I'm really more interested in all the different ways of killing the image.'

Temple disappears for a few minutes. He is checking that the crowd milling around on the street outside – who we see in the film through the window of Big Jill's basement flat – have got the right tempo. That is Temple's style of direction – he is more likely to be found explaining the rhythm of movements than the psychology of his characters, and he orchestrates action so that even the smallest bit-part becomes a cameo. There's no way *Absolute Beginners* will end up as *théatre filmé*.

Big Jill, played by Eve Ferret, is not just big. She is also blonde with a very generous cleavage – and the shocking pink ribbon in her hair matches that on the collar of the poodle sitting on her knee. The fifties set is suitably outrageous: an orange and black panther-skin fur-fabric sofa, neo-Afro-Matisse curtains and a jungle – literally hundreds – of cacti and thick-leaved succulents. Sitting next to Big Jill, looking awfully cute, is Colin. Temple compares him to a young Robert Mitchum – and there's no doubt that his fresh-faced looks and unmannered air are the make-or-break role of the film.

Smash! – Big Jill has just kicked in the television set. The smoke machine plugged in to the television immediately begins to belch smoke and banks of film lights bathe the scene in red and yellow. Colin and Big Jill leap up and the crowd starts running and shouting. Then the window shatters. The scene ends with a close-up of a can of cat food that has flown through the window – on the side a juvenile hand has scrawled 'Wog Shit'.

Absolute Beginners almost never saw the light of day. The project limped hesitantly along for nearly four years, hampered by the reluctance and wavering commitment of the original producers, Virgin, whose other recent films – *1984* and *Electric Dreams* – had not been spectacular successes. 'A lot of the time we came up against the predictable film industry attitude,' comments Macpherson, 'To simply get the film made as quickly and as cheaply as possible. If some people could have had their way, it would have starred Wham!, the Eurythmics or Duran Duran, and it would have been transposed to the eighties. People kept saying, 'We like the idea, we like the style, we love it all – but we want it to be happening today.'

The project really took off thanks to Palace and Woolley's enthusiasm, with Virgin and Goldcrest leaping on to the bandwagon and Orion, the American distributor, advancing the balance of the money needed to make up the production budget. Says Woolley, 'Temple is not just another young English hopeful with pretensions to film-making. He has the ability to provoke the kind of excitement produced by Welles, Hawks, Vigo and Cocteau. He has a true passion for the cinema. And he's also an anarchist – someone who likes to shock audiences, to wake them up. I know *Absolute Beginners* is going to be a triumph.'

Temple doesn't make the same claims for himself, or his film. But he has equally few kind words for the 'new' English cinema. 'There aren't any British films, just vehicles for the way Americans want to see and show England – films like *Another Country*, *Passage to India*, or *Chariots of Fire*.. Otherwise they're just tellyfilms – which may show Burgess and Maclean as gay public-schoolboys, but never at work as spies. Yet Burgess was obviously so much more than a drunken faggot, which is the way they portray him. Can you imagine the self-discipline needed to outwit the Foreign Office for ten years? What an amazing achievement! But of course they would never make a film about the glorious, epic side of his life. They would never have the nerve.'

He continues. 'And the so-called new British cinema just makes me want to laugh. It is just films for festivals – not for the general public, who would never bother to go and see them. I prefer to make two or three points and slip them into the film. I've got only one aim — to see people flocking back into the cinemas, to give them back that amazing sense of excitement which seems to have disappeared from the movies.'

These English — they are not just mad. They are *completely* mad. Not only have they built two extraordinary sets of Soho and Notting Hill, which would knock a gaping hole in any Hollywood budget. They have been far cheekier than that — they have actually built the ramshackle houses and mean streets of Notting Hill in the open air. Doesn't that put the shoot at the mercy of the English weather, I ask. 'Sure', they reply without hesitation. 'But if you don't believe in something enough to take risks, you might as well not bother at all.' End result: they are just about to start again on a scene which they had struggled through the day before, using four huge spots to compensate for the lack of sunshine. This time they are shooting with daylight alone. It is a scene with Colin and his buddy Cool, an elegant, mysterious black guy who plays the trumpet and loves Miles Davis. They part and Colin walks the length of the street — an excuse for a wonderful panning crane shot, which takes in street urchins on the pavement, blacks enjoying the cool of the day up on the rooftops, and a string of other interlocking vignettes, each of which slots in with extraordinarily tight precision.

But it is the next sequence they shoot which gives an outsider the best feel of the film. Main character: Ed the Ted, a half-starved rocker in a king-size frock-coat, played by Tenpole Tudor, better known for his notorious punk hits, *Who Killed Bambi?*, used by Temple in *Great Rock 'n' Roll Swindle*, and *Wunderbar*.

Here, he is Gene Vincent-like with his scavenging skinniness and his piercingly bright blue eyes staring out from a face littered with plastic pimples. He bounds across a bombsite, chucks a brick at a monstrously fat passer-by and screams, 'Go home, Yank!' For a moment, it looks as if there is going to be a fight. Then, suddenly, the music explodes out of nowhere.

Seven or eight kids aged from twelve to fifteen suddenly spring up around the bombsite and start backing Ed in a hysterical, raucous chant, which proclaims loud and clear that 'Ted ain't Dead' — not by a long way. One small kid grabs a tyre, and a couple of the others — Tedlets, real Blitz babies who have survived the war years — launch miniature planes into aerial spins. A self-contained world, the bombsite shakes frenetically in a vicious, snarling ballet which eventually comes to a screeching, grinding climax.

'The music has to literally explode off the streets', says Woolley, 'Because each group — the Teds, Trad Jazzers, Modernists and Rock 'n' Rollers — had their *own* music. It's hopeless when there's only one kind of music around, as there is at the moment. The same thing is true of film: right now there is nothing but Spielberg's soft-core science-fiction, kid's stuff. Now that is what I call decadence.' Temple agrees. 'The real problem in England is this all-embracing mafia of good taste. For instance, they hated me giving the part of the gay pop impresario, Harry Charms, to Lionel Blair, who is an ex-television and variety actor. They wanted someone intellectual — subtle like Alan Bennett. Which is ridiculous. Blair is brilliant, perfect for the part —

he is supposed to be the kind of manager whose teen idols' stagenames describe their performance in bed.'

Absolute Beginners will be an aggressively English film. 'I want people to rediscover their own — our own — fifties,' says Temple, 'To forget the stupid American clichés. It's not that I'm necessarily against clichés, but they should be our own, not those of other people.' Macpherson is fascinated by the same issues. 'The real question, the only one that matters, is 'Why do English people want to be Americans?' It's a dilemma in so many people's minds, and it's completely pointless. Don't forget — Elvis never came to England. He spent forty-five minutes in an airport in Scotland, and then took off again as fast as he came.'

A stream of jazz suddenly pours out around us. Can it be Mingus? 'Absolutely. This comes at the very beginning of the film. You meet the main characters and suddenly the screen is torn apart, literally forced widthways into Cinemascope.' Confidentially and very quietly, Macpherson is playing us bits from the soundtrack. It's only a rough mix, but it's enough to get the flavour — a wild, loose, hybrid mix of jazz and rock 'n' roll. 'This is the music in Colin's head, almost an extension of his character.' Even the Bowie number has an unusually jazzy feel — not so surprising, though, when one remembers that all the music is arranged by Gil Evans.

'When I first said I wanted Gil Evans, the producers virtually collapsed with heart failure,' says Temple. 'What? Jazz!!! Now, of course, it's all 'Wonderful!' 'Marvellous!' etc, etc. The person I really did want to have was Miles Davis — I would just love to see him playing *So What*. There's still an outside chance that he might do it — but we aren't black which makes it more difficult and, anyway, he's asked for a fortune.' Macpherson adds, 'I think we feel that the film could maybe both change chart music and open up jazz to a much wider audience — even that people might stop listening to Wham!'

Temple again. 'Colin adores jazz. And through his photographs you pick up the wonderful feeling which ties him to his time, living from day to day, for the moment.' Back to Woolley, 'The film is about the birth of a new spirit and state of mind — it's something which we've all been through at some time or another. In *Absolute Beginners* it happens to be the discovery of jazz, rock and roll, freedom during one brief summer. But for other teenagers it was the Beatles or Culture Club. I remember going through it myself. It was wonderful. I would wake up thinking 'Waaaaah! What's today going to bring? What'll it be this time?' Every kid goes through that — when they haven't a care in the world, when everything is fun, when everyone is your friend. No need for money — there is a magic password instead. And you've got it.'

Woolley hits his black shorts and scratches his stomach. Under the skull on his white T-shirt are the words 'Wings of Death'. Nearby, in a corner of the set, are a second pair of shoes — pointed grey mock-crocs identical to Colin's own. Gossips say that Steve Woolley never did discover punk, that he has always been a hippy. But that, as the saying goes, is another story.

Text © Louis Skorecki, *Libération*, 14 August 1985

Choreographer, tap dancer and director: David Toguri, David Bowie and Julien Temple

A City of the Imagination

Julien Temple

" At the heart of *Absolute Beginners* was the idea of telling a story of London as if it were Baghdad, a magical place, a city of the imagination. In contrast to the way television and the tradition of British films have made London smaller than life and far less interesting than it should be, I wanted to create a heightened version of the city which used the full spectacle of cinema to recreate the excitement I feel living in it. Although a musical is always a stylization of reality, I didn't want this film to be as deliberately unreal as *One From the Heart*. I simply wanted it to conjure up something of the experience I remember the first time I took speed in the city. I walked around Camden Town thinking, 'This is amazing!', feeling very *pleased* to be part of London. I still feel that. I love walking from where I live in Marble Arch to Notting Hill: the feel of the time of buildings getting later, the layout of the squares, the mews and the trees, the big terraced houses. It's a very *clear* city.

I love MacInnes's book because it shows London during a decade when it was really under pressure to become one thing or another. In that sense, making a film about London in the fifties is, rather strangely, like making a film about Iran just before the Shah fell. In both cases, you are dealing with a culture being pulled in different ways. I remember when I was in Iran at Shiraz, a famous religious town largely destroyed by an earthquake, in the late seventies. You could walk around at sunset when everyone went out to pray near the ruins, and suddenly they would be surrounded by huge Coca-Cola signs. These mullahs and men in turbans were completely freaked out. You could feel the electricity in the air. You could see them being pulled two ways: people had spontaneous nosebleeds as I walked around.

In the same way, the fifties were really the decade when America took over in England. People were pulled two ways. I wanted to convey that tension between an English culture which was emerging from the war with all its consequent deprivations, and, at the same time, being seduced by the American dream. Rather than treat the

Teds, for instance, as obvious Showaddywaddy-dayglo-crepe-sôled-ITV rockers, I wanted to place them in an older English tradition. They were around before rock 'n' roll and they dressed in a style which was not American but a piss-take of Edwardian costumes worn by nobs in Mayfair and the Queen's Guards – it was altogether a very *English* thing. Their heads were being pulled around. Having won the war and been schooled in the legacy of the British Empire, they were then plunged into a period where they could not have milk without signing for it and were very poor, with incredibly dull lives. Then, suddenly, in the late fifties they – and everyone else – were deluged by a plethora of American goods forced through television sets at them. The great thing about MacInnes was that he was aware that what was new was American, and that the people who were responding to it were not.

It's an irony, of course, that we've made a film which climaxes in the riots of '58 and that there have been the same kind of riots in '85. Rioting London is an image that has become known across the world: it's like the Blitz with St Paul's in flames. It is unfortunate that the attitudes of the people who were then on the streets of Notting Hill throwing stones through black people's windows are now so prevalent in the police force. The film is also a celebration of the black presence in London. The fact that a new wave of West Indians and Africans arrived in London in the fifties is very important. To me, it certainly made London more bearable as a place to live, and I am still very excited by that.

What comes through the book, no matter how many times you read it is a mixture of cynicism and optimism that is a very powerful combination. MacInnes was interested in writing about ordinary people, who weren't stupid. So I hope the film is an attempt to treat ordinary people in an important way. Why should a movie always have to be about Gandhi or an Olympic runner rather than a young guy? And why copy all those BBC angst-dramas that show the agonies of being poor and young? Why not try to make it on a more optimistic and expansive level, and treat the subject as American cinema treats working-class people –

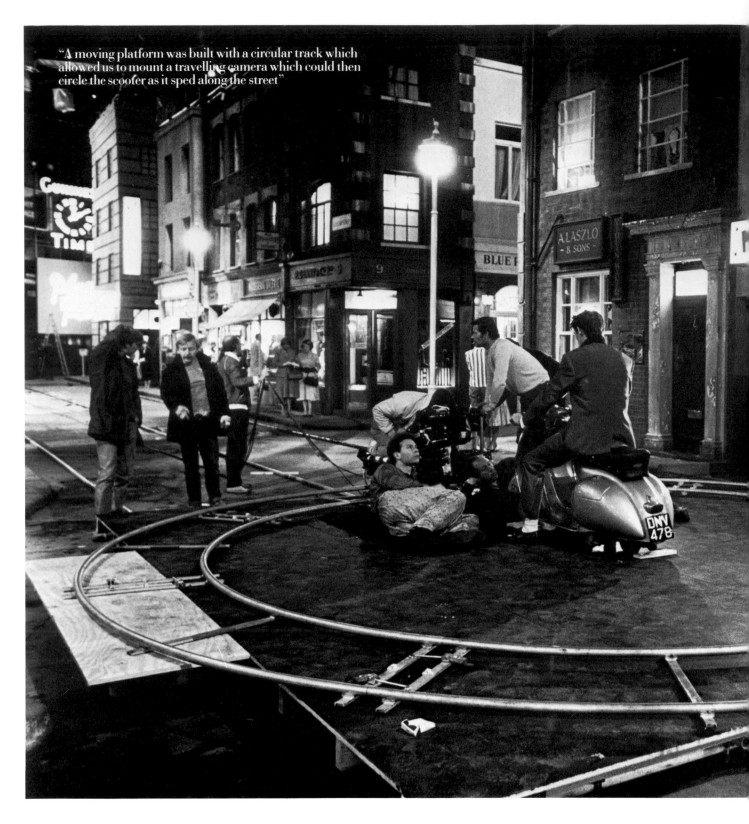

"A moving platform was built with a circular track which allowed us to mount a travelling camera which could then circle the scooter as it sped along the street"

that is, like anyone else, like people who've got a mind and an intelligence of their own?

Absolute Beginners was a film we could make without compromising a total belief in what we were doing, as well as at the same time trying to make it a popular success in the cinema. The truth which makes the film both interesting and commercially viable is the energy behind teenage in post-war Britain. Those different teenage styles are really this country's only recent achievement — other than its spectacular plummet, it's the only reason the rest of the world still notices Britain. The model is 1976. To me, that

was the last heroic summer of the teenage thing in England. I was involved with the Sex Pistols then. It was very exciting. It happened to be a real heatwave, a hothouse for a strange growth of characters like Sid or Catwoman who sprouted like mushrooms in sweaty basements of Soho clubs. There was something very epic about it, especially if you were in Oxford Street at the right time to see the sun go down in Hyde Park. That was an inspiration. You would see a girl walking down Oxford Street wearing nothing except a see-through polka-dot mac and American tourists walking past saying, "God! Is this the end of English teenage?"

power now. I hope the film can serve as a challenge for kids today to do something as powerful as their parents.

A basic element to the story is that it's about a young guy who gets seduced by the success that's available. That's very much part of the 'pop' process which is so dominant in London: young people are used, sucked dry, then thrown away. The character in the film is tempted, used and then discovers that is not what he wants. Since it is a fairy story, he is rewarded in the end. But the film *is* saying that you should be true to the idea of why you did things in the first place. The best thing about being young is questioning the things people tell you. That is the secret of eternal youth.

I think the only reason I have been able to be around and make a film is by playing a whole game with the media. The best position is to try and be hated in a curious kind of way because if you're hated, then they can't place you. Once you're loved, they have you on a shelf with Madonna, on top of the TV set. And you're out next week. You've been done. On to the next one. But if you refuse to be microwaved in the way they like you to be, then you can carry on. You need the media, but the media needs you. It's symbiotic. Like Benny Hill and his girlfriends.

The only way to approach any of this culture is to love it because you love it and to hate it because you hate it – to use that as a motor because you have that friction. Everything I have done in this area, as with my videos, is very much to do with hating things as much as loving them. The more absurd it gets, the nearer it gets to a resolution. I was brought up to believe that Jean Luc Godard had suddenly invented a new language of films and started off persuaded by that idea, but now I find Godard irrelevant to the way I'd like to make films. I find Minelli or Michael Powell, and Emeric Pressburger or Robert Hamer far more relevant. They loved and hated things from a very different perspective, but I'd now far rather see *The Band Wagon* than *Une Femme Est Une Femme*. There's just no comparison.

I react very strongly against the puritanism of some of the left and those worthy artists who feel that they always have to suffer in order to do something. I hate it. I don't see the point. People play football because they enjoy it; people drink because they like drinking. Education and enlightenment have to be about enjoying yourself or they're not worth doing. I'd love people to go and see *Absolute Beginners* like a James Bond film. I hope it is more about England than James Bond ever was, and just as entertaining – in terms of being educated, I remember that the more laughs, the more filth, the more pornography in history, the more interesting it always was.

That's why I have a real respect for Tex Avery's cartoons – I love his cartoons about American culture because they become surreal in the most effortless ways. It is not worked at. It is not people growing their moustaches like Dali. It just comes from living in the middle of it all. Tex Avery is, to me, like stretching your emotions between love and hate, then letting them go and – bang! they collide in the middle. That's very subversive to me. It's wonderful."

That was the only reference I could use for the idea of youth as a shock tactic – I'm sure that was what the buzz of being a teenager in the fifties was largely about. 1976 was the end. The Sex Pistols were the gunpowder that blew it all up. I'd like it if young people were doing something really unpredictable today, but they're not. There are characters hanging on to bits of the wreckage and saying, 'It's still afloat!' But there isn't anything special about being a kid anymore – not when your grandfather was a Teddy Boy. It's more special now to be a young married. The Baby Boom generation had numerical power then, and still has

ACKNOWLEDGEMENTS

The Musical

VIRGIN and GOLDCREST present a PALACE PRODUCTION
A JULIEN TEMPLE FILM

Based on the novel by COLIN MACINNES

STARRING

EDDIE O'CONNELL as COLIN   PATSY KENSIT as CREPE SUZETTE

DAVID BOWIE, JAMES FOX, RAY DAVIES
EVE FERRET, ANITA MORRIS

with special appearances by STEVEN BERKOFF and SADE ADU

WITH MUSIC BY DAVID BOWIE, RAY DAVIES, GIL EVANS, PAUL WELLER,
PATSY KENSIT, SADE, JERRY DAMMERS, NICK LOWE,
EKOW ABBAN, SMILEY CULTURE, TENPOLE TUDOR, SLIM GAILLARD, TOT TAYLOR

Choreographer DAVID TOGURI

Music arranged and conducted by GIL EVANS

Screenplay by RICHARD BURRIDGE, CHRISTOPHER WICKING and DON MACPHERSON

Executive Producers NIK POWELL, AL CLARK, ROBERT DEVEREUX

Produced by STEPHEN WOOLLEY and CHRIS BROWN

Directed by JULIEN TEMPLE

MADE AT LEE INTERNATIONAL STUDIOS, SHEPPERTON, MIDDLESEX, ENGLAND

SOUNDTRACK AVAILABLE ON VIRGIN RECORDS LTD.

A PALACE/VIRGIN RELEASE

THE BOOK

The Beginners' Guide to Absolute Beginners
A CORGI BOOK 0 552 99237 2

First publication in Great Britain 1986

Copyright © Goldcrest Films and Television Limited and Virgin Vision Limited

Corgi Books are published by Transworld Publishers Ltd., Century House, 61–63 Uxbridge Road, Ealing, London W5 5SA; in Australia by Transworld Publishers (Aust.) Pty Ltd., 26 Harley Crescent, Conell Park, NSW 2200, and in New Zealand by Transworld Publishers (N.Z.) Ltd., Cnr. Moselle and Waipareira Avenues, Henderson, Auckland

This book was conceived, prepared and produced by DREW AND HAYWARD for Goldcrest Films and Television Limited

ILLUSTRATIONS

Unit photography for Absolute Beginners, the Musical, by Graham Attwood
pp. 1, 71 Illustrations by Graham Humphries
p. 5 David Lachappelle, textile The Design Council
p. 13 Ellen von Unwerth; signature Jo McKenna
p. 17 Frank Spooner
pp. 21, 82–83, 94–5 Roger Mayne
pp. 30–31 Map by Graham Humphries
pp. 46, 62–3 Kays catalogue
p. 50 Sunday Times Picture Library
p. 54 Kevin Cummings
p. 96 Portrait of Colin MacInnes by Roger Mayne
pp. 102–3 Davies and Starr

TEXT

pp. 1, 3, 7, 18, 28, 55, 75, 76, 86, 93 extracts from *Absolute Beginners* screenplay
pp. 22, 25, 46, 52, 66, 72, 94 lyrics from *Absolute Beginners* soundtrack, as credited
p. 7 Colin MacInnes, *London – city of any dream*, 1963, by kind permission of Thames and Hudson Ltd.
pp. 21, 79 Samuel Selvon, *Ways of Sunlight*, 1957–8, by kind permission of McGibbon and Kee
pp. 22, 87 Michael Malik, *Michael de Freitas to Michael X*, 1968, by kind permission of André Deutsch
pp. 22, 83 Colin MacInnes, notes on Roger Mayne's photographs, *The Observer*, January 1962
pp. 45, 83 Colin MacInnes, 'Pop Songs and Teenagers', 1958, from *England, Half English*, 1985, courtesy of the Hogarth Press and the author's estate
pp. 45, 51, Colin MacInnes, *Absolute Beginners*, 1959, (1980 edition), by kind permission of Allison and Busby and the Colin MacInnes Estate
p. 55 Frank Norton, *Soho Night and Day*, 1966, by kind permission of Transworld Publishers Ltd.
p. 55 R.A. Norton, *Through Beatnik Eyeballs*, 1961, by kind permission of Pedigree Books
pp. 79 (Interviews with a Trinidadian and man from Antigua, extract from *Going to Britain*), 87 and 93 (*The Manchester Guardian*), Ruth Glass, *Newcomers, The West Indians in London*, 1960, by kind permission of George, Allen and Unwin. (*The Manchester Guardian* article was used by MacInnes as a source for his description of the riots in the novel.)
p. 83 The Fanatic's speech by Steven Berkoff
p. 95 Colin MacInnes, 'The Anarchists', by kind permission of *Queen*, May 1962
p. 98 Mary Quant, *Quant by Quant*, 1966, Cassell and Co.
p. 99 Jack Kerouac, *On the Road*, 1957
p. 100 Interview with 'Teddy Boys', *The Observer*, 7 September 1958
pp. 109–111 Translation © *Beginners' Guide to Absolute Beginners*

Care has been exercised to trace the ownership of copyright material used in this book. The publishers will gladly receive information enabling them to rectify any reference or credit in subsequent editions.

Typeset by Phoenix Photosetting, Chatham
Colour separation by Fotographics Ltd.

A DREW AND HAYWARD ORIGINAL ACCEPT NO SUBSTITUTES!

Editor: Vicky Hayward
Design and Art Direction: Tracy Drew
Original text: Don Macpherson
Research: Christine Vincent

Production: Landmark Production Consultants
Additional Layout: David Black, Stella Crew, Andy Chambers, Elizabeth Waterworth

Cover design: Tracy Drew
Photographs: Front: Graham Attwood, right Davies and Starr
Back: Graham Attwood, top left: Roger Mayne

SPECIAL THANKS TO *Belle Anscombe, Olivier Auscher, Chris Brown, Roger Burton, Hannah Charlton, Davies and Starr, Elizabeth Drew, Julia Ethell, Ewa Glazer, Stephen Hayward, Diana Hawkins, Denny Hemming, Rose Jennings, Mike Leedham, Barry Lewis, Cynthia Lole, Bogus Machnik, Roger Mayne, Amanda Pirie, Pollyana Music, Sue Steward, Julien Temple, Stephen Woolley*